She Needed Killing

She Needed Killing

Book 3
in the
Needed Killing Series

Bill Fitts

She Needed Killing

ISBN 978-0-9883893-6-6

Cover design: www.EbookLaunch.com

Printed in the United States of America

www.billfittsauthor.com

For Anne,
without whom this book too never would have been written,
and for my mom,
who wanted her kids to love what they did for a living

CONTENTS

PRINCIPAL CHARACTERS

Coba Boucher, assistant director of The Festival

Crawford (James F. "Ford"), university retiree; private investigator

Stan Dowdy, friend of Crawford; AV specialist at university

Dot Fields, director of The Festival

Joyce Fines, Festival board member

Ellen George, Festival board member; married to Rufus George

Rufus George, university provost; married to Ellen George

Ben Gibbons, an immigration lawyer

Jack Harlon, friend of Bobby Slater; married to Rebecca Perry

Chad Harris, artist at The Festival

Harry Johns, homicide investigator, Shelbyville

Levi Keith, gospel singer; married to Mary Keith

Mary Keith, Crawford's house cleaner; gospel singer; married to Levi Keith

Ted Lowe, artist at The Festival

Lenora Maisano, Festival board member

Frank Manning, University Press employee

Morgan Moore (Dr. Snake), Shelbyville native and snake expert

Mr. Whiskers, Bobby Slater's cat

Guy Nelson, chief of security for The Festival

Pauline, Frank Manning's date

Rebecca (Bex) Perry, Bobby Slater's sister-cousin; married to Jack Harlon

Paul Simms, Stan Dowdy's assistant

Bobby Slater, Crawford's lady friend; University Press employee

Mose Smith, owner of Mo' Music; sound specialist at The Festival

Kurt Snoddy, chief of police, Archibald

Ralph Stark, head of volunteers at The Festival

Tan, Crawford's dog

The Black (TB), Crawford's cat

Sammy Thompson, sheriff, Jemison County

Jim Ward, friend of Crawford; head of homicide, Shelbyville

Whittlin' Woodrow, artist at The Festival

"Approving license application for private detective for James F. Crawford." My heart jumped. I had known that it was coming. After all, it had to be printed in the paper, but even so it was exciting to see it in black and white—or newsprint and ink. Someday there will be the Internet equivalent of publishing notices in the local newspaper—but not yet. There it was, an item on the Shelbyville City Council agenda for tonight. The agenda for a meeting I wasn't going to miss.

Alabama doesn't have statewide licensing for private investigators—just a state business license. The cities and towns are allowed to set their own requirements. In Shelbyville, the standard wording was "for private detective and uniform security guard" but I'd kicked up a ruckus on that. Evidently most people petitioned to be both private investigator and security guard. Since I couldn't see myself working as a rent-a-cop for fraternity parties, I'd made sure to limit the petition to just private investigation. It seemed like a reasonable thing to do at the time.

I was sitting at my kitchen counter reading the paper. I smoothed out the notice making sure there weren't any wrinkles in it. My dog, Tan, and I had done our morning walk. I'd showered, shaved, and dressed for the day before making breakfast. My current uniform—shorts, T-shirt, and sneakers—had been a comfortable change from my preretirement garb. Not that, as a geek, I'd been required to go the coat and tie routine. But there is casual and then there's *casual.*

Eventually the weather would force me to move to long sleeves and long pants. October in Alabama can have some cool days—it can also be as hot as June and July, which is why I was still in shorts. I hadn't been retired from my day job for a year as yet, so I was learning on the job, as it were, about retiree apparel.

Once the city council approved my application I was going to have to start saying that I was retired from the university and "in between jobs" in my new career. I smiled to myself. What do private detectives wear to work anyway? I was pretty sure that I wouldn't have to run out and buy a new wardrobe.

Retirement had altered some things, but breakfast hadn't gone through much of a change. Today was sausage biscuits with mustard and cheese. The cheese was a culinary wrinkle in my breakfast biscuit world that a new friend had introduced me to. Well, she wasn't really a new friend—it was the degree of friendship that was new.

I had opened up the *News* to get the morning started. I had my ritual for reading the newspaper. It was based in part on how I read the *Saturday Evening Post* when I was growing up. I think it was the *Post*. I started at the back since that's where the cartoons were and worked my way to the front. Same story with the newspaper. Comics, sports, local news, and finally the national news and editorials. Certainly I had not started with the city council agenda until recently.

I checked the back of the page the council agenda was printed on and decided that I'd forgo whatever story it was a part of. I stood up, got a pair of scissors out of the catch-all drawer, and headed to the table in the breakfast nook. I wasn't going to risk tearing the agenda item.

Once I'd spread the newspaper out, The Black jumped onto the table, walked across it until he was in the middle of the newspaper, and sat down. "Thanks," I scratched the cat's ears. "Now get off the newspaper—and the table." The commanding tone I used fell on deaf ears and I knew from experience how successful such entreaties would be. So I picked him up and poured him onto the floor. I had the agenda cut out of the paper before he got back on the table.

. . .

I tucked the clipping away in a folder I had sitting on the kitchen counter. There were a couple of other items in it, all things I thought I should do something with, but couldn't decide just what. Occasionally I'd flip through the folder item by item, decide I'd been wrong about one of them, and throw it away. But usually I just saved them all for another day.

In the folder were articles from the *News* about my old boss Sean Thomas dying from food poisoning, one about the accidental death of Albert Worthy, and another reporting the arrest of the person who'd killed both of them. There was an odd editorial from the student newspaper in which I was depicted as the provost's secret agent. It attempted to paint an ordinary business arrangement as mysterious and covert but was offset by the nearly universal respect accorded the provost. More *News* articles about the shooting of the University Press's director, the suicide of the last member of a once-prominent Shelbyville family, and another call for increased campus security from the student newspaper.

The folder contained, in fact, a history of events that had led to my applying for a private investigator's license. Maybe I should make a scrapbook. I shrugged. My muse must be busy somewhere else. I closed the folder to await another day.

Things had been slow in the detecting business since those two weeks in September that had dumped me headfirst into my new career. If by *slow* I meant nonexistent. But that was okay since it had taken until the middle of October for my application for a license to get on the council's agenda.

Today would be the start of my licensed career. My business cards were supposed to be ready so I'd stop by the printer and pick them up—along with a small supply of invoices, envelopes, and letterhead. I hadn't thought to order those items until the graphic artist I was working with brought it up. Since then I'd received her invoice with a pleasant cover note on her letterhead, all enclosed in an envelope sporting her business logo. I could see how handy these things were going to be. Along with the business credit card my accountant had strongly encouraged me to get. At least her suggestion was more altruistic than the artist's—having my business expenses separate from personal spending was going to make her job easier and she billed by the hour.

I'd been told that the council's approval of my application was all-but-assured. Still I'd been encouraged to attend the meeting and to try and appear as if I was a solid citizen. I assumed that meant wearing a suit and tie since that's what our politicians always wear. Misery loves company. Of course it might be they wore suits just in case a funeral happened to pop up.

The fact that I was going to be wearing a suit had prompted me to think at first that it would be a good time to take Bobby out for a celebratory meal. We'd started to go to Trey's one evening—gotten as far as being seated—but I'd gotten distracted by the outfit she was wearing, and we ended up back at her house and, eventually, had a late supper. Operating on the principle that "life is short; eat dessert first," we'd gone straight for dessert.

Retirement isn't the end to life, it's a beginning. I was glad I'd taken early retirement, and my new relationship with Bobby was one of the reasons. Bobby was short for Barbara. She'd put the *y* at the end in honor of Bobby Kennedy. And she put a smile on my lips every time I thought about her.

But the council meeting didn't start until six o'clock, I wasn't first on the agenda, and she had to go to work tomorrow. So the celebratory meal was on for tomorrow night—Wednesday evening that is. I'd made reservations for six o'clock. This time we'd save dessert for after dinner.

And, at the end of the week, across the river in Archibald, was The Festival. It had been an annual event for going on thirty years now, part folk festival—arts and crafts, primitive and contemporary—music festival; outdoor performances; and food. As close as it is to Halloween, costumes abound at The Festival. Sunday was Bring Your Pet to The Festival Day; Saturday celebrated Alabama beer and wine; and Friday—opening day—was the day to shop before the artists sold out of what you wanted. Thursday was the day I'd promised to meet Stan so he could shoot a video promoting The Festival. He'd asked if I'd bring The Black with me since he wanted a black cat in the video—what with Halloween coming up.

Remembering this, I guiltily looked around to see if The Black was still around. I'd neglected to mention to him that Stan wanted to video him at The Festival since this involved riding in the car, which meant he had to be in the cat carrier. Historically, this is not one of the things TB enjoys. And after the photo shoot, I was going to take him to the vet for his annual shots though I wasn't sure he was going to appreciate my rationale: he was going to have to go to the vet's anyway—what harm was a short delay?

I'd brought the carrier out from storage yesterday and put it down on the floor in the den. The Black had sniffed at it. So had Tan, who couldn't fit into it even if she'd wanted to. Then they had both ignored it. So far so good.

I went back to the clippings folder, opened it up, and wrote a note on the inside cover—Tan and The Black. I was careful to use seniority in determining priority. If this was going to be a history of my detecting career I needed to include my confidants.

I looked around the kitchen. Tan was on one of her dog beds and The Black was curled up asleep in a patch of sunlight on the floor. I, James F. Crawford, Private Investigator, went to clean out the kitty litter. Best not to get too puffed up about myself.

. . .

That evening The Black followed me into the bedroom as I was getting out of my suit and into something more comfortable. He was fussing about something—probably my not paying him enough attention—but I wasn't paying much attention. "You know TB, I don't think I do my best work in a suit. Maybe it's the tie."

I don't know what I'd expected the City Council meeting to be like but I had found it unsettling. The council room was impressive—heavy wooden paneling—twenty-foot-plus ceiling—rectangular—wider than it was deep. Seating for the public was sort of pew-like to your right as you entered the room. Across the room the civil service types sat behind some railing like where the choir would have been, if it had been a church—but there wasn't an altar. No, no altar—just an imposing wooden wall behind which city council members sat in high-backed leather chairs on a raised platform—looming over the populace. They had the high ground for sure.

The room was old but it had been retrofitted with the amenities—air conditioning, sound system, microphones, projector screens, laser pointers, computers, wireless network, and the like. Everything you needed to conduct today's business of governing but they'd left that part alone—the part that made it clear who were the governed and who governed.

I had sat there waiting my turn in my suit and tie, dress shoes freshly shined, file folder in my lap, cell phone turned off—the picture of a dutiful applicant—while the council worked its way through the night's agenda. I was the fourth item—not counting the pledge of allegiance, opening prayer, and approval of last meeting's minutes. I was so nervous that it was a wonder butterflies weren't flying out of my ears.

It was clear that the first three items were routine by the way everybody was only half paying attention—almost sleep walking. The city clerk would read a summary of the application, city attorney murmur that there was no legal reason to deny it, police department representative say the police had no problem with it, the applicant would walk to the podium, no one would have any questions, council chair would bang his gavel, ask for a motion and then a second, get mumbled responses, ask for ayes and nays, slam the gavel again, and say "approved." Then it would start all over again.

I'd been so hypnotized by the routine that I found myself standing at the podium wondering how I'd gotten there. I was still nervous. So nervous that I'd been surprised when the chair asked the clerk a question and broke the routine.

"This the guy who caused all the trouble? The uniformed guard thing? Changing the application?"

"Yes, sir."

He frowned and leaned forward to peer down at me. So far no one had asked me a question so, for once, I had kept quiet. I had a sinking feeling that it might have been wiser to have let the joint application stay joint.

Another councilman stirred in his seat and leaned forward to peer at me too. "The same one that Rufus George wrote to us about?"

"Yes, sir. Same one." The clerk was positively verbose.

The second councilman shook his head. "Interesting."

The application had required references and Rufus had agreed to be one. I wondered just what Rufus had written. After all he'd gotten me started doing this.

"If he's good enough for Rufus George, he's good enough for me." A councilwoman looked up from the file folder she'd been reading and looked at me over her half-moon glasses. "I move to approve."

The second councilman leaned back. "Second."

The chairman shook his head. "Troublemaker." He leaned back. "Any opposed say 'nay.'" There was silence. "Those for approval say 'aye.'"

Scattered "ayes" were uttered by the council.

Slam. "Approved. Next."

. . .

"So, I got approved all right. Maybe it was the suit. I can pick up my license tomorrow afternoon at city hall." I picked up TB and draped him over my shoulder. He began to purr. "Because mine has to be specially made."

The Black was in his carrier nestled in the backseat of my car. He wasn't happy. I could tell because he wasn't suffering in silence. He wasn't suffering at all as far as I could tell. This was the same carrier that he sometimes slept in while it was out, but he didn't care for it once I closed its door while he was in it. And when I put it in the car and we drove off? At least he'd settled down into an angry silence with an occasional mew of protest at any change—whether it was direction, speed, or road surface.

I pulled into The Festival grounds and was surprised to see what it looked like before it had its party face on and all the artists, vendors, and festival-goers descended on it. There were volunteers setting up the festival grounds. Wide pathways had been created over the years and people were raking them smooth, clearing out the underbrush on either side of the paths, repairing fencing, staking out booth locations—so you could see the skeleton, if you will, of The Festival being put together. Tomorrow the bones would be clad in booths and festival-goers.

Once paths had been shaped and locations for booths staked out, other volunteers followed along placing trash cans and recycling bins at intersections, between booths, along straightaways, within the food court areas—literally all over the grounds. Festival-goers, vendors, and artists alike always commented on how clean The Festival was. The Festival believed that people would be neat if you gave them a place to put their trash. There were also signs asking people to stay on the paths—"Do not even leave footprints." And every piece of it—from tents to trash receptacles to notepads—everything except the wooden stakes had been labeled Property of The Festival. Like I said, I've been coming to The Festival for years and have even worked as a volunteer, but that was always while it was going on—not before it opened. I usually parked my car in downtown Archibald and took a shuttle bus to the grounds since traffic was always a mess despite the best efforts of the Archibald police.

I found what looked like a parking spot near the decorative metal gates where the opening and closing ceremonies were held. Originally a simple metal gate, essentially a triangle with parallel horizontal bars for braces, the gate had evolved over the years and was now quite ornate.

Under a tree near the ceremonial gate were two parking spots. The one labeled Director was in full shade; the assistant director's wasn't. I was a little surprised that The Festival went in for perks like that. I had always thought of it as a pretty egalitarian bunch of people. I mean if you think some backwoods, unskilled, untaught sharecropper could make something that you would call art, you have to be pretty open-minded, right? There was a pickup truck parked in the director's slot but the assistant's spot was empty.

The Black had fallen silent as soon as I parked. At this point he must have been wondering where we were. He hadn't been any further from our house than the vet's office since the woman from the humane society had delivered him to his forever home. At which point in time, Tan and I had begun to learn how to live with a cat.

The carrier had a door made out of metal bars spaced about half an inch apart, sides of some kind of plastic with air holes, a solid bottom, and a top that opened—making it easier to get a reluctant cat into it. The top was made out of metal bars too, with a metal handle made out of wire the same thickness as the bars.

I picked up the carrier, noted, not for the first time, that the handle design was flawed—they could have put some cushioning on it—and headed onto The Festival grounds. Stan Dowdy had said he would be shooting around the fortune-teller's tent and I remembered where it had been pitched the last few years. That was one of the good things about The Festival's traditions. Artists' booths were generally in the same location year after year—if the artist was invited back. It was a juried show and competition was pretty stiff, or so I'd been told.

The grounds were essentially an old pine grove that had been surrounded by farm fields before the owner had given the land to the city thirty or forty years ago. The city of Archibald had started turning the cleared land into baseball and soccer fields but hadn't done anything to the grove or the pond that bordered it on one side. It hadn't cost very much to turn a cornfield into a baseball diamond. And the reason the farmer hadn't turned the grove into farmland was that it was too much trouble. The ground wasn't level and the soil—sandy, thin, and rocky—was fine for longleaf pines, brambles, briars, scrub oaks. And for an annual fall festival as it turned out.

I had shifted the carrier from one hand to the other and back again before I saw the tent. I made a mental note to ask the vet just how much weight The Black had gained. Eleanor used to tell me that black was slimming and what was true in basic black dresses apparently was also true in cat fur.

Dot Fields's fortune-telling tent had already been set up. It was an odd kind of tent, octagonal, each side or wall going straight up for seven feet before the sides began to taper and meet in a center peak—basically a cone set on top of a cylinder. Every time I saw it, it made me think of the tent where knights waited between jousts in the Danny Kaye movie *Court Jester*. Each side was a color of the rainbow—red, orange, yellow, green, blue, indigo, violet, plus black. (There is some mnemonic that's supposed to make it easy to remember the colors of the rainbow, but I can never remember what it is, which makes it, for me, a useless mnemonic.)

Stan and his assistant Paul Simms were already at the tent setting up tripods for cameras and lighting. Whenever anybody asked Stan if he liked reality shows on TV he would lose it—and them—with a comprehensive denouncement of how "unreal" it was that there were never any shadows on the actors' faces no matter what time of day the "real" event was occurring. It was years of doing shoots like this one that added to the intensity of his response.

As I closed in on the tent, I saw that Stan had commandeered a picnic table just outside the entrance to the tent to use during the shoot. Good thinking to shoot outside. It would have been impossible to illuminate the interior of that tent well enough to eliminate shadows and still be able to move around. Not to mention the heat. Wait, Stan was using the new LED lights so it wouldn't be that hot. Not like the old days with incandescent lighting. I reminded myself to try and keep current.

"Yo, Crawford!" Stan had turned around and caught sight of me.

"Hey, Stan, Paul." I put TB's carrier down on the table and proceeded to clench and unclench my hand trying to work the blood back into it. The so-called handle had made a dent in my palm. Why hadn't I used both hands to carry TB? Macho pride? I needed to get over that for my hand's sake.

Stan had been over to the house countless times and was on good terms with The Black. He walked over and looked through the top of TB's carrier. "Hey, TB. Thanks for coming." It was easy to tell that there was an angry cat in the carrier so Stan wisely didn't stick his finger through the wires. The Black was radiating rage. Paul followed Stan over.

Paul had been one of Stan's student assistants before I retired. Stan referred to his students as "minions," fully realizing it made him sound like a B-movie villain. Since my retirement, Paul had been hired on as a full-time employee.

"Wow! What a handsome cat. Is he solid black?"

"Pretty much."

"Aren't you the handsome beast?" Paul continued to talk to TB in the way any cat lover speaks to a cat. "Now I know why Mr. Stan wanted to take your picture—what a great cat. What's his name? TeeBee?"

"His real name is The Black but I call him TB for short." I could tell that Paul was having a calming effect on the cat. Of course, he loved being talked to and told how wonderful he was—he the cat, that is. Although I guess Paul wouldn't have minded some praise himself. I mentally kicked myself.

"Congratulations on getting on the university's payroll. Glad they made you full time. I know Stan's glad to have your help."

Paul looked up from TB's cage and grinned. "He told me that after you retired the department discovered there was a little extra money available for payroll—so thanks for retiring."

I laughed and grinned back at him. "Then it was a win-win situation."

Stan coughed into his hand. "Do you suppose you could let The Black out of the carrier? I really wasn't thinking of pictures of him in a carrier when I came up with this idea for a promotional shot."

"I think Paul may have soothed him down—nothing like compliments to turn a cat's head." I unhooked the top of the carrier and lifted The Black up out of the container. He stiff-armed me when I tried to drape him over my shoulder, so I knew I hadn't been forgiven. I moved the carrier to the side and set the cat down on the table. Paul grabbed the carrier and moved it out of sight of the cameras and I started to stroke The Black's ears.

Stan waved me to one side and I stepped back as he and Paul started shooting. At first The Black just sat on the table, tail wrapped around his feet, then he began to stretch. Maybe he'd felt cramped in the carrier. It wasn't a big picnic table, but it was big enough for a Ouija board or a tarot tableau.

I'd forgotten just how long TB can be when he stretches out.

"That is one *big* cat," whispered Paul. He let his camera hang around his neck as he stepped back to the video camera that was on a tripod and started filming.

Just then the flap of the tent swung open and Dot Fields, director of The Festival, stumbled out of her tent, staggered several feet, and almost ran into the table.

"Damn that door lip! One of these days I'm going to fall flat on my face." I saw where the floor of the tent was curved up by three or four inches, presumably to keep water from seeping into it. Dot had turned around to glare at the offending tent then turned back to face us.

Tall, heavyset, with her long, black hair in a single braid draped over her shoulder, she was wearing a pair of faded bib overalls and work boots. "Howdee, folks! Sorry about that entrance," she bellowed. She must have been in the tent putting on her gypsy costume, at least that was the only excuse I could come up with for her having a couple of scarves tied around her head, garish earrings dangling from her earlobes, and costume jewelry rings on every finger.

That's right, I reminded myself, Stan was doing promotional pieces for The Festival and Dot, as director, had demanded he include a piece on her fortune-telling tent. The university was going to run the spots on its TV station as part of its ongoing support of The Festival. Stan was trying to give the pieces a Halloween flair to justify highlighting Dot's booth over the others. It was easier to do it that way than to fight with Dot, or so he said. I'd never met her until today.

We humans had all at least seen Dot before, I guess, since none of us reacted to her appearance the way The Black did—or maybe it was just because we'd been taught to try and be polite. Not so the cat.

TB arched his back, every hair standing on end, opened his mouth wide, and hissed at the creature that had appeared before him. I could see the claws extend and contract as he continued to wail at her. I'd seen The Black express his displeasure at other cats and at dogs, but nothing like this. Stan and Paul were falling all over themselves trying to get as many shots as possible. Dot, for her part, stood there looking surprised and, for the first time this morning, not saying anything.

I'd say that Stan got the shot he was looking for.

. . .

Dot took a half step back. "My," she said. "Animals always love me." For a brief moment Dot seemed to be uncertain, then she began to bluster. "Oh, she must smell the snake. That's what it is. Dogs and cats always love me!"

The human's step back had broken the confrontation as far as The Black was concerned and he had won. He sat on the table and began to vigorously wash himself. The human had flinched and he was willing to leave it at that. I stepped back up to the table and scratched him behind the ears. I didn't want TB to bolt or to attack Dot though I'm not sure what I thought I could have done about it if he'd tried. "He's a he. The cat that is."

"What's that about a snake?" Stan, having captured The Black in full fury, was trying to smooth things over as usual. I bet that was just the shot he was hoping to get—not with Dot in it, mind you, just the classic Halloween black cat.

"All cats are female."

Dot had returned to what appeared to be her normal behavior—full bluster. I've had other people tell me the same thing—or that all dogs are male—and it never bothered me. In fact, some of the people are dear friends. In this case, all I can say is that Dot had a way with her.

"Well, this one isn't." I picked up The Black, draped him over my right shoulder, then turned so he could keep an eye on Dot as I talked to Stan.

"You got all you need?"

Stan hesitated and Dot broke in. "You must get a picture of the cat with our snake! It will be like one of those animal pictures on the Internet that everybody loves! It won't take long. Coba should be here any minute."

I had my own idea of how The Black was going to react to a snake and I wasn't sure we'd want to post it on the Internet.

"Coba?" I looked at Stan.

"Coba Boucher—the assistant director of The Festival."

"My *current* assistant," added Dot. "Who won't be my assistant for long if she keeps me waiting. You must be that Craw-*ferd* fella, the one with the cat Stan told me about."

"Crawford." Stan corrected Dot and then pointed down the path at a figure walking our way carrying a box in both hands. At least she had sense enough to use both hands.

. . .

As I watched her approach, I realized how little I knew about the workings of The Festival. And having finally met Dot Fields, I was not inclined to learn about it from her. The Black began to purr quietly as I continued to scratch his ears. Maybe he was ready to forgive me for this escapade.

Dot began to harangue her assistant even before the young lady got to the tent. I tried not to pay attention. Dot's management style reminded me of my late boss's: berate in public, praise in private. It wasn't a particularly successful approach when Dr. Sean Thomas used it on me and I doubted it was working any better with this Coba woman. Despite Dot's loud complaints about how slowly Coba was walking I didn't see any increase in her assistant's speed.

From a distance, she looked pleasant enough. Short, petite; blond hair cut to frame her face; not much tan, suggesting she paid more attention to health warnings than to fashion. She was wearing the volunteers' uniform of the day—jeans and a Festival T-shirt. In her arms was a rectangular box covered with some kind of cloth.

When Coba got close enough to be heard, she spoke. "I'm trying not to disturb the snake, Dot." Her tone was matter-of-fact. She must be used to Dot and Dot's tongue lashings. It's a shame any employee has to get used to that kind of behavior. "By the way, I brought your bag. You must have picked up mine by mistake."

"It was hardly my mistake. They look the same." Dot pointed at the tent. "Yours is in there."

Coba was carrying a large carpetbag, its rope handles draped over one shoulder. "They're identical and reversible." Her voice was quiet. "I try to change which side is out when I notice that you've changed yours. I must have—"

"Never mind. Just put the snake down on the table. Why do you have that cover on the cage?"

Coba kept on in her quiet little voice. "You know this has to be disorienting to the poor thing. I read somewhere that they don't like to be moved. That's why I've got the cover on the cage. It's just gotten used to being at the office downtown."

As she went to put the box down on the table, I stepped back making sure I had as good a grip on TB as possible. If I hold him too close, he struggles to get loose. There was something about her accent that made me think she wasn't from around here. Coba Boucher? Is that what Stan had said? Boucher? Maybe Dutch? German?

Dot snorted. "Silly girl. Since when do you know anything worthwhile about snakes?" With that Dot jerked the cloth off the box, revealing it as a snake cage. It was made out of clear plastic with a metal top that looked similar to TB's carrier. The bottom of the box was filled with an inch or so of some brown mulch—bark maybe. I didn't see a snake, but there was a small boxlike thing in the cage that looked like a snake could be hiding under it. I didn't get a good look at it because Dot snapped open the top, stuck her hand in the cage, flipped the box over, grabbed whatever was hiding there, and pulled it out.

Coba made a half-hearted gesture as if to protest Dot's actions but didn't speak. I recognized the signs. Why speak up? Dot wasn't going to pay any attention anyway.

Dot had grabbed the snake somewhere about the middle of its length and either end of it had begun to writhe—trying to find something to hold. Before it could find anything, she put it on the back of her neck, head draped down one side, tail on the other. The snake continued to writhe, twisting its body into coils and wrapping part of itself around Dot's braid of hair. It, the snake, not Dot's hair, was red fading to orange with square blotches on its back. The belly, when you could see it, was checkered with white and black markings. It must have been a yard long.

"That's a beautiful snake! What kind is it?" Stan looked at Dot then Coba.

Coba spoke softly. "It's a corn snake." She looked over at me, wondering, I suppose, what I was doing there. A closer look and her features seemed a little pinched, eyes too close together, and I wasn't quite sure how I felt about her stare. If she'd been staring at my cat it would have been different. TB was beginning to get restless. I could feel him starting to squirm.

"You a city boy, Stan Dowdy? What's the matter, you never go out to the corn crib and find a snake in it? Growing up on a farm like I did, you learn how to handle life. Reach out and grip it with both hands." Dot shrugged her shoulders and the snake seemed to settle down. Its tail was wrapped under and around one of the straps that held up the bib of her overalls while, on the other side, its head had lifted up and it was tasting the air with its tongue. "It's a corn snake and a mighty fine one at that, if I do say so myself. Right 'purty' as we say in the country."

Stan laughed. "Can't say I even know what a corn crib is, much less what I'd find in one. I would have guessed it was some place, other than the refrigerator, where you kept corn, not snakes. I can see where you wouldn't want a snake where you expected corn."

Stan had an amazing ability to put up with all sorts of characters while he was on a shoot. And, because he could deal with them, he got footage that no one else could have gotten. Like now.

. . .

I was ready to pack up and leave. I circled around the table to where Paul had put TB's carrier on the ground. Paul kept on shooting. Stan was going to have plenty of footage on which to work his editorial genius. Heck, from all the footage of the snake he was getting he'd be able to do a one-snake documentary.

Dot guffawed, laughing at Stan's expense. "That's rich, city boy! The thing is you'd rather see a snake than the rat it just ate! A snake in the corn crib is good news for the farmer. That's why I decided The Festival needed snakes!"

I thought to myself that better news for the farmer would be nothing but corn in the crib. Coba was watching me as I edged toward TB's carrier. When she saw what I was trying to do, she jerked forward with a start, grabbed TB's carrier, and put it back on the table.

"Thanks. Would you open the top, please?" She did so without a word and I slipped TB in and latched the carrier. It had been so easy that I suspected my cat was ready to leave. I know I was.

"The Festival needs snakes?" Stan was moving around with his camera, getting close-up shots of the corn snake. Paul continued to operate the video camera.

"Its offices and gift shop do! Ever since that new store, the Bird House, opened up next door to The Festival gift shop we've been having problems with mice and rats."

The Festival's year-round office and gift shop were located in the old downtown section of Archibald built when merchants and residents alike depended on the river, instead of highways, for interstate traffic. Archibald's historic downtown had been in a decline ever since the drawbridge across the river to Shelbyville had been replaced with an overpass bridge that encouraged shoppers to bypass Archibald and Shelbyville and go shopping in the malls.

Historic downtown Archibald had been fighting for survival for more than thirty years. The Festival was part of the battle and as it had become increasingly successful the nature of a small southern downtown had changed from auto parts stores, barber shops, shoe stores, haberdasheries, ladies clothing, jewelry stores, and mom-and-pop grocery stores to antique stores, artists' galleries, boutiques, health food stores—the specialty stores that changed with the fads of the boomer generation. The newest was the Bird House. It sold bird feeders, bird baths, lawn ornaments, and bird seed to the growing generation of bird-watchers. Nothing the store sold was less than first class—even the bird seed was mixed especially for the climate and was species-specific to the area.

"Oh, we're glad to have them as neighbors—don't get me wrong—better to have a store next door than an empty building. Still the bird seed that's 'specially mixed to attract our feathered friends' does a hell of a job attracting rodents too! Of course,"

Dot leaned back and tucked her thumbs under the straps of her overalls, "growing up on a farm like I did, I knew just what to do." She nodded, clearly hugely satisfied with herself.

I glanced over at Coba and saw the almost imperceptible shake of her head and wondered what it was about.

Dot went on. "I was going to put out mouse traps, but this one's too squeamish for that. Can't kill anything, even a mouse. You can tell Coba wasn't raised on a farm."

Uh-huh, I thought to myself, that's what Coba's look was about. She knew what was coming.

"Oh don't kill it, Dot." Dot imitated Coba's voice in a squeaky falsetto. "Don't kill this. Don't kill that. Why the silly twit won't even step on a roach."

She gave up on her falsetto and glared at Coba who didn't say a word.

"So what did you do about the mice, Dot?" Stan has way more patience than I do.

Dot turned away from Coba and back to Stan. "Snakes. Can't depend on cats—some are good mousers, some not. But snakes, snakes you can depend on for rodent control. I had Coba here get us some snakes to let loose and, sure enough, problem solved. This one," she patted the snake that was around her neck, "was just too pretty. Made this one the official pet snake of The Festival. Keep it in a cage at the office."

"Stan." I jumped into the conversation when Dot took one of her infrequent pauses for breath. "If you've got the shots you wanted with the cat, I'll be heading on." I nodded my head encouragingly at my friend and grabbed the handle of TB's carrier. A little of Dot Fields went a long way.

Dot jumped back in before Stan could speak. "No, no! I want some pictures of my fortune-telling tent and a black cat! That's why I wanted Dowdy to find a black cat we could use in the pictures. The snake handling is just a new wrinkle I'm trying out this year. The fortune-telling is the big thing."

. . .

"See!" She pointed at the tent. "I had some volunteers set it up for me, but when I was doing the circuit I used to pitch it all by myself all the time."

Stan, Paul, and I turned our attention to the tent with slogans painted across its brightly colored panels—all about seeing the future, hearing the past, knowing the unknown. At the very least it was colorful. I was impressed with the tent underneath the decorations but skeptical as to anybody's ability to put it up singlehandedly. The tent was designed with a floor attached, so the sides were zipped to it—great for keeping water and cold air out, crawly critters too for that matter. There wasn't much chance of extremely cold air this weekend—or rain, though The Festival had survived both.

There were two entrances—sort of front and back doors. The front entrance faced the path; the back door, the park grounds. It was a sensible arrangement. Dot could slip in the back door, put on her fortune-telling clothes, set up the crystal ball or other props, then open the front flap for business.

She opened it now and gestured for us to enter. Stan glanced over to Paul and ran his forefinger across his neck. Paul stepped back from the camera tripod, looked at the tent and then back to Stan. Stan shook his head no. I was interested to see that they practiced sound stage discipline even when no audio was being recorded. Or were they recording sound? The cameras did have built in microphones—I think all of them do now.

I think Stan knew that looking at the inside of the tent was a waste of time, but he went anyway. He knows how to work the customer. I followed them in since I'd never seen the inside of a fortune-teller's tent. I peered around at the dim interior. In the middle of the tent was an eight-sided table covered with a black cloth that must have been sprinkled with glitter. In the middle of the table was a large cloth bag or purse. On either side were two metal folding chairs—one with a cushion, which must be Dot's. A narrow rectangular table was set against one wall. It held a couple of electric candles and an incense stand. Stacked beneath were what looked to be supplies—a small medical kit, some kind of metal screen, incense, lighters, batteries, light bulbs, tissues, and the ubiquitous water bottles. I'm old enough to remember when water didn't come in bottles, but that's another story.

"I've got a tablecloth that will cover up the stuff beneath it." Dot waved in the direction of the rectangular table. "I'm planning on putting the snake cage on top, and this time," Dot raised her voice so that everybody standing outside could hear, "this time we're not leaving that silly hide box in the cage. I don't care if the snake does like to hide. I want the customers to be able to see the snake." She rolled her eyes and muttered, "Coba's always worried about upsetting the snake—makes me tired."

Neither Stan nor I responded. Tired can run both ways.

Dot reached into the bag on the table and started pulling things out of it—a crystal ball, tarot cards, and a Ouija board with it's what-do-you-call-it-pointer-thing—right, a planchette. "What do you think, Stan? Should we just shoot the crystal ball or add a tarot tableau?"

I glanced around the rest of the tent and saw what I thought was a golf club leaning up against the back door. Puzzled at what a fortune-teller would be doing with a golf club, I picked it up and realized that while the shaft was the same, no golfer was going to want to try and hit a golf ball with just a curved metal strip. It was a snake stick. The kind professionals—and serious amateurs—use to deal with snakes.

"Wow, look at this. You really are serious about snake-handling!" I hadn't said much since my attempt to leave had been thwarted, just a few murmurs about how nice the tent looked.

"That thing! Huh, that's just Coba not wanting to get her hands dirty. I'd never use a thing like that. I catch them with my hands. That's what growing up in the country will do for you."

As I replaced the snake stick, I noticed another metal pole in the corner. This one had a handle grip that could be squeezed and released to open or close a pair of tongs at the other end. Looked like something else Coba used for handling snakes but I decided not to ask.

Stan, meanwhile, responded to Dot's earlier question. "Inside the tent?" He shook his head in that manner experts employ when they want to disabuse novices of foolish choices while not hurting their feelings. "I'm worried about the lighting, we didn't bring any portable lights and without them, inside shots aren't going to work."

"Electric candles don't throw off enough light, huh?" Dot grimaced. "Those were purchased because they were the closest thing I could find to actual candlelight. Fire marshal won't let me use candles and you can't tell a good fortune in a hospital operating room." She shrugged her shoulders. "So much for that idea—and it was such a good one, too. Let's see. What else do we need. Oh, that's right." Dot led us out of the tent. I had the sinking sensation that we were going to pursue the corn-snake-meets-cat idea, but I certainly wasn't going to mention it. Maybe she had forgotten.

. . .

Coba was standing a few feet away from the tent talking to a man I recognized—one of the top network guys out at the university. What was he doing here? Right—the university, through the Department of Technology, provides a wireless network every year just for The Festival—actually, two networks. One for the general public, the other just for vendors, artists, suppliers, and staff. It started out as a way for vendors to process credit card transactions, but, like so many things, technology was being used in ways no one had anticipated. Let's just say that everybody was thrilled with Internet access.

Standing behind the guy I knew—drat, I still couldn't remember his name—was another volunteer. I thought back and realized I'd noticed but not really processed the fact that a stream of workers had come up, talked to Coba, and then gone away. Volunteers looking for instructions—are we doing this like last year or not? Dot could go and work her fortune-telling booth because between the volunteers and Coba, The Festival ran itself.

"We've got shots of the outside of the tent and the black cat. We just need some more of you and the snake and I'll have everything I need for the promotional shots." Stan glanced in my direction and winked. "I think we can send the cat on his way."

I took the hint, headed for the table, and started to pick up the carrier, using both hands this time. As I lifted the cage, The Black made a sound—one I wasn't familiar with. Putting the box back on the table I peered in, trying to see if anything was wrong. Do you know how hard it is to see a black cat inside a cat carrier that's in the shadows?

Dot was yapping something about what an opportunity we were missing. I think she even called it a "photo op."

I opened up the case, reached in, pulled The Black back out, and put him on the table. He stared straight at the corn snake as it moved around on Dot's shoulders. It had been circling Dot's hair braid like it was a braid on top of hers; now it started to wind down her left arm, headfirst, leaving a few diminishing coils of tail on the braid.

My cat's eyes were locked on the snake's head as it lifted off of Dot's arm and turned in his direction. The snake began to taste the air with its tongue. TB was standing on the table as the snake lifted its head higher and higher. I had my hand on his back in case he made a break for it, but he was clearly fascinated by the snake. I looked from cat to snake and back again. They seemed hypnotized, eyes locked on each other.

"Look! Just as I said!" I hated the thought but it did seem that Dot might have been right about the photo. Snake and cat had obviously noticed each other, and there might have been a chance of capturing a truly memorable photo. Patience, however, was yet another virtue that Dot did not possess. She stuck her left arm, snake and all, out at The Black. The snake had wrapped itself around her arm at the elbow. To get the animals close, Dot's hand ended up in the cat's face. The Black decided that Dot had once again invaded his personal space.

Maybe Dot had forgotten The Black's earlier reaction. Maybe she thought The Black was harmless. Maybe she thought her flesh was sacred. Whatever maybe she used to explain her action, it was wrong.

I would have to watch the video in slow motion to know exactly what TB did to Dot. A mixture of teeth and claws I imagine. I didn't think there would have been that much blood if he'd just used his claws. The snake wasn't harmed. Dot's left hand, on the other hand—if you will—wasn't so lucky. Fortunately when she jerked it back, The Black let go. Watching the blood run down Dot's arm, I made a mental note to have the vet clip TB's claws.

While all the commotion was going on—Dot demanding and getting attention—I picked up TB and put him in his carrier. He didn't resist. In fact, he was quite calm. I think he thought he'd made his point.

. . .

Fortunately, the emergency medical technicians who were going to be on duty during the three days of The Festival were on site and quick to respond. Dot was taking blood thinners so the damage the scratches had done wasn't as extensive as it had seemed.

I carried The Black back to my car. Once we were on our way, TB reminded me that he didn't care for riding in an automobile. I was tempted to forgo the vet visit but, in the end, decided to get it over with. Both of us wanted to put the carrier away once we got home.

. . .

As it turned out, late Thursday morning is a good time to take your pets to the vet—on that Thursday, anyway. There was no waiting, so we were in and out quickly. The Black got his shots, a clean bill of health, claws trimmed, and fawned over by the new assistant who couldn't have been more smitten. I tried to point out to TB that she probably said things like that to all the cats but he was sulking in his carrier and didn't respond.

Mary's car was at the top of the driveway so I pulled into the carport so as not to block her in. Thursday was her day to clean but I'd left before she'd arrived this morning. I wondered what she was going to fuss at me about today. Ever since Eleanor, my wife, died five years ago, Mary felt she was responsible for nagging me. Truthfully, I'd needed it at first. Now I think it was just habit.

"Hey, Mary, we're back!" I shouted as I entered the kitchen from the carport. I set the carrier down, opened the front door, and The Black sauntered out—showing me that he wasn't in a hurry to exit. Holding his tail straight up he walked out of the kitchen into the den and disappeared from sight. He hadn't even checked to see if there was food and water. Yep, he was mad at me.

I went through the den to the screen porch to let Tan back in the house. She only wanted in because I'd come home, which meant she was now on the wrong side of the door. I'd been to unfamiliar places and carried their scent with me so Tan had to sniff me over. With Tan sniffing away at my feet and pants legs, I headed back to the kitchen.

Just as I got there, Mary walked up the stairs from my basement office, mop and bucket in hand. It must have been time to mop something downstairs. Not for the first time, I idly wondered how she decided *what* needed cleaning *when*. I knew if I asked she'd try to explain it to me but I also knew it was hopeless so I didn't.

"You need to clear off that thing you call your desk so I can clean it. There's so much stuff on it that I can't see the dust I know is there."

"Okay." I made a mental note of it since the fact that my desk was covered in paper notes was the cause of the problem. Wait, hadn't I decided to give up on mental notes? I picked up my cell phone and added a reminder to my electronic list. Hmmm. I needed to remember to check it more often.

"And how're you doing? You and Levi ready for The Festival?"

Mary and her husband, Levi, sang in their church choir, which performed at The Festival once it had turned Sunday into gospel music day. Mary walked past me to the laundry room, where the mop and bucket lived when they weren't in use, and disappeared from my sight. "Levi's in good voice and I guess I'll do. Sometimes I wonder about missing church to go sing with the choir. Still, if the preacher's okay with it, who am I to say?"

"Audience is bigger at The Festival than it is at your church."

"If we're singing to praise the Lord and not glorify ourselves, why do we care how many people are in the audience?"

I'd been sort of half paying attention to the conversation while thinking about what to have for lunch. That got my full attention. I walked into the laundry room and found Mary folding clothes on the ironing board.

Being totally unequipped to handle a crisis of faith, I tried to sound supportive. "Maybe it's a good thing to bring to so many people the pleasure of listening to you sing?" It was weak but it was the best I could do. Mary took pity on me and changed the subject.

"Where did you and The Black go this morning? I missed him helping me change the sheets."

"It was time for his annual shots so we went to the veterinarian's via The Festival."

"The Festival? Sunday's Pet Day. The Festival's not even open until tomorrow. What are you doing taking The Black out there? I thought he got mad enough at you when you took him to the vet's."

I shrugged my shoulders. "I knew he was going to be mad at me anyway, what with the vet visit, and Stan needed a model for some Halloween shots he was doing for The Festival."

"For The Festival?" Mary sounded skeptical. She put the folded clothes on the washing machine and collapsed the ironing board so she could put it away. The laundry room wasn't large enough to leave it set up and still be able to use the back door or get to the freezer.

Mary headed back to the kitchen and I followed. "Well, as Stan explained it, Dot thought publicity for her fortune-telling was the same as publicity for The Festival.

"Oh."

The almost silent sniff Mary gave at the mention of Dot Fields was indicative of her high regard for the director of The Festival. I remembered something about how Mary had represented the choir in dealings with The Festival one year and hadn't ever since.

"Yeah. I got to meet Dot Fields for the first time today." I thought for a second. "Somehow she managed to mispronounce my name. Anyway, I didn't introduce her to The Black and she never introduced her snake."

"She got a snake now? At The Festival?"

I nodded.

"Levi will want to see it. What kind of snake she got?"

"Levi likes snakes? I didn't know that."

"He's taken up studying them, but not because he likes them. He's been scared of them all his life and then one day he decided he was too old to be scared of snakes. Says learning about them makes it better."

"It's a corn snake and she's keeping it in her fortune-telling tent. I'll see if I can arrange for Levi to see it. I'll have to get Stan to set it up. Don't imagine she'll be doing me any favors."

"How's that?"

"Oh, she had a run-in with The Black. She stuck her hand in his face and he took exception." I shook my head. "The EMTs didn't think she'd need stitches."

"The Black?" Mary smiled. "Got to love that cat."

As if on cue, The Black strolled into the kitchen, walked up to Mary, and began to rub up against her legs. As far as the cat was concerned, I didn't exist.

"Did you scratch that director woman, TB? You shouldn't have done that. You know that, right?" Mary reached down to pet the cat. "If I had a treat to give you, you'd be getting one."

"Doesn't sound like you care much for Dot Fields."

"Two-faced." Mary picked up the cookie jar that sat on the small table beside the door to the carport and got her cash out. After Eleanor died, I started leaving cash in the jar for the times I'd forget Mary was coming or forget to buy the cleaning supplies that she'd bought out of her own pocket since I'd forgotten to go shopping.

"How's that?"

"The woman is two-faced. Sweet as she can be to the rich folk; mean as a snake to those not so lucky." Mary shook herself. "Well, that's not a Christian thing to say, but it's true. Woman makes me lose my religion. And that's another thing I don't like about her."

Mary opened the door and then closed it back again. "I forgot. I was going to ask you first thing when I got here and then you weren't here. Did you get your license—that private investigator license?"

I opened a small box that was on the counter, and, with a little difficulty since it was packed so full, pulled out a business card. "Absolutely. The Shelbyville City Council approved my application last Tuesday night. Here I am, James F. Crawford, licensed private investigator, at your service." And I handed her my card.

Mary looked at the card, feeling the weight of the heavy stock it had been printed on. "Why did you choose a color? Aren't most business cards printed on white paper?"

"It's tan. The graphic artist I used wanted to make my cards stand out so people would remember them. When I insisted on a plain design she wanted to use brightly colored ink." I smiled. "After insisting on black ink, it only seemed fair to use tan card stock."

Mary stared at me for a heartbeat and then laughed. "You and your pets. I swear, I never—anyway, congratulations. Now you've got to stop saying you're retired. You're only retired from the university."

She opened the door, said she'd see us next week, and left. I turned around and saw that The Black had turned his back to me. Still mad, but I knew how to get back into his good graces. I went over to the pantry and pulled out a can. Now I knew what to have for lunch—tuna fish salad.

The Black was a sucker for tuna.

Having reestablished cordial relations with The Black and played a little fetch with Tan, I headed back to The Festival. The University Press had decided to have a booth at The Festival for the first time. The prior director would never have approved of such a thing, but the interim one couldn't see a problem with it. Bobby had volunteered to help set up the booth and I had volunteered to help her.

I had known retirees who complained about being busier after retirement than when they worked full-time. It always seemed to me that it was their own fault. Certainly it was in my case. I'd agreed to help Stan out this morning, this afternoon was the Press's booth, and tonight was The Festival artists' party. Every year The Festival threw a party the night before the grand opening, ostensibly as a welcome for the participating artists and patrons of The Festival—and I guess that's what it really was. I rarely went, even before Eleanor died. I'm not really comfortable at big parties. I guess it's because—I guess I really don't know why. But when Bobby said she wanted to go, it sounded like fun.

There was more traffic on the roads leading to The Festival grounds than there had been this morning and more vehicles parked in the artists' lot. Campers, RVs, vans, and pickup trucks were scattered around the area reserved for people who were setting up booths. By tomorrow morning the parking lot would be filled with vehicles and there would be lots of tents pitched around the perimeter. Many of the artists made their living going from festival to festival and paying for a hotel room cut into profits.

I parked in the general lot just outside the grounds. Tomorrow that lot would be reserved for festival-goers. The area closest to the gate would be handicapped parking—with the exception of the director's and assistant director's reserved spots. I don't know why those parking spots bothered me, but they did. Silly, really, why not give the employees a perk or two?

If I had seen the bones of The Festival this morning, now I could see muscle and tendons forming, filling out the framework of The Festival.

Once the paths were cleared, volunteers had started staking out plots to assign to artists and vendors. Working with wooden stakes and string, they had made their way along the paths marking each plot with letters and numbers so that vendors would be able to find where to set up their booths and festival-goers would be able to find the artist they were looking for. Booths were popping up left and right, on either side of the pathway. The Festival grounds were beginning to fill up.

This was the first time the Press had had a booth so I couldn't head to its *usual* place. I looked around. There ought to be a way to find it without walking the full circuit.

Duh. I pulled out my phone and texted Bobby. "What is booth number?" I had long since figured out the numbering pattern they used here at The Festival. It was the same numbering system the U.S. Navy used for ships and buildings. Numbering starts at one end (the stem) and stops at the other (the stern). Standing at the stern, the left-hand side (port) is assigned even numbers while the right-hand side (starboard) gets odd numbers.

Bobby messaged back that the tent was next to the fortune-telling tent. So much for figuring out the numbering system. I chuckled to myself as I retraced the path I'd taken this morning.

. . .

I was still feeling amused when I got to the booth where Bobby and her coworker Frank Manning were checking out the situation. The tent had already been set up and faced the path so that it and one identical to it flanked Dot's colorful fortune-telling tent. Dot's tent was farther off the pathway so that there was room for a small picnic table in front of it. Right. A waiting area for her customers. Can't have them in the tent while a session's going on. Where's the mystery in that? The Press's booth opened onto the pathway so that potential clients could walk right in.

"So I'd figured out the numbering system The Festival uses and then Bobby texted 'next to the fortune-teller' instead of the booth number."

Bobby laughed. "Good! I don't want to be too predictable. Besides, you know I'm not a numbers person."

Frank continued to stare at the tent, stroking his mustache. "We *all* know you're not a numbers person, Bobby. But then neither am I. Editors work with words, not numbers."

"So it wouldn't do me any good to tell you they use the same method that the U.S. Navy does? Even numbers port side, or left. Four letters in port, even, and left. Makes it easy to remember which is which." The white tent looked brand new and I wondered if that was what Frank was staring at.

"Crawford, that's silly. Starboard and right hand have the same number of letters—nine—and nine is an odd number."

I had to stop and count before I was convinced. "Huh," I finally responded. "Never thought of that." I wasn't sure just how useful Bobby's mnemonic for remembering "starboard" was, but I wasn't about to argue. "How'd you get the tent up so fast? And where did it come from? Did the Press buy it?"

Frank turned around and exhaled, fluffing out his mustache hairs. "Okay, I think I know how we want to set it up. Hey, Crawford, how have you been?" He stuck out his hand and we shook.

"Did I tell you that it was Frank's idea for the Press to have a booth at The Festival?"

"Is that right? What made you think of it?"

Frank paused and then shook his head. "Nayh, I really can't take credit for the idea. Coba came to me and asked if the Press might be interested in having a booth this year. If Philip had still been alive I wouldn't even have mentioned it, but the interim director had been asking for suggestions."

"So there was a woman involved! I knew it." Bobby smiled. "Your secret is safe with me."

"There's no secret." Frank frowned and his mustache drooped dramatically.

"So things aren't working out that well with Coba, huh?" I'm supposed to be a detective, I told myself. I should be able to detect these things. But I had had no idea Frank was seeing the assistant director of The Festival.

"Whaaa— no." Frank looked surprised. "I took her out for a drink after last year's Festival and there was nothing there. One drink and that was it. We even split the tab." Frank reflected. "Which was a good thing. I had a beer and she had some fancy South African wine. She should have paid half."

"So that was it? One date a year ago?"

"That's right. Are we going to talk or set up the booth?"

"Then what's this about her coming to you?"

"She came to me and asked if the Press would like to have a booth at The Festival. We had met and she knew where I worked. She told me she knew it was at the last minute but there was a spot available and she could help us with the tent." Frank threw his hands up. "The university has supported The Festival for years now—helping with the publicity and everything. It seemed like a little tit for tat. The Press could use some free publicity—not the- director-shot-dead-in-his-office kind of publicity either. So I talked to the interim director and here we are."

Bobby and I looked around. A spot next to the director's tent and the tent itself. "You got a prime spot and a tent from The Festival? Wow, good work!" I had some mental reservations about how *prime* the location was having spent some time in Dot's company. I couldn't imagine Dot assigning herself a bad location, but I had doubts about how many regulars would want to be close to her.

"Will you shut up? Coba told me the Press could have those things but we couldn't tell anybody. All exhibitors pay to be part of The Festival—except the artists of course. That's been the rule since the beginning and it's still the rule. The Festival doesn't let organizations exhibit for free and it doesn't provide tents. Got it?"

I blinked. Now that Frank was rubbing my nose in it, I realized that none of the not-for-profits exhibited here. None of the charity groups that had to host their own fund-raisers. There were a number of organizations that raised contributions with folk art sales and I couldn't think of a one that had come to The

Festival. Wait, what about the organizations that entertain the kids?

The university's School of Music had a tent filled with musical instruments and grad students letting kids get some hands-on experience. Did they have to pay for a place? At a guess, no. Anybody entertaining the kids was doing it for free. Face-painting, tie-dying, working with clay, even the skits were there just so families would come to The Festival. I bet those groups didn't have to pay. But the Press, yeah, in years past I bet The Festival would have made them pay.

Bobby spoke up. "Makes sense, doesn't it? When The Festival started, nobody thought it would be successful. They would need to do things like that—everybody pays. Maybe now they're trying to help out without letting everyone know."

Frank tugged at his mustache. "All I know is that I promised to keep it a secret and I'd appreciate it if you'd keep your mouths shut too."

"Sure!" said Bobby. "Now how do you want to set up the tables? We've got some displays we can use."

Frank pointed to the back wall of the booth. "Since there's no back exit—just a wall of canvas—we can set up our tables against it and the side walls too. That will make a big U of displays all around the tent. We'll set up our computers and whatnot here in the middle, facing the pathway."

I kept silent while Frank was talking. I wouldn't go around telling people that The Festival had grown a heart and was letting select organizations exhibit for free—even throwing in a tent. But I wasn't going to promise that word wouldn't get out. Heck, Frank had already blabbed to us. Wonder what kind of story he had told the interim director?

Whoever had pitched the tent for the Press had put it right on the front of the plot. They'd pulled out the wooden stakes used to outline the plot to drive in the ones that held the tent. I knelt down and picked up the original stake that had been tossed aside. Funny. It was made of oak. Nobody made throw-away things like this out of oak—pine or poplar, but not oak. It was a short piece of wood, I grant you, but still. I tapped the pointed end on the ground to knock the dirt off. The end had been made with two cuts—left and right to make a perfect triangle—a single cut would have made a good enough point and saved some wood. Here's a puzzle I thought. Who puts that much effort into making a throw-away stake? And it didn't even have a Property of The Festival label.

"Hey, Crawford! Feel like helping us out over here?" I looked up and saw Frank struggling with one end of a long folding table.

"Sorry! Lost in thought!" I grabbed the table's other end.

"Maybe if you tried thinking more often you wouldn't lose your way so easily."

"Maybe if you treated volunteers better you'd have more than one."

I had fed Tan and The Black early since I was headed out to The Festival's Artist Appreciation Party—stopping along the way to pick up Bobby. The Black's lack of interest in his treat had worried me at first, but then I remembered he'd gotten his annual shots. Sometimes it takes a day or so for him to get over them. Same with Tan, I realized. Maybe there was more to their reluctance to go to the vet's than I had thought.

Anyway, I assured them that I wouldn't be out that late and would drive with caution. Tan curled up on her dog bed in the den while TB decided to hide. I suspected he was under the guest room bed for reasons that he alone understood.

The party was basically a beer and BBQ affair so the dress was casual—no question of white tie or black tie here. Blue jeans would be the uniform of the day except for the fact that it was late October and Halloween was in the air. I've never been one for dressing up in a costume, although I enjoy those who do. Some people I'd worked with in the Department of Technology were serious about Halloween costumes—serious to the point of being willing to wear something uncomfortable. I enjoy looking at the results but don't envy the pursuit.

Anyway, there were those who took advantage of The Festival's timing and wore costumes to this party as sort of a warm-up to the real events—Halloween parties. For that matter, there would be people in costume at The Festival itself. I would be too if you considered blue jeans and a long-sleeved T-shirt a costume.

I'd toyed with the idea of getting a plastic pocket protector, a white short-sleeved shirt, black slacks, heavy, Buddy Holly-style glasses held together at the nose with adhesive tape but decided against it. It was too close to my geeky roots to work as a costume.

I stopped at the doorway to the carport and wondered what had become of the mirror Eleanor had used to check her appearance one last time. My responsibility had been to make sure that no tags showed. I'd gotten so used to tucking in clothing tags that I'd had to stop myself from doing it at the university. Maybe the mirror was in the living room? I was pretty sure I hadn't gotten rid of it.

· · ·

Bobby was ready when I pulled up in front of her townhouse. I had gotten out of the car and started forward when she appeared at the door, stepped out, and locked it behind her. It was dusk, darkening into night, but the light on her porch caught the silver of her hair and flash of her smile.

"Sorry! I'm really looking forward to this party. It's one of my favorites. Did you need to come in?"

The only reason I could think of for going back inside would have made us late to the party—if indeed we'd ever have gotten there. I walked around to the passenger door and opened it.

"No, that's fine. Accepting delayed gratification is a sign of maturity. You look great by the way."

She didn't break stride, just smiled even broader, and patted my cheek as she got into the car. "Anticipation can make everything better."

· · ·

The party was at Dot's farmhouse, which was in the country. It wasn't that far from Archibald, as the crow flies, but it didn't take long for that crow to get into sparsely populated country. Like I said, I didn't usually go to these parties, but over the years Bobby had and claimed she had learned how to spot the turn-off that marked the dirt road that led to Dot's driveway. The map and the numerous signs that lined the route were pretty helpful as well. The Festival wanted people to find the party.

The party started at six and Bobby had decided that, while she didn't want to show up before six, she wanted to be there not much later. I think she wanted to people-watch as long as possible.

In October, the sun sets at six, so I'd picked her up just as the sun was setting. Once on the way, I was glad we were generally headed north. Every once in a while the highway would veer west and I'd be staring into the setting sun, almost blinded by the light.

Years ago, I'd been told that—all things being equal—houses to the east of cities were more expensive than houses to the west because commuters preferred not to drive into the sun going to and coming from work. I was now a firm believer. Oh, that's right, the guy who told me about the phenomenon said it was only true in the United States since the rest of the world believes in public transportation.

Bobby spotted the turn on the right just as the To Dot's signs proclaimed it. Following Bobby's directions, I turned east onto a dirt road and immediately slowed down as the car started vibrating wildly—washboarding. The road ahead was as rippled as any I've ever driven on. Clearly, it had been some time since Jemison County had sent their road graders down this section. Fortunately it was less than a quarter-mile to the gate to Dot's place. Which wasn't really a gate but a cattle guard. The parallel, horizontal metal bars set in the ground across the entrance kept cattle from wandering through the opening in the fence with no need for a gate.

As a child I had always wondered why the cows didn't jump over them to get to the other side. I suspect I had actual cattle behavior mixed up with nursery rhymes.

I eased down the driveway following signs that led to parking near the lights coming from the farmhouse. There was a large oak in the center of an open area bounded by the farmhouse, a small barn, and a large open-sided tent.

. . .

Bobby had been to the party often enough to have picked up a few tricks. Even though the parking area was not close to full, she had me drive down to the end of the field and park. There was an exit there—behind the portable toilets—that most people didn't know about. And it made a perfectly good entrance, too.

I backed into the parking space so that I could drive straight out. I had learned a few tricks myself.

We made our way past the toilets and found ourselves at a bar. Bobby ordered a red wine and I, after determining that the draft beer was of the light variety, settled on a bottle of nonlight beer. It had been too much to expect The Festival to be serving Red Stripe and, indeed, they weren't. Still I should have been thankful that not all the beer was light beer and I was—thankful that is. She had a tip jar set up and I contributed.

. . .

Drinks in hand, we headed toward Dot's farmhouse—toward a small group of people who'd beat us here. Bobby was talking about other artist appreciation parties she'd attended as we approached the people, who were standing in a rough line facing the house. At the front of the line, but still twenty or so feet from the house, was a small round table where a couple of people were seated.

I surveyed the backs of the people in line and didn't recognize anybody. That wasn't so surprising. There were a goodly number of people on the guest list I didn't know and many people in disguise—Halloween costumes, true, but disguises nonetheless. And you have to know somebody really well to recognize them from the back.

"What's going on?"

"Oh, you remember, I told you. It's Dot telling fortunes. She does it every year." We walked past the end of the line and could see who was sitting at the table. "I had forgotten where she sets up her table. She starts off telling fortunes for free. Sample readings, much shorter than the ones she charges for. I guess these are kind of teasers—appetizers—to promote business."

Dot was sitting with her back to the house, so her face should have been cast into shadows by the lights behind her but it wasn't. The light from the crystal ball sitting in the middle of the table made it easy to see her face. She had her gypsy costume on and was gesturing at the crystal so that the rhinestones and other faux jewels caught the light. Her subject—the person sitting across the table from her—was the one shrouded in the early evening shadows.

What do you call the man who has his fortune told? From the point-of-view of the fortune-teller, that is. The mark? The john? The client? This client of Dot's didn't look like he was enjoying himself or entering into the spirit of the thing. His body language—slumped posture, pushed back from the table—made me wonder if he'd been "volunteered" to have his fortune read.

I glanced over at a one-eyed pirate who was chatting with a red-headed vampirette—vampiress?—as they stood in line. I noticed her fangs but was distracted by how much neck she had on display. The pirate flipped his eyepatch up and glanced in my direction.

I pointed at Dot's victim. "Who's having his fortune told? Doesn't seem to be having much fun."

The pirate flipped the eyepatch back down before answering. "Arrgh. Nay, laddie. I be thinking young Chad there would rather be walking the plank than being the center of attention." His pirate's accent faded as he talked.

The vampirette nodded her agreement. I suspected it wasn't easy to talk through those fangs.

"I bet Dot picked him out, didn't she?" Pirate and vampirette nodded at Bobby. "I've seen her do it before. I have no idea how she knows just which people will be most miserable having their fortune read, but she does."

"Well, if you'd been around Chad a while you'd know he doesn't much care for the spotlight." The voice came from behind the pirate.

At first I couldn't decide if the guy who'd spoken was just *dressed* as a hippie or *was* hippie. He'd been standing behind our friends the pirate and vampirette and had joined in the conversation. At a closer look I realized he was barefoot and his clothes had that authentic hippie lived-in, slept-in, look. This was the real thing.

"Oh come on, Chad, let her look at your palm." Somebody at the front of the line called out. The crowd was getting restless.

Another heckler joined in. "Yeah, come on, buddy, what have you got to hide? You're not one of those hanging Chads are you?"

We all turned to look at the man in question. Dot appeared to have given up on the crystal ball and was trying, unsuccessfully, to get Chad to let her read his palm. Suddenly, he stuck his hand out, palm up.

Dot immediately grabbed the hand and bent over it. Her head was down as she stared at the palm, running her finger across the different lines. Her lips were moving so she must have been saying something but nobody but Chad could hear her.

The crowd, satisfied that progress was now being made, went back to the idle chit-chat people indulge in while waiting in line.

"I thought for a minute there that Chad had gotten his back up and was going to tell Dot what she could do with her fortune-telling." Our hippie sounded almost wistful. "Oh, well, peace, everybody." He wandered off, giving up his place in line. The people behind him closed up the space between them and the rest of the line as we watched him shuffle away.

"Probably got the munchies or forgot why he was in line." The pirate shrugged his shoulders with the careful movement of a man with a bad back. "Say," he looked at Bobby and me, "you're not trying to get in line are you? Because the end of the line is back there." He pointed toward the barn.

"You can go to hell! Just leave me alone, damn you!"

With that shout, every eye turned to Dot's fortune-telling table. I wasn't the only one who had missed whatever had happened to spark the outburst but we were all paying attention now.

Chad was on his feet staring down at Dot who was looking up at him wide-eyed. He must have jerked his hand out of her grasp, jumped to his feet, and exploded all at once. He was wiping the palm of his hand on his shirt as he shouted at her.

"I haven't done anything wrong. I don't know what you're trying to get at. No. I don't feel guilty. No. I don't have anything to hide. No. I haven't lost sleep over anything that I've ever done. And I'm for damn sure never coming back to The Festival no matter how big you make my stipend. Guest artist? Some way to treat a guest. No matter how you dress it up what you're talking about is blackmail."

Standing, his face and chest were caught in the light coming from the porch. He was tall and thin, wearing blue jeans, boots, and a leather vest over a Festival T-shirt. From the look of him, I'd guess he was in his late twenties. His hair was pulled back into a ponytail and that might have made him look younger. He was panting, gulping down big breaths of air, so angry that he was fighting himself for control. He went on in a somewhat quieter voice. Not that it made a difference. There was no other sound; everyone was listening to Chad.

"A spider. No, no, not a spider—a mosquito." He leaned forward until his face was close to Dot's. "That's what you are. A blood sucker. And you ought to be squished just like a mosquito." He snapped his fingers under her nose. "Stay away from me unless you want to get swatted—because that's what you deserve. You are a loathsome leech. A blackmailing bitch."

He straightened up, looked at the people staring at him, shook himself, and said, "Right. You're all too civilized to tell the truth aren't you? Too polite to say anything that might upset somebody—even if it is the truth. When I get older—when I've seen more of life—when I've realized I'm not perfect—then,

then, then, I'll understand how things work." He spat on the ground. "Bullshit. Art is truth. I know that. You know that—some of you do—or you did—once upon a time." With that he stalked toward the parking lots, his hands pressed against his thighs and his head held high.

For some reason I noticed how large his hands were. Pressed against his legs they seemed to cover his thighs. What kind of art did Chad create? What could you do with hands that large?

. . .

Dot had started laughing as soon as Chad turned to leave—loud, raucous laughter—and some people had joined in. Not many, but some.

"Let me tell you, friends, fortune-telling is not for the weak of heart!" Dot stood and shook her arms and hands. "Let me get rid of the bad juju! Got to shake it off." Her booming voice was heard by most of the ears that Chad had reached. "There's power in reading the palms, like the power in the crystal, the Ouija, and the tarot cards. A power so strong that it can be easily misunderstood—misunderstood like poor Chad Harris must have misunderstood it tonight."

Since I had formed my own opinion of Dot Fields and it didn't differ too greatly from what the young man had said, I was surprised to see how quickly she was able to get the crowd to accept her version of what had happened. I looked around and saw some people nodding their heads in agreement.

"Now, I don't rightly remember just what I said to set poor Chad off like that. When I'm filled with the gift, I let the words flow through me like water. Clearly some of my words struck poor Chad hard—not my intent. Chad and I will meet tomorrow—I'll see to it—and we'll patch this up—you'll see. Meanwhile, I just got to wonder what it was I said that set him off. After all, we all know it's the hit dog what barks."

Dot sat back down at her table. "Now who's next? Who wants their fortune told for free?"

I watched as a short, round woman took the chair that Chad had so recently vacated. Free fortune-telling seemed to be pretty popular. Most of the line stayed in place. Our pirate friend and his lady vampire and a few others—maybe friends of Chad— were wandering away but they were the exceptions.

"Dot was lucky Chad didn't wait until later to call her a blackmailer. Another thirty minutes and it would have been all over Archibald." I looked at Bobby and she shook her head in disagreement.

"Everybody is going to be talking about this from now until the end of The Festival—maybe longer. A guest artist accusing the director of blackmail? And Dot is neither loved nor revered. The story will be repeated—and believed."

"What's a guest artist? I heard him mention a stipend."

"The Festival is juried, which means artists have to have their work approved in order to be able to be part of The Festival. Just because you get accepted one year doesn't mean you'll automatically be back the next year. Every year the artists have to apply and be approved."

"Right. I knew that, but what's this guest artist deal?"

"I'm not sure I understand everything that's meant by the term. Some of the original artists have been coming to The Festival from the beginning and, I think, aren't part of the screening process. There's bound to be somebody here that can explain it to us." She smiled slyly. "Did you see the dress the lady vampire was almost wearing? I think the front was cut down to her navel."

"Was that what it was? I did think there was a lot of neck exposed."

Bobby punched me in the arm and we both laughed.

"Lots of neck. Yeah, that's what you were looking at—you and the pirate."

I had noticed that most people—those who'd come through the proper entrance—were wearing name tags. We hadn't been offered the opportunity to get ours since we'd used Bobby's shortcut.

Bobby had gotten an invitation to the party because she was a patron of The Festival. She'd responded to the invitation saying that she and a guest (me) would be coming, so our tags should have been made. We agreed that we might as well pick them up and began strolling toward the "real" entrance, where there was a long row of tables covered in name tags.

When we got closer, we saw that there was a another table separate from the ones with the name tags. The person seated behind it stood up, leaned forward, shook hands with the person across the table, and briskly walked away from the table. There was a hint of urgency in her stride. The individual who was left walked around the table and stood next to the chair. A recruited replacement, I deduced, which explained the urgency in her stride.

Even from the back, the recruit's silhouette looked familiar. He was handing out flyers or something as people walked by.

"Is that Frank?" I asked Bobby.

"Looks like his back." She agreed. "But I don't know, there's something odd about his head."

He turned slightly and we could see that he was wearing eyeglasses—with big, thick, frames—and he was holding an enormous cigar. Frank had come to the party as Groucho Marx. When Bobby called his name, he turned fully around and waggled his cigar at us.

"Say the secret word and the duck comes down."

I shook my head. "Frank, that has got to be the worst Groucho Marx impression I've ever heard."

"Well, who else could I impersonate without shaving my mustache off?"

"Uh." I was stuck. For the life of me I couldn't come up with anybody else who sported a mustache—a few civil war generals, but who else? "Teddy Roosevelt?"

"Do I look like a Roosevelt?"

Frank was right. He didn't resemble either President Roosevelt—with or without a mustache.

There was a pause in the stream of arrivals. It looked like the first field they were using for parking had filled up and people were starting to use one farther away.

"Ah-ha!" Frank grabbed a brochure off the table and turned to Bobby. "Have you seen this? Do you know what they're doing?"

Bobby took the offending piece of paper from Frank and glanced at it. "What are you fussing about?"

"The Festival." His frown deepened. "Look at the text. It's just wrong!"

Bobby laughed and handed the brochure back to him. "Give it a rest, Frank. You're not going to get the board to change that 'the.'"

I looked from Frank's frowning countenance to Bobby's smiling one. "I have no idea what you're talking about. Anyone care to enlighten the ignorant?"

"It's the 'the' in 'The Festival.' The capital T offends Frank's editorial sensibilities."

"Well," said Frank, giving the offending flyer one last glare before setting it down with the stacks of other brochures and the flyers advertising The Festival, "it violates standard editorial practices."

"It does that," said Bobby. She set her drink down on the table then reached over and began tidying the stacks of paper, aligning them with straightedge precision.

I smiled to myself. I had noticed that she was a compulsive neatener. Was that a word? I'd have to ask the neatener herself. She rearranged dishes in the dishwasher, straightened boxes on store shelves, and tidied magazines in the checkout line. I wasn't sure she was always aware of what she was doing. Like now.

She finished her tidying and picked up her drink.

"But exceptions to the rule are part of what keep our job interesting. And challenging."

Frank looked anything but convinced. He huffed, making his mustache quiver, and waved the cigar. "But why should 'The Festival' get to be an exception?"

"Why shouldn't it?" Bobby retorted. She turned and bestowed one of her high-wattage smiles on me. "Frank reminds me of me a few years ago. Rules are rules and exceptions to them should be few and far between and have a compelling reason for their existence."

I glanced at Frank then gave Bobby a quizzical look. "I wouldn't have pegged either of you as a stickler for the rules. Quite the opposite in fact."

She laughed and even Frank smiled. "And you'd be right— except when we put on our professional editor's hat." She took a sip of wine. "In any case, I have mellowed over the years. Frank, however, is still throwing himself on the barricade of editorial purity. Hence, his loudly and frequently expressed distaste for the capital *T* in The Festival. It's a lost cause—and he knows it. But he remains 'a tattered knight on a spavined steed.'"

Spavined steed? Wait, what or who did that remind me of? Frank snorted, "Look, do you two mind watching the table while I go get a drink? The young lady who is supposed to be staffing the table had to go 'powder her nose' and I was kind enough to say I'd cover for her. She must have found a line at the powder room."

Bobby looked at me and I nodded my head. "Sure," she said, "we can stay here for a while."

"Thanks." Frank gave us each a nod and walked off toward the nearest bar.

I snapped my fingers. "Travis McGee! The tattered knight!" I said triumphantly. "As described by his creator."

Bobby smiled at me again. "Clever you."

"I read them all in my misspent youth. Every title had a color in it—made it easy to remember if you'd read it before. I like that in a series of books. Reread a couple of them not too long ago." I sighed. "Sadly dated in my opinion; they did not age well."

"I'll introduce you to some other authors to take Mr. MacDonald's place."

"Why, thank you kindly, ma'am."

The break in the arrivals ended and Bobby handed out brochures on the benefits of becoming a dues-paying patron of The Festival as we waited for Frank to return with his drink or for the freshly powdered young lady to reappear.

. . .

While Bobby was discussing the pros and cons of becoming a patron of The Festival, I decided to get our name tags. Crawford was easy enough to find but Bobby's proved to be harder. I had

finally found a row of Smiths and was working back to where
Slater should be when somebody tapped me on the shoulder.

"The Cs are toward the front of the line, Crawford. You're
not going to find your tag down here."

"Thanks for the tip, Stan." I turned around and found Stan
Dowdy dressed all in black, with a guitar hanging from a strap
around his neck. His usual short hair had been covered with a
dark wig. "I mean, Mr. Cash." If he'd been wearing sunglasses
I'd have called him Roy Orbison, but he wasn't and besides, he
was a big Johnny Cash fan. "Did you really shoot a man in Reno
just to watch him die?"

"Worst reason for killing somebody I could think of." Stan
grinned. "I see you found your name tag. You must be looking
for Ms. Slater's." He stepped up to the table and began running
his finger down the row of badges.

"Yeah, Bobby's handing out 'don't you want to be a patron
of The Festival?' brochures for Frank. So I thought I'd get our
name tags."

"For Frank? Here it is." Stan straightened up tag in hand.
"Looks like they got it right this time. Bobby with a *y* instead of
an *ie*."

"Great. Come on, you can give it to her. Unless you're
waiting for somebody?"

He shook his head and we started walking back up the line of
tables giving the name tag searchers a wide berth. Stan was
evidently traveling single tonight. I never knew whom he might
appear with.

I explained why Bobby was subbing for Frank. "Frank was
standing in for somebody who needed to go to the bathroom and
Bobby took his place so he could go get a drink."

"Frank is always willing to help an attractive young lady in distress."

"That may be true, but I have to give him the benefit of the doubt tonight. Haven't seen the lady in question."

"Huh."

Stan seemed pretty confident that he was right.

"Hi, Bobby. Crawford said you might want this." Stan handed her the name tag.

"Thanks, Mr. Cash. Where's June Carter Cash?"

Stan dropped his voice. "Because she's mine, I walk the line."

"Wow, I'm impressed. Can you do 'Burning Ring of Fire'?"

"Oh, I can do it. Whether you'll recognize it is another question."

"I think Stan should let Bobby go back to pushing Festival membership."

Stan gestured at me with his thumb. "And I think he's heard me sing." We walked around the table to stand beside Bobby.

I laughed. "Let's just say that Bobby is supposed to be pointing out the pros and cons of being a patron right now. Once Frank gets back we can talk about you singing. No, make that once Frank gets back and we get another drink—then we can talk about you singing."

We stood quietly for a while as Bobby continued to hand out brochures. Stan picked up a brochure, glanced at it, and put it back down. "So, what are the pros and cons, Bobby?"

"It's really simple, Stan. If you become a patron you get all sorts of fun stuff for free. Like invitations to this party."

"That sounds like the pros," I said.

"Right," replied Bobby.

"What are the cons then?" Stan asked.

"You have to pay to become a patron in order to get the free stuff."

. . .

We were all laughing when Frank, in his Groucho Marx outfit, returned. He was escorting an attractive young lady—score one for Stan—who apparently had found a St. Pauli Girl-type outfit and decided to wear it even though the top was obviously several sizes too small. She looked like she was one deep breath from embarrassing herself—well, not that deep a breath.

"I'm glad to hear you're having fun. Sorry it took me so long to get back." Frank was still waggling the cigar but I was glad to hear he had given up trying to sound like Groucho.

"You've all been so kind." Miss St. Pauli Girl had the sound of the Magnolia State in her voice. "Something happened to the elastic in the blouse's neckline while I was sitting here. When I realized how low-cut it made the blouse, I just had to go pin it up."

"A sort of wardrobe malfunction," said Bobby with a grin. She stood up and gestured at the chair. "Here let me give you back your seat. I'm sure I speak for all of us when I say how relieved we are that you were able to fix the problem.

"And what a gentleman you were, Frank, to step into the breach like that." Bobby's voice promised that Frank was going to hear about what had happened, maybe for years.

Frank glanced at Stan and me, who were giving him astonished looks, shrugged his shoulders, and said, "Some are born great, some achieve greatness, others have greatness thrust upon them." With a grin he lifted his cigar.

"Say the secret word and the duck comes down. Hey, nice costume, Mr. Cash!"

. . .

We wandered away from the table, leaving incoming guests to marvel at Miss St. Pauli Girl's display of décolletage, unaware of what they might have seen.

"So, tell me, Frank." Bobby's voice was pitched so only the four of us could hear her. "Just how low-cut was it before?"

Frank struck a pose, cigar in hand. "I was glad I was wearing glasses otherwise my eyes would have popped! Just like the elastic did when she took a deep breath. Poor elastic never had a chance."

"And that is the closest you've come to sounding like Groucho all evening!" I laughed. "Who was she supposed to be?"

Frank shook his head. "I asked and she said that she didn't know. Somebody had given her the costume."

With that we were all silent for several paces.

"Some man," I said.

"Without a doubt," agreed Bobby.

"Anyway, she knows a lot about bicycles," said Frank.

I didn't want to know how he knew that and, evidently, neither did anybody else.

"So how's the party going?" Stan looked around. "I meant to get here earlier but didn't make it. Did I miss anything?"

"Just some artist calling Dot a blackmailer to her face then storming out of the party."

Stan perked up. "Crawford, what's this? What did she say?"

"She denied it—blamed it on the power of fortune-telling or some such." I looked at Bobby for confirmation.

"Right, Dot didn't seem very concerned. Said they'd patch it up tomorrow."

"Hey," said Frank. His eyes seemed to be magnified by his Groucho glasses. "I overheard somebody mention blackmailing when I was on my way back from the bar."

"Blackmailing is a pretty serious charge."

"Good point made by the man in black. How about you, Bobby? Have you ever heard anything like that about Dot?" I'd been inclined to discount the charge in part because it was so serious and partly because Dot had made so little of it.

"I haven't heard any hint of Dot doing anything illegal, but I don't know if I would have heard."

"Well, it can't be true," said Frank sounding certain.

"Why is that?" asked Bobby.

"Because it would be too wonderful if it were true and Dot got what was coming to her. Things that good just don't happen."

We all laughed, then walked along in silence thinking about good things that never came to pass.

. . .

"Are you coming to the Press's Halloween party, Crawford?"

"I've been invited." I glanced over at Bobby and smiled. "And accepted."

"So what's your costume going to be?"

"My costume?" I looked back at Bobby. "I thought costuming was optional."

Bobby smiled sweetly. "Coming to the Press's party is optional, Crawford. But I thought I'd made it clear that once a couple is committed to coming to the party, the woman gets to determine whether the couple comes in costume or not. Now start looking at the costumes and see if one appeals to you."

"Can I pick your costume? If so, do you mind if—"

"Crawford!"

"I'd say that was a no, Crawford. What do you think, Stan?"

Johnny Cash grinned. "Sounded like that to me."

I decided a dignified silence was my best approach. Particularly since I couldn't think of anything to say.

As we walked I made a point of looking at people in costume. Comic book characters were popular among the menfolk, not so much the women. Since the comic books I grew up with always had the female superheroes dressed in skin-tight outfits, I could understand the women's reluctance. Men, on the other hand, usually got to wear a cape, which helped cover up less-than-heroic figures. Padding to create muscles wasn't difficult, hiding extra poundage was.

In addition to our Johnny Cash and Groucho Marx, I saw two Elvis Presleys (male and female), Indiana Jones, vampires of both sexes, bride of Frankenstein—but no Frankenstein's monster, as yet—cowboys, cowgirls, Indian braves—no squaws—Tolkien characters—elves, hobbits, dwarfs—of both genders. Wait, I'm not sure about female dwarfs.

"Why is it that nobody comes dressed like our legendary coach—the god of college football? All you'd need is a rolled-up program, a coat and tie, and the right kind of hat."

Stan answered immediately. "I don't see anybody dressed up as Jesus, Muhammad, or Buddha either."

Right. Sacrilege. "Good point."

Bobby stopped walking. "Columbo."

Frank and Stan stopped and looked at me, assessing the possibilities. I hadn't been that big a fan. I don't watch much television now, actually never have.

"Columbo?" Stan sounded skeptical.

Frank slowly started nodding his head. "I can see it. Rumpled raincoat, no hat, right? And the cigar. He doesn't really look like Falk, but who does? It's the spirit of the thing, right?"

"Didn't Columbo carry a hat?" Bobby cocked her head to one side.

"I'm not sure," said Frank. "Crawford, can you squint out of just one eye? Give it a try."

I opened both eyes wide and looked at Stan who shrugged his shoulders and turned up his hands. "Doesn't sound like that bad a costume. Could be worse. Much worse."

He was right, I decided after glancing around. "Great! So that's settled. I'll check at a thrift store for a raincoat." It wouldn't do to pout about it. "So we've got a deceased comedian, a deceased country music legend, and—what? Mrs. Columbo?"

Bobby shook her head no. "I intend to go to the party, and no one ever saw Columbo's wife. It was one of the intriguing parts of the show. Was she thin, fat, old, young, pretty, not so pretty? No one knew what she looked like."

Frank looked at me thoughtfully. "Take a couple of steps away from us and then turn back and say 'one more thing' just like he did."

"Like *he* did? Like Steve Jobs did?" That would be an even simpler costume. Black T-shirt and jeans—I'd have to grow a beard, well stubble, but that was doable.

Bobby and Frank looked at each other and then back at me. "What a geek," said Bobby softly, and admiringly—I hoped.

"Yep. Once a geek always a geek." Frank nodded.

"Hey," Stan had been thinking about what I had said and was a little slow in responding. "That's right. Jobs was always doing that right before he introduced the product we were waiting to hear about. He'd start to walk off the stage and then come back and announce a product that would blow your mind."

"Well then," said Bobby firmly, "another thing Jobs did was watch TV because Columbo did it first. He stole Columbo's line."

Actually, that didn't surprise me. There had been plenty of tales about Steve stealing from Xerox—supposedly Gates had too. "Okay, so I'm going to the party as Columbo. Glad to have that settled. Who needs another drink?"

Bobby looked into her glass and seemed surprised to find that it was empty. "Sounds good to me."

"I'm fine." It stood to reason that Frank still had most of a drink left. We'd been nursing our drinks while he went to get his. "But I've got another vice I'd like to scratch. I'm for the smoking court. Anybody want to join me?"

"You're not going to light that thing up are you?" I pointed at Frank's cigar.

Frank looked down at the cigar and laughed. "If I did, where's my costume? No, just a little dose of nicotine will do me." He crouched into the Groucho position and waggled the cigar. "And that's the secret word—nicotine!" He waved and walked off to one edge of the clearing where you could see the red ends of cigarettes glow and fade, and the occasional glint of a flame.

. . .

"I think I'll find the food before the bar." Stan was always the practical one. "I'd like to find it before they run out."

"Run out? What do you mean run out? Of food?" I had never heard anything about The Festival running out of food.

"That was years ago, Stan. And I'm sure The Festival is using a different caterer than they were back then."

"Don't know about that. It's the same food year after year." Stan looked skeptical. "It's good BBQ, mind you, but I want to be able to have seconds."

I'm fond of eating but Stan is a little bit fonder than I am. "I'm guessing they're serving under the tent over there or inside the house, otherwise we'd have seen people with food."

"Thanks, Columbo. See you guys later."

We watched him walk away and then headed toward the bar that was in front of Dot's farmhouse.

Bobby had told me that it was a three-B party—beer, BBQ, and beans. As we made our way to the bar I thought she should have said four Bs—she'd forgotten bourbon. Those oversize Dixie cups that some of the partygoers had clutched in their hands held more than cola. You could smell the bourbon in the air, just like a tailgate party.

. . .

"Craw-*ferd*! How you doing!" It had skipped my mind that, unless we were incredibly lucky, we were bound to end up speaking to the hostess. "You didn't tell me you knew Ms. Slater! I'd have thought a literary type like her would be out of your reach—ignoring the fact you're a little old for her."

Dot Fields was standing on the porch of her farmhouse, seemingly without a care in the world, holding a pint Ball jar in her hand. Based on the head of foam floating in it, she was using the jar as a beer mug. As usual she was dressed in overalls—Archibald tuxedos was how she referred to them—but she still had her fortune-telling costume on—multicolored scarves draped over her head and shoulders and gaudy, cheap rings and bracelets. The very picture of a gypsy fortune-teller who was born in the country, and the country wasn't Romania.

I wondered how long I was going to have to put up with her mispronouncing my name. She'd probably continue to do it the rest of my life just because it irritated me.

Bobby spoke up. "Crawford! You didn't tell me that you knew Dit!" She turned and looked up at the porch. "Just want to compliment you on a terrific party, Dit. Just as wonderful as last year's. Why even the food is the same."

"It's Dot, not Dit."

"And his is Crawford, not Craw-*ferd*." Bobby smiled sweetly and batted her eyelashes while she held onto my arm, fingers digging into my flesh. "Thanks, again." We turned and walked away.

"She quit telling fortunes pretty quickly, didn't she? How long since we saw that scene? Not more than twenty minutes or so, right?"

Bobby loosened her grip on my arm as we got farther from Dot's house. "Long enough for her to tell some fortunes, distract some people, then quit for the evening. Her free session is never very long."

"So tell me about Dot, good ol' country girl that she is. I know she's not from around here. Seems like a farm girl would have some farm animals around—chickens maybe?"

"She's a jerk."

I thought Dot had made her angry. I was right.

"That was pretty much the conclusion I'd come to this morning. Don't know how people like that keep jobs.

"See the young woman over there behind the bar?" I pointed discretely with my free hand. "The girl with short blond hair who's delivering ice? Wearing blue jeans and a T-shirt? You should have heard Dot haranguing her this morning. Reminded me of how Sean used to speak to people who were in no position to answer back."

"That's Coba isn't it? The assistant director? The one Frank didn't hit it off with?"

"That's right. Coba Boucher. I met her this morning too. She's got an odd way of staring at you—made me uncomfortable. Of course, that was while Dot was making me uncomfortable with the way she was acting. Does that happen often?"

"Does what happen?"

"Frank not hitting it off with an attractive young lady."

Bobby laughed. "No, not that often according to Frank. I'm sure we don't hear about those, but we do hear about the ones where he does 'hit it off.' Not in any detail, mind you, just that he's dating someone. The turnover in someones is pretty high."

I looked ahead and saw Rufus George, the university's provost, and his wife, Ellen, walking in our direction. Rufus was wearing khakis and a casual shirt with the university seal on it. The slacks had creases so sharp that they might cut. His wife, on the other hand, evidently was one of those who enjoyed the costume part of Halloween. She was dressed like a fairy godmother, maybe? Anyway, she was wearing some kind of gown and carrying what had to be a magic wand.

I waved and caught Rufus's eye. He and Ellen stopped.
"Come on, there's somebody I want you to meet." I took her
hand and cut through the crowd.

"Rufus, Ellen, I don't know if you're acquainted—."

"With Bobby Slater? We've known and loved her for years!"
Ellen hugged Bobby, wand poking up behind Bobby's head.
"When Rufus told me that you two were dating I couldn't think
of a better match for you."

Ellen was from Tidewater Virginia—related to the Byrds or
one herself, I believe—who had never lost that lovely accent.
She and Rufus both had the sound of the Old South in their
voices—educated, cultured, refined, intelligent.

While the women were hugging, Rufus and I shook hands.
He smiled and winked, but didn't speak. Ellen turned and
hugged me while Bobby got a hug from Rufus. Sly old fox, he'd
never given me a hint that they were friends. Not even when she
was a murder suspect.

Ellen stepped back and tapped me with her wand. "Bobby, of
course, could do better—much better—so make sure she's happy
or I'll cast a spell on you."

I always forget that Ellen is short—she's just about Bobby's
height. But Ellen is so slender and carries herself so erect, with
head held high, that she seems taller—regal even. She's also got
a natural vivacity lurking just below the surface that keeps her
from seeming stern or stuffy.

"I don't think you have to worry about 'casting spells,' my
dear." Rufus had a broad smile on his face. "I'd say Bobby's
done a fine job of that all by herself."

"I'd like to cast a spell on Dot Fields. And not a nice spell
either."

"Oh my, what has she done this time?" Ellen looked concerned.

"Oh," Bobby laughed. "Made me so irritated mispronouncing Crawford's name that I called her Dit. I hate it when people make me act petty. I should have just ignored her instead of behaving in a fashion that I'm sorry for later. She brings out the worst in me."

"She mispronounced Crawford?" Ellen looked puzzled.

I volunteered an explanation. "She was giving it the country sound—*ferd* instead of *ford* and with the accent on the last syllable. But, what the heck, she is from the country."

Ellen tapped me with her wand. She handled it well—as if she might actually be a fairy godmother.

"Now, James, even if she were poorly educated, it wouldn't be an excuse for mispronouncing your name. But the fact is she was *not* born on some hard-scrabble farm to parents who could barely eke out a living. She merely chooses to pretend that she was. Deplorable, I think." Ellen gave a little sniff of disapproval. Hmmm. My guess was that Dot Fields better not ask Ellen George for a letter of recommendation.

. . .

Rufus and Ellen are some of the few who call me by my first name. Of course, I wasn't going by my last name when I met them. I was what—eight years old—ten?

"Huh?" I hate it when I resort to monosyllabic responses. "I mean, I beg your pardon? She didn't grow up on a farm?"

"No, James, she did not. I'm really disappointed in her. She likes to pretend, you see, and now she's made up all these things she's pretending to be. Poor thing, it must be hard for her to keep up with it herself."

Ellen continued. "She is from a farming community in the Midwest, that's true enough, but she didn't grow up on a farm. That is," Ellen stopped and looked thoughtful, "unless she lied to the hiring committee and is now starting to tell the truth. No," she shook the wand slightly, "that's not right. She's lying now. That's all there is to it. I was one of the board members who interviewed her before she was hired as assistant director. Now I'm president of the board and she's the director."

"Oh, I almost forgot. Have you heard that one of the artists accused Dot of trying to blackmail him? Because if you haven't you will. Bobby and I were there when it happened."

The vivacity that normally lit Ellen's face disappeared. "I beg your pardon? James Crawford, what are you saying?" Rufus stirred behind his wife and then held still.

I wondered for a moment if I was speaking out of turn— repeating something that shouldn't be repeated, but, no, she needed to know—the board needed to know that the director had been publicly accused of blackmail. Speaking truth to power, however, has its dangers.

"I asked if you'd heard that Dot was accused of blackmail by one of The Festival artists."

"I have not yet heard the story. Please enlighten me." I was glad the frost in Ellen's voice wasn't actually directed at me.

I shifted my weight from one foot to the other and felt like I was about twelve years old. I reminded myself that I was professional. A licensed private detective. An adult. I told myself to stop fidgeting. "Dot was telling fortunes and tried to read the palm of an artist named Chad. I don't think anybody heard what she actually said to him, I know Bobby and I didn't. But whatever she said, he took exception to it.

"In a very loud voice he called her a few choice names, accused her of trying to blackmail him, and said he wasn't going to put up with it. After he walked away, Dot blamed the whole thing on a misunderstanding—something to do with the power of fortune-telling."

I looked at Bobby. "That's pretty much the way it went, right?"

"That's right, Ellen. And now she's acting like it never happened."

Ellen paused for several seconds, her face still and eyes hooded. Then she nodded as if she had made a decision. "Thank you, James—and Bobby. Now," the vivacity returned, "you haven't said a word about my costume." She spread out her arms so we could see the glitter and sequins.

"I thought you were dressed as president of the board of directors of The Festival. Doesn't the president always wear that kind of outfit?"

"Silly boy. Enough about the board." Ellen's eyes glittered and a smile toyed at the edge of her lips. "It's *Oz* of you not to know who I am."

"Well," I glanced at Bobby and Rufus—no help. "It's just that I rarely take the yellow brick road and I'm not much of a Judy Garland fan."

Bobby relented and came to my rescue. "She must be Glinda the Good Witch."

Ellen nodded and curtsied. "At your service."

I pointed at Rufus. "I see you couldn't get him to put on a costume."

"I am in costume. It's very obvious." Rufus gestured at his slacks and shirt. "I'm dressed as a university football fan." We all laughed. Would that more fans dressed so tastefully—discreetly.

Rufus smiled. "The good witch and I were headed to the food tent to see what they have to offer. I'm sure the board president already knows the answer, but I would rather find out for myself. Care to join us?"

. . .

Rufus refused to confirm or deny whether the menu was the same. He claimed that he'd attended too many banquets to remember any of the menus except the exceptionally bad ones. For example, the dinner when the coffee was served cold ranked up there with memorable meals. Ellen and Bobby were certain the menu was the same. We wisely took their word for it.

Manlike, neither Rufus nor I was concerned that the menu was the same as last year's and the year's before that, and so on, and so on. Ellen believed that the menu hadn't changed since the first year Dot had been director. It wasn't exotic certainly, but as far as I was concerned, it was perfectly adequate. Ellen and Bobby, on the other hand, were incredulous that someone would serve the same food year after year. "She hasn't even tried chow-chow instead of sliced dill pickles."

The food was served cafeteria style. There was shredded BBQ pork, baked beans, potato salad, coleslaw, sliced dill pickles, and buns, rolls, or cornbread. There was iced tea—sweet or unsweet—hot coffee, lemonade, water, or whatever you brought in from the bar to drink. The only dessert was what I took to be banana pudding—a disappointment for the chocolate lovers. Actually, as it turned out, it was a disappointment for traditional southern banana pudding lovers too. From a glance you could tell there weren't any vanilla wafers in it—a bad sign.

The food tables lined the side of the tent nearest the house. The plates were stacked at the end of one table, so we knew where to start. Say what you will about the lack of variety in the menu, I was happy to see that the dining utensils and napkins were at the end of the line of food instead of next to the plates. I hated to carry that stuff along with the plate I'm filling up through the line. More often than not, I'd drag my napkin through the sauce—or put the utensils down and forget them.

It made much more sense—to me—to pick up knife, fork, spoon, and napkin *after* your plate was full. How else would you know if you needed all of them? Or how many napkins you were likely to need? I also thought the drink table should be separate from the food and preferred a separate dessert table. I had my opinions—and had enough sense to keep most of them to myself. The Festival was run by volunteers who—if criticized— were only too happy to let *you* try and do it better next year. Rightly so perhaps.

We started at the end where the plates were and worked our way down the line, serving ourselves.

Bobby led the way, then Ellen, then Rufus—I brought up the rear. As Bobby got to the cold dishes she raised her voice, "Crawford, there's paprika on the coleslaw but none on the potato salad. Any idea what that means?"

"That's right." Rufus was stirring one of the two bowls of BBQ sauce trying to determine just by looks if it was the hotter of the two. "Ellen, did you know that James is now an expert on the progressive change of the paprika pattern on party potato salad? How the pattern changes as the party progresses, I believe. Are you going to publish a paper on your research, James?"

The academic description of discovering clues in a murder investigation left me speechless. Ellen, on the other hand, rose to the conversational challenge.

"I wouldn't doubt that for a moment. I'm sure it was worth at least a master's degree and might have served as a dissertation topic." Ellen was juggling her wand and plate in one hand while serving herself. "I've heard of odder dissertation topics."

The table arrangers had miscalculated, in my opinion. I hoped they had ordered enough BBQ. They should have put the buns next to the BBQ meat instead of with the other breads. If the buns had been there, I might have made a sandwich or at least an open-faced one. Since they weren't, I went with a serving of the meat sans bread—more meat than if I'd made a sandwich.

Rufus had decided to put both sauces on the meat and was now dribbling the second sauce over his BBQ.

I snorted. "Ellen, it was nothing to do with dissertations or higher education, for that matter. It's just how I figured out that the potato salad at my retirement party had been tampered with."

"So that's how you solved the Sean Thomas murder. I thought it was something about the other man's suicide that made you suspicious."

"Oh, it was Albert's death that made me go back and look at the pictures of the party and the potato salad. That's all." I followed Rufus past the rest of the dishes until the four of us were standing at the end of the buffet looking at the rest of the room. I didn't see any reason to keep on talking about the party where my ex-boss died of poison and some of my ex-coworkers suffered from food poisoning. Not at supper.

The rest of the area under the tent was filled with tables and chairs. The tables were round, and designed, I suppose, to seat eight. Anyway, I'd guess that there were eight chairs at each table to begin with. But as nothing had been bolted down, eaters had added chairs to some tables as dining gave way to conversation. As there was still plenty of room for the newcomers to find a place to eat, lingering at the tables seemed acceptable and was easier on the feet. We picked a table and headed toward it.

I was starting on my dessert, poking around trying to find some evidence of banana or vanilla wafer in its yellow gel, while Rufus was working on his own concoction of cornbread and honey. I think the honey had been intended as a sweetener for the coffee, but Rufus had other ideas. I was beginning to think he remembered the menu just fine and had learned to avoid the dessert. Bobby and Ellen had long since finished with food and were enjoying some after-dinner coffee while reminiscing about Festivals of the past.

Every year at The Festival at least one gadget, gizmo, toy, whatever seemed to catch the public's fancy and become a hit with The Festival-goers much to everybody's surprise—even the artist's. Things that had been for sale in prior years could suddenly become the rage. Or things that hadn't sold at other shows or festivals would come to Archibald and become the hit of The Festival.

Bobby and Ellen were trying to match item with year when Peter Pan appeared at our table.

Really. Peter Pan. Tinker Bell wasn't with him, but this person could have walked right off the peanut butter jar or the movie screen. If Captain Hook or Wendy had been present, they would have agreed with me. He was the right height and size for the boy who refused to grow up—wearing a green tunic, hat, leggings, and a sword thrust through his belt. If he'd been standing legs apart, fists on his hips, ready to crow it would have been perfect—but he was carrying a plate of food and a plastic cup.

"Mind if I join you?" Peter Pan glanced at our plates. "Oh, you're finished." The voice was all wrong. That was no boy who refused to grow up—that was a grown woman's voice—husky and warm. With another glance at the tunic I wondered how I thought there had been a boy's body in it.

Rufus started to stand and I began to get out of my seat as well.

"Oh, don't get up." She tried to stop us.

The words were wasted on Rufus George and, I was pleased to see, on me as well. Rufus was a good influence. As a child, I had had drilled into me the behavior expected of any southern male over the age of six. My generation had rebelled against the status quo, as every generation does—only more so. And I sometimes regretted the fact that we had all too often been successful in changing the rules of etiquette.

"Lenora, what a delight to see you. Please do join us." He looked around the table. "Ellen, of course, you know. Do you know Bobby Slater and James Crawford?"

Peter—that is Lenora—put her plate down on the table and nodded at the women. "Ellen. Nice to see you again, Bobby." Then she turned to me and stuck out her hand. "Lenora Maisano. I teach introduction to art history to freshmen, sophomores, and the occasional football player. Because it's a survey course with huge enrollment, I'm stuck in one of those enormous lecture halls where none of the audiovisual equipment works like it should when it should. You may not remember me but I remember a bunch of times when your part of the Department of Technology saved my butt."

I grinned. "Professor Maisano, what a pleasure to finally meet you. An art professor ought to be able to show art to her students. Your requests always seemed reasonable to us.

Particularly since you phrased them as requests, unlike some
faculty members." I hadn't met Dr. Maisano before; now that I
had I could see why our guys were always happy to go out when
she called.

Lenora raised her eyebrows at Rufus. "And I remember
when the department began to act like my requests were
unreasonable and showed a 'lack of vision.' I'm glad to report
that they've gone back to being helpful."

I grabbed the chair next to me and held it for her. She smiled,
pulled out her sword, set it on the table, and then sat. Rufus and I
reclaimed our own chairs.

. . .

"Where did you get that wonderful costume?" Bobby leaned
forward to talk to Lenora across me.

Lenora laughed. "It's a long story. When I was younger,
more acrobatic, and at a much smaller campus, I agreed to do
some stunts for a campus production and ended up with the
costume. I've had to alter it since, but I like playing Peter—
we're simpatico." She nodded across the table. "And your
costume is beautiful too, Ellen. Glinda the Good Witch?"

Ellen smiled and nodded her head in regal
acknowledgement.

"And that's a real sword?" It sounded to me like Bobby was
still on the hunt for what to wear to the Press's Halloween party.

"It's real—an épée." Lenora agreed. "But with a practice
button covering the tip."

"Interesting," I said. "Since there's no scabbard you're not
carrying a concealed weapon."

"And the button means the safety's on." Lenora unwrapped the paper napkin from around the plastic set of dining utensils.

I pointed at the sword and asked a question with my eyebrows. Lenora nodded agreement so I picked up the épée. It was sized, I decided, for her. The handle and guard were too small for my hand. The sword too light. The blade was three sided and thin instead of the broad, heavy blade of the sabers favored by Civil War cavalry—the swords I was most familiar with. In truth, it would have been more accurate to say they were the swords I was least ignorant of. I must have looked puzzled.

"Dueling swords, James. Designed for dueling to first blood. Part of a movement to make dueling less lethal, while preserving the function of a duel."

For half a heartbeat I thought Rufus was speaking as a southern gentleman who'd won his share of duels then I remembered he had a doctorate in history. He still taught an upper-level course in the spring. I gave the button that covered the only dangerous part of the épée a tug and it didn't budge.

"James, are you speculating that your next murder case will involve a sword?" Rufus leaned back in his chair with a satisfied smile on his face. "You've had poisoning, hanging, and shooting. Time to add stabbing?"

We all laughed, Lenora joining in after we started. "That's right. I knew Mr. Crawford had retired from the university and now was solving murders. How's that going?"

"You can call me Crawford," I responded. "Rufus and Ellen have known me since I was James. I have names like trees have rings—both mark the passage of time."

"I don't think tree rings are a good simile, Ford." Bobby grinned. "I think you've got circles of friends who use names that reflect how old you were when you met and how close the relationship is—more like a Venn diagram."

I kept my mouth shut. I could have said I'd been called Jimmy as a young boy. When I started grade school I informed everybody that I was done with "Jimmy" and they could call me "James." It had taken a little while and some perseverance but I'd eventually put an end to Jimmy.

"And, Rufus, you know I don't choose cases—or haven't as yet—they seem to choose me. I have no control over the murder weapon." I was struck by a thought and this seemed like a good group to broach it to. "As a licensed private investigator should I start carrying a weapon?"

" A weapon?" Bobby looked surprised.

"It was just an idle thought." I was uneasy about carrying a gun, thinking that if I carried one, sooner or later I'd use it just because I had it—not because it was really necessary. Of course, none of my murder investigations to date had included a threat to my safety. If they had, I might be more interested in a weapon.

"What about a squirt gun? Like one of those that were so popular at The Festival a couple of years ago. Remember? You hid it in the palm of your hand, made a fist with the nozzle poking out between your fingers, and squirted people without their having any idea where the water was coming from." Bobby pointed at Ellen. "We were just talking about them and couldn't decide at which Festival they were a hit."

"Lenora might remember," said Ellen. "She's a die-hard Festival-goer and a member of the board."

Lenora swallowed a bite of food before speaking. "Of course I remember. It was called the Little Squirt and that was two Festivals ago. It was shaped more like a bulb than a gun—put the nozzle between your fingers and cup your hand around the bulb. A quick squeeze and out comes a stream of liquid. It didn't hold that much but boy was it hard to figure out where the water was coming from. Last year's hit was that toy snake that actually bit you. Fun gadget."

"Right," agreed Ellen. "It was a wooden snake—made of sections—with a rattle on one end and a head on the other. There was a rubber band that you twisted—what did you turn—the head or the rattle?"

"The tail, don't you remember?" Bobby made a motion as if she were turning a wheel. "You locked the mouth open then turned the rattle to twist the rubber band as tight as you wanted to. Then you put the snake down, set the head upright, and flipped the tail down. It was locked and loaded. All you had to do was flick the tail up. It would rattle wildly then—just as it was dying down—the tension released the jaws so it would snap shut. It was lots of fun."

Bobby paused. "Well, it was a three-day wonder. That's what most of the hits are at The Festival. You never know what's going to catch the public's fancy."

"That's the truth! Who would have thought those copper-roofed bird houses on a pole would be so successful?" Ellen tapped her forefinger on the table. "Which Festival was that—four years ago or five?"

"Five years ago because I missed that one," answered Bobby. "The next year everybody was talking about what a hit they had been the year before. That year—four years ago—it was the hand-made bread knives. The ones with industrial bandsaw blades with beautiful wooden handles. You could have your pick of exotic woods and the knives were specifically designed to be either right- or left-handed—something about the handle."

. . .

The banana pudding was served in clear, squat plastic glasses. The kind you'd serve an old-fashioned in, sometimes called a rocks glass. There was no evidence of vanilla wafer or banana on the outside and my investigations of the interior had convinced me that all the glass held was yellow goo. There is a special spot in hell for people who take a dish that can be surprisingly good even when made in enormous quantities and screw it up. Why leave bananas out of it?

I put the pudding aside and glanced over at the dessert table. Judging from how many puddings were still there, I might be the only person who had taken one.

"This is the first time I've been to one of these pre-Festival parties and I've got no complaints except for the worst banana pudding I've ever tasted."

"Oh, that's not banana pudding. Didn't anybody warn you?" Lenora shook her head. "Dot claims she doesn't like bananas so the caterer makes faux banana pudding without bananas, vanilla wafers, or meringue. I think she's the only person who eats that stuff."

I wondered if a frustrated caterer could murder somebody that way—poison a dish that no one else was going to eat?

"Who's the caterer and why haven't they gone out of business?"

"He hasn't gone out of business because he caters for most of the old Shelbyville families and does a wonderful job. His true southern banana pudding is ambrosial," explained Ellen. Rufus smiled and nodded his agreement.

"So Dot and the caterer got into an argument about banana pudding and they took it out on the food?"

"Say rather, they took it out on the pudding," said Ellen
judiciously. "He still provides the food for this party. I'm not
sure why, but he refuses to be listed in the program so I would
be going against his express wishes if I told you his name."

That was that, then. I could name names all night long and
Ellen George wasn't going to confirm or deny it.

"You're not sure why he still provides the food? It's
interesting that someone just made a loud and very public
accusation against Dot. Could that be how she gets people to do
what they don't want to do?" I pushed back from the table. "As
in, 'I don't why he does it . . . unless it's blackmail.'"

"So you've heard it too." Lenora glanced around the table.
"The rumor that Chad Harris accused Dot of trying to blackmail
him. I didn't want to mention it—just in case."

"It's not a rumor—the accusation part, anyway. Bobby and I
were there when he made it—along with twenty or thirty other
people. We all heard him shout that she was a blackmailer—and
heard Dot claim—after Chad had stormed off—that it was just a
misunderstanding."

. . .

Ellen glanced at her wrist. She was wearing a bracelet that went
perfectly with her outfit. At first I'd thought it was costume
jewelry, but the presence of a tiny-faced watch set in the midst
of rhinestones made me rethink the rhinestones.

"Do excuse me," she glanced around the table. "I have to go
meet this year's judge for The Festival. Bob Freight has agreed
to judge the artists. He refused our offer to dine on BBQ and
beans but assured us he'd attend the party after dining
elsewhere."

"Really?" There was a little chill in Lenora's voice. "Bob's getting a little full of himself, isn't he? I mean he does have an amazing collection of folk art, but no BBQ?"

"He pleaded a delicate stomach." Ellen met Lenora's gaze. "Did you know he'd been sick?"

"No," Lenora looked a little abashed. "I hadn't heard. How's he doing?"

"I haven't seen him yet, but I heard he looks frail. Anyway, he said he was honored to be asked to judge and was looking forward to the party. You know Bob, he loves parties."

Ellen fiddled with her wand for a moment. "Lenora, I think the board—at least those of us on the executive committee—needs to discuss this blackmail accusation as soon as possible. Would you meet me back here? Say in thirty minutes?"

"Certainly, Ellen. I'll be here."

Rufus stood up and held Ellen's chair for her. "Sorry to eat and run but I don't want to keep our judge waiting."

Ellen and Rufus left amid a chorus of good-byes, so-good-to-see-yous, and see-you-laters.

Lenora turned to me. "Did you say you don't come to these parties? Then you won't have seen Dot's house. Have you?"

I smiled. "Just from the yard. Dot was on the front porch being gracious to the peasants."

Lenora turned to Bobby. "How about you? Have you seen the inside? The original part of the house was a dog-trot built in the late 1800s."

"Sounds interesting," I interrupted. "But we'd just as soon not run into Dot any more this evening. Right, Bobby?" Dot wasn't my kind of people but I didn't really care if I ran into her again or not. Bobby, however, had clearly been angry at how Dot had treated me.

"Do you think I want to run into her? Bob Freight is arriving at her party and Dot's going to be part of the greeting. Don't worry, she's not in her house right now—that's why I suggested it. There's no time like the present to see Dot's house and not see Dot. Besides, I've got thirty minutes to kill."

I glanced at Bobby and she nodded her head and grinned. "Sounds great. Let's do it."

. . .

The crowd had gotten thicker while we'd been eating and talking. I let Bobby and Lenora go ahead and I followed behind as, single file, we squeezed our way through the mixture of party-goers—costumed and un-costumed. I had assumed that the locals would be the only ones to show up in costumes and I might have been right. It was hard to tell if some of the artists were in costume or if that's just what they wore.

If Lenora was talking I hoped Bobby could hear her because I couldn't. There was a steady roar of crowd noise that was so loud I couldn't tell if there was a band playing. I could hear snippets of conversation, mostly about The Festival, as we squeezed between clumps of chattering people.

Some were complaining that the food was the same as last year—others were delighted to hear there was food and where was it? Artists and vendors were generally pleased with where their booths were located—because it was the same as last year's or not the same. "If you don't like the booth location, see the little blond—Coba is her name—don't bother with Dot. Coba knows how important location is to us regulars."

We paused as Lenora tried to find a path around a knot of people who had apparently just found each other after an absence of several years. While we were stopped, my eavesdropping picked up complete sentences.

"Oh, Dot is just impossible to deal with—always talk to Coba."

"As far as I can tell, Dot wants to do the worst job possible."

"She thinks the harder she is to deal with, the less she'll have to do."

"If she keeps that up, the board will fire her and keep the little blond—odd as she is—at least the blond tries."

"Why hasn't the board fired Dot? That's what I want to know."

"Oh, I've heard she's got pictures of board members performing unnatural acts with goats. Or maybe playing golf with Satan."

"I did hear that she tried to blackmail an artist this evening."

The crowd parted, Lenora took advantage of the opening, and we surged forward toward the house so I never heard more about the pictures of board members. I had difficulty picturing Ellen George playing golf—with anybody—or giving in to threats.

We'd worked our way through the space between the entrance to the food tent and the bar nearest to it so the crowd was thinner but the going didn't get easier. Why, I wondered, do people stop at the head of the stairs? Or at the foot, for that matter. Or at doorways? As if nobody else was trying to walk up the stairs or go in or out the doorway. Lenora led us up the wide front steps to the porch that wrapped around the house.

The porch floor was painted a glossy shade of gray and had been painted so many times that it was thick and slippery. It was hard to tell but I'd say it was made of tongue-and-groove boards. It was old, but not that old.

"The wrap-around porch isn't original." Lenora had read my mind. "It was added sometime in the 1900s we think. Now the core of the house," Lenora crossed the front porch and headed toward a double screen door, "the original part, that is, is from the 1860s."

We stepped through the doors and were in a wide hallway that stretched through the house to the screen doors leading to the porch at the other end. "This is all original. The kitchen and dining rooms were off to the left where we're standing, the rooms on the right were bedrooms and private rooms—reading or music rooms."

I nodded my head. It made sense to build like this in the South. "So the kitchen heat was on one side of the house—I bet the washroom was off the back too—and a breezeway between it and the rest of the living space."

"There are fireplaces on both sides of the house, but the ones on the bedroom side were only used in winter."

"All of this was under the same roof?" Bobby was looking up at the ceiling. I was looking at the wide plank flooring. It looked original, and, if it was, it had to be heart pine.

"That's right. This was before screening was common so a dog could trot right through the house. If it wanted to. Some people call them possum-trot houses."

I had to grin at the thought. "I'd guess that would be an either/or kind of situation."

Lenora and Bobby looked puzzled.

"If you had dogs, no possum was going to trot through here. If you didn't—who knows what might trot through the house."

. . .

Lenora led us through the rest of the house with the exception of Dot's bedroom. The house had been lovingly restored or preserved but I didn't much care for the way Dot had furnished it. The authenticity of the structure quarreled with the primitive style of the furniture she'd filled it with. Except for the gun safe.

I stopped and looked at the safe. It was old and built into the wall. I bet Dot hadn't put it in and I was glad she'd had enough sense to leave it. The manufacturer's name was faded and the metal knob on the dial was worn by countless years of being spun. Even the numbers on the dial were faded.

I nodded at the metal door with the combination lock knob and handle at waist level. "Nice gun safe. How old is it do you imagine?"

"It's probably from the turn of the century—the early 1900s. I was glad to see Dot hadn't had it taken out. I asked her if she felt she needed guns for protection living so far out of town. She just laughed and said that she liked storing her protection in that safe." Lenora shook her head. "If you're going to have guns I agree they need to be under lock and key."

I grinned. "I'm glad to see she keeps both her guns and her ammunition locked up. It's much safer than just locking up the ammo." I looked over at Bobby and she smiled. We were both thinking that if Philip Douglas had kept his rifles as safe as he had his ammunition he might still be alive.

"Is that what happened when the Press director was killed? He left a gun out and the murderer used it?"

Lenora was clearly interested in finding out some of the details around Philip Douglas's murder. Details that Rufus had wanted kept from the public. Not from a love of secrecy so much, more a love of the university. He hated for it to be in the news for bad things that happened on its campus and the less said about them the better.

I smiled and shook my head. "This is awkward. Sorry. Really the less said about Philip Douglas the better. Bobby will tell you that the man needed killing. But just because he needed it, didn't make killing him right. Rufus is correct. We don't need to be talking about it."

Bobby took Lenora's arm and said in a stage whisper, "Don't take offense, Lenora. Rufus hired him and doesn't want it talked about so Crawford is going around being reticent. You know how men can be. I know all about it. See me tomorrow at The Festival and I'll tell all." Together they turned toward me and smiled.

"And she'll probably do a better job of it than I would. Words are her business, after all."

We turned to leave Dot's house. Lenora was on The Festival board and some of the things I'd overheard or seen with my own eyes made me ask, "Speaking of awkward questions, I've got one for you. Why does the board keep Dot on as director? I've heard murmurs about her."

"A big reason is Dot's own commitment to The Festival." Lenora shrugged her shoulders. "She's turned down raises and suggested diverting the money to the artists stipend fund—and I shouldn't have said that much. Board meetings are not public meetings and it is the consensus of the board that our discussions—particularly about employees of The Festival—are not disclosed."

I thought to myself that I'd never heard of such a dedicated employee. "That's two awkward questions. Want to go for three?"

Lenora put the palm of her hand on the sword's hilt. "Curiosity killed the cat, Crawford. What's the question?"

"How about Coba? Can you talk about her or does that board of director's reticence still apply?"

"Coba? What about her?"

"Why she puts up with the way Dot treats her? I retired early just so I didn't have to put up with that kind of treatment."

"Oh, that! Well I can't tell you the reason as a member of The Festival board, but I can as her landlady."

"Landlady?" The thought of Peter Pan owning property surprised me.

"Oh, I'm not a slumlord or anything. When I first moved here to teach, I bought a small house in Archibald. After I got tenure I moved closer to campus—across the river, but a colleague who was visiting wanted to rent for a year. It worked out for both of us, and now I have a small two-bedroom, one-bath house I rent. I just cover costs. Lately I've rented it to Coba—subsidizing The Festival's poor pay scale."

"Did you rent it to Dot too? Before she became the director?"

"Dot? No, Dot bought this farm, well farmhouse, and some acreage right after she started work as assistant director. I always figured her family had money no matter how she poor-mouthed them. Coba is another story.

"Coba has applied to become a naturalized U.S. citizen, and if she quits this job she jeopardizes her chances. She might have to find another job and reapply, which is like starting all over again from the beginning. Not something anybody wants to do. Same thing would happen if she moved, so I've decided to double or triple her rent."

"Lenora!" Bobby was horrified. "You can't mean it!"

"Of course I don't mean it. Who would do something that mean?"

"Dot?" I ventured a guess.

Lenora chuckled. "Yes, well that is possible. But what's most important in Coba's life right now is getting her citizenship. She's headed over to Atlanta at the end of The Festival to meet with her immigration lawyer and the USCIS case worker. The board's given her approval to leave right after the closing ceremonies."

"Us cuss?" I pulled on my earlobe. "You lost me there."

"Sorry, I've dealt with the immigration bureaucracy for so long that I forget not everybody else has—U.S. Citizenship and Immigration Services. It's the new user-friendly name for what used to be called INS—Immigration and Naturalization Service."

"I would have recognized INS, now that you mention it." I smiled at the name-change-game organizations play. You get such a bad reputation that you eliminate the name. Management decides it's easier to change the name than to change the way they do business. "And Dot agreed to let her leave? Wow, I wouldn't have thought she'd do that." That didn't match the petty tyrant behavior I'd seen. I'd have predicted that any request like that Dot would automatically deny—or cancel at the last minute.

"She didn't." Lenora's voice was dry. "Coba made the request directly to the board and we approved it. If you're serious about naturalization you don't tell the USCIS to reschedule. You meet them when they're ready to meet you."

"Really?" Bobby and I exchanged glances. "Had no idea it was that complicated."

"Oh, the U.S. bureaucracy is pretty puffed up with itself when it comes to dealing with powerless foreigners. I've had other friends who've gone through the process. One of them moved down here from Connecticut to go to graduate school and had to start the immigration process over from the beginning. The same thing would happen to Coba if she moved to Connecticut or anywhere else that's not part of the Atlanta district." We must have looked interested since Lenora continued.

"Coba's from South Africa and came to the United States as a student at the university on a student visa. While she was a student she volunteered at The Festival and caught Ralph's eye. He suggested that we hire her—a good worker, dependable, catches on fast, all good traits for an assistant director. Even better, she was willing to work cheap."

I scratched my head trying to remember. I'd met a lot of people in the last twelve hours. "Who is Ralph? Is he a member of the board?"

"Ralph Stark. He's sort of our head volunteer—straw bosses the volunteer work crews during The Festival. We've tried to get him to agree to be on the board but he refuses. He says it takes a volunteer to manage volunteers. He threatens to quit if we elect him to the board." Lenora shook her head and smiled. "Don't know what we'd do without Ralph."

"So how does he deal with Dot?" The exposure I'd had to Dot's management style—the way it reminded me of the late Sean Thomas—had me wondering how people got along with her. The possibility of blackmail had added to my curiosity.

It was odd to see Peter Pan look thoughtful. It's not something that happened that often in Never-Never Land.

"What an interesting question. He's not the type to put up with nonsense, but he's never complained—not that I'm aware of." She paused. "But he wouldn't complain. He'd just take care of it—somehow. Do you know what time it is?"

I reached for my phone. The Velcro strap on my wristwatch had gotten so that it tried to grip things it shouldn't so I had stopped wearing it after I retired. Just like the younger generation I now depended on my phone for checking the time.

"Never mind, it doesn't matter. I don't know what time it was when Ellen said to meet her in thirty minutes."

"Oh that." Bobby thought for a second. "Twenty-five minutes ago—give or take five minutes."

"Really?" Lenora looked surprised. "You can do that in your head?"

Bobby smiled and nodded.

"Guaranteed," I said. She had proved it to me more than once. Bobby had her own built-in timepiece.

"Then I've got to scoot. I'd rather be early to meet Ellen George than late!" Lenora waved and started off, making her way through the crowd that still filled the area between the bar and the food tent.

Too bad she didn't have any pixie dust—otherwise she could have flown—or did Peter need dust to fly? I couldn't remember.

"Did Peter Pan need pixie dust to fly?"

Bobby looked at me and smiled. "No, Peter could fly on his own—the Darling children had to use pixie dust."

I wasn't quite ready to leave and Bobby was willing to keep looking at Halloween costumes, hoping for inspiration. We decided to stay another thirty minutes then head for Shelbyville. Bobby had guests coming in Friday night and I'd invited them over for supper Saturday night, so we both had things to do outside The Festival. We would get a drink and work our way back across the party grounds to our semiprivate parking space.

Looking at the crowds around the three bars, I decided there was a shorter wait at the bar closest to the entrance. Earlier it had been the one to avoid; now most of the partygoers had clumped around the food tent and the bar closest to it. We started strolling, not quite hand-in-hand. The idea of walking hand-in-hand made me self-conscious. Should I take her hand? Do adults do that? What kind of public statement would that make and did I want to make it? More importantly, did Bobby? This deserved a serious, adult conversation.

"Big party, isn't it?" I said as we walked along. Three bars, a food tent, portable toilets, fields turned into parking lots, parking lot attendants, bartenders, food handlers, and who knew how many others working behind the scenes. People called it Dot's party but it was clear that Dot wasn't running it. No, the person in charge was Coba. She was doing some of the work herself, but that didn't make her a bad manager in my opinion. Some management philosophers would disagree, but I like a manager who knows how to get her hands dirty.

The clean night air had a chill but wasn't cold. It would have been unusual for Shelbyville to have a night in late October too cold for an outdoor party. Of course we weren't in Shelbyville, nor Archibald for that matter. Dot's place was out in the county, Jemison County. If I was going to split hairs, I might as well be precise. I was really sorry that there hadn't been an excuse for a fire—not a bonfire mind you, just a campfire. How long had it been since I'd been near one—flames, pops, crackles, heat, smoke—the noises and smells of an open fire?

"Is it time for a Johnny Cash impersonation? Ready to hear a really bad version of 'Burning Ring of Fire'?"

I was startled by the sound of Stan's voice. His all-black apparel had made him hard to see in the deep shadows between the lighted areas.

"Whoops. Didn't mean to scare you." He slapped his gut. "I'm not used to being overlooked."

"It's the costume, Stan. You be sure to walk on one side of the road or the other going back to your car—better yet make sure you walk with a group of people. You blend in to the dark too well." Bobby's tone was a little sharp. Stan's appearance had surprised her too.

A big smile spread across Stan's face. "Don't worry. When I go trick-or-treating I'll put reflective tape on my guitar."

"Be sure to put a strip across your mouth too." It was feeble but it was the best I could come up with at the moment.

"And then how would I say 'trick-or-treat' huh?"

I gave up trying to engage in witty repartee. "So how are you liking the party? Did you get plenty to eat and drink?"

"I stayed away from the coleslaw because it had paprika sprinkled on it and I didn't recognize the pattern. I ate the baked beans and potato salad though. BBQ was good but the sweet tea was too sweet for me."

He shrugged his shoulders making the guitar on his back move. "Other than not getting to talk to Coba and missing out on Dot being called a blackmailer, it's been a pretty good party."

Having told Stan about the blackmailing scene, I ignored that comment and went back to Coba. "Not getting to talk to Coba? Is there something you've forgotten to tell me?"

"Or that's none of his business?"

"Thanks, Bobby. But there's nothing there to be 'none of his business' or much of a topic of conversation. She's South African."

"I'd heard that—explains that hint of accent—and her last name. Boucher doesn't sound like somebody from around here, neither does Coba for that matter."

"With first names it's getting so you really can't tell—region-wise that is." Bobby thought for a second. "You can make a pretty accurate guess as to what TV shows were popular when they were born though."

Stan laughed. "Well, Coba is originally a Dutch name. Other than that, I can tell you that Halloween isn't a big deal in South Africa and I thought she was attractive so I tried to make some small talk. She's working, so the talking didn't go very far. She's got The Festival and then an immigration meeting over in Atlanta. When she gets back she'll give me a call—or I'll call her."

. . .

We had been walking as we talked and had arrived at the bar nearest the entrance—which was becoming the exit. A few people were making their way back to their cars. The party had peaked and was beginning to wind down.

I was tired of beer and had been careful about how much I'd had to drink up to that point. "Last call. I'm going to see what the bar scotch is. Bobby, what would you like to drink?"

"The red wine will be fine."

I glanced at Stan and he nodded his head. "One for the road. They can't make a Cosmo so I've been getting by with rum and Coke—with lime if they haven't run out."

I headed into the mass of people in front of the bar. It might be the least crowded, but that didn't mean it was deserted. Stan and Coba—or the possibility of Stan and Coba—I couldn't see it myself, but I hadn't been that fond of his first wife. She'd decided she wasn't that fond of him. Stan was fine for the here and now but she wanted somebody for the long haul. She wanted somebody for her like Eleanor was for me, or so she'd told me back before Eleanor died. She'd ditched Stan and was last seen in the company of an older—and wealthy—man. Idly I wondered why she'd talked to me about it all those years ago.

Service was quicker than I'd expected. It might have helped that I had the money for the tip jar in my hand when I was trying to get the bartender's attention. I turned around and headed away from the bar holding the drinks in my hands. I looked around trying to get my bearings and spotted Bobby and Stan who were now talking to Frank Manning and Mose Smith.

Frank was still in the Groucho costume. He had the big cigar in his hand and would wiggle it now and again. It was hard to tell if Mose was in costume or not. He was pretty much wearing what he usually did—faded blue jeans and a T-shirt advertising some music event. He had curly gray hair encircling his round face. The hair on his head was longer than his beard but it made the circle complete. He was a man who had found himself during the 1970s and was happy staying there—appearance-wise that is. Mose was the founder, owner, and operator of the Mo' Music stores in Shelbyville. If it had to do with music, Mo' Music was involved in it.

It looked like the conversation was hot, whatever they were talking about. Lots of gestures, hand-waving, cigar-pointing, okay, there was only one cigar—finger-pointing.

"I'm telling you it all makes sense! Think about it." Frank was jabbing at the air with his cigar to make his point. "Dot must be blackmailing people. Look at all the exhibiting artists who come back to The Festival no matter how she treats them. Why come back?"

"Because The Festival pays guest artists to attend." Stan was holding his own. "Guaranteed money makes a difference when you're depending on making sales to the public. You might be able to sell more at another venue but you might not."

Mose was standing beside Bobby his arms crossed over his stomach. "Frank's got a point, Stan. I've wondered why some of the musicians keep coming back. Some of them don't need the exposure and The Festival doesn't pay enough to justify the cost to get here."

I walked up and handed Bobby her wine. "Howdy, Mose. You in costume tonight or not?"

"Jerry Garcia." Mose replied without hesitation. "Can't you see it? This is a genuine Dead T-shirt." He pulled the front of the shirt forward. "It's from one of their tours in the '70s."

I waved it away. "Come on, Mose. On a regular day you look more like Jerry Garcia than Jerry Garcia does—or did."

Stan took his rum and Coke and I got to test the bar scotch. I took a sip. Not bad, I'd had worse and had to pay for it.

"Crawford's right, Mose. You might as well claim you're impersonating Garcia every day of the week." Frank paused and then added with a grin. "Oh I get it. Say you are. Call it a costume because you're carrying. Then you'd be able to tell the police the drugs were props 'cause you were pretending to be Jerry. Clever."

Frank looked impressed at his own cleverness and we all laughed. As far as I knew Mose had never been implicated in any illegal drug use—surprising since just as Frank had pointed out, he looked the part. Maybe that was the issue. Mose looked too much like a pothead to be any kind of challenge to the narcs. But then the police keep on busting Willie Nelson so that theory didn't hold up.

Mose smiled. "Are you kidding? At one point I was getting hassled regularly. I finally decided that the Shelbyville Police Department was sending out its rookie patrolmen to my store so they'd get practice in how to arrest somebody on suspicion of possession. I called Chief Boyd and complained. Now I am a guest lecturer and do a little role play in their training program."

"So what do you think—about Dot being a blackmailer? I heard Frank saying it made sense to him." I was having trouble visualizing it. Nowadays, it seemed people weren't ashamed of anything they did. Didn't that make it hard to blackmail somebody?

Mose stuck his hands in the back pockets of his jeans and flapped his elbows. "Maybe a petty one, I guess. I'm of the opinion that Dot puts on a show and there's less behind the scenes than in front." He ran his hand through his beard. "I can see her threatening to 'snitch' on people—like in grade school—but I can't see anybody being really scared of Dot."

"Come on, Mose," Frank defended his opinion. "What you're saying is that when you get hassled you call the chief of police and that's the end of it. What about the people who think the title 'director' means something? Dot's a bully and she'll bully anybody she can."

I nodded my head. Frank had the right of it. Dot was a bully and bullies are always looking for victims. She'd recognize the ones she would never be able to bully—the ones like Mose—and leave them alone. But others? The Festival had given her a position of authority and that had been a mistake.

While I was chewing on that thought, I looked back to the farmhouse and saw four people standing on the porch looking our way—looking, as far as I could tell, at me. They were Ellen George, Lenora Maisano, Joyce Fines, and a man I didn't recognize. I turned back to the group.

Bobby started to speak. She had been pretty quiet. Unusual—sort of—but not when she was working things out in her mind. "I didn't realize what kind of person Dot was before tonight." She looked at me. "I'll bet there are those that say, 'Dot Fields? There's a woman who needs killing.'"

The hairs on my neck stood up. "Let's hope it doesn't come to that. Is Joyce Fines on the board of The Festival?"

"The ecologist?" said Mose. "Sure, she's been on the board for years. What about her?"

I pointed at the four people who were standing together on the porch. "Who's the guy?" As I spoke, the three I had identified walked down the steps and began marching across the grounds toward us. I waved at them and Ellen waved back.

"The guy on the porch? That's Bob Freight. He's this year's judge for The Festival." Mose scratched the left side of his face with his right hand so his lips were covered. "Ellen, Lenora, and Joyce—that's The Festival's executive committee and I believe they are headed our—no, your, way.

. . .

"Mr. Crawford." Joyce Fines spoke as the group walked up.

"Dr. Fines. Nice to see you—"

"One of the reasons I agreed to this is that I've met you and between what Rufus has said about you and my own observations, I believe this can work."

Dr. Fines had been identified as a suspect in Philip Douglas's murder and I had questioned her. I hadn't seen her since. No costume for Dr. Fines. She was wearing khakis and a blue chambray shirt, open at the neck, with a dark red quilted vest.

"I'm a member of the board of The Festival and chair of its executive committee. It's a working subcommittee and reports back to the full committee but is empowered to act for the full board. Understand?"

"Would this committee have the authority to hire consultants without prior board approval?"

I saw Ellen and Lenora glance at each other and nod. I hoped nobody thought I was so stupid as not to have seen that coming. Once Chad Harris had publicly accused Dot Fields of blackmail, the board of The Festival had to investigate. They could have gone to the police but that would have made the investigation public. Better to keep it private.

A hint of a smile appeared on Joyce's face. "A consultant such as a private investigator—yes, we have that authority."

"You do know that I've only investigated murders—up to this point." I said that out of some feeling that full disclosure was necessary.

The smile grew more apparent. "You're supposed to tell me that you've worked on a number of blackmail cases—zero being a number."

"And solved every one I've undertaken to my customer's complete satisfaction."

Both of our smiles faded.

"I'll take the job. I'll do everything I can to determine if there is any basis in Chad Harris's claim."

Joyce raised her voice slightly so that we heard her clearly. "Acting on behalf of The Festival at the board's request, you will determine to the best of your abilities and to our satisfaction whether Dot Fields is, indeed, a blackmailer."

"What you said."

The next morning—the first day of The Festival—I got an early start. I was going to meet Bobby at The Festival and, together, we would finish setting up the Press's booth and man it until noon. I had one of the two vendor parking passes The Festival had deemed appropriate to allocate to the Press. Frank had the other one. He and somebody else from the Press were going to be our relief.

Bobby's plan was to drive close enough to historic downtown Archibald to park in one of the lots serviced by the shuttle buses that ferried the public to The Festival grounds. She'd catch one and meet me at the grand opening of The Festival. I had the Press's inventory and other supplies in my car.

While I was driving, I picked back up on what I had started thinking about last night. How do you investigate a blackmail case? I didn't have any kind of technique or standard procedures on investigating murders and I'd solved two of those. I'd hung around the party last night until The Festival board members made up their minds to have the allegations investigated because I wanted the job. There was nothing like being on the spot for getting hired.

I wanted the case because I was bored. The murder investigations had been exhilarating so I'd gone ahead and applied for my private investigator's license and gotten business cards. I missed the thrill of investigating.

This was going to be trickier than I had originally thought. Murder victims—once discovered—didn't resist the investigation. But victims of blackmail? They were as likely to resist investigation as the blackmailer. The blackmailer would want to hide the fact that she was blackmailing and the victims would want to hide the fact that they had done something they were willing to pay money to keep secret.

I thought about that tangled stretch of logic and wondered if I'd had more to drink the night before than I'd realized.

I stopped at the traffic light that marked the center of Archibald's old downtown. The Festival gates didn't open to the public until nine o'clock—after the opening ceremony—but there were plenty of signs of preparation for the crowds of people that would be coming and the traffic they would create. The Archibald police were still letting the stoplight go through its normal cycle of green, yellow, red. Once traffic thickened, there would just be a blinking red light at the intersection with a police officer beneath directing traffic.

The light changed and I eased on through the intersection and headed west toward the park, all the while looking for the signs that would point the way to the back entrance of The Festival grounds and vendor parking.

After solving two murders—actually three murders, I corrected myself, but only two murder cases—now I had a case that didn't involve murder. I came back to the question I'd started out with.

How do you investigate a blackmailer—okay—an alleged blackmailer?

I decided that I'd better see if I could buy Jim Ward lunch. He was head of homicide for the Shelbyville police but he might dabble in blackmail as well—investigating it that is. And I better talk to Chad Harris. He could tell me what it was like to be a victim of attempted blackmail. Wait a minute! I caught myself. I was trying to find out if it was true that Dot was a blackmailer. I had to give her the benefit of the doubt. Maybe I'd better talk to her too.

Yep, I nodded to myself. Maybe I should talk to her first. Give her a chance to explain. Briefly I wondered why The Festival's board hadn't wanted to handle it that way and realized that's what they'd hired me to do.

. . .

The vendor parking lot—a recently bushhogged field—was beginning to fill up despite the early hour. Volunteers had strung rows of heavy twine propped up on tall sticks to mark lanes for cars to park in and I parked with my hood inches from a section of string. Before long there would be Girl Scouts directing vendors to parking spaces in this lot just as they'd direct customers in the other lots.

I opened up the hatch and looked at the boxes of books and computer equipment. After we'd loaded up my car at the Press, I'd made a point of putting my old hand truck in the car too. It was a great alternative to hand-carrying the stuff to the booth. Even so it was a relief to get onto the pathway. I wished I had a handcart with wheels the size of bicycle tires—or maybe a golf cart instead.

I reminded myself that if wishes were horses, beggars would ride, dropped the cartons of books off at the booth, and went back for the computer equipment. I'd moved the heaviest stuff first to get it over with and the second load went faster. I hid the monitors, cables, power strips, keyboards, laptop, and mice under the tables that lined the booth. Bobby and I had covered them with cloths so that the skirts would hide whatever was stored underneath. I doubted that anything would disappear but didn't want to put too much strain on the moral integrity of passers-by.

I stepped out of the tent and glanced around. I could see into the next tent past Dot's pavilion. Whoever was going to use it was getting off to a slow start. There was no sign of activity. I had to go past our tent and turn away from the pathway to see Dot's tent. It looked like she'd added some signs and plaques since yesterday morning. Other than that, it was as deserted as the other tent—and the Press's tent as well. I set out down the path toward the official entrance to The Festival where Dot would be conducting the opening ceremony. I'd never seen it, and when Bobby heard that, she decided we should meet there and then head back to the booth to open it up. I had refrained from pointing out to Bobby that the fact that I hadn't seen the opening ceremony before was probably a pretty good indicator of how interested I was in seeing it. Besides, seeing it with her would make it more interesting.

I had pretty much ignored everything else that was going on in the park while toting and fetching. I was now free to gawk all I wanted. So I did. And as I did, I tried to figure out how what I saw could be related to blackmail—or to detecting it.

I needed to talk to the two people who'd brought up the whole issue—Dot and Chad. Dot wasn't likely to confess to being a blackmailer. No use in sailing up to her and asking that question—still, I needed to know her explanation. Same thing with going around asking random people if Dot was blackmailing them—except, of course, Chad Harris. I wondered just what he had done that made her think she could blackmail him.

One of the things that bothered me in trying to think of Dot as a blackmailer—a successful one—was that I'd figured her for a braggart. There seemed to be a conflict between the persona of someone who demanded to be paid in order to keep quiet and one known to brag about everything she did. If I was one of the people Dot was blackmailing, how comfortable would I be that she'd remember to keep her mouth shut?

There was plenty of time before nine o'clock, so I was taking the long route to the entrance. Here and there, people were setting up their booths. Metro Shelter, the local animal shelter, had set up in an area next to the fence so they could show off adoptable dogs and cats. I wondered if they brought other animals as well. The shelter ended up with all sorts of abandoned animals, some of them exotic.

The Festival didn't allow pets in the park until Sunday. But that worked out all right, you couldn't just walk up and adopt a pet—the process was more complicated than that. The shelter people had learned how effective it was to take the pets to the people instead of trying to get people to come to them. They still had their rigorous screening process—they weren't going to let the animals go to bad homes—but they generated a lot more activity when they went to where the people were. I made a mental note to steer clear of the outside pathway for the same reason I didn't visit the animal shelter. It was easier to remain a one-cat and one-dog household that way.

I made my way past the emergency medical booth with its ambulance, stretchers, oxygen tanks, wheelchairs, two miniature ambulances—basically glorified golf carts—and a card table with four folding chairs. The EMTs played bridge to pass the time between emergency calls. I'd asked about it years ago, thinking they'd be playing poker, but they told me they were too cerebral to play poker. Firefighters play poker, I'd been told. Personally, I had my doubts about how serious they were about their card game. The golf carts were equipped with sirens and flashing lights and somehow the EMTs had to use them every year. In front of it all was a large sign that hid the card table from casual view. The sign explained that the local ambulance service was the official Festival emergency service with a phone number that was just for The Festival—1911. I checked to make sure it was still in my phone contacts while I headed on toward the gates. Emergency numbers were best obtained *before* an emergency, it seemed to me.

. . .

A local potter and his wife were setting up a kiln behind his booth, having finished putting his wares on display. I liked his work and made a note to drop by and see what he had this year. With the kiln onsite he'd do one or two firings a day while at The Festival—replenishing his stock as he sold it. Listening to him explain how he created different glazes and finishes through using various firing techniques was fascinating to me. I waved as I went on by. Today's weather was pleasant but in other years there had been days when the heat off the kiln had made this booth a pleasant place to linger.

I thought about stopping to ask them whether they thought the rumor that Dot was a blackmailer was true and immediately thought better of it. They could only be certain if they were one of her victims. My asking the question would imply that I thought they might have done something Dot could have used to blackmail them. Hmmm. This investigation was turning out to be much more complicated than I had thought.

Coffee.

I decided I needed more coffee and maybe a sugar boost to get my mind going. I picked up my pace and headed straight as possible to the Public Radio booth. They sold coffee and breakfast biscuits to the public. The coffee was good and I knew that they kept a stash of doughnuts under the counter. Their board had decreed that they wouldn't sell "empty calories" and would provide Festival-goers "healthy alternatives" instead. The first year they tried it was the worst year they'd ever had in sales and pledges at The Festival.

I got coffee and two sugar-glazed puffs of airy dough—products of a local franchise of a national doughnut chain. So much for healthy alternatives. A smattering of folding chairs and small tables clustered in front of the booth offered a pretty clear view of the entrance gate, so I sat down to eat. I found it easier to lick the sugary glaze off of my fingers if I wasn't walking.

. . .

The gate, much like The Festival, had evolved over the years. It had started life as a simple metal pole gate—the kind you find on private driveways out in the country, though in this case, either side of the gate would have been wide enough to let a car through. Each segment was essentially a triangle attached to a large metal post—a right triangle if you remember your plane geometry. A simple padlock held the two parts of the gate closed in the middle.

To the resident blacksmith the metal gate had been an empty canvas. It cried out for decoration. How The Festival came to have a resident blacksmith is another story. He had added metal flowers, leaves, vines, butterflies, berries, and the like. The simple metal gate had been transformed into a piece of blacksmith art.

As a result, each side was so heavy that the gate sagged in the middle. The blacksmith had reinforced the posts and added ornate counterweights at the ends. Even so, he'd had to put a large wooden brace in the middle for the poles to rest on when the gate was closed. Worried about the poles bending, I guess. The gates had worked nicely yesterday when I saw them being tested.

With my index finger, I made sure I'd gotten the last flakes of sugar off the corners of my mouth and stood up. There was one of the omnipresent oil-drum/trashcans nearby so I tossed my crumpled napkins and coffee cup into it.

On one side of the gate were the reserved parking places I'd noticed the day before. Dot's pickup truck was in its accustomed place in the shade, and today there was a bicycle with some kind of rack over the rear wheels parked in the assistant's spot. Must be Coba's bike. She probably used it for shopping and the rack held those saddle-bag things bicyclists use.

I looked back at the gate, Dot and some other people were clustered around the middle of the gate trying to do something. I took that as a sign that the opening ceremony was about to begin. As the crowd gathered on the other side of the gate I spotted Bobby standing near the front. If she hadn't been at the front of the crowd, I'd never have seen her. Her silver hair gleamed in the morning sunlight and I found myself grinning from ear to ear for no particular reason.

I moved and waved so she'd see me and she waved back. When I got a little closer to the gates I could see that something was out of whack but I couldn't tell just what was wrong, partly because Dot kept moving around blocking my view. She was wearing her everyday outfit—denim overalls, T-shirt, work boots, and baseball cap. She'd have to toss on her fortune-telling garb before she opened her booth.

"What's wrong with it?" bellowed Dot as she tried to get the padlock to move. I was glad she wasn't bothering with the speaker system. She was noisy enough without it. "It's broken. That's what's wrong with it. What are you? Some kind of idiot? Yes, I know it was working yesterday, but it's not working today!"

I couldn't hear what anybody else was saying, but I could see Coba shake her head and see her lips move. Whatever she said it must have been the wrong thing.

"Oh, get out of my sight you pitiful excuse for an assistant director! Make yourself useful and take the snake to my tent." Dot waved in the direction of headquarters. "Or are you too scrawny to do even that?"

I watched Coba shrug her shoulders, turn around, and head back toward the building.

Dot ignored Coba and turned to scan the crowd that had gathered on this side of the gate until she spotted some volunteer workers. "Ralph! You and Dawson come out here and help me move these gates. I can't move them myself, it's going to take three of us."

Ralph Stark stepped out of the crowd, pulled a pair of work gloves out of his back pocket and started putting them on. "Dawson's got a bad back." Ralph turned back to the volunteers. "Darryl, why don't you and William Allen give us a hand here." Two men stepped out of the group, one heavy-set, the other wiry, and followed him as he joined Dot at the gate.

. . .

As soon as I realized Dot was looking for help opening the gates, I started doing my best to blend into my surroundings. I was looking as inconspicuous as possible when Coba spoke to me.

"Mr. Crawford, do you remember the corn snake? Want to see it again?"

Sure enough, Coba was standing there with the snake box she'd had yesterday. She seemed to be handling it fine despite being "scrawny." I wondered how Stan would react to the scrawny comment when I told him. Coba had dressed up for opening day. She had on a leather skirt with fringe, leather vest, and knee-high boots instead of yesterday's blue jeans and T-shirt. Now that I thought about it, I had upgraded what I was wearing too. But those boots were going to get hot.

I peered into the box and saw the snake with its bright markings easily visible among the wood shavings or whatever it was that covered the bottom of the box. I pulled out my phone and took a couple of pictures. "He's a handsome snake all right. I thought so when I saw him yesterday—or is he a she?"

"Oh, I'm sure I don't know. Does it matter?"

"To another corn snake? Surely, but nobody else, I suppose."

A man standing next to me leaned over my shoulder to look. "Is it poisonous?

I briefly considered explaining to him that the correct term was "venomous"—poison is ingested; venom is injected, as through the fangs of a snake—but decided against it. He probably wasn't interested in a vocabulary lesson. I wouldn't have been either except it was Bobby who had taught me.

"Oh no, a corn snake is a good snake. Eats rodents and protects the corn."

There was a faint lilt to Coba's "oh" and "good" that hinted of another country—another language. I couldn't have said it was South African if I hadn't been told. I wondered if that hint of foreign accent was part of what Stan had found attractive.

As I stepped back and let a small crowd that wanted to see the snake form around Coba, I heard one of them ask, "Did you catch him or get him from the animal shelter?"

"That did it!" Dot's excited shout turned everybody's attention back to the gates. She was holding up the padlock in triumph while Ralph, Darryl, and William Allen were half-dragging, half-carrying the right-hand section of the gate to the side. They must have had to align the holes in the poles that the padlock's shank had been inserted through so there was no pressure on it. Once the padlock wasn't being squeezed, Dot could get the shank of the lock free. Not as easy as it might look to maneuver those overweight poles.

With the gate unlocked and being moved out of the way, the crowd settled down for the opening ceremony—whatever it was. I glanced around and saw that everybody had turned toward the gates.

Everybody but Coba. The small crowd of people who'd been looking at the snake had turned their attention back to the opening ceremony. I could see Coba's back as she walked on up the path toward Dot's fortune-telling tent, head held high, snake box clasped firmly in her arms.

Dot was panting from her exertions but was able to make what sounded like the standard preopening announcements—stay on the paths, throw trash into trash cans, put recycling into recycling bins, no smoking, and call 1911 if you needed the emergency medical technicians who were on site because of the generosity of whoever owned the local ambulance company—announcements that would be made again and again throughout the days of The Festival.

Ralph and the others had, by now, moved the other pole out of the way and the official entrance to The Festival was clear. Dot paused for a second, straightened up, took a deep breath, and bellowed The Festival's traditional start:

"All who have kept the spirit of The Festival in their hearts rejoice! Let The Festival begin! Rejoice in The Festival."

. . .

I met Bobby at the gate and we walked back to the Public Radio booth to get coffee and a sausage biscuit for Bobby. She'd skipped breakfast—a bad habit to get into as far as I was concerned. I saw Dot at the counter and grabbed Bobby's elbow—holding her back. She glanced up at me and I nodded in Dot's direction. Once she spotted Dot, she smiled and nodded. We didn't exchange a word while we waited for Dot to finish her business and leave before we got any closer.

Dot rummaged through her magic bag and pulled out a ceramic travel mug—one with a top you can sip through—unscrewed the top, tilted her head back and drained its contents. "Gack, that's bad coffee." She wiped her mouth with the back of her hand then set her mug on the counter. "Even though the director drinks free, I'm not sure it's worth it."

The woman behind the counter didn't say a word but held her hands out like "what can I do?" Dot snorted and said, "Don't just stand there. Fill it up again. Coffee, black."

I watched as the woman quietly wiped out Dot's coffee mug with a paper towel and then filled it up again. "That's a lovely mug, Ms. Fields."

"Of course it is. I had one of the artists make it for me years ago." Dot snatched her mug out of the woman's hand and walked away.

Since the crowd—the coffee-drinking crowd anyway—was still sparse, Bobby and I were able to step forward and take Dot's place at the counter. I spoke to the woman who had waited on Dot. "Two coffees, please."

The woman was looking past me, so I turned my head to see what she was watching. It was Dot. She sipped her coffee and made a face.

I turned back and saw a satisfied smile spread across the woman's face.

"I'll be right with you, sir." I stood there as she took the carafe she'd used to pour Dot's coffee, dumped its contents into the sink, picked up two paper cups, filled them from one of the large urns that were sitting in a row behind the counter, and brought them to us. "Creamers and sweeteners are over on that table. Would you like anything else? Sausage biscuits? Doughnuts?"

"I'd like a sausage biscuit," said Bobby. "I skipped breakfast so I could have one of yours. Public Radio's biscuits are always so wonderful."

"And the coffee is always good." I took a sip.

The woman smiled at us. "That's what everybody says, so it must be true. Let me get that biscuit."

I took another sip of coffee while we were waiting for Bobby's order and idly wondered how old the coffee was she'd poured Dot, or if she'd made it especially for the director—gratis, of course.

. . .

Coffee cups in hand and biscuit in a bag, we started walking up the pathway toward the Press's booth.

"Oh," Bobby stopped short. "Frank says we need to get an account and password for the secure network—something about not wanting to depend on the public network. Does that make sense?"

"Yeah. The Festival has two wireless networks working out here. One's for the public so they can tell their friends about how wonderful the stuff for sale is—send pics if the artist allows—stuff like that. The other is for commercial transactions—credit card charges and database access. At least, that's how I'd have set it up—back when I was working for the university."

I thought about the equipment I'd unloaded this morning. "I'll need that information to set up the computers. Did Frank say where we were to get this information?"

"Headquarters?"

"And how do I prove that I'm from the Press and worthy of said account name and password?"

"Do you miss working at the university?"

"Huh?" One of the things about Bobby that I was adjusting to—or so I thought—were abrupt changes of subject. "No, of course not—I mean—sort of I did, but—where did that come from?"

Bobby had been watching my expression from the moment she'd asked her question and whatever she read there seemed to satisfy her. "Never mind, we can talk about that later. Now, go get the accounts and passwords and I'll meet you at the booth." She got up on her tip-toes and gave me a quick kiss on the cheek and a hug then set out for the booth.

Bemused I turned back and headed to the only permanent building on the park grounds. During the rest of the year when

The Festival grounds were used for more parklike activities, the headquarters building was the perfect multipurpose building. It did it all—bathrooms, concession stand, meeting room, information booth, and office. But The Festival was too grand, too big, too successful, for the building to remain multipurpose. It could serve only one purpose during The Festival—headquarters.

As I closed in on the building I remembered that I had forgotten to warn Bobby about the animal shelter booth. Well, she was a grown woman. She could take care of herself. Whether I was mature enough to ignore pets in need of a home was another question.

The Festival had stuck a small booth in front of headquarters as an information center for Festival-goers. It was stocked with programs, maps of The Festival grounds, lists of exhibiting artists and what media they worked in, this year's version of The Festival T-shirt, and volunteers—some of whom looked familiar. I picked up a program, folded it up, stuck it in a back pocket, and went on into the building.

In one corner, with a line of people in front of her, was Coba, sitting at a table with a large map of the grounds spread out before her, walkie-talkies, cell phones, a covey of clipboards, and two small nylon coolers sitting side-by-side on the floor—lunch and soft drinks at a guess. There wasn't anybody on her side of the table so she was handling everything by herself. Coba had taken off the leather vest, but still had the leather dress and boots on. She was working her way through the line of people at a good clip. Unfortunately just as fast as she solved one person's problem another person would get at the tail of the line.

The network guys had their own table in another corner of the room. I had thought it might be some people from the computer center that I might know, but these were student workers. If I'd given it any thought I'd have known the department would have sent student workers on Friday morning, saving the staff for later in the day and weekend duties. The table was covered in cables, sticky notes, empty boxes, antistatic bags, laptops, mice, and a printer. There were boxes behind the guys—probably replacements if something died—things to keep the networks up.

I asked for the vendor account name and password for the Press and—after a short wait while the student helper flipped through a stack of paper—was handed a bright yellow sheet of paper that had the account name and password at the top of the page and directions on how to set up network connections for different operating systems and multiple versions of said operating systems. I was happy to see that the instructions for the Mac were much shorter than those for any version of Windows. I took it as a sign that the instructions might even work.

Walking toward the door, I realized no one had asked for any identification—they had just handed over the account information. It made sense. There wasn't much I could do with it and if I did screw it up, they could just change the password and lock me out. There was no need to make it any more complicated than it needed to be. If I'd had to go to campus to pick it up, there would have been forms to fill out, signatures to verify, all that kind of crap.

Looking around I realized there was a hum in the air. The kind of noise people make when they're doing a good job of handling responsibilities—no shouting, yelling, or cursing. It struck me then that Dot wasn't in the room. She must have gone on to her fortune-telling tent. I wondered how much the dynamics in the room had changed once she'd walked out the door.

. . .

Back on the pathway headed to the Press's booth, I could hear sounds coming from the stage area. There was live music every day of The Festival and Friday was Celtic music day. Last night I'd asked Mose Smith why they didn't mix the music up. Have a little gospel, Celtic, country/folk, rock, and blues every day. That way you wouldn't have to put up with music you didn't like for the whole day.

He'd looked at me over his circular, wire-rimmed eyeglasses and said in a voice dry as toast, "Don't come the day we play the kind of music you don't like. It's that simple."

So for today we were going to be entertained with songs—most in a minor key—about border wars, poaching, treachery, death, dying, grief, fairies, unfaithfulness, and love gone wrong. Country music would kick in tomorrow and would add mama, trains, pickup trucks, hangings, liquor, whiskey, and beer to the things they sing about. We would have to wait until Sunday for the gospel singing before religion got added to the mix.

The occasional howls from the sound system indicated that yesterday's monologue of "test, test, test" had somehow failed overnight. The first couple of screeches were so loud that people in their cars on their way to The Festival must have heard them.

Were there any songs about blackmail? I tried to think of one but couldn't. I'd have to ask Frank when he showed up or maybe Mose if I ran into him. It sounded like something somebody must have written a song about—Long Black Veil? That wasn't really blackmail, was it?

I kept on thinking about blackmail and how to detect who
was being blackmailed or who was doing the blackmailing—
what to do after talking to Dot and Chad. All I could come up
with was money—money would be the way to track it. Who was
paying somebody money they shouldn't be? Making somebody
do something they didn't want to do by blackmailing them
seemed much harder to prove. After all, if you were being
blackmailed into coming to The Festival would you go around
complaining that you didn't want to be here and wouldn't be
except that somebody forced you? No, you wouldn't.

The flip side—now that might hold some promise. Being
able to brag that you could get somebody to do something that
they didn't want to do? Yeah, I could see somebody doing that.
The problem there would be finding out who Dot brags to—to
whom Dot brags. Clearly, she hadn't been bragging to Ellen,
Lenora, and Joyce or they'd have mentioned their suspicions last
night. Who were Dot's friends?

I passed the booth that was on the other side of Dot's tent
from the Press's and saw that a few people had shown up and
were setting up some tables and chairs. I was glad to see there
wouldn't be an empty booth near ours. An empty booth would
not be good for business.

Dot had added a few more items to her area since last I'd
paid attention. I got to the picnic table that served as her waiting
room, stopped, and sat down to take in the whole setting while I
finished my coffee. There was a new sign that said Wait Your
Turn—The Gypsy Has Someone with Her on one side; I knew
the flip side said The Gypsy Is Within—Please Knock. Beside it
was another sign with the hours fortune-telling was available
during The Festival. She was scheduled to open up in ten
minutes or so. But I knew things were running behind schedule,

which explained why the Please Knock side wasn't turned outward.

Lenora had told me that Dot used to have a sign that said the Witch Is In/Out with the In/Out reversible. She'd gotten rid of it because some joker kept changing the *W* to a *B*.

Would you do that to somebody who was blackmailing you? Probably not. But I didn't really know. I brought my attention back to Dot's signs.

Fortunes were free but contributions were accepted. Like anybody got out of there for free. It was a sliding scale. Reading your palm went for five dollars. For ten, the crystal ball was consulted. Lucky thirteen combined the palm reading with a crystal ball consultation. Twenty dollars and the gypsy would break out the Ouija board for a fifteen-minute session. Hour-long tarot readings went for fifty dollars.

There was no mention of snake handling. It might be so new that she hadn't had time to add it, or maybe she was waiting to see how popular it was going to be. Personally, I felt that the snake handling might not work out so well. And there was no mention of blackmail.

Did Dot give The Festival a cut of what she made telling fortunes? And if she did, how would they know if she was cheating them? I made a note to ask Ellen about that. If Dot lied to The Festival she would certainly lie to the IRS. Or would she? Lying to the federal government can have serious consequences.

The walls of the tent—rainbow colored themselves—were covered in brightly painted come-ons promising to reveal true and unfaithful lovers—future and past. Promises of wealth, health, and happiness—communications with the dear or the not-so-dear departed plus predictions of fame and fortune.

Everything looked okay once you accepted the idea of a fortune-telling tent at The Festival. I'd have to ask Ellen how that had happened. I suspected Ellen had inherited that situation and wasn't able to put a stop to it. I swallowed the last dregs of coffee, got up, dusted off the seat of my jeans, and glanced around the ground. Litter free. There was a trash barrel next to the table so the area was likely to stay clean. I crushed the coffee cup in my hand and tossed it in the trash.

There was small sign at the entrance to Dot's tent: Watch Your Step. I was glad to see she'd thought to put up a warning. Further on there was a bulge at the bottom of one side of Dot's tent—right along the line where the floor was zipped to the wall. Probably something she'd stored too close to the wall this morning.

I pushed thinking about blackmail back into my subconscious and headed to the next tent over. It was time to get the Press's computers set up. It was time to get to work.

. . .

When I stepped into the booth, Bobby was wrestling with one of the iMacs I'd stored under the tables—the ones with the twenty-seven-inch screen. Frank and Bobby had decided to go with a slideshow of all the Press's titles that were in the fall catalog—an endless loop of the dust covers.

Once I heard what they were thinking about doing, I'd wanted to jazz it up a little so that a potential customer could click on the cover art and be connected to a short description of the book, reviews of the book, links to the author, other books by the author—if the Press had published them—and other books in the series or about the same topic—if they were available from the Press.

Of course, I'd figured on adding a shopping cart application too. All features that ought to be in their website already but weren't. I had thought about adding a link that allowed a customer to order an autographed copy of the book for a small additional fee—a flat charge for the signature plus a per word charge for personalizing. It seemed like a gimmick the Press could handle that the big online bookstores couldn't.

I'd been excited about the ideas and might have gotten a little carried away with the technical details. Okay, more than a little carried away. When I had finally looked at Frank and Bobby the glazed, stunned, glassy-eyed look of technological overload was on their faces. I'd forgotten that the recently deceased director of the Press had resisted using personal computers much less marketing innovations. They were used to being the ones pushing to use modern technology. I'd overwhelmed them.

So the booth was going to have three iMacs running slideshows of dust covers for the current book catalog. We had agreed not to have a soundtrack since we didn't need to have out-of-synch noise issues.

"Need any help with that?" Bobby was hidden behind the computer and I didn't want to startle her.

She peered over the top of the monitor. "Nope. I've got this." She cocked her head. "Why? Don't you like the way I'm holding the computer?"

It had looked awkward to me, but she obviously had things under control. It wasn't the first time she'd done something not the way I would have done it and her way had proved to work quite successfully. If I learned to control myself and keep my mouth shut there was a chance she'd keep on letting me hang around watching her do things her way. It was something I was working on.

"Since you obviously don't need my help setting up the computers, I'll get to work configuring our network router to connect to The Festival's private network and then set up our own subnet." I started pulling out other equipment from underneath the tables.

"You'll need to set up the printer."

"Right! I was going to connect it to the subnet instead of hanging it off one of the desktops. If I do it that way, printing shouldn't impact any individual computer's performance." I was about to start discussing the pros and cons of connecting printers locally to computers that were on the network versus a separate network connection for the printer so that each computer could send directly to it. It was something I knew a bit about.

"Crawford?"

"Yes?"

"I can handle the computers. The printer is large and heavy. You set it up. Okay?"

"Absolutely." Sometimes I try to explain things that don't really need explaining.

. . .

Setting up the network, printer, and computers hadn't taken as long as I'd thought it would. The printer had been a little tricky but I expected that. Moving data from the binary world to the printed one is tricky. Crossing the border between worlds.

The slideshow was running on all three of the display monitors. Bobby could access the warehouse to check on stock, and we could print invoices and accept credit cards from any computer in the booth. The Festival's private network was secure as was the Press's subnet. It looked like we were good to go. I'd been assured that things started slow on Friday morning. There weren't that many customers and nobody was in a hurry—in comparison to the rest of the weekend.

Friday afternoon, things picked up, and Saturday and Sunday could be extremely busy. And everybody connected to The Festival hoped they would be. Sunday morning would start slow—until the churchgoing crowd got to the park. Then things would get busy as customers gave in to their desires or jumped on bargains, as vendors started cutting prices on things they didn't want to pack up and take back with them. Things would finally slow down for the closing ceremony, by which time everybody would be exhausted. Originally The Festival had only been Saturday and Sunday but they'd added Friday—instead of extending Sunday's hours.

. . .

Bobby was talking to a couple who were interested in the ecological publications of the Press. She had it under control so I stepped out of the booth and looked around. I could tell that the sound technicians at the stage had got their system straightened out. The musicians had moved in and were practicing. We could now hear fiddles, mandolins, flutes, guitars, banjos, and the occasional voice tuning up. It had to be practice since their first performance wasn't until ten o'clock.

I like Celtic music—don't get me wrong, some of my best friends are Celtic musicians—but I couldn't see it at nine-thirty in the morning. For that matter, I had some serious doubts about people who wanted to start the day listening to that music and having their fortune told. Why would they want to do that? Then I remembered the horoscope column in the morning paper. Sure, maybe it made more sense in the morning. Your future might suggest you'd be better off going back to bed—and avoiding depressing music.

I stepped away from the booth so I could see Dot's tent and realized there were people waiting in front of it. They wanted to start the day by hearing their fortune told.

The Gypsy Is Within—Please Knock had been turned to face out, so Dot must have gone into her tent and put on her gypsy outfit and flipped the sign. There she was—ready for customers. The time was right. I was glad not to run into her—another thing I didn't want to start my day doing. I'd have to talk to her soon about the blackmailing but there was plenty of time.

There were three teenage girls standing before the tent, apparently trying to get up the courage to knock on the door. I wasn't sure if they were in costume or not and didn't really know if they were teenagers. There had been a time, years and years ago, when I would have known within a couple of years how old they were. The flip side of that was I couldn't have told the difference at the other end of the age spectrum. Okay, not the real other end, more toward the middle.

The girls started to giggle and push each other toward the entrance of the tent so I dropped my estimate of their ages slightly. I wondered why Dot hadn't broken the ice and come out of her tent to greet them. She must have been able to hear them from inside the tent.

The tallest of the girls—two of them looked enough alike to be sisters—tossed her head and her long hair whipped around her. I was thinking when she stuck her head through the flap into the tent that the length of the hair was another sign of youth.

I had a theory that as women aged they moved to lower-maintenance hair styles. Unfortunately, I haven't been able to get the data to jibe with my theory. I'm working on corollaries.

. . .

When the scream split the air, I jerked and felt adrenaline slam into my bloodstream as my body went on full alert. The girl's head had reappeared with the scream and now she stood wide-eyed with her hand over her mouth. Her scream had set the other two screaming. Understandable. But that must have startled Dot as well.

I headed toward the girls standing at the entrance of Dot's tent. The taller girl was crying with her hands covering her face as her friends tried to comfort her.

"What was it, Lydia?"

"It's—awful—blood on her face—her neck—she's lying on the floor." The sobbing made her words come out in bursts.

I heard what she said just as I got to them. I tried to project confident competence or competent confidence—I never can decide just which one I'm projecting. "It's okay, girls. Let me just take a look, okay? I'll handle it from here."

As I herded them out of my way I saw Bobby headed toward us with other people following. It seemed wildly incongruous that some of them were in Halloween costumes. I pushed the girls forward. Anybody who'd heard that scream was wondering what had happened. I pointed at the picnic table. "Go sit down while I see what we're dealing with."

They seemed relieved to have an adult take charge. Once I stepped into the tent I wished for an adult to show up too.

It was dark in the tent. The light from the entrance flap caught Dot's face—foam on her lips and nose, blood on her throat, eyes open but fixed—the rest of the tent was in darkness, with some electric candles scattered on the floor casting weird shadows. I switched on my phone's flashlight app and was immediately sorry. Dot was lying on the floor of the tent up against a wall, perfectly still. Her convulsions must have twisted her body into the unnatural shape—wedged into the side of the tent.

What the hell had happened? I flashed the light around the area. The octagonal table was buckled; she must have fallen on it. Chairs were overturned. Her magic bag was on the floor, its contents—crystal ball, tarot cards, Ouija board, planchette—scattered hither and yon. Next to the crystal ball was the snake cage with its top off and the bark scattered around. There was no sign of the corn snake. Mentally, I snapped pictures of the scene. The images would be burned into my memory.

I knew what I had to do. I'd forced myself to take those Red Cross classes before applying for my PI's license. I knelt beside the body and tried to find a pulse in her throat—nothing. My hand was wet—presumably with blood. Moving as quickly as I could, I wiped my hand on my jeans, pulled my cell phone out, put it down, and placed both hands on Dot's chest. Hands-only CPR. It might be pointless but I wasn't qualified to decide that. I started the routine, then spoke to my phone. I tried to keep my voice calm—voice recognition can only do so much. "Phone, dial 1-9-1-1." I swear I'd saved the number under a really good contact name but my mind drew a blank. I was glad I remembered the number. Now, what song was I supposed to use?

A cheerful voice answered. "Emergency Services at The Festival. How can—"

"Emergency! In the tent." Duh! The Festival was full of tents. "Dot's—the fortune-teller's tent! Body down—no pulse, repeat, no pulse!" I heard the sounds of the sirens as I got to the second "no pulse" so I shut up.

I kept rocking forward, pushing on the center of Dot's chest to the beat of "Staying Alive" just as I'd been taught. The adults were coming. They'd know what to do. My mind skipped around. I wondered if disco was coming back, then wondered where I'd come up with "body down," all the while muttering "staying alive, staying alive." I turned my head and stared at the floor, the tarot cards, anything but Dot's face. Part of my brain wondered if she did many tarot readings—the cards looked brand new—clean and shiny—the other part of my brain tried not to think at all.

The sirens got louder as they approached the front of the tent. I kept rocking back and forth but shifted slightly so I could look over my shoulder toward the entrance watching for someone to come in when the flap on the other side of the tent opened. I jerked my head around and saw a man silhouetted against the light.

"Here, let me take over." He crouched down beside me moving his hands close to mine. It was one of the EMTs. "On three—one, two, THREE."

I lifted my hands and stood up as he slipped into my place. Other people in uniforms started coming in the front entrance and I realized how small the tent was, how much in the way I was, and how very, very much I didn't want to be there. I got out as someone was cutting through the tent so they could have access to Dot from both sides. Outside were the two golf carts, lights flashing, sirens silent. A crowd was growing, but a couple of uniformed Archibald police officers were keeping them from getting too close.

I was surprised to see the police here so quickly then realized they'd already been on the grounds. They didn't have a booth like the EMTs but I'd noticed them at The Festival before.

I glanced around, looking for Bobby, and saw her seated at the picnic table with the three girls. The box of tissues must have been something she'd packed for the Press booth. I'd never seen it before. I raised my hand and she waved back.

"Snakebite!" The voice came from within the tent. It was loud enough for everybody in the crowd to hear, and it got an unintended but instant reaction. We all looked down at our feet. People moved uneasily, peering at the leaves and debris that covered The Festival grounds.

I had barely had time to start wondering what had happened when the medic had figured it out. I had thought maybe a heart attack or seizure—but snakebite?

The voice from the tent spoke again. "She was bitten on the neck. Venom must have gotten into a vein for it to affect a woman her size so quickly. That would also explain the blood." Standing just outside the tent was an EMT on her cell phone, relaying the information.

She was on the phone to the emergency room—no, I corrected myself, to a physician who was in the emergency room. I shook my head hoping that it might get my brain going again.

"Sir?"

It was one of the EMTs. It struck me how young he looked standing there in his blue uniform. One of the adults I'd been so happy to turn responsibility over to. He was holding out a cell phone.

"Is this yours? I found it by the body. You must have used it to call us while you were doing CPR."

I reached out and took the phone. Obviously this was the man who'd taken over CPR from me. "Sorry. I didn't recognize you, but boy was I glad to see you."

"Happens all the time, sir. Don't worry about it." He turned around, stopped, and turned back. "You did a good job there, sir. Calling us and the hands-only CPR? Nobody could have done any better. No one could be expected to have done any better." He stared intently at me. "You understand?"

I understood. "She's dead?"

He shrugged his shoulders. "It's always better to try. We're waiting for a physician."

"Say." I remembered the silhouette against the light. "You came in the back of the tent—the back entrance?"

"Oh, that." He looked very young again. "The scream. That must be why you entered the tent. I was trying to figure out where it had come from when your call came in. It confirmed what I already suspected." He pointed back toward HQ. "I just cut across the grounds—it was the quickest way to get to her tent on foot."

I watched him walk back to the tent. So much for talking to Dot first. There was a life lesson I thought I'd learned: plenty of time had turned into no time at all.

. . .

Bobby and I were watching when the doctor showed up and was escorted to the tent by one of the EMTs. He was young but he knew his business. It wasn't long before he'd pulled the blanket over the body confirming what we'd all thought. Before he left, the doctor stopped and talked to a policeman and one of the EMTs. I put my arm around Bobby's shoulders and we stood together in silence.

The deep grumble of a man's voice came from behind us. "You the one that found the body?"

Bobby and I had been standing near the picnic table talking quietly while watching the EMTs. The girl who had actually found the body was sitting at the table with her mother, who was patting her daughter's shoulder and being comforting while the young girl cried.

I turned around. "Actually that young lady sitting over there saw her first."

The man was about my height and half again as wide as he was tall, maybe more. He was dressed in the khaki uniform of the Archibald police, only his hat had a lot more gold braid on the brim—scrambled egg we used to call it, we enlisted men, that is. He'd spoken slowly and he looked sleepy-eyed. I wondered if he moved as slowly as he looked.

He had glanced over at the picnic table and then back at me. "You the second one who found the body? I'm thinking the first one isn't going to tell me much of what I'd like to know. I'm Chief Snoddy." He pointed at his name tag.

"Yes, sir." I stuck out my hand. "James Crawford. I live in Shelbyville."

He took my hand and I watched as mine disappeared into his. Hands as big as bear paws, fingers so thick they made themselves look short. Firm grip but not so firm as to crush my hand—although I was pretty sure he could have. I'd heard of Kurt Snoddy, chief of police of Archibald. Heard how he used to be an offensive lineman at the university, then spent some time in the pros. I wondered how many times he'd been penalized for holding.

"You the James F. Crawford who just got his Shelbyville private investigator license? The one who's too good to be a uniformed security guard. You that one?"

Ouch. I guess some people could interpret my changing the standard wording to leave out "uniformed security guard" that way.

"Truth is I'd make a lousy security guard—not sure I'm that good a private investigator."

"Huh." Chief Snoddy rubbed the side of his nose with his thick forefinger while sizing me up. "You got that license on you?"

I nodded and reached for my wallet. It was the first time I'd been officially asked to produce it. I flipped my wallet open to display the license. I confess I'd practiced. Personally, I thought it looked professional.

"Uh-huh." He glanced down at the license. "How about your business card? That way I won't have to write all that stuff down."

My heart sank. I hate to carry a bunch of stuff in my pockets. "I left them in the car. Didn't think I'd need them. I can go get them. Won't take a minute."

The chief shook his massive head. "Well they can't be doing you or me a bit of good sitting in the car, now can they? What were you thinking?"

I swore to myself that I was going to the car as soon as I was through here. I was going to carry those cards.

He turned to Bobby and nodded his head politely. "Howdy, miss. I'm Kurt Snoddy, Archibald chief of police, and you are?"

"Bobby Slater, Chief." She flashed one of her brilliant smiles at him. "And I've got one of his business cards with me." She reached into her fanny pack, found her wallet, and pulled out the card I'd given her.

A broad smile slowly spread across Kurt's face and he reached out and took my card. He nodded at Bobby again. "I wasn't that impressed with him, but you might make me change my mind. You with him?"

"He's here helping me set up the booth." Bobby pointed at the Press's tent.

Kurt took off his hat. "You mind if I borrow him? I'd like for him to tell me what he saw before he forgets it."

Bobby smiled. "Sure you can borrow him. He's more interested in what you're doing than selling books. But don't worry about him forgetting anything he's seen."

. . .

Chief Snoddy put his hat back on and tipped it at Bobby. "I won't keep him long." He nodded toward Dot's tent. "Come on, Mr. Crawford. Let's see how much you do remember."

"It's just Crawford, Chief Snoddy. Mr. Crawford was my father."

"That so? Can't say as I ever met him. Did you see Ms. Fields enter her tent this morning—Crawford?"

"No, the last time I saw her was just after the opening ceremony. She was getting coffee. When I got back up here that sign, the one that says The Gypsy Is Within—Please Knock, was turned the other way, telling people to wait. She must have gotten to her tent afterward."

"It was turned the other way? What time was that?"

I stopped and took a second to go over what had gone on. The opening ceremony had started late. We'd gotten coffee and a biscuit afterward. Bobby had come on up to the booth while I went to get the networking account information and password. That went pretty quickly and then I walked up here and looked at the signs. I snapped my fingers. "It was about nine-twenty. I remember thinking she had about ten minutes before she was supposed to start." I pointed at the sign that displayed the time schedule.

"Then I went in there." I pointed to the canvas side of the Press's booth. "And set up the network for the computers, connected the printer, and tested the connection and how well it printed. By the time I had it all set up it was nine-thirty. I came back outside and the sign had been turned."

Snoddy had stopped and turned to face me while I worked on setting up the timeline. "Ten minutes to set up computers, network, and printers?"

"Bobby set up the computers. It's a wireless subnet that connects to The Festival's wireless private network and it was only one printer. Besides, I've done it before."

I ventured to guess that his experience with computers and networking had never gone well, hence the doubt in his voice and look. "They're Macs. It makes a difference."

We stared at each other for a moment.

"If the application had been for private investigator and computer geek I wouldn't have changed a word."

Chief Snoddy threw back his head and laughed—a deep rumbling series of haws that eased into chuckles. He lightly patted me on the back and I staggered forward three steps.

"All right, Crawford. You just might do at that. Why don't you try calling me Kurt for the time being."

"For the time being?"

"Until I can't stand it and tell you to stop."

. . .

An Archibald police officer had walked up while we were talking and stopped just out of listening range. He was tall, over six feet, with no hint of a paunch. He stood just close enough that his chief knew he was there, but not so close as to suggest that his news couldn't wait. Kurt waved him closer.

"What's up?"

"One of the EMTs says the victim was on blood thinners, which explains the amount of blood in the tent."

"That's right!"

Kurt looked at me. "And how do you happen to know that?"

"Well," I grinned involuntarily, "my cat scratched her yesterday during a photo shoot and there was a lot of blood."

"Your cat, eh?"

"Yep."

Kurt shook his head and turned his attention back to his deputy. "What else you got?"

"I've finished up with the other interviews. Nothing you didn't hear when you were talking to the assistant director—the Boucher woman—about the accident. So far everything matches up with what she said." He stuck his finger in his ear and wiggled it. "Seemed to me she got more upset as the news sank in. She's still working. Says 'The Festival must go on.' But she's crying." He shrugged his shoulders. "She's sending some volunteers to screen off this tent to cut down on the gawkers."

"Good. When the volunteers get here, make sure they don't put the screens in our way—and find out if the doctor had anything to say other than accidental death by snakebite." The police officer nodded and turned away.

"And try to get used to women crying, will you?"

The chief turned back to me. "Once the water fountain starts, he turns to mush. Where were we?"

"Accident?" I said.

"Well, what do you call it when somebody gets bitten by a poisonous snake? Suicide?"

"Venomous. Snakes are venomous."

"Huh?"

"Arsenic is poisonous. Snakes are venomous."

"Is that a fact?" The chief rubbed his finger along his nose. "You don't figure this for an accident?"

"I just got hired to find out whether she'd been blackmailing people. Seems kind of odd for her to have a fatal accident the next day." When I said it aloud I heard how stupid I sounded.

"What is it about the word 'accident' that you don't understand?" Chief Snoddy bent forward and peered at me. "Is there a normal time to have an accident? Oh, I forgot you started out solving murders—first taste of investigating right there in the deep end. What was it? Two murders in two months? No, three murders in one month. And at first nobody thought the first two were murders." He stood up straight. "You're just like a rookie police officer. So fired up that you're seeing murder and mayhem everywhere."

"You've got to admit it seems a little unnatural. Her death, so sudden."

"The day after Chad Harris calls her a blackmailer? I heard about that first thing this morning. You figure Chad was so insulted that he had to kill her?"

"I know it sounds stupid, but—"

"Sounds stupid! Boy, it not only sounds stupid it is stupid! You're talking about somebody killing somebody with a snake! How do you figure it? We got a killer who trains snakes to attack on command?"

I opened my mouth and then shut it.

"Good." Chief Snoddy said the word emphatically. "Come on up to the tent here and I'll tell you what we think happened. Oh, and don't be worried about getting bitten. The way we figure it that snake was just about as surprised as the dead woman. It must have made itself as scarce as possible once she stopped thrashing around."

Dot's body had been moved out of the tent, placed on a stretcher/gurney kind of thing, covered with a blanket, and strapped to it.

"We're still talking to witnesses, but, so far, we've been told that Dot sent her assistant up to the tent with a corn snake in a box. This is while Dot is performing the opening ceremony. Her assistant comes back, meets Dot at headquarters. They talk, Dot talks to the guy in charge of volunteers, the woman responsible for ticket sales, head of the Girl Scouts, and a few others. Spreads her charm around, if you know what I mean, and then heads up to her tent to get ready for fortune-telling. Everybody confirms that was the last time she was seen alive."

. . .

We stopped at the front flap of the door. The chief pointed at the bottom of the entrance—at the three- or four-inch lip where the flooring curved up to keep water from getting into the tent.

"See that toe-catcher? Nine times out of ten, maybe nineteen out of twenty, you step over it—no problem, right? But occasionally you don't and you stumble over it. Our theory is that she stumbled coming in and fell to the floor of the tent." Kurt squatted down and ran his hands along the lip. "You can tell somebody has tripped over it. What we can't tell is whether it was today."

"Yesterday morning she tripped on it coming out of the tent."

"Did she now? Yesterday. And how did you come by that information?"

"I saw her. We all did. I was here with Stan Dowdy, his assistant, and my cat. He was taking promotional pictures. Stan that is, not the cat."

"That the cat that scratched her?"

I bit my lip to keep from saying something smart and just nodded.

"That before or after you got hired to see if she was a blackmailer?"

"Before. I didn't get hired until the party—after Dot had been publicly accused."

Kurt frowned and muttered to himself. "Don't like hearing she tripped yesterday morning. That's two times in less than twenty-four hours. Still—."

"Why are you saying she fell?" She had been on the ground when I found her but that happens when you don't die in bed. You end up on the ground.

He stood and dusted off his hands. "Because the snake bit her on the throat. We don't figure she stood there while it crawled up her body." He looked at me. "Most snakebites are on people's arms, hands, legs, or feet. Parts of a human the snake can reach."

"But if she fell on the snake—." I was beginning to catch on.

"Exactly. Look at it from the rattlesnake's point of view. You're resting. Things are nice and quiet and all of a sudden Dot Fields comes crashing through the tent—knocking the table down—and landing almost on top of you or, maybe, actually on top of you. Most natural thing in the world would be to strike at what was attacking you. Once that venom got into a vein, Dot was history. And so, I figure, was the snake."

"The snake is long gone?" I looked around the tent.

"I don't hear any rattling, do you?"

"What was it doing in here anyway? Are you sure it was a rattlesnake? What about the other venomous snakes?"

"Look around, Crawford. What are you standing in the middle of? Don't bother answering, I'll tell you. A pine grove in west central Alabama. A pine grove that most of the time is just a pine grove—except for the weekend it becomes The Festival. What kind of poisonous snakes live in pine groves?" He held up his hand. "Okay. Venomous."

"Well, rattlesnakes, for sure, but—."

"I rest my case."

We stood in Dot's tent, a trouble light hanging above—the EMTs must have put that up. One of the eight walls was open where the EMTs had cut it to get access to their patient. The only really clear spot on the floor was where her body had been; this and that were scattered about the floor or up against the walls. The bark that used to be in the snake box was scattered all over. I could see spots of dried blood on some items, but it blended in with the clutter. I pulled out my phone and started taking pictures. I could see in my mind's eye how it had all been before the EMTs had gotten there—and see how they'd disrupted the area—but pictures seemed like a good idea.

I stuck my phone back in my pocket and nodded my head. "It's a good theory. Holds together well and takes into account everything we—you know. An accident—the simplest answer that explains everything."

Chief Snoddy nodded and a smile spread slowly across his face. "The answer is even simpler than I'd thought. There's something in that bag that's moving and I'm guessing it might be that snake that disappeared. It's not 'long gone' after all."

The bag was Dot's magic bag—I'd have called it a carpetbag but what do I know—the one she used to carry her crystal ball, tarot cards, Ouija board—the tools of her fortune-telling trade. All those things were scattered on the floor, but there was something in the bag—something that had just moved.

"Damn it to hell!" Chief Snoddy slapped his leg and the sound filled the tent. "I hate being wrong!"

He glanced around the tent and picked up the snake handling stick leaning up against the tent wall next to the back entrance. I remembered it from yesterday.

"It could be the corn snake. We know Coba brought it here. That's its box." I pointed at the cage but certainly didn't get any closer to the bag.

The chief didn't reply. He just slipped the end of the stick into the mouth of the bag and with a little fumbling lifted up one side of it. It was a rattlesnake all right. As Kurt opened the bag, it drew itself into a coil and began the telltale rattling. "Sure don't look like any corn snake I've ever seen. What do you think?"

I couldn't tell how long the snake was since it was coiled, but the coils themselves were thick—forearm thick—not Kurt's forearms but Bobby's certainly.

"Big one." Kurt squatted down, making sure to keep the stick between his body and the snake. "Well if this isn't a hell of a thing. Two snakes loose in the same tent and only one had the sense to get the hell out of Dodge."

"Looks like it found a hiding place before it found a way out." It had stopped rattling and was now smelling the air with its forked tongue.

"You mind going over there and getting that snake box and its lid? I'm going to need a way to restrain our suspect once he's apprehended and I don't think my handcuffs are going to do the trick."

I looked at the box, its lid, the snake, and Chief Snoddy and worked out some triangulation. "Sure. Just a minute." I stepped out the front, walked around to the back entrance, and picked up the box, scraping one edge against the tent floor to recapture some of the barklike stuff that had been in the box. I could see a jumble of supplies under the narrow table that still stood against one of the tent's eight walls. There might have been more bark there, but I didn't plan on searching for it. Not until the snake was in the box, if then. I edged around behind the snake and retrieved the lid. It was comfortingly solid, made out of metal mesh on a wooden frame.

I was directly across from Kurt, the snake between us. "How you figuring on apprehending him? Aren't you going to read him his rights first?"

"You just be ready to put that box down when I tell you to."

"Got it."

Without another word Chief Snoddy slipped the curved end of the stick behind the snake's head, pulled the head forward, pinned it to the floor, lunged forward, and with one hand grabbed the snake behind its hinged jaws. With those hands it was a cinch the snake's head wasn't going anywhere. The snake was writhing, its body twisting, but it couldn't move its head.

"Put the box next to my hand."

I didn't need to ask which hand. I put the plastic container parallel to the snake. While still holding the snake behind its head with one hand, Kurt reached under the middle of the snake's body and lifted the creature up chest high. He then leaned forward and carefully placed the snake into the box, With a suddenness that made his hands a blur, he moved both hands away and closed the lid. After making sure the top was securely latched, Kurt stood up, pulled a handkerchief out of his pocket, and wiped his hands.

"No hard feelings about not letting you help, Crawford, but it all had to happen at once."

I was too impressed to say anything.

For a big man he had moved awfully fast. I wondered how many fumbles he'd recovered during his football career—fast feet and fast hands. That answered the question if he moved as slowly as he looked like he would—the answer was no, emphatically no. It was only then that I glanced to the corner where the snake tongs were leaning against the wall. Too late now but it looked like they would have been a safer approach.

I looked at the snake through the clear sides of the box. It was a pretty thing, with brown and yellow striping on the side of its face and brownish diamond shapes down the back, each with a yellow edge. Being deadly doesn't keep something from being beautiful. "So that's what killed Dot Fields."

"Sure looks like it." He showed me the bright red stain on his handkerchief. "Still had a little of her blood on it. I'm no snake expert, but you can't mistake those rattles. We'll get an autopsy—I've already let them know that I want one—to see what that tells us. Hell, she might have died from fright." Kurt slowly shook his head. "You know, in all the years I've been in police work, I've never seen anybody killed by snakebite— accidental or otherwise."

"Is that right? How big do you think he is?"

"Oh, I'd say five, six feet—a big one for sure." He rubbed the side of his nose with his thick forefinger. I'd seen him do that before and wondered what he was thinking.

"Like I said, this looks like an accident to me. We've got tents pitched on natural habitat for rattlesnakes. And, it's been a warm fall."

I agreed with him without really knowing that much about it. "Uh-huh."

"But then you turn up with a story about her blackmailing people." I looked up from my study of the alleged murderer and found Kurt Snoddy studying me. "You've got a knack for turning what looks like accidental death into murder, don't you?"

"Only when it is. That was the first case—the poisoning and the hanging. The second was a bullet to the back of the head. Nobody thought that one was an accident."

"Still," he kept talking as if he hadn't heard a word I said. Maybe he hadn't. "A rattlesnake seems like an iffy kind of murder weapon. How you even going to make sure the snake bites the victim?"

"You've asked for an autopsy, right?" Kurt was making me nervous the way he seemed to be staring at me and gazing into the distance at the same time. "Why not wait until you get those results? Like you said, she could have died of fright."

Kurt jerked himself out of his reverie. "You've got a point. I'll send a message with the body asking for somebody to take a quick look."

. . .

We walked out of Dot's fortune-telling area and looked around. There were Festival volunteers quickly re-pitching the booths that had flanked the entrance to Dot's tent so that they blocked the public's view. In another ten or fifteen minutes it would look like the pathway had never passed by Dot's tent.

Kurt had stopped to talk to one of his deputies. I stepped back a little so I wasn't intruding. I was still eavesdropping, but I gave the appearance of minding my own business—I hoped.

"Found a rattlesnake in the victim's tent and stuck it in a snake cage that was in there." Kurt held up his hand. "Don't go trying to tell me that I tampered with evidence. Take charge of the box and make sure no one meddles with it. Don't leave it unattended."

He tugged on one of his earlobes. "Check with some of the veterinarians—the ones with clinics—and see if any of them would take a rattlesnake for a few weeks."

"How about the Metro animal shelter?" I put my two cents in, thus blowing my pretense of disinterestedness. "They've got an adoption booth over there—on the outside of the perimeter pathway. Heck," the thought had just crossed my mind, "the snake might have escaped from there. They get all sorts of pets dumped on them."

Kurt looked at me and then turned back to his deputy. "Check out the animal shelter first. That's a good idea. If they lost a rattlesnake out here, I want to know about it."

The deputy hustled off. Kurt nodded his head. "Thanks, Crawford. I hadn't thought about Metro."

"No problem."

I heard the sound of a siren, far off but getting closer. "Is that the ambulance for Dot?"

"Eh? EMTs sent for a hearse. They didn't want to use their ambulance in case something else happened while they were moving Dot and they needed the ambulance. But no siren, we're trying to keep this quiet. No need to stir things up with sirens and flashing lights. The Festival wants things to go on like nothing happened."

While he was talking, the sirens got louder and closer. At first I thought they were coming straight down the road that led directly to the park, but then the noise seemed to drift off to the side.

"Shit," said Kurt not quite under his breath. He pointed at two plumes of dust coming across the field. They must have turned off the road and taken to the open ground. As they got closer I could tell that it was a police car—lights flashing, bouncing across the fields—with a TV van from the local station following behind.

Kurt took a massive breath of air and let it out. "I was hoping a snakebite might not be important enough for Sammy to take notice. Must be a slow news day." He shook his head. "You know Sammy? Ever meet him? He'll remember even if you don't."

"Sammy Thompson? Sheriff of Jemison County?" That had to be who Kurt was talking about. I'd never met the man, but I'd seen him on local TV and in the newspapers. "No, but I would recognize him."

"Of course you would. Every potential voter in Jemison County knows what Sheriff Thompson looks like. Why else would he have his picture plastered all over the place? I am surprised, though, to hear he hasn't shaken your hand."

Kurt looked at me and laughed. "'Course that would have been before you got that private investigator license. Sammy has got some issues about PIs, but you'll find out about that soon enough, I expect."

. . .

We watched as the police car got close to the barbed wire fence that marked one edge of The Festival's grounds. The TV van had slowed down going over the rough ground, so it was a hundred or so yards behind, moving at a much more cautious speed.

The police car stopped, both front doors flew open, and two figures exited the vehicle. Its lights were still flashing, but the siren had been shut off. The taller of the two figures jogged ahead of the second to the fence, pushed down on the middle strand of wire with his foot, and then lifted up the top strand with his hands. Without breaking stride the smaller man ducked through the opening and headed straight toward where we were standing.

"My, makes an impressive entrance, doesn't he?"

Kurt just grunted and crossed his arms across his chest. I thought for a second that he couldn't have made himself look bigger if he'd tried, then I looked at the smaller man headed his way, and wondered if he had tried.

Chief Snoddy's uniform had started the day clean and crisp, ironed and starched, I'm sure, but by now there were wrinkles here and there, and smudges of dirt. The sheriff's uniform was still starched smooth and the creases on his pants looked sharp enough to shave with.

The ground throughout the park was pretty level but not parking-lot-flat. Whatever high ground there was, Kurt had claimed it. I stepped back and to the side.

"Snoddy," Sammy spoke the chief's name, stopped beside him, turned so they were facing the same direction, and crossed his arms across his chest—equals looking out over the landscape. "What have you got?"

Kurt glanced down at the smaller man. "Not much more than what you heard on the radio, Sammy. Snakebite. The victim is the director of The Festival so there'll be some publicity. She entered her tent this morning sometime between 9:10 and 9:30. What happened then is subject to speculation."

"Speculation? You know I don't like speculation in police work. What have you got that's certain?"

Kurt nodded over toward the stretcher that held Dot's body. "A dead body that's got what looks like a snakebite on the neck and a five-foot rattlesnake in a cage."

"Accidental death then."

"Well, Mr. Crawford and I were just talking about that." Kurt pointed at me with the thumb of his right hand. "Mr. Crawford here is a private eye who was hired by The Festival to investigate allegations of blackmail activity on the part of the deceased."

I noticed that I'd become Mr. Crawford and wondered why, as I leaned forward holding out my hand.

Sheriff Thompson looked at my hand, then looked me in the eyes. His were a pale shade of gray. "Huh." He turned back to Kurt. "I guess he's out of a job now that she's dead. That should save The Festival some money."

I dropped my hand. I looked over at Kurt and saw the hint of a smile tugging at the edges of his lips.

"So how do you see it happening, Chief?" It was clear that Sheriff Thompson didn't want my input.

Kurt shrugged but kept his arms crossed. "Today's a nice bright day. Victim walks up to her tent—tent has a three-inch lip all the way around—stiff plastic stuff. Looks like people have stumbled over it before—can't tell about today. Say she stumbles this time, falling into the tent. Table in the middle of the tent breaks her fall but can't stand up to her weight. Table crumbles, she's waving her arms, can't really see—eyes haven't adjusted—falls to her hands and knees."

He uncrossed his arms and started to point at me, then brought his hand back and stroked his chin. "That's when the rattlesnake comes into it. The snake bites her on the neck—she convulses—making more of a mess in the tent while shaking the snake off—and dies. EMTs think the venom must have hit a vein to work so fast. We'll know more after we get an autopsy."

"Snake just happen to pick her tent?"

I answered him. "Snake had to be somewhere. Why not there? She kept a nonvenomous snake in the tent. Might have made a difference—made the space more attractive, maybe."

Sammy didn't even acknowledge that I'd spoken.

"Don't see anybody using a rattlesnake as a murder weapon," said Kurt. "Do you? Hell, it's a wild animal. If somebody had let it loose in the tent, what was to keep it from escaping? The other snake took off quick enough."

The TV van had pulled up beside the sheriff's car and a camera operator and newscaster were standing next to it. It looked like they were setting up an on-the-scene segment.

Sammy looked at the camera and then back at Kurt. "Anybody hear anything?"

Kurt smiled then winked at me. "I've got a witness who didn't hear anything. Said The Festival's stage was having problems with their sound system about that time. Might have covered up any noises from the victim's tent."

"Okay. Then we'll go with accidental death for the time being. We're waiting for autopsy results and further investigations." Sammy nodded to himself. "While there's been a death, we see no need to call in the Multijurisdictional Homicide Unit. I'll go handle the press. You carry on here."

He started to leave then turned around. "Did you say you had the snake? Is it dead? And you sure it's poisonous?"

"We apprehended the snake. It's a rattlesnake, which means it is venomous—not poisonous."

That got Kurt the gray-eyed stare. "Venomous—not poisonous?"

Kurt just nodded in my direction. Damn, I thought, he's enjoying this.

Sammy continued to ignore my existence. "Go ahead and get rid of the snake. No use keeping it alive—waste of resources. Kill it."

"Oh, don't know about that, Sammy. I've got the snake in custody but I can't decide if it's a material witness or a lethal weapon. Don't want to do anything rash either way."

There was a vein throbbing in Sammy's forehead that hadn't been there when he'd walked up to us. "Right. Your decision, Chief Snoddy."

Kurt and I watched him head toward the camera.

"So, what did you think?"

I couldn't decide if Kurt was kidding or not. "Maybe he's got some control issues?"

"Mebbe."

"And a touch of small man syndrome."

. . .

I'd excused myself while Kurt was still laughing about the small-man syndrome comment and headed over to the booth to catch up with Bobby. The volunteers had finished moving the booths so that they blocked access to Dot's tent from the pathway. The computer monitors still were going through their slideshows and people were either watching them or looking at the few hardback samples on display. I caught Bobby's eye and she gave me a thumbs-up, which I took to mean the network and printer were still working. She was talking to Batman and Robin; I decided I'd better wait before going over to her. That reminded me that I was supposed to be assisting her so I looked around the tent to see if anyone looked like they needed help.

I saw Ellen George and Joyce Fines standing together. Ellen had left her Glinda the Good Witch outfit at home. She and Joyce were dressed in slacks, blouses, jackets, and sensible walking shoes. I headed over to speak to them. Neither one could be considered in need of help, on the other hand I was pretty sure they weren't here to buy books.

As I closed in, Joyce Fines cut straight to the issue—as she saw it. "You are to continue to investigate the allegation against Dot Fields despite what has happened. The board will want the question of blackmailing to be resolved even if the employee who may or may not have perpetrated those actions is now deceased."

This was good because I had already decided that it would be good experience for me to continue to try and figure out how to investigate blackmailing. The fact that they weren't interested in calling it and me off made it easier.

Ellen George raised her eyebrows and glanced around the tent. Joyce's voice was normally carrying and this time she'd made no attempt to be quiet. Suddenly, we had something of an audience. The people turning our way may have come into the tent wondering about the books the university's press had published but I was sure they'd be interested in The Festival director's death as well.

Ellen spoke in a quieter voice. "Why don't we take this outside and let these people get back to The Festival?"

I swept my arm toward the front of the booth. "After you, my ladies." There was something about the manner with which Ellen George and Joyce Fines conducted themselves that made me feel like I should bow—or take off my hat if I was wearing one. We Americans don't really know how to behave around royalty.

. . .

Stepping out of the booth, we were on the pathway, blocking traffic. The crowd was growing. People were wandering from booth to booth while drinking their Public Radio coffee out of souvenir cups. Some brave souls were in costume—wizards, cowboys, cowgirls, and vampires were mixed in with uncostumed Festival-goers. I thought to myself that Friday morning certainly wasn't the time I'd pick to dress up in costume but reminded myself—to be fair—that I wasn't inclined to wear costumes at any time of day.

Expanding the audience wasn't the point of leaving the tent so I led the board members between the booths back to the fortune-telling area. Having gotten us out of eavesdropping range, I turned around to face Ellen and Joyce. Ellen started right in.

"Now, James, as members of the executive board of The Festival, we'd like to be briefed on this unfortunate incident."

I was tempted to tug my forelock but I controlled the impulse. It helped to remember that I wasn't thirteen explaining to my friend's parents how I'd accidentally kicked a Coke bottle into their brand new color television. I'd already done that. Once, I assure you, was enough.

I pointed in the direction of Sheriff Thompson who was still in front of the camera—the face of law enforcement in Jemison County. "If you want to catch the noon news, I'm sure the Sheriff will be on it."

"I'd rather we were briefed by someone who doesn't refer to himself in the third person," said Joyce Fines. She was fairly imperious herself. Fortunately for me, she and I didn't have any history of shared childhood disasters to make her even more formidable.

"Right."

"What do the police know about this terrible accident? Bobby told us that Chief Snoddy had taken you away to discuss what you found when you discovered Dot's body."

The chief was still standing where I'd left him, so I led the ladies toward him. "You might as well get it firsthand. Chief Snoddy might be pleased that somebody wants to hear it from him instead of Sheriff Thompson."

Kurt had his right hand up to his ear and, until I heard him speak, I had no idea he was holding his cell phone—it was swallowed in the palm of his hand.

I slowed down when I realized he was on the phone but he urged us closer while continuing to talk. "If you'll send some of your people to handle the traffic that would be terrific. Thanks, Andrew, I owe you one." He lowered his hand. "Chief Boyd— head of the Shelbyville police. This accident has stretched us a little thin, what with The Festival and all.

He stuffed his phone in his pocket then extended his right hand. "Mrs. George, how are you and the provost doing these days?"

"Fine, Chief Snoddy. How's your family?"

"Fine, thanks for asking." He looked at Joyce.

"Do you know Dr. Fines?" Ellen looked surprised when they both shook their heads no. "I'm sorry, I thought you two would have met by now.

"Joyce, this is Chief Kurt Snoddy. Don't try to get him to fix a parking ticket for you. He always claims Archibald needs the money."

"Chief, this is Joyce Fines—she's professor emeritus in environmental studies here at the university and chair of The Festival's executive committee."

Kurt held his hand out and Joyce put her hands behind her back. "No disrespect intended, Chief Snoddy. I've got arthritis and shaking hands just stirs it up."

"No problem." He gave Joyce a considering look. "Environmental studies?"

Joyce laughed. "When I graduated my degree was in botany, if that's what you're asking. Nobody got degrees in environmental studies back then."

His face fell. "Botany, huh? Guess that means you don't know much about snakes."

"Snakes and reptiles are clearly within the field of environmental studies." There was an edge of frost in Joyce's voice. "So I do know about snakes to some degree—not to the degree I would if my graduate degree had been in herpetology, of course."

Kurt looked a little confused. Ellen stepped up to take charge. "Joyce and I wanted to ask you about the director of The Festival—as representatives of The Festival board."

"Sheriff Thompson is over there talking to the press about it right now. I'm sure he'd be happy to brief you as well."

"Kurt?" I spoke up.

"Yeah?"

"I suggested that the sheriff would be happy to speak to them but they indicated that they wouldn't be that happy to hear him. I thought you'd understand what they meant."

A smile lit up the chief's face. "I see. Well, as it looks like Sheriff Thompson has pressing business elsewhere, I'll be happy to try." He nodded in the direction of the police car that was now leaving the grounds as rapidly as it had arrived.

"Unless you need me, I probably should go back and help Bobby. If you'll excuse me." I looked from Ellen to Joyce before walking away.

Joyce shook her head. "I think you'd better stay, Crawford.

We may want your input on this."

So I stayed.

. . .

Kurt summed it up quickly and clearly.

"Dot Fields, the deceased, was the victim of an accidental snakebite—rattlesnake bite—this morning sometime between 9:10 and 9:30. The bite was on the neck, which, we believe, contributed to how quickly the venom entered the deceased's bloodstream and resulted in her death. The location of the bite and the condition of the tent indicate that Ms. Fields fell upon entering the tent and was subsequently bitten. An autopsy will be performed. The rattlesnake has been captured."

Ellen and Joyce nodded, and I added, "Good summary."

"Are you satisfied that this was an accident?"

"Accident?" Kurt stared at Ellen for a moment or two. "Yes, as far as us humans are concerned. The snake might have meant to kill Dot but that wouldn't fit our definition of premeditated murder. Call it a crime of passion."

Ellen continued. "All right. In light of this unfortunate accident, should we be concerned about the safety of our volunteers or the Festival-goers? Should we evacuate the grounds?"

Kurt took off his hat and scratched his head. "I don't have a degree in—what was that Dr. Fines—herpetology? But as far as I know, rattlesnakes aren't pack animals, they don't travel in pairs, and they shouldn't have any little ones with them. Fall has been on the warm side so I'm not surprised that the snake wasn't hibernating. As I pointed out to Crawford here, this is a pine grove—native habitat for rattlesnakes. We've caught a rattlesnake and I'd be surprised if more than one could make a living around here. It should be safe."

Joyce stirred beside Ellen. "I don't disagree with anything Chief Snoddy has said regarding the snake. In fact, a 'crime of passion' might be the best way to describe it. There have been a number of studies that indicate an adult venomous snake would hesitate to waste venom on something that wasn't prey. As adults, they learn to regulate the amount of venom they inject and don't waste it on things too big to eat. When they do bite humans, which isn't as often as many people think, it's often a 'dry bite.'"

Kurt took off his hat, wiped a hand across his hair, and then returned the hat to his head. "Dry bite, eh? Even more reason not to use a rattlesnake as a weapon."

"Oh, no," said Joyce in a most professorial manner. "As far as using one as a weapon, none of the venomous snakes indigenous to North America would be good choices—in my opinion. But if you want an authoritative opinion, I can put you in contact with an acquaintance of mine who has a more extensive knowledge of snakes than I do. You may know him—or have heard of him. He grew up in Shelbyville."

Kurt nodded. "Over in West End. I forget his real name but all the kids called him 'Snake.' He was the same age as my older brother, so I grew up hearing about him—him and his basement full of snakes." He grinned. "My brother used to tease me about going down into that basement."

"His name is Morgan Moore and he is an internationally renowned expert on reptiles and amphibians. He no longer has to keep his snakes in the basement—that's what his herp lab is for. He's a top-notch scientist and has a flair for communicating with the public. Shelbyville ought to be proud of their native son."

"Wasn't there a football player with that nickname?" I was trying to remember if I'd ever heard of this guy.

Joyce looked at me blankly, Kurt snorted, and Ellen rolled her eyes.

"And that is what the people of Shelbyville are proudest of—football." Ellen sighed.

"The gymnastics team is pretty popular too." I didn't get the opportunity to tease Ellen George very often.

"James—"

I interrupted before she got started. "Dr. Fines, do you know how to get in touch with Dr. Moore—I assume it's doctor?"

"He lives in Alton, South Carolina. He works at an ecological laboratory near there where a very dear friend of mine works. I've got his contact information, if you'd like it."

"That would be fantastic. If I had his email address I could send him some pictures of the snake we're dealing with. It might help."

It was too much to expect Dr. Fines to have the Bump app so she could transfer Dr. Moore's email address to my iPhone, but she did have it written down in her address book. And she had the book with her. She carefully spelled it out for me as I typed it into my phone.

Joyce assured me that he was used to getting all sorts of questions about snakes from all types of people, but I could say she'd referred me to him.

That settled, Joyce Fines and Ellen George excused themselves and left for headquarters to see if they could offer Coba anything more than moral support.

"I hope," said Ellen, "that Joyce and I can persuade her to take a break—to get out of headquarters for at least a little while. She lives close enough she could even go home. She's doing a magnificent job under the circumstances. The Festival is very fortunate to have her."

Kurt and I watched them walk away and he said what I was thinking. "If I was Miss Coba, I'd be taking that break. Those are some formidable women."

"I agree. And speaking of formidable women, I think I'd better go see if I can help Bobby. That's supposedly why I'm at The Festival."

. . .

Once I got back on the pathway, the crowd was even thicker. That was how it was supposed to happen. People were still coming and going, it was just that now the arrival rate was exceeding the departure rate.

I popped back into the Press booth and saw that things weren't that crowded. Batman and Robin had left, and the people who'd followed them weren't in costume. Frank wandered over to me.

He had a broad grin on his face. "Must be interesting to be you."

"How do you figure?" I spotted Bobby talking to an elderly man who was using one of those odd-looking four-footed canes. Good idea on these unpaved, uneven paths. But why four? Surely three would be sturdier.

"Finding murdered bodies all over the place. This is the fourth one in what, three months?"

"Frank—." I was about to start correcting him, but he knew the truth; he was being deliberately provocative. This was actually the first dead body *I* had found. "She wasn't murdered. It was an accident."

"Oh, I got the faith—don't think I don't. A great detective like you will discover that she'd been blackmailing the rattlesnake. You know," he paused to make sure I got it, "Dot was putting the bite on the snake."

I like puns. "Frank that's awful."

"You're just saying that because you didn't think of it first."

There might be some truth to that, but, as there was no way Dot had been blackmailing the snake, my chance of using "putting the bite on the snake" was extremely limited. I was sure he'd already sprung it on Bobby and, in my opinion, there was nothing unfunnier than a secondhand pun.

"I like the way they moved the booth—lining us up with the AIDS booth." Having inflicted his pun on me, Frank was willing to move on to other topics. "I was a little disconcerted when I got here and you couldn't even see the fortune-telling tent. They did a nice job moving the booths."

"Probably made it easier that the two tents are identical—whose tent is it, by the way?"

Frank looked startled. "Are they? Identical? I hadn't noticed."

"Not only are they identical, they're both brand new." Sometimes I'm baffled at what people don't see but then the amount of stuff I overlook stuns me too.

"Well, that would explain why they could move it so easily. It's The Festival's tent, only I'm not supposed to tell anybody that. The Festival doesn't want anybody to know they supply some tents."

"Yeah, you've already told me that and I still haven't told anybody—yet. I meant who's in the other tent?"

"I told you—AIDS—the local organization. It's a group trying to raise awareness, educate the public, and help the unfortunate."

"Its official title is West-Central Alabama HIV/AIDS Outreach—shortened to WAHO—unless they've changed it. I used to be on the board."

"Really? On the board?" Frank sounded sincerely surprised. Actually, it surprised me too—then and now. I'm not much of a group person and I'm suspicious of good intentions.

"It was a number of years ago." A friend of Eleanor's and mine had asked if I would help the group. A friend who has had great success doing things with the best of intentions. Go figure.

Bobby and the elderly customer parted company and she walked over to where Frank and I were standing.

"So was Frank right? Had Dot been putting the bite on the snake?"

I was right. Frank had already shared the pun with Bobby. "I can't even prove they had ever met before. This might have been the first and last time."

"Does Dot's death mean no more case for you to investigate? The Festival board happy enough to know Dot's not going to do it any more—if she ever did?"

"Not according to Joyce and Ellen. They still want to know if Dot had been a blackmailer."

"I saw you leave with them. Did they just want to tell you to keep on working?"

"Nope. They wanted a briefing on what happened to Dot—or what the police think happened to Dot, anyway. So I took them over to Chief Snoddy and let him sum things up for them."

"Not the sheriff?" Frank spoke up. "I saw him in front of the news cameras when I was coming here."

"No, they wanted a private briefing."

"Huh," scoffed Frank. "They didn't want to hear it from a man of the people. Sammy's something of a publicity hound and that's not the way well-bred people behave."

"Chief Snoddy's not exactly a blue-blood himself."

"Right," agreed Frank. "But he fits in the culture—the milieu—of big burly policemen deferring to those above his class—in their eyes—while—."

"Whoops! There he goes with the social revolution! Let's get out of here." Bobby grabbed my arm and pulled me toward the exit, a movement I was in total agreement with.

"Frank, you're in charge of the booth from now until closing! Crawford and I are off to enjoy The Festival!"

Bobby bounded out of the tent. "Now it's time to have some fun!" I moved a little slower, but was right behind her. I was ready to put Dot's death aside for the time being.

"I want to scout out the exhibits so we can be sure that Jack and Rebecca won't miss anything."

"Are they into anything particular? Ceramics, painting, woodcarving, metalwork?"

"Oh, Bex enjoys everything. She's interested in all sorts of things and has an amazing capacity for enjoying life! She's such fun and so is Jack."

"Bex?" I knew who it had to be but didn't remember Bobby calling Rebecca that.

"Oh that's Rebecca's nickname—what we called her growing up. There was Bex and Bunny and me—we called ourselves the three Bs."

It sounded to me like it was a waste of time to try and pick out things they'd enjoy—since they enjoyed it all. But I wasn't complaining. I was enjoying being with Bobby. There was one thing though.

"How about food?"

"Oh, Jack is an amazing foodie—fearless. He loves to try different foods. If he hasn't had it he'll try it. He figures somebody enjoys it—why not him?"

"Great, because I'm starving. Let's see if we can find some food for him to try tomorrow!"

Bobby laughed and grabbed my arm. "You silly, all you had to say was that you were hungry."

"Wait, wasn't that what I just did say?"

Bobby pointed up the pathway away from The Festival's headquarters. "That's the quickest way to the food court and we can look at what's in the booths on the way!"

. . .

I was able to convince Bobby that it would be best not to dawdle too much on the way to the food court. We could take pictures of the booths as we walked by them and then look at them while we were eating—to see which ones were worth coming back to. I would have been more patient but we were downwind of the food court.

As we made our way along the path, I could hear Festival-goers discussing Dot's death. They sounded more shocked at the death being by snakebite than they were at the death itself. The mood of the crowd was festive. There didn't seem to be any pall cast over The Festival because the director had died today. Maybe it was a reflection of how powerful The Festival had become—how much a part of people's lives—or maybe not.

The hickory smoke in the air hinted at all sorts of possibilities of the edible variety. I knew there would be boiled peanuts, cotton candy, funnel cakes, hot dogs, and hamburgers. That was a given even at the smallest southern county fair. But The Festival was more than a county fair—much, much more. As the cooking odors in the air competed for my attention—the familiar versus the unfamiliar—I began to understand why people would object to Dot's having the same menu year after year at the artist appreciation party.

We entered the cul-de-sac that was the food court and stopped to consider the booths scattered around the periphery of the opening and the signs advertising their menus.

"Jack loves this. There's always something new."

"Jack, hell, I'm loving it!" The signs promised varied taste treats—some with cryptic names—turkey legs, craw taters, gumbo, red beans and rice, fried gumbo, bourbon chicken, BBQ shrimp, beignets, corn dogs, blooming onions, spiral potatoes, Frito pie, chicken skewers, Conecuh sausage, Polish sausage, boiled crawfish, and kettle corn.

Two or three stands offered soft drinks, lemonade, or water. The Festival sold beer only on Saturday, so none of the beer stands were open. Jack had that to look forward to tomorrow— and so did I.

After a brief consultation, we split up to stand in different lines. I'm usually a sucker for gumbo but the spicy-chicken-on-a-stick, a variation of the fried-chicken-on-a-stick taste treat, called to me, as did the ever-popular spiral potato chips. To finish it off, I went with the fresh-squeezed lemonade in a souvenir Festival cup. The Festival cup was an extra charge but I was thinking about claiming the whole meal as a business expense. Bobby settled on a gyro and a bottle of water—having elected to share my spiral chips.

Food in hand, we grabbed some seats at a long picnic table near the music stage. It was crowded but everybody cheerfully made room for us. We shared bites of chicken and gyro and agreed that we both had chosen well. The tzatziki sauce was particularly wonderful and I thought about having the gyro tomorrow. But tomorrow I had a choice of beers to consider as well. Life is so delightfully complicated sometimes.

While we were eating, the Celtic music issuing from the sound stage changed. Actually, the only thing I can say with absolute certainty is that the lead singer changed—the lead female singer. The songs she sang weren't different—they were still lamenting treachery and betrayal with occasional snide remarks about the English—but the woman's voice certainly was. What was a world-class talent doing singing on The Festival stage? Maybe Dot had blackmailed her into performing? Here was a potential start—maybe I could talk to her after her performance?

"Listen to that woman's voice," I said to Bobby between bites. "I wonder what she's doing singing here?"

The man seated next to me wiped his mouth with a paper napkin before speaking, "She's a student at the university whose getting performance credits singing with this group. We're really lucky to have the university here. Get to hear lots of talent just getting started. I forget her name, but it's in the program."

He went back to his bowl of chili and I scratched off another potential blackmail victim. But the exchange wasn't a complete loss. "Where did you get the chili?"

His mouth was full so he pointed at a booth I hadn't noticed.

"The one with a sign for a grilled jalapeño and cheese sandwich?"

The guy nodded, big grin on his face, pointed at a crust of bread on his plate and gave it a thumbs up. It sounded good. I made a mental note to remember the grilled sandwich and chili.

Bobby and I poured some of her water on a paper napkin and washed up before heading back onto the pathway of The Festival.

Having been reminded of the existence of a program for The Festival, I pulled the one I'd gotten at headquarters out of my back pocket and tried to find where Chad Harris's booth was in relation to the food court. The other end of the park. Of course.

We began working our way to Chad's tent. It was close to the Metro Shelter's adopt-a-pet booth. Oh, they didn't call it that— they weren't that blatant, but that was what they were hoping for. The last time I'd gotten around animals in need of adoption it had been a house full of cats. I had been arrogant, knowing that I was a dog person, and discovered I was a dog and a cat person—at least for one dog and one cat. I had no desire to add any more to the menagerie. Two to one was as outnumbered as I cared to be. Bobby and I had agreed to look the other way when we passed that booth.

The section where we were was filled with artists who specialized in jewelry. Earrings, bracelets, necklaces, pins, brooches, and the like. Occasionally one would have hand-made sun-catchers or silk scarves painted by the artist, but they were sidelines to the jewelry.

"Wonder why they put all the jewelry booths together like this?" I was watching an attractive young woman peering at herself in a hand-held mirror; she had backed up enough to be in front of the next person's booth. "Seems like you'd want them spread out."

Bobby shook her head. "It's just like car lots."

"Huh?" I was full; it was a pretty day for meandering; and my mind was not fully engaged.

"Car dealers. You know how the lots are all out on the highway south of town? One cheek-by-jowl with the other. Just like you see on I-20 east of Atlanta. I forget the name of the town but it's one car dealer after another for miles. If you're in the market for a new car, that's where you go. You can look at and compare all the models, makes, what-have-yous without driving all over the place. If you're at The Festival and want to buy some earrings, this is the place to be."

It made sense now that she'd explained it to me. I'd thought, if I'd given it any thought, that the car dealers wanted to be near the highway so buyers could test drive the cars. Maybe that was why one built out there and then the rest all followed. Same kind of marketing that there used to be for gas stations. If there was a Texaco on one corner, then a Pure would open up across the street. I hadn't thought about that in ages.

We'd gotten to a fork in the path. One side looked like fabrics, textiles, quilts, and weaving; the other fork had some pottery set up; there were paintings and sculpture down both forks. The fork to the left was the more direct route to Chad Harris's booth—and the Metro Shelter. Bobby started down that direction and stopped when she realized I wasn't following. I waved at her to come back and pointed straight ahead.

In the center of the fork was Whittlin' Woodrow, one of the legendary folk artists who'd been coming to The Festival since the very beginning. Scattered around the delta that split the paths, were some of his creations—some blending in, others standing out in this natural setting. In his salad days, Woodrow had worked on large pieces, using an array of knives and chisels of various sizes and shapes to bring out the odd shapes and mysterious creatures that he'd found hidden in logs, stumps, and tree trunks. He'd gotten too old to handle the big pieces of wood now—too old, too wizened, and too arthritic.

There were still some of those early pieces standing, leaning, arching in place to mark the ground as his—his studio—his works. Some of the big pieces were ones he couldn't part with no matter how much money he was offered. Others were here on loan from their owners—owners who'd agreed to display the pieces at The Festival if he'd part with them. Festival legend said that over the years he'd given one or two away—but nobody knew why or to whom—and you never could be sure what he might sell.

He was sitting in a rocker, dressed in new overalls, plaid shirt, and baseball cap. He was neat, clean, and tidy like the tools he worked with. At the moment, he had in his hands a branch as big around as a softball and about three feet long. Bark still covered most of its surface and Woodrow was running his hands up and down the stick, turning it this way and that, occasionally twisting it in his grasp and putting it next to his ear listening to what the wood said to him. I was fascinated and stepped closer to watch.

His long fingers were calloused and showed the wear and tear that you'd expect from a lifetime of dealing with sharp knives. He wasn't looking at the wood. His face was lifted up while his hands learned the wood. I have no idea what I expected him to do but I was enthralled watching him.

"You in my sun." His voice was thin and curt.

I jumped and stepped back.

"Sorry. Just fascinated watching you work with wood."

"Used to not mind the cold." His voice got a little stronger. "Nowadays like to sit and soak up the sun—like a snake on a rock." He cocked his head to one side and looked at me. "You know snakes?"

I chuckled. "I know more about them now than I did when I woke up this morning, but that's not saying much."

"Word is you found her dead—Miss Festival Director Woman Fields—and the snake that killed her. That true?" He looked directly at me and I could see the cataracts in his eyes.

"Yes sir, it is. Dot Fields is dead. Looks like it was a rattlesnake bite."

He flexed his hands and the branch he'd been holding snapped in two. He dropped it on the ground. "Rotten inside. Just like her. Thank you, sir." He smiled. "And thank you Mister Rattlesnake. Did you think to use a stake?"

I thought I'd misheard him. "It was a snake that killed her. The chief of police caught it and they've got it in a cage."

"Good for the chief. I hope they treat that snake kindly. But it's not enough. You need to use a stake—somebody need to drive a wooden stake through that woman's heart. Otherwise she likely to be comin' back."

He bent over and began sorting through a pile of wood by his side. The sticks varied in size, thickness, and shape. They probably varied by species too, but a stick is a stick is a stick to me.

"Sounds like you didn't like Dot Fields."

"Momma didn' hold with talkin' ill of the dead. She was tiresome about it sometimes, but even she would'na had nothin' good to say 'bout that woman."

I had wondered how to find somebody Dot had been blackmailing. Was it going to be this easy?

"My name is James Crawford. I'm a private investigator that The Festival hired to find out if Dot Fields was blackmailing people. Mind if I ask you a few questions?" The words came out effortlessly—as if I'd been saying them for years.

Woodrow put the stick he'd selected in his lap, dusted off his palms, and reached out to shake my hand. "Go right ahead, Mr. Crawford. Most folk here call me Woodrow." His hand was dry and cool.

"Most folk call me Crawford."

Woodrow went back to the stick, twisting and stroking it. Listening to it. He was so used to handling wood, I don't think he was even aware he was doing it while he talked to me.

"So The Festival people beginnin' to wonder about their director woman. 'Bout time they did."

"Last night one of the other artists—Chad Harris—accused her of trying to blackmail him."

"Heard he'd done that." Woodrow shook his head. "Hotheaded young man—she got his blood boilin'. She was good at that." He smiled. "Nice usin' 'was' to speak of her." He discarded the stick and picked up another.

"Do you mind my asking if she was blackmailing you?"

Woodrow's chuckle was dry and raspy. "'Course she was. She had a tale she threatened to tell 'bout somethin' I'd done years and years ago. It wad'n true. Leastwise, it wad'n the way I remember it. If she'd spread it around, it'd been her word 'gainst mine. She had me 'tween a rock and a hard place. Kept me there too. Oh, she didn' use it that often. Ever' year or so she'd offer to sell one of my pieces for me. One I didn' wannna sell—so she'd jus' keep the money. Her way of helpin' me help myself. Otherwise I'd've kept too many of them. She just helped me get rid of some."

"But if it was her word against yours, couldn't you do something? Go to The Festival board?"

The old man shook his head. "Crawford, you sound like a man who grew up around here. You oughta know a man like me didn' do himself no good sayin' a woman like her was lyin'. People got hung for less. Those early lessons are hard to unlearn."

I couldn't argue with him. I couldn't walk a mile in his shoes.

"Do you know if she was blackmailing anybody else?"

"You think that leopard had only one spot? Oh, she was blackmailin' others. I seen her talk so mean to people. . . . But I never asked, so I can't say for sure."

I got out one of my business cards and handed it to Woodrow. I'd made a special trip back to the car to get them and they were already coming in handy. "I'd appreciate it if you'd try and remember who else she treated so poorly. I'd rather not involve you."

He tucked my card into a pocket of his overalls. "It don't really matter. It was her story 'gainst mine and now she can't tell her version. What she can't say, can't hurt me. Anyway, I'm gettin' old and tired. If she'd tried that trick on me this year, I might just have let her have her say. Gettin' too old for such foolishness."

He looked at the stick he had in his hand. "Might do. Seems like it might have somethin' in it." He propped it up next to his chair. "I'll be thinkin' about the old-timers here and who else she might've been blackmailin'. Give you a call if I have anything to say."

"Thanks."

. . .

"I wasn't sure what I should do." Bobby appeared at my elbow. "I realized that you were 'detecting' so I didn't want to interfere. Clever of you to start with Woodrow, he's been part of The Festival since the beginning."

"Bobby," I stopped walking and turned to face her. "It's kind of you to think that I'd planned on starting my investigation with Woodrow but I hadn't. I'd forgotten that he'd be here, much less thought that he'd be a good person to interview. Once we started talking I—." Damn. How could I expect a woman like Bobby to put up with me acting the way I just had. "I'm sorry, I just forgot what we were doing."

She reached out and hugged me. "That's what I thought had happened. You got so caught up in what you were doing that you forgot about me and I forgive you." She squeezed and then stepped back and pointed a finger at me. "But only because you were honest enough to admit it."

We turned and headed down the path. Bobby took my hand and it felt natural to walk hand-in-hand with her. Fortunately I had learned long ago that I was too stupid to lie. But how was I going to balance investigating with the rest of my life? I needed to think about this—seriously think about it.

The hand-in-hand worked for a few more paces and then we had to give it up. The path was neither wide enough nor empty enough to make it practical. It felt like we were walking against the traffic—swimming upstream. No, the salmon swim *upstream* to spawn. If we were swimming against the crowd, we would be going downstream, dodging people headed in the opposite direction.

The pathway that led to Chad Harris's and the Metro Shelter's booths—one to avoid, one to visit—was unusually crowded. I was following Bobby when we hit a bottleneck. On one side of the path, an artist was creating something using a blowtorch and a bunch of plastic buckets and pipes that had been arranged around a wire frame. Based on the other sculptures, this was a potential dragon, dinosaur, or coat rack. People had stopped to watch, and the heat and smell of melting plastic had forced them to step back into the pathway.

Bobby turned around and shrugged her shoulders. There was nothing to say. We couldn't make our way through the crowd without physically pushing people out of the way. The heat and smell of melting plastic repelled me more than the sight of said melting plastic enthralled, so I retreated. Bobby followed and we found ourselves standing at a booth that was surprisingly understocked this early in The Festival. There wasn't that much for sale.

The artist worked in oils, apparently, primarily portraits judging by the few pictures we could see from where we were standing. He was seated in a cloth director's chair facing a canvas, back to his booth, palette and brush in hand. He was concentrating on his work and seemed to be oblivious to whether he had an audience. He was sitting at an angle so he didn't block the entrance.

I checked the booth number with the program. The artist's name was Ted Lowe and the blurb he'd supplied—I had to assume every artist wrote his or her own piece—said he painted in oils, usually did commissioned work, and had recently returned from England where he'd made a reputation for himself with portraits of the nobility. He'd been classically trained in New York. What the hell was he doing at a folk festival?

Bobby had gone past the artist into his tent to look at what he had on display while I was reading about him. I followed her in thinking that I might never know why he came to The Festival in the first place, but I could guess what had brought him back, and why he might never return.

The paintings were varied—several nudes, male and female. Demonstrations of his skill and ability to depict the human body I thought to myself. A self-portrait—the kind of thing a prospective client might want to see—how faithful he could be to the original. There were two very interesting portraits in which he had juxtaposed the face of a person at about age twenty with the same face at about eighty. Next to the portraits were photos of the person. He had painted a young woman as she looked now and how she would look and an old man alongside how he had looked at twenty. Even I could tell this guy could paint.

I took a look at the prices and decided his work was probably worth what he charged. But he wasn't going to sell anything at The Festival—not at those prices. If he sold even one, he'd have made more than any two artists at the show.

We walked back out of the tent to find the artist cleaning his brushes. There were tubes of paint, brushes soaking in liquid, blank canvases in various sizes, a palette covered with smears of paint, and cans of turpentine. Tools of the trade. Nothing unusual there. I glanced over at the canvas he'd been working on, but Bobby beat me to it.

"Why that's Dot! You're painting The Festival director's portrait!"

I could see he'd finished Dot's face and hair but the background was empty and her head floated on the canvas.

"The late director. Or hadn't you heard the news?" He pushed back the brim of his hat with a thumb, the rest of his hand being covered in turpentine and diluted paint. "Not sure what I'm going to do with it now."

"Who commissioned it?" Surely he wasn't doing it on speculation with the hope somebody would buy it?

"Oh, she did. She," he was wiping his hands on a rag that showed signs that he'd wiped his hands on it more than a few times before and paused as he spoke—choosing his words carefully, "made—arrangements—to have me paint her portrait.

"You see," he shrugged his shoulders, "I did a portrait of the original director when I was just getting started. She told me that it's hanging in the offices of The Festival in downtown Archibald. In a way, it was my first step to success. I've been able to build on it."

"Dot wanted her portrait to hang in the office along with the first director's?" Bobby looked puzzled.

"That's what she told me."

She turned to me. "Doesn't it seem like the board of directors would make that decision, not the director herself?"

I looked at the artist. "Who paid for the first portrait? Do you remember?"

"The board, I'd say. It seems like that's the way it went. First director didn't much care to have his portrait painted. Didn't take it out on me, you understand. He just felt like the board could have used the money better."

"Was that the last time you came to The Festival?"

Ted's gaze moved from Bobby to me. I didn't blame him. I preferred to look at Bobby myself. "No, I came back a couple of times—next two years."

"That would have been while Dot was the assistant director? You'd met her then?"

"Yeah." Ted looked like he'd prefer a different topic for discussion. "I guess I have—or had."

"Did you give her a special price on her portrait? Some kind of bargain rate?"

He didn't speak but his gaze was becoming a glare.

"I mean, just looking at the prices on what you've got in there—I'd say you're used to showing to a more well-heeled bunch of customers."

"Who's asking?"

"James Crawford." I stuck my hand out but he shook his head and continued to wipe his hands with the rag.

I shrugged. "Maybe you should leave it unfinished and see if anybody will buy it?"

"You interested in it?"

"At those prices?" I pointed at the paintings he had on display.

"Maybe I should just burn it. Excuse me." He brushed by me and went into his tent.

I looked at Bobby and she returned the favor. "A warm human being."

"He's an artist. And you were asking hard questions."

"Not subtle enough, eh?"

"Well, maybe being subtle isn't one of your strong points?"

"I'll work on it."

. . .

By this time the artist with the blowtorch had shut down and the pathway was relatively clear. We were walking past the booth when I realized that Ralph Stark and a couple other volunteers had erected some poles beside the booth and were attaching fire extinguishers to them. They looked like chemical rather than water-based extinguishers—better to handle plastic that caught on fire. Of course, they had the ubiquitous Property of The Festival lettering stenciled on them. The artist must be new to The Festival else the fire extinguishers would have been in place.

We passed a few more booths with less exotic artwork—or maybe just as exotic just not on as large a scale as dinosaurs. There were birdhouses with copper roofs; baskets, large and small; wooden boxes and bowls, and old-fashioned handcrafted toys. The farther we went, the louder the sounds of dogs barking and yipping got until we knew we had to be close to Chad Harris's booth.

There was a young woman sitting in one side of a booth that had been divided. It was a normal-size area, but half of it was set up as a work area—propane tanks, burners, glass-blowing tubes, gloves, pads, clamps, and a bunch of other things that I couldn't put a name to. The other half held shelves under a canvas shelter. In the program, Chad Harris had been described as a glassworker. Apparently that was correct.

The woman, wearing a wooden badge that identified her as Artist's Relief, assured us that this was Chad's booth and he'd just stepped away for a few minutes. "The Festival offers booth sitters to all the artists and the ones that travel by themselves really appreciate it." She laughed. "And we love being mistaken for a real artist."

"I've been wondering," I held out the program, "how The Festival goes about classifying artists that work in so many different mediums. You know—earrings, statues, wall hangings, paintings, scarves—all from one artist."

Miss Artist Relief smiled. "I can answer that one. The Festival makes the artist pick the niche—or niches they want to be listed under." She laughed. "So they have to do it themselves."

"So where their booth ends up is up to them?"

"Well sort of. When Dot—the director of The Festival—she died today—snakebite! Have you ever?"

We agreed it was sad and unusual.

"Anyway, when she handled booth locations—not to speak ill of the dead but the truth is the truth—she was forever putting artists that didn't like each other next to one another. Coba is so much better at it than Dot ever was. For instance, Chad wanted this location because he does some animals in glass and he hoped being near the Shelter's booth would help sales—pet lovers, you know."

"So he does animals? In glass?"

"Oh! I'm so sorry. I'm supposed to help the artist sell things and I haven't even gotten you to look at anything. Come on, come on, take a look at what he's done. I can answer *some* questions."

She shooed us in the direction of the shelves and we went, laughing. Chad did *do* animals. Birds in fine detail—feathers filled with color, alligators displaying their teeth, bears, lions, snakes, fish, horses, unicorns, dragons, and—here and there—dogs and cats. There was a spectacular rattlesnake head—with its mouth open, fangs glistening, and tongue showing—you wondered where he got his inspiration. I was taken by a cat he'd done. It was a solid rectangle of glass with a black cat, seated with its tail around its feet, encased inside.

Besides the animals there were vases, and balls, and—interestingly enough—knives—more like scalpels. Sharper than steel and never need sharpening! That was according to the sign propped up beside them.

We examined his art, waiting for Chad to reappear. On closer inspection, it looked like he was experimenting with using color inside of clear. There was a little snake whose open mouth was black as jet inside, but clear everywhere else. I wondered if he'd tried the technique with leopards—the spots would be spectacular.

Finally I pulled my phone out of my pocket and checked the time. The Festival closed at five o'clock just in time to really mess up what passed for rush hour in Jemison County. Rush hour wasn't—an hour that is—but for fifteen or twenty minutes the bridges were crowded, people had to wait several cycles of traffic lights to get through intersections, horns got honked, fenders were bent, tempers flared, and then traffic would begin to flow "like it should." Friday afternoons were closer to real rush hours because college students were getting out of town for the weekend. When you add traffic from an event like The Festival, well, even people from California and New York agreed that the traffic was heavy.

It was well after four, Bobby wanted to be back at her house by five-thirty, and I was her ride. Either I gave her a ride or she'd have to find a spot on one of the shuttle buses. I'd have to catch up with Mr. Harris tomorrow.

We thanked the volunteer for her cheerful assistance and headed back across the fairgrounds to the field where my car was parked. At least we were headed away from the adopt-a-pet booth. As we walked along we could feel the crowd joining us in our exodus all the while volunteers worked to empty trash cans and recycling bins and otherwise keep the grounds neat. They wouldn't have to start cleaning up when The Festival closed because they cleaned it all day long.

. . .

There was a line of cars to get out of the lot I was parked in, then another line as we crept past the other lots, taking turns as we edged onto the only road that led directly into historic downtown Archibald. There were Shelbyville traffic officers trying to speed things along, and I remembered that Kurt had called "next door" for assistance. It didn't take that long before we were in

Archibald and I was trying to get out of the traffic flow and into the lot where Bobby's car was parked.

We'd passed The Festival's gift shop and offices on our way to the lot and caught a glimpse of Chief Snoddy with some of his officers standing in front of the shop's entrance talking to somebody. Bobby thought it might have been Coba Boucher, but what would the assistant, now acting, director have been doing away from The Festival itself? I wasn't even sure the gift shop and the offices were open during the big event—everybody needed to be at The Festival.

I finally forced my car into the lot by blocking one of the exits—actually it was the entrance but some drivers were ignoring that fact and were trying to go out the in. From the glares I got, some of them thought they should have had the right of way. Not caring if your paint gets scratched or your bumper gets dinged is empowering in parking lots—particularly if it looks like you don't care.

Bobby gave me a quick hug and a kiss before she hopped out of my car and got into hers. I blocked traffic so she could pull out of the space, waved at her, and then took her parking space.

Bobby was off to get ready for her weekend guests, Rebecca and Jack. Her dear friends and cousins—okay Jack wasn't a cousin, Rebecca was the cousin—as close as sisters was the way Bobby put it. Of course, Bobby didn't have any sisters so how did she know? Maybe that made her better than a sister?

Anyway, they sounded like good people and I was hoping I could depend on Bobby's judgment as much as I imagined Rebecca and Jack were hoping they could. We'd find out tomorrow.

I put the car in park and shut off the engine. I was interested in what the Archibald chief of police was doing in historic downtown Archibald when all the action was out at The Festival grounds. Something was up.

. . .

It *was* Coba that Kurt was talking to—in between her phone conversations with the staff at The Festival grounds. She must have just arrived when Bobby saw her. They would talk a little and then the phone would ring, she would raise her palm, speak into the phone, drop her hand, then continue her conversation with Chief Snoddy. It was anybody's guess as to how long the chief was going to put up with the interruptions.

As I got close enough to eavesdrop, I heard her speaking into the phone. "Look, run all the questions by Ralph—Ralph Stark. Don't let anybody call me except Ralph. Okay? As soon as I'm finished talking to the police I'll be back at headquarters."

She put the phone in her back pocket and nodded at Kurt. "Sorry. It's like everybody's ability to make a decision died when Dot did. Where were we?"

"You had been explaining that you didn't have the keys to the door with you because The Festival gift shop and office were closed while The Festival was running. That you didn't bother with the keys anyway because—?"

"Oh," she started forward and knelt next to an empty bicycle rack that was next to the doors. One of the slots had a lock and chain on it but no bike. It was like The Festival to promote riding your bicycle—it went along with all the recycling bins. The rack itself had a sign proclaiming it to be Property of The Festival and the spot with the lock in it had a label reserving it for the assistant director. No sign for the director. Made sense to me. Dot wasn't the type to ride a bicycle to work. Coba probably did ride to work and left a lock and chain here for convenience.

Coba fumbled around with one end of the base of the stand and stood up with a key. Of course, hide a key outside for those times people forgot to bring their keys to the office. She unlocked the doors and started to put the key back.

"No, Ms. Boucher. Let's not leave a key outside—not until we've secured the offices and seen what's missing." Kurt took the key right out of her hand and slipped it into his pocket. He nodded at his officers who then entered the building.

"They're going in to take pictures of everything inside. We've got shots from the back but want ones from the front too. You can wait out here or go in. If you go in be careful. Stay in the gift shop area. We don't want to disturb any evidence from this side. Don't touch anything."

"I'll just stay out here then." Coba pulled her phone back out and glanced at it. "Reception is better out here."

"What happened?" Everything looked normal to me.

"Burglary—we think. Somebody could have heard about Dot's death and decided to seize the opportunity to break into the place. Like those sickos who read the obits and break in during the funeral."

"How'd they get in?"

"Back door. Opens onto the alley." Kurt waved toward the back of the building. "The alley provides access to the warehouses."

"I think I'll look around outside before going in."

"Suit yourself. Just don't touch anything when you do go in." Kurt pulled his phone out of his pocket and stepped inside the building.

. . .

I walked past the bike rack and turned at the corner. The Festival building must have originally been some kind of a store— probably not a gift shop. I wondered when gift shops had first appeared and was glad The Festival had resisted the temptation to call it a gift shoppe. There were display windows facing the street on the front and side. Not all the way down the side—just about half-way. I walked past the end of the windows to the corner of the building and turned into an alley.

I'd never noticed the alleyway before. My excuse was that I didn't come to historic downtown Archibald very often. I wondered if there were apartments here like there were across the river in Shelbyville. The Festival's building was two stories, but I think the second floor was rented out as workshops to sponsored artists.

The back of the building showed the age of the building more than the front did. Here were the electric and gas meters, HVAC units perched next to the brick wall, each with its own orifice drilled through the brick. They all looked like afterthoughts, just stuck onto the building. The Festival's trash can sat next to what must be the back entrance.

As I walked down the alley, I looked to the other side and saw several warehouses in a row. Windowless, with barnlike doors facing the street. They must have common walls since there wasn't any space between them. Archibald had paved the alley recently, otherwise I would have looked for cobblestones and train tracks. Back in the day, railroad cars would have been used to stock the warehouses.

The trash can had been kept next to the back door. Actually, it was still standing there—the door, however, wasn't. It hadn't been that much of a door in the first place. You could see that somebody had replaced the original lock with a bigger, fancier, deadbolt but they hadn't done anything about the wooden door frame. It probably hadn't taken more than a determined kick or two by a good-size man or woman in boots to kick it in. Dot could have done it easily. A bar across the door inside would have been more of a challenge than the deadbolt, medieval as it might have been. What was that lyric—"get up and bar the door"? Where had I just heard that? Oh, right, The Festival. I'd heard that song one time too many—too much Celtic music.

I peered in the doorway and could see that there was some kind of powder scattered all over the floor and somebody—the perpetrator maybe—had left footprints. I nodded to myself. That explained Kurt wanting to come in from the front. Coming in from here would just stir up the powder. Other than that, I couldn't see anything that looked out of order.

The alley I was in continued on behind another building and then out to the next street. Past the building a low wall bordered it on one side and on the other side there was a building that was oriented to face the side street—backing up to the warehouses. I'd heard something about Dot and Coba's neighbors, but what was it?

Walking past The Festival's neighbor's back door—it looked just as flimsy as the one that had been kicked in—I was intrigued by the low wall at the end. It had been an empty lot on the corner ever since whatever had originally been there had been torn down. Now there was the low wall, and the brickwork looked new.

The Bird House. When I got to the end of the building, I suddenly remembered what Dot had called it. I stood looking over the wall and realized that the vacant lot had been enclosed and turned into an outdoor showroom for the Bird House. It was pretty clear that they sold more than birdseed—a heck of a lot more.

Access to the lot had to be through the Bird House. The wall covered all three sides and I didn't see a gate. The lot was probably level to start with, but it wasn't now. It had been landscaped with a small self-contained stream with an occasional waterfall, pools, and delicate but functional bridges. Here and there were bird feeders, birdbaths, fountains, lawn art, sculpture, tables, chairs, and a gazebo or two. The pergola was probably hiding the entrance into the store. I couldn't tell if there were fish in the stream but couldn't imagine that there weren't. It was a garden out of a fairy tale.

There were bird feeders—platforms, cylinders, fanciful shapes, serious metal mesh—squirrel-resistant at a guess— fortified types, some designed for a particular seed, some for mixes. There were even some feeders that looked like they had been designed for squirrels. And the birds appreciated them all. This late in the day there were mostly cardinals feasting, but a few other species were there as well.

I pulled out my phone and started taking pictures. This was the kind of landscaping that made you think you'd like to have something similar in your backyard. Which was why they'd built it.

But the same things that attract birds, attract rodents. And when you've attracted birds and rodents, you get the animals that prey on them—such as cats and snakes. And there, lying in the late afternoon sun on the top of the wall, was a snake. At first, I'd dismissed it as a branch but now I could see that it was animate. It must have moved and caught my eye. I took several pictures of it as it started to work its way off the wall. Maybe it was the angle of light but it looked like it had yellow stripes down its side. Garter snake, I said to myself; I'd heard they had yellow stripes.

Impressive. It took some money to turn an urban building lot into a nature display like the one I was looking at. The Bird House must have a pretty good markup on its products to cover that kind of overhead. Not the kind of store for those who were pinching their pennies. But maybe I was wrong. After all, I reminded myself, this wasn't the high-rent area of Archibald—not even close. How else could The Festival afford to be here? For when all was said and done, it was a nonprofit organization that supported the arts.

I turned around and headed back to what was left of the backdoor. They should have finished photographing everything by now. The sun was so low that the whole alley was in shadow. It must be getting close to five o'clock, I thought to myself. This time of the year, the sun set at six.

A police officer had just finished sweeping up the white powder into a pile near the open door and waved me on through. At least I wasn't going to leave tracks—or disturb any.

I walked in and tried to fit the outside of the building with the inside. The back fourth of the building—the windowless part—was basically a storage room. The door that led to the offices and then into The Festival gift shop was opposite the kicked-in back door. On either side of it were shelves filled with stock for the store. The back wall—the alley wall—had hooks for coats, mops, and brooms. Next were trash cans, recycling bins, cases of bottled water, a hand truck, cardboard cartons, buckets—the usual odds and ends of an office building. On the left, the outside wall, was a staircase to the floor above, with a short landing, then metal stairs marching up the wall. A sink, water heater, coffee machine, microwave, hot plate, toaster, and an old refrigerator were underneath the steps. In front of those things—out from under the stairs above—was a rectangular table with a linoleum top and several straight-back chairs. Across the room were two unisex bathrooms on the inside wall—the common wall with the building next door—and more storage. With the exception of what was left of the powder on the rough cement floor, it all looked pretty much undisturbed. No messier than you'd expect.

. . .

I stepped through the doorway and found myself in a short hallway flanked by offices. Well, there was one office on the right—clearly the director's and smaller ones to the left—offices and workrooms.

Kurt and Coba were standing in front of the door to Dot's office. Kurt had a long-suffering look on his face, an interrogator politely asking questions and getting little if anything useful in reply.

Coba, on the other hand, was clearly distressed and confused. "I don't understand who would do this."

"We've been through that, miss. It might help us to find out *who* did this if we had an idea of *what* they did."

Coba was staring into Dot's office and Kurt looked at me over her head. From his expression I'd say his patience was wearing thin—it had been a long day for the Archibald chief of police, and Coba's inability to understand his questions wasn't making it any easier.

"But I don't know *what* Dot had in her desk. It was *her* desk, how would I know what she put in it?"

I looked into Dot's office while thinking that Coba's logic was irrefutable. She should know what was in her desk—ask her about that. How could she know what Dot had in hers?

Anyway the answer was—not much—not anymore. Desk drawers lay on the floor next to their contents—or what looked like normal desk drawer contents: rubber bands, paper clips, pencils, pens, pads of paper, sticky notes still in their packaging, paper of all sizes and colors—most with printing or writing on them. There were built-in bookcases on the back wall—to the right of the safe—whatever she'd had on them was on the floor as well—except for some knickknacks. It looked as if somebody was making sure there was nothing hidden in the office—if I'd been a comic strip character you'd have seen the light bulb go on above my head.

"They were trying to find out where Dot kept her blackmailing evidence." Not everybody was like Woodrow—willing to knuckle under to your-word-against-mind. She'd have needed pictures, documents, physical evidence.

Kurt grunted agreement. I didn't know if he'd figured that out already or not. Probably so. Coba, on the other hand, had no idea what we were talking about.

"Blackmail? Evidence?" She looked from Kurt to me and back again.

"Yeah, maybe evidence is the wrong word to use. Where she kept the stuff—you know what you have to have to be able to blackmail somebody?" I looked at Kurt and he shook his head. No help there. "The stuff that she could use to prove you'd done something that you didn't want people to know about?" Coba still looked baffled.

"Is blackmail a word they use in South Africa? Do you know what it means? Blackmail?"

"Dot?" said Coba. Her eyes were so wide that her narrow features looked even narrower. "Dot? Blackmail? No!"

Good. We'd given up on complete sentences. Soon we'd be grunting at each other. I was sure Kurt appreciated my help. I looked at him. The expression of frustration that had been on his face was now giving way to one of amusement. I, on the other hand, was not amused.

"Are you saying that Dot wasn't a blackmailer? I hate to bust your bubble there, but she was. Woodrow said she'd been blackmailing him. Ted Lowe all but admitted it. Yep, she was blackmailing people. You didn't know?" A thought popped up into my mind then disappeared before I could seize it. Maybe it would come back.

"Dot Fields? Blackmail?"

"Right." I wondered how far I could push that budding belief. "Let's just say she was blackmailing people and you didn't know anything about it. But she was and then she died unexpectedly—accidentally. The people she'd been blackmailing would have to feel some relief at her passing.

"Then they'd begin to wonder where she'd kept that—that picture she had of them doing something they didn't want anybody to know about, for instance. Stuff like that."

Both Coba and Kurt had begun to nod their heads. I was pretty sure that Kurt's nods were limited to approving the way I was explaining things to Coba. He'd no doubt figured this as a possibility as soon as he'd heard of the break-in.

"Dot was a blackmailer?" Coba looked at the chief and then at me.

"You didn't know?"

Coba shook her head.

"Don't worry about it. It's okay. People are incredibly multifaceted, Coba. Having worked with her like you did, you knew her in ways that other people didn't. I mean, well—Hitler was kind to his dog for instance."

Having said that I wondered if it was true. Was Hitler kind to his dog? Where had I heard that and why did I repeat it? What did it matter anyway? There was a good side to Hitler? Yeah, Stalin had a great mustache, Genghis Khan was a hell of a horseman, and Julius Cesar was fluent in Latin. So what?

The cop who'd been sweeping the floor came into the room and told Chief Snoddy that some volunteers from The Festival were here to nail the backdoor shut and was that okay.

Kurt looked at Coba who spoke to the policeman. "That would be great. Tell them to go ahead."

"Tell them to make sure it's secure," I added. "Whoever did it might be back. Or we might have some opportunists." I wondered if anyone would try to take over Dot's blackmailing business.

The policemen looked at Kurt, who nodded. "And be sure to tell the night patrol to keep a closer eye on the building while The Festival is running."

The founding director's portrait was hanging on the wall next to Dot's door. I stopped to check and, sure enough, Ted Lowe's signature was there on the bottom. Hanging next to it were photographs of board members and local artists. I half expected to see the first dollar The Festival had ever made framed and hung on the wall. Although, on second thought, maybe not.

I stepped into Dot's office and looked at the items scattered about the floor. The contents were all covered in a layer of fine powder, but the floor had been swept clean. Even through the powder, I could tell that among the items on the floor were a checkbook, loose change, a nice pen, credit cards, business cards, coupons, and a letter opener. I glanced over at the shelves; they were free of the powder. There were ornaments there that would be easy to sell.

I wished there was a wad of cash sitting somewhere in the office so we could eliminate simple burglary as a motive. On the other hand, even someone whose objective had been to get hold of whatever compromising material Dot had would probably have taken the money.

Frowning, I looked up at the back wall of Dot's office and dismissed the idea entirely. Surely no one would leave a large amount of cash in a desk drawer if they had a safe.

The back wall of Dot's office consisted of shelves and a built-in, walk-in safe. Well, you might not have been able to walk into the safe but that was only a question of depth. The door was big enough to walk through. I gave the handle a tug and it didn't move. Locked.

"Was it locked when you got here?" I turned around and looked at Coba and Kurt. "And what's with the safe anyway? This thing is a monster."

Coba just lifted her shoulders.

"The reporting officers said both this safe and the one in the front were closed when they got here. Coba says they were always locked unless she or Dot was getting something out of them. This used to be a jewelry store back when Archibald was a happening town—in the old days. The jeweler kept valuable pieces in the front and supplies—gold, silver, unmounted jewels—in this one. I'd say no tenant since then has been willing to pay to have the safes removed. They're built into the wall. It'd be a mess taking them out. And what good would it do?"

I looked at Coba and briefly considered asking her to open the safes. Since we had no idea what was supposed to be in them, what good would it do? Besides it was getting late.

"Two safes?"

Kurt nodded his head toward the front of the building. I followed him into the gift shop, which was set up like the jewelry store it had once been. There were earrings and the like for sale, mixed in with the folk crafts of other artists. Kurt pointed at the wall.

There was another safe identical to the one in Dot's office. The powder hadn't made it into this room and the displays looked normal. Another bit of evidence against burglary.

"What's with the powder, anyway?"

"I was wondering when you'd get around to asking about it." Kurt stroked his chin. "We figure the burglar or burglars tossed it around right before they left."

"Why did they do that and what is it?"

"It's plaster. Evidently there were several bags of it in the back room." Kurt nodded at Coba. "She recognized it."

"We have an artist who volunteered to paint some frescoes on the walls here—scenes of The Festival. It's a kind of painting on the wall that becomes part of the wall." She looked at my expression and added hopefully. "You use lime plaster to make frescoes."

I stared at Coba and then turned to look at Kurt who was smiling. "Do you mean to tell me that somebody kicked in the door to The Festival's offices and gift store, ransacked the director's office, dusted some rooms with plaster powder, and left? And we've got no idea what they were trying to do with the plaster?"

Kurt chuckled. "I think you're about to catch up with me on this one. Doesn't make a damn bit of sense, does it?"

"Is somebody trying to make us think some kids broke in and trashed the place?"

Kurt was still chuckling. "Glad to see you so puzzled. I thought about that. But if you were trying to make a mess there are cans of paint back in the storeroom that would have done a better job. Heck, throw the paint on top of the plaster. That would be a good, gooey mess, now wouldn't it?"

He turned and walked toward the front door. Coba and I followed. "Best explanation I've been able to come up with is that they wanted to cover up any clues they might have left." He opened the door and held it for Coba. I followed her through onto the sidewalk. He locked the door and put the key back in his pocket. I suspected he wasn't strictly entitled to keep the key, but I wasn't going to say anything about it. It made more sense than leaving it where somebody else could find it.

The chief's car was parked at the curb. The sun was setting on the horizon with shades of red, pink, and purple. They contrasted nicely with the thin plume of black smoke that was climbing up the sky.

Something was burning. Something to the west of where we stood.

The Festival grounds are west of downtown Archibald.

. . .

It was Dot's fortune-telling tent. You'd be surprised at how much smoke a tent can generate when it burns to the ground. Or maybe you wouldn't be. By the time we got back to The Festival grounds, the firefighters had turned their hoses on Dot's tent and had wet down the area around it to keep the fire from spreading.

Kurt Snoddy was standing in the tent—technically, he was standing in a couple of inches of water that was trapped by the bottom of the tent, the part that had kept rain from seeping in from the ground. That only worked when there was a tent above it of course. Without the tent it just caught the water from the firefighters' hoses, turning whatever hadn't been consumed by the fire into a soggy mush. On top of the water was an oily sheen. No telling what was causing that. Coba had been relieved to find that the damage was confined to property not owned by The Festival.

Kurt told me that it had taken a while to convince her to come down to The Festival's store. It was only after he mentioned the possibility of damage to Festival property that she'd agreed to leave the fairgrounds. She was the driving force behind the ubiquitous Property of The Festival labeling.

After we got to the scene of the fire, once she'd satisfied herself that it didn't look like any Festival property was involved, she'd headed straight for headquarters.

Kurt was standing in the pool of water, shaking his head, muttering to himself, and occasionally turning something over with his foot. I hadn't noticed that anything he was doing was making a difference, but I hesitated to mention it.

My shoes and socks were soaked and I felt like the water was making its way up my pants legs. The sun had set and the temperature was dropping. It hadn't been a particularly good day for me. I admit that Kurt's was worse—snakebite, break-in, and fire—and all of it having to do with the biggest annual event in Archibald. I wasn't sure what kind of temper the big man had and wasn't interested in finding out. Not tonight, not ever.

Even though The Festival was closed for the evening, the park lights were on, such as they were. The area wasn't as well lit as a high school football field would have been—not by a long shot—not a football field in Alabama, anyway. There were pockets of darkness and areas of shadow. On top of being wet and chilled, I was tired and hungry.

I'd turned on the flashlight app on my phone and was casting light here and there on the ground. Seemed like the kind of thing an experienced investigator would do. I shone the light out a little farther and it caught the edge of a red plastic container that was in a clump of brush. Any litter at The Festival was unusual. This looked promising.

"Hey, Kurt." I shone the light on the brush.

"Got something?" He walked toward the light and I thought I heard his shoes squish. He had a real flashlight—government issue—one of those with a barrel that held four or five batteries. My light had style points, but his was a heck of a lot more effective.

It was a gasoline can, if we still call them cans when they're made out of plastic. Kurt squatted down beside it, slid his pen down the neck, and set it upright. The black lettering, Property of The Festival, contrasted nicely with the red plastic. It also made it easy to figure out where it had come from.

"I noticed a storage shed next to the headquarters building. It looks like that's where the volunteers keep their tools—and gasoline."

Kurt sighed. "I had figured it was going to be arson when I saw the smoke. This pretty well proves it."

"We all thought it was arson, Kurt." I switched apps and took a picture of the gas can. "Well, I can't say what Coba thought. She seemed obsessed about whether any Festival property had been damaged."

"Now we've got to figure out what the arsonist thought he was doing."

"He or she." I automatically corrected him. It helped me to keep my mind open about suspects when I read mysteries.

Kurt glared at me and the look reminded me that I had just been thinking I didn't want to see him angry.

"Whatever." I tossed my gender-neutral ideals aside. I'd fight another day. "He either wanted to burn something up just to burn it or he had a deeper motive. What would somebody gain by burning the tent and contents?"

"If there was any evidence in there, it's pretty much gone now." Kurt looked at the remains of the tent. "And if there had been something and he took it before setting the fire—."

I could see him mentally kicking himself for not having the contents inventoried when it was only an accident scene. "I took a lot of pictures." I held up my phone encouragingly. "And I remember what it looked like."

"Good. At least we've got that."

I knew what was bothering him. It was bothering me too. Three big things had happened today in Archibald. A person had died of snakebite. A person's office had been ransacked. A person's tent had been burned. And Dot was the person—the connection. Coincidence? If I changed today to the last twenty-four hours, I could include Dot's being accused of blackmail. I couldn't square the accidental death with the blackmailing pattern, but accidents do happen.

"Somebody is determined to find or destroy Dot's blackmailing material."

Kurt grumbled. "Somebody or somebodies. One might be looking to recover what she had; the other to destroy what she had. One burns; the other searches."

"Oh, I don't like multiple suspects. Too messy."

"Well, how sad-making for you. Just think how many people she could have been blackmailing—each one of them is a suspect—and how about those who knew she was a blackmailer—that Chad Harris for instance. Plus, was there someone who would like to take over her extortion business? We've got a mess of suspects for sure."

He waved at my phone. "Download those pictures for me. We're going to need them."

"No problem." I'd burn copies onto disks. The pics should have automatically been uploaded to my online storage, but I'd better make sure tonight.

"Good." He pulled his phone out of his pocket. "I've got the pleasant task of telling Sheriff Sammy Thompson how to do his job."

"How so?"

"Dot's house is out of my jurisdiction. If somebody or somebodies are burglarizing and burning Dot's stuff, then he needs to have that house watched. It's obvious. But he's not going to want to hear that from me." Kurt shrugged. "Maybe he'll have already thought of it and he can tell me so with a sneer."

I thought about how the sheriff had acted. "Tell him it was my idea and that I insisted you call him."

"Your idea? What good is that going to do?"

"Since I don't exist and you're saying it's not your idea, he'll have to think it was his own."

It was a quick conversation and I made sure not to hear Kurt's side of it.

Kurt put the phone back in his pocket. "At least he volunteered to call the state and get a deputy fire marshal up here tomorrow. Saved me that trouble."

We started walking back to a lighted area. "What about the gas can?"

"Thanks. I'll get somebody out here with an evidence bag so we can tag it before we leave. Meanwhile," he glanced in my direction, "I'll run you into town so you can get your car."

I wasn't sure what I wanted more—a hot shower or a scotch. I'd been debating with myself ever since I got in the car. I pulled into my driveway and heard Tan barking. Since she knows the sound of my car, the barking was a greeting not an alarm. I glanced at the dashboard clock. Yep, it also was a reminder that her suppertime had come and gone.

Tan guilted me into going for the drink first. I could shower after she'd been fed. After all, it was her *only* meal of the day and it was going to be my second shower.

I parked in the garage, entered the kitchen, and went straight to the back door to let Tan in—then headed for the liquor cabinet. Tan stuck right to me—more than usual. Her nose was all over my slacks and shoes. They must have smelled of wondrous, mysterious, and magical things—things beyond her imagination. To me, I smelled like burnt canvas.

The Black wandered in, jumped on the counter, and promptly gave my shirt the same treatment that Tan was giving my shoes. Their attentions made it difficult to get liquor and ice in a glass but I persevered. I took a sip and decided that while a shower would be nice a hot bath and a scotch would be even better.

It took a little longer to get the dog her supper and the cat his treat. I thought for a moment or two that Tan was going to keep sniffing me even after the food bowl was on the floor but she came to her senses. TB never hesitated. He went straight for the canned food. Of course the cat doesn't consider me a pet owner. I'm just staff.

Once Tan had finished and gone back outside, I headed down the hall. The hot bath still sounded good but a shower was quicker and I realized that the problem with food from The Festival was that you're hungry again after an hour—okay, make that seven hours.

. . .

Clean, dry, dressed, and hungry I was back in the kitchen. I'd decided to throw the clothes I'd been wearing into the washer considering how much attention the dog and cat had given them. I didn't think they'd smell better tomorrow—aging wouldn't improve them. Tan might have disagreed but she didn't get a vote.

Bobby was bringing her friends Jack and Rebecca over for supper tomorrow night. She'd thought about eating out, but local restaurants are always packed on the weekend of The Festival. On top of that, though the football game was away, it was at night and televised. That meant the game would be on in most every restaurant in town, adding to the noise. If we wanted to be able to hear one another, going out to eat wasn't an option.

Anyway, I like to cook and it had been a while since I'd grilled steak—I had a recipe I wanted to try—so we planned on eating here. Bobby was going to make a salad; Jack and Rebecca were bringing imported wine and dessert—imported from Tennessee; I was going to make scalloped potatoes.

I pulled some potatoes out of the pantry, washed them off, dropped them into a pan half filled with water, put the pan on the stove, turned on the burner, and ignored them.

Tan was barking to come in so I opened the door. The Black had eaten and left the room. He'd be back when it suited him.

"Did I tell you that we were having guests tomorrow night?" Tan was on her way to her dog pillow but she stopped to look at me. Her tail wagged tentatively.

"Bobby's coming over." Tan's tail picked up speed. They got along great. "And she's bringing two friends with her—Rebecca and Jack. I think you'll like them."

Having gotten the potatoes going for tomorrow's supper, I was faced with the decision of what to have tonight—something easy and tasty—out of ingredients I had on hand. Hmmm. Potatoes tomorrow night—had potatoes for lunch—rice or pasta then? I like to rotate my starches. Rice. Okay. I'd had chicken for lunch and planned on steak for tomorrow's supper. Fish? Shrimp? I like to vary the protein too.

I pulled a box of flavored rice out of the pantry. I'd tinkered with one of their suggested recipes to make a variation of dirty rice with sausage and shrimp—forget the chicken livers—and the so-called Cajun holy trinity—chopped onion, celery, and pepper. All Cajun recipes start with sautéing the holy trinity. The original trinity calls for chopped green pepper. I cheat and use red, yellow, or orange instead of the common green pepper. To me, the riper peppers have a better flavor. I already had all of the chopped ingredients in the freezer. People wonder what a single man is doing with a full-size freezer. Freezing things I tell them.

Tan went to her bed and began her elaborate settling-down ritual. I'd read somewhere that dogs have to turn around at least three times before lying down because their ancestors had done the same to mat down the tall grasses out on the plains. I wasn't convinced, but Tan took it seriously.

I waited to speak to her until she was through. When I interrupt her ritual she forgets where she was and has to start over.

"What do you think about coming with me to The Festival on Sunday?" Tan lifted up her head and cocked it to one side.

Sunday was pet day at The Festival just like Saturday was beer and wine day. While pets were forbidden the other days, you could bring them on Sunday. Equally, you couldn't buy beer or wine any day but Saturday.

"I just thought that the weather was supposed to be good and you'd enjoy getting out of the house." The fact that I felt guilty because we weren't getting our daily walks in wasn't the point. Besides Tan was a pretty good judge of character and I needed some help—judging characters.

The potatoes were just coming to a boil.

I went into the laundry room and got the frozen ingredients for the Cajun trinity—checking to make sure I also had the shrimp and sausage I needed.

Characters—yep there were some characters at The Festival for sure. Coba Boucher, Ralph Stark, Chad Harris, Ted Lowe, Woodrow—did he have a last name or *was* that his last name— all interesting people. And what was the name of the woman at the Public Radio booth who'd made Dot the worst cup of coffee she could? Were any or all of them being blackmailed by Dot? Had they been, I corrected myself. Woodrow admitted it. Ted, I was pretty sure, had been. Chad—Chad had set off the fireworks that started this investigation—refusing to be blackmailed. Or was he refusing to continue to be blackmailed?

I chewed on that while I dropped the trinity along with crushed garlic into a frying pan with some butter and olive oil and turned the heat on low. If I heat the oil first, the frozen stuff sputters and spits.

I adjusted the heat under the potatoes. Since the rice concoction was a simple one-pan meal, I planned on getting the potatoes ready for tomorrow's meal while cooking tonight's supper.

"What do you think? Would Dot have tried to blackmail somebody for the first time at her party—and in front of several dozen people?" Tan stretched her head forward until it was almost off the bed. It looked uncomfortable, but she keeps on doing it.

"Either she did, and it blew up in her face, or she didn't and Chad was lying. But Woodrow confirmed that Dot was blackmailing him." I was finding it difficult to get into the mind of a blackmailer.

The butter had melted and the trinity was beginning to give off a little odor—great smells. I stirred the onion, garlic, celery, and pepper mixture, making sure it wasn't sticking to the pan and turned down the heat. I was waiting until the onion was soft before adding the slices of hot Italian sausage. I'd been hungry when I started and the aromas were making me even hungrier.

"I need to talk to Chad tomorrow. Maybe camp out at his booth. See if he'll tell me whether Dot had tried to blackmail him before. What do you think?"

Tan sighed and closed her eyes.

. . .

I went over to a cupboard and pulled out a can of peanuts, poured myself a handful, and put the can back. Tan didn't stir since dog treats never came out of that cupboard. It was dangerous to leave the can out. Its contents had been known to disappear without my noticing. I put the handful on a paper napkin. Handfuls had been known to disappear too.

"Chad is one of the artists who get a stipend to attend The Festival. This was his first year. Think there was a connection?"

The water for the potatoes was still at a boil so I hadn't turned it down too much. I know cooks who like to add salt to the water but that lowers the temperature at which water boils—meaning that you have to cook the potatoes longer—or anything else for that matter—and potatoes have to boil a while.

"I wonder if the artists who get stipends are more likely to get blackmailed? Dot would know how much they got and when they got it. I wonder if she handed the checks out herself. Need to talk to Ellen George about how that works or worked." I put both notes to myself into my phone—Ellen and Chad.

The onions and celery were translucent so I added the sausage. It and its grease would add flavor and color to the vegetables as the sausage cooked. I stirred the mixture some more. Things were beginning to come together so I fixed myself another scotch. Checked the potatoes by piercing them with a long fork and they had cooked enough. They didn't have to be done—just well on the way. I took them off the stove, poured the water off, then dumped them in a strainer to cool.

"Did I tell you what happened when I took The Black to The Festival? First he hissed at Dot and then he scratched her—drew blood. That was yesterday—Thursday."

I was glad I'd mentioned it to Kurt—might show up in the autopsy—scratch by cat or cats unknown. Interesting man Kurt Snoddy.

"Should I include him as somebody Dot might have blackmailed?"

Tan sat up with just her front legs pushing and yawned.

"That's right, you haven't met any of these people yet. But you might recognize the smell once you do meet him. You'll like him." It would be unusual if Tan didn't like him—unusual but not unheard of. Another reason to take her to The Festival.

"I need to call Jim Ward. Ask him how to investigate a blackmail when the blackmailer's dead."

The dog walked to the water bowl and drank loudly, splashing water around. When she looked up, I could see water dripping from her muzzle. That reminded me. The Festival was good about providing amenities for the pets but it wouldn't hurt to take a water bowl.

After putting those additional to-do items in my phone—the reminder to call Jim and to bring a water bowl—I went back to the frying pan and added some frozen shrimp to the sausage—about the same amount of shrimp as I had sausage—the shrimp were already cooked and peeled. The ice on the shrimp made a lot of noise as the shrimp hit the hot grease. I slapped a cover on the pan and left it, trapping what little water was left. Cooking can be a lot of fun.

I picked up one of the potatoes and quickly dropped it. Not quite cool enough for me.

I took the lid off the frying pan and gave the mixture a stir. Everything was cooked or close to it. It was time to add the rice. I looked at the back of the box and got the amount of water needed. I never can remember how that works. Bobby knew how to make rice without looking at a recipe. I called her the Rice Queen. Satisfied, I poured the water into the pan and listened to the swoosh of steam that formed. I stirred the mixture, scraping bits off the bottom of the pan, then emptied the contents of the rice's special seasoning package into the pan. I stirred the mixture until the package contents had dissolved, then I added the rice and a chicken bouillon cube. I kept stirring until the water came back to a boil, put the lid back on, and turned the heat down to low.

What else did I need to do about this blackmail case?

I kept thinking about the blackmail as I started working on the potatoes while the rice part of supper cooked. I got out a baking dish, sprayed it with nonstick stuff, and put it next to the cutting board. The potatoes were cool enough to handle now, so I sliced them and arranged them in layers in the dish.

Money was the trail I'd like to follow, but how?

Once the potatoes were in place, I made a mixture of sour cream, egg, milk, garlic, and dill and poured it over them. I topped the potatoes with pads of butter and salt and pepper. The dish was ready to go.

I couldn't figure out a way I could get to the money trail—legally. And it would be hard to hack her online banking account if you didn't even know which bank she used. The police were watching her office and her house. Maybe Kurt would be interested in subpoenaing bank records?

I covered the dish in plastic wrap and slipped it into the fridge. Tomorrow I'd decide whether to top off the potatoes with cheese or bread crumbs. Tomorrow was going to be a diet-busting day.

I checked the rice dish. The rice had absorbed all the liquid so I turned off the burner. I like cooking with gas; you don't have to take the pan off the burner.

The Black came back into the kitchen as I was starting to dish up my supper. He decided to stop in the middle of the kitchen floor and leave it up to me not to step on him—a not uncommon decision on his part. I'd made a ridiculous amount of food for just one person—particularly one who'd like to lose some weight—so I split it into four portions, one for tonight and three to freeze. I walked around TB and got three plastic containers of roughly the same size.

"So do you remember that woman you hissed at yesterday morning at The Festival?" I reminded myself to label and date the plastic containers before putting them in the freezer. I might tell myself I'd recognize a rice-sausage-shrimp dish once it was frozen, but I'd be mistaken.

TB yawned, his pink tongue curling almost into a circle, and then started to lick his paw.

"Not so impressed with her that you remember, huh?" I left the plastic containers on the counter by the stove. They were pretty warm and I wanted them to cool a bit before I put them in the freezer. Besides, I was hungry.

Beer was generally my beverage of choice with this dish. Sometimes I'd have red wine with it, but mostly beer. I pulled a Red Stripe out of the fridge, pried open the top, and set it on the kitchen counter next to an empty glass I'd had chilling in the freezer. I'd been hoarding the Red Stripes but tonight I decided to splurge.

"Well, if you had remembered her, I was going to tell you that she died today—this morning. It was an accidental death by snakebite." I checked to make sure I had everything I wanted—beer, glass, spoon, bowl of food, hot sauce, and a couple of paper napkins. I thought about some crackers to go along with it and decided the dish wasn't soupy enough to justify them. Satisfied, I pulled the bar stool back from the counter and sat down.

The Black was looking at me intently, his head cocked slightly. I poured some beer into my glass—two or three inches deep—and took a sip. "That got your attention, huh? It wasn't the snake that you saw—that one was a corn snake and it escaped, but we caught the rattlesnake."

That seemed to make an impression on TB. He straightened his head and sat up straight, curling his tail around his feet. I took a couple of bites of food, gave it some thought, and added a little hot sauce. I had to use the spoon to cut the shrimp into bite-size pieces, but that wasn't a problem. I was used to that.

The morning newspaper was still on the counter so I pulled a section over to read. The cat still hadn't moved. "What's up, TB? Accidents happen all the time. People die of snakebite all over the world, even in the United States. Well," I thought about it, "I don't know exactly how many die from snakebites every year, but it happens." A few more spoonsful and I poured some more beer into my glass. I like for them to come out even—the beer and food, that is.

"Okay. Maybe it is unlikely that she got bitten by a rattlesnake but unlikely things happen all the time. It's been a warm fall."

When cat owners talk to each other we're always telling stories about how aloof our cats are. I guess we're also confessing that we try to amuse them, else how would we notice how aloof they are? It was clear to me that The Black didn't believe what I was telling him. And the more I tried to justify what I was saying, the weaker it sounded.

TB gave up his place on the floor and leapt on top of the fridge via the counter. It was one of those flat-footed jumps that always impress me.

I finished up my food and poured the remaining beer into the glass. There was only a swallow or two left. Perfect.

"I've got to admit the corn snake's escaping while the rattlesnake didn't seems far-fetched when you think about it." I swallowed the last of the beer, stood up, picked up my bowl, and carried it to the dishwasher.

Tan, who was still on her bed, lifted up her head and looked at me. I had scraped the bowl so there wasn't any reason to let her lick it. I closed the door of the dishwasher.

"I was just telling The Black that a woman died at The Festival today." Tan sat up.

"It was an accident—snakebite." What the heck. I took the bowl back out and put it down next to Tan's food dish. She got up and walked to the bowl, stuck her nose in it, sniffed it tentatively, and began to lick.

The Black jumped down from the top of the fridge and walked over to see what I'd given Tan. Tan ignored the cat and licked harder. Possession was the key here. If they had gotten to the bowl at the same time, TB would have gone first.

"Don't bother the dog, TB." As useless a comment as I've ever made.

I put the containers in the freezer, which was in the laundry room, and came back into the kitchen to find both dog and cat standing in the middle of the room facing me.

"Look, there's going to be an autopsy. We'll find out more tomorrow. But tonight—." I'd been thinking about watching some TV. Staying home and watching TV on a Friday night. There had been a time . . . Tan's plume of a tail began to slowly move from side to side.

"Tonight is as good a time as any to learn a little more about snakes. Let me finish cleaning up and we'll see what the Internet has to tell us."

I debated whether to drive to The Festival grounds or to one of the parking lots that the shuttle buses serviced. Usually I take the shuttle. Sort of a sop to the environment—no, more like an acknowledgment of the environment. But I wasn't sure what to do today.

The plan was to meet Bobby and her friends at The Festival, spend most of the day there, and then come back to my house for supper. But plans don't always work out. For instance, yesterday's plan hadn't included death, a break-in, and arson. Sometimes it pays if you're not dependent on public transportation—a little more flexible. Of course, that's part of the problem here in Alabama. We're way too un-dependent on public transportation so the people who can least afford private transportation have no choice but to use it.

I stood up—firmly undecided. Absently, I patted my pockets identifying what was in them—wallet, keys, phone, business cards. My PI license was in the wallet. I had cash and a credit card. The disk with the pictures Kurt wanted was with The Festival program. Last night, after I'd finished learning how little I knew about snakes, I'd remembered Kurt had asked for the pictures. I wanted to talk to Kurt about bank records and the blackmailing—the disk gave me an excuse, if I needed one. I looked at the to-do list on my phone. Yeah, everything was on there. Now I just had to do it.

Jim Ward was going to The Festival today and would try and catch up with me. Meanwhile he'd said he'd give some thought to how to investigate a blackmailer—particularly a dead one.

Tan was outside and had water. The Black had seen the signs that I was getting ready to go out and had disappeared. The house was as neat as it was going to be. I had done everything ahead of time for dinner tonight that I could. Hmmm. I put my coffee cup in the dishwasher and started it. It was a small load and I'd have time to empty it before my guests arrived.

I stood at the door to the garage and wondered if Archie Goodwin or Spenser had ever taken public transportation. Crap. So I'd be the first. I had plenty of time. I could be the PI who took public transportation.

. . .

I was late. Not very late, but late. I'd parked in a lot in plenty of time, I had just missed the first shuttle bus—the one that runs before The Festival starts. It had pulled out as I pulled in. No problem. There'd be another one along in ten minutes. And there would have been too, except one of the volunteer bus drivers came down sick and you had to have a commercial license to drive the school buses they were using because of insurance requirements.

Turned out the insurance agent had a commercial driver's license and after they'd called him to verify the need for a CDL he'd volunteered to substitute. I made a note of the agent's name. I might need a helpful agent.

The buses don't drop you off right at the gate. They stop a short walk from the gate, load up, and head back downtown. As I was walking to the gate, I spotted Bobby right away despite the crowd. It might have been because she was one of the few figures standing still or it might have been something else.

Bobby was talking to a woman about her age who must be her cousin Rebecca. She had a smile on her face and was talking animatedly, using her hands for emphasis. Bobby was in jeans, but the other woman was wearing a skirt. I didn't see anybody that could be Jack. Then a man who must have been squatting down looking at the gate stood up next to them.

I waved and the man spotted me. He said something to Bobby who turned, looked my way, nodded her head, and waved at me.

"Sorry I'm late. They ran out of bus drivers and had to find some more." I started talking as soon as I was in earshot.

"I figured it was something like that." Bobby took a few steps forward to meet me, gave me a hug, and turned to her friends. "Rebecca and Jack this is James Crawford. Call him Crawford."

I put my hand out but Rebecca pushed it aside and gave me a hug. "I'm a hugger. Didn't she tell you? So you're the reason my sister-cousin has been so cheerful on the phone lately." She looked up at me and turned back to Bobby. "He's taller than I thought, but I'd have recognized him anywhere."

I reached around Rebecca to shake Jack's hand and once again lost my hand in another man's grip. Oh, his hands weren't as big as Kurt Snoddy's but they were big enough and calloused. A man who worked with his hands; that's right, Bobby had said Jack was a contractor.

Rebecca had turned to Bobby and they were chattering at each other simultaneously. It was like two conversations taking place at the same time. Jack and I stood there looking at the women for a minute, then Jack turned to me. "They're like that for the first twenty-four hours or so, then they slow down—a little.

Jack was about my height only bigger, a little broader across the shoulders and heavier in the torso. His beard and hair were a salt-and-pepper mixture that was more pepper than salt. He had a calm, steady air about him. Judging by how animated Rebecca was he seemed to be a perfect balance.

He nodded at Bobby and Rebecca. "Most times I'm just along for the ride with those two. Glad to have some company."

"Does it tire you out just to watch them? Or listen to them?"

"Not too bad. Sometimes they'll leave me alone and go off on their own but when they do, they usually make sure I've got food and drink." He smiled and I smiled back.

I pointed at the gate. "How do you like The Festival gate? I noticed that you were looking at it."

"I've seen it when we've come down for The Festival before." He reached out and touched one of the metal leaves. "The blacksmith has loaded this thing down with three or four hundred pounds of extra weight. I like the metalwork. It looks nice, but, golly, they should have reinforced it."

I nodded. "Yeah, they had some trouble with it during the opening ceremony."

Jack chuckled. "I guess they did. I talked to the guy in charge of the volunteers. Ralph? He said they had to replace the bolts in the top hinges. That somebody had taken them out. You can see they're brand new."

The gate along with all of its decorations had been painted black and I could see the shiny steel of the new bolt. "What a funny thing to do."

"Yeah, vandalism is a laugh a minute. You won't believe what people will do at construction sites. This piece of vandalism had to be done while the gate was closed—when there was that brace in the middle for it to rest on."

"Huh?"

"That's what the guy who fixed it and I figured, anyway. When it was open he had to have two or three guys lift up the end so he could get the bolt in. It shouldn't be that far out of balance. Wouldn't be except for the artwork."

"You mean somebody unbolted it while it was closed? Unscrewed the nuts and took them and the bolts?"

"Yeah, the guy I was talking to said somebody was probably wanting souvenirs. Well, they got 'em. He's going to weld these nuts on and then paint them. It'll look good as new."

"They got them from both sides?" I remembered Dot demanding volunteers to help open both sides.

Jack and I walked through the incoming crowd over to the other side and, sure enough, a new, unpainted bolt secured the top hinge to the post. I looked over at the two reserved parking spaces. Today the director's spot was empty, as was the assistant's. Somebody had gotten Dot's pickup truck then. I wondered if Coba had walked to The Festival today. Ellen had said her house was within walking distance.

I tried to fit the missing bolts in with blackmail and couldn't. There didn't seem to be any connection.

"People can be weird, Crawford." Jack shrugged his heavy shoulders. "You run into all sorts in construction."

"You do in my line of work as well."

"That's right," Jack's eyes sparkled. "Bobby tells me you're a private investigator. You must have some tales to tell!"

I laughed and reached for my business cards. "Here, be one of the first people I've given a card to. I've only been a PI for a couple of months. I was actually talking about my old job, when I worked for the university. I'm telling you there are some strange people out there."

Jack held the card in one hand and finger thumped it with the other. "Nice. I'm on vacation so I don't have mine on me." He stuck it in his shirt pocket. I was glad I'd gotten the heavy paper stock. "Oh, professors you mean?"

"Them too."

"Are you two going to stand there all day talking?" Bobby and Rebecca had noticed that we'd moved to the other side of the gate. Bobby was standing in front of us with her hands on her hips. "I thought we were going to The Festival."

Rebecca joined in. "I didn't drive all the way down here from Cranbury, Tennessee, to *not* go to The Festival."

Jack and I looked at each other and shrugged our shoulders. What could we say? I reached for my wallet. "I guess that means we need to buy some tickets."

. . .

The quickest route to the Press booth and the Metro Shelter booth was counterclockwise from the gates. Once the four of us were properly fitted out with a two-day Festival pass around our necks, we headed clockwise. The width of the path varied, as did the amount of foot traffic headed our way. It was impossible to walk four abreast—barely possible two by two—so the walking arrangements were fluid at first. Rebecca and Bobby seemed to feed off of each other as they found things to show each other, Jack, and me. That's not to say we males didn't find interesting things to look at. It's just that not all of them were in booths.

We'd stopped at a booth of sculpture—primarily faces— made out of old metal machine parts that had made it to the junkyard years ago. Bobby and Rebecca were thrilled with the different faces and their expressions, but Jack was more interested in identifying where the parts had come from. He'd identified a tractor seat and several car engine parts; he and the artist were trying to decide if something was from a '56 or '57 Chevy before I eased out of the booth. That was part of the fun of going to The Festival. The next booth might have stuff made out of computer parts to delight an old geek like me. You never knew what was around the bend.

Today's music was country/folk so lyrics about bars, honky-tonks, trains, momma, preachers, and pickup trucks were added to the loss, betrayal, revenge, and grief themes of the Celtic songs. I didn't think I'd hear the one about "get up and bar the door" today, but who knew? Were there songs about blackmailers? Hadn't I wondered about that already—songs of the blackmailer?

I was watching the crowd walk by—people-watching, one of my favorite pastimes at The Festival, when I recognized two of the people headed my way.

"Hey, Levi. Mary." I stepped into the pathway. I'd talked to Mary Keith last Thursday when she was cleaning my house, but I hadn't seen Levi in months. He stands a head shorter than Mary but that doesn't make him a small man. He was stocky—in keeping with his deep, bass voice.

"Crawford. How you doing?" Choir directors all over the South probably drooled in anticipation when they heard Levi speak and wept tears of joy when they heard him sing.

We moved next to a pine tree to get out of the crowd traffic.

"Pretty good. How about yourself? I figured on seeing you tomorrow, not today."

"We decided to come to The Festival today to see things. Tomorrow we're singing with the choir and we never see much of The Festival the day we sing."

"Well that's great. I'm looking forward to Sunday's music. Your choir always makes it special."

Mary smiled and crossed her arms. She knew the choir was good and didn't mind hearing people say so. "Don't forget to ask him about that snake, Levi."

Levi snapped his finger. "That's right. This Dot Fields who died of snakebite—she the one with the corn snake you told Mary about?"

"That's right, Levi. She had a beautiful corn snake that escaped in the confusion when she died. Evidently she knocked the cage over and the snake got out."

"That's a shame." Levi shook his head. "Both her death and the snake escaping." I decided not to add Levi to the list of potential blackmail victims.

"Didn't Mary tell me you've taken an interest in snakes?"

"Been scared of them too long and—."

Mary interrupted. "While you two men are talking snakes I'm going down here a-ways. I think the quilting society's booth is this way."

"I'll be right there," said Levi.

"And I've heard that before." Mary laughed and waved good-bye.

. . .

"Had a birthday six months ago," Levi went on. "One of those big ones with a zero at the end. The ones that make you take stock, you know? I decided then that I was tired of being scared of snakes. Decided to find out something about what I was scared of and I'm learning there ain't much to be scared of. I read up on the good snakes like the corn snakes, rat snakes, king snakes, ones that kill rats and the like. Been trying to see some too. Pictures not as real to me as—" Levi laughed, "as the real thing."

"Hey," I remembered that I'd taken pictures. "I can at least show you what the corn snake looked like. The rattlesnake too." I pulled my phone out and started sorting through the pictures.

Levi was still laughing. "Crawford, I never said that I'd studied up on bad snakes. And the one that killed Ms. Fields must have been one bad snake. She was no little woman. Why she must have been as big as Mary."

"Here." I handed my phone over to Levi. "I've got several of the corn snake."

"My! That is a pretty snake. Look at those colors."

Levi was slowly scrolling through the pictures when Jack walked up and joined us next to the tree. He stuck his thumb over his shoulder pointing down the path. "The ladies are looking at baskets and I volunteered to tell you not to get lost."

Levi grinned. "Don't much care for baskets, eh? I understand. My wife's looking at quilts."

"Jack Harlon, I'd like you to meet Levi Keith. Levi, this is Jack Harlon from Cranbury, Tennessee."

They shook hands.

"Tomorrow you'll get to hear Levi sing gospel music and you'll be proud to say you've met him."

"I'm looking forward to it." Jack smiled. "That would be the bass part, I'm guessing."

"Oh, I might surprise you with some soprano," squeaked Levi in falsetto. "But mostly not." He gestured at my phone. "Is that the rattlesnake? I don't see any rattles."

"If it's not the rattlesnake then—oh." I'd forgotten about the snake at the Bird House. "No, those are pictures I took of a snake I saw after the corn snake and before the rattlesnake. It's a garter snake sunning on a brick wall. Here, I'll show you the rattlesnake." I took the phone back and swiped through a bunch of shots before I got to the rattlesnake.

"Sorry to hear about that woman dying." Jack shook his head. "Snakebite. I don't know the last time I've heard of anybody dying from snakebite."

"That's just it, Mr. Harlon. That's what's weird about this."

"Call me Jack, Levi."

I handed my phone back to Levi who looked at that picture and some others of the rattlesnake.

Levi went on. "Every other accident you hear about somebody's always got a cousin or a friend of a friend who has had the same thing happen to them. But not this one. Bitten maybe—but not dead. Ever since Genesis, been blamin' it on the snake, but this strikes me as odd. Does it you, Jack? Crawford?"

"We just got into town last night, so I haven't heard that much about it."

"Don't matter. You just another one of us who ain't heard of people dying of snakebite."

I tried to think. I'd heard lots of comments about Dot dying of snakebite but—

"I think you're right, Levi. Everybody is surprised."

Levi handed my phone back to me. "You take all these pictures here?"

Jack looked interested so I handed my phone over to him.

"Sure enough. Why?"

"Well, see that's the problem. All I've learned is from pictures. I ain't seen that many snakes live, you know? But I don't think that was a garter snake you took a picture of. I'm thinking maybe rat snake."

Jack handed my phone back. "Can you find them for me?"

"Really?" I found the Bird House pics, handed the phone to Jack, and turned back to Levi. "I'd heard that garter snakes have yellow stripes and just assumed that since that one looked like it had stripes it was a garter snake."

"But that's just it, Crawford." Levi's forehead was furrowed.

Jack handed the phone back again. "Corn snake too?"

It was a good thing I hadn't taken the time to delete this stuff off my phone last night. I found the first of the corn snake pictures.

"What about the snake, Levi? The one you think's a rat snake."

"We don't have yellow rat snakes 'round here—I don't think—gray or black."

"Really colorful snakes." Jack looked at Levi. "I don't know anything about snakes. I go my way and they go theirs."

Levi looked fretted. "I don't know much about snakes, I know that, but I don't think these snakes are from around here—something about their colors."

Jack looked at me. "It's a cinch I don't know. All I can do is agree that you've got pictures of snakes. Sounds to me like you need to check with an expert. Somebody that knows. Maybe their colors change when you keep them captive?"

I stared at my phone. I'd learned last night that colors in a species vary widely. I just hadn't learned which colors change and what causes them to change.

"What do you think, Crawford?" Levi still looked concerned.

"I think you know more about snakes than I do and if you've got concerns I ought to do what Jack suggests and check with an expert—or tell Chief Snoddy he ought to check with an expert. And you know what else I think?"

Jack and Levi exchanged glances and then looked back at me.

"I think it's a good thing that this is Alabama beer and wine day at The Festival 'cause I will be glad to have a drink."

We all laughed. Then Levi went off to catch up with Mary while I got out my cell phone and composed a short note to Morgan "Snake" Moore, Joyce's snake expert. I made sure I attached pictures of the rattlesnake before I sent the email. Should have done that last night. That chore out of the way, Jack and I headed off in the opposite direction from Levi. I was keeping my eye out for the Archibald chief of police, too.

Jack was still giving the coloration of snakes some thought. "It could be the diet, right? I'm trying to remember."

"Sure," I agreed. "Flamingos aren't as pink if they don't eat the right stuff—shrimp I think or maybe it's algae. The pinker they are the more whatever-it-is they eat. Maybe that applies to snakes as well."

"Well, okay then." Jack nodded. "It could be diet. Feed a snake a different kind of Purina snake chow and you get different colors."

"Purina?"

"Yeah, you know how they've got a chow for everything—dog chow, cat chow, hamster chow, rabbit chow, horse chow, goat chow. Why not snake chow?

I laughed. "Right. Dry snake chow and an occasional can of mouse." I didn't know if Jack was kidding, but I decided to leave it alone for the time being. "Let's catch up with the ladies."

. . .

The ladies had investigated the baskets, moved on to a potter who made jugs of all sizes with human or quasi-human features, another artist who covered everything with dots, and another who made wooden whirligigs in bright colors and fanciful shapes. We finally caught up with them at the booth of an exhibiting artist who made wooden furniture that incorporated the shape of vegetables in their design.

Bobby was standing in front of a perfectly functional table that just happened to have legs that looked like red chili peppers.

Rebecca was reading from a scrapbook that was sitting on a podium made out of an asparagus spear. It must have been filled with pictures of what he'd made over the years plus clippings of news articles about the artist.

"Did you know he has stuff in the Smithsonian?" Rebecca sounded surprised.

Bobby and I nodded. Jack said, "Huh? Who?"

"This guy. Some of his stuff is on display in the Smithsonian—airports—places like that. He's really well known," she added.

"It's beautiful work. There's no doubt about that." Jack ran his hands across the smooth inlaid surface of the top. He flipped the price tag over, looked at it, turned it back over, and carefully stepped away from the table. "Does he sell much of this stuff?"

Bobby shook her head no. "I don't think so—not at The Festival. I think most of his works are commissioned these days. He's from here, got his start in Shelbyville, and exhibits—I guess you'd call it—at The Festival. He's a woodworking genius with a sense of humor—and whimsy."

I'd forgotten about this guy when I thought Ted Lowe's paintings were overpriced for The Festival. Still, this guy was just exhibiting his work. Ted was trying to sell his.

"Why don't you three go stand behind the table and I'll take your picture?" I pulled my phone out and waved Jack and Rebecca over to stand by Bobby and took the picture. I glanced at the mail and saw an automated response from the snake expert. It warned me that he might not get back to me right away. That happened once you got into the weekend.

Bobby ran her hand across the tabletop. It was so beautifully smooth it was hard to resist. "Let's go see how Frank's doing at the Press's booth and then get some lunch."

She got no argument.

. . .

The University Press booth wasn't that far away. We approached it from a direction I hadn't used since Thursday when I carted all the gear in from the vendor lot. The reoriented booths for the Press and the AIDS organization hid the old path that had led to Dot's tent. If it hadn't been for the police crime scene tape, you really wouldn't have been able to tell where it had been.

Just as we were passing the other tent a woman called my name.

"Crawford! You going to walk by without even a wave for old times' sake?"

I turned to my right and saw Wanda Madison standing behind a table filled with brochures and under a banner that said, West-Central Alabama HIV/AIDS Outreach.

"Wanda!" I waved and turned to Bobby. "I'll just be a minute."

"Go on, we'll be next door."

I headed into the tent. Wanda was the first full-time director of the AIDS Outreach program. I'd been on the board of directors when she'd been hired and thought then we were lucky to get her. She'd since proved just how amazingly lucky we'd been.

"How are you? You look great!" She did look great. She'd matured in the position—grown with it as she developed the program, expanded its reach, increased its services, and widened its support.

"I heard you retired." Wanda gave me the once over. "And it looks like retirement agrees with you."

"I'm retired from the university but that doesn't mean I'm retired. I've got a new gig." For the second time today I pulled out my business card. This time I bowed as I handed it over. "James F. Crawford, private investigator, at your service." I was getting the hang of this.

Wanda took the card and gave me hers so smoothly that I decided I wasn't there yet—I needed more practice. "Too busy to do any volunteer work?"

I held up my hands. "I'm working even as we speak. You wouldn't have been being blackmailed by Dot Fields would you? Besides you know I'm not the volunteering type."

And that was the truth. I wasn't much of a joiner either. The only reason I'd been on the board in the first place was as a favor to a friend. By herself she'd started several very important volunteer programs that were still making life better for West Alabama residents. When she asked me to join the board I was flattered and learned for myself how persuasive she could be. I was to bring some "balance to the board" was how she put it. To this day I don't know what kind of balance I brought to it, but I did what I could.

"Any chance of you coming back on the board?" Wanda seemed hopeful.

"None whatsoever," I replied cheerfully. "Look how well you're doing without me." I pointed at the tent. "We'd never have been able to afford this when I was on the board."

Wanda leaned forward and dropped her voice. "I shouldn't tell you this. I was sworn to secrecy—we still can't. You can guess just how excited I was when The Festival approached us. They waived the fee. They even provided the tent." She looked around. "We'd never have been able to get this kind of publicity without their help."

"Really!" I looked around at the tent—brand new. "Nice tent."

"Well, it really isn't as open as I would have liked. You can't see anything to either side or behind you, but the price was right. Who am I to look a gift horse in the mouth?"

It was the way she could be aware of the tent's shortcomings while taking advantage of its availability that helped make her so effective as AIDS Outreach director. Wanda waved her hand at the walls of the tent and the flash from a diamond ring reminded me. "Hey, I forgot, you've gotten married since I saw you last! How's that going?"

That got a great big smile but a short reply. "It's wonderful."

"Now that he's swept you off your feet is he going to take you away from us?" She'd married an instructor at the university who was over here from England. I had heard that there was some concern in the AIDS community that he'd take her away from Shelbyville.

"No. In fact he's in the process of trying to immigrate to the United States. If I hadn't already experienced how complicated dealing with the government could be I wouldn't have believed what he's had to go through with USCIS—Immigration."

"Really? That bad?"

"We had to hire an attorney—an immigration lawyer—it's a specialty—to help us deal with them. Best thing we ever did, too. He's really helped. And the funny thing is that he's an alumnus of the university—and gave us a discount. Says he gives everybody from the university a discount." She paused for a moment, looking thoughtful. "He tried to explain it to us. Something about a field goal kicker who'd been a soccer player—never played football before he came to the university from some soccer-playing country? Won the game as time expired? Games? He can never repay his debt?"

I laughed. "Sounds like a true alumnus of the university. The kicker probably covered the betting spread."

There had been that ebb and flow of people coming into the tent around us when Wanda and I suddenly realized that there were people standing in line waiting to speak to her.

"Great to see you. Felicitations on your marriage!" I smiled and left the tent.

It bothers me to hear how hard it is to deal with parts of the federal government. I know some career bureaucrats who work hard—and successfully—to do their jobs competently, efficiently, and effectively. They serve their country well, and it's a shame that lazy or incompetent employees give civil servants a bad name.

I was almost at the Press's tent when I remembered that she'd never said yes or no to my blackmail question.

. . .

There was a crowd of people in the Press's tent, I was glad to see. I was getting so used to seeing people in costume that the outfit had to be really striking for me to notice it. Lady Godiva would have worked, but short of that—nope. The Press had had some bad luck for awhile and deserved some good. Bobby and Frank knew their clientele better than I did. People seemed happy to fill out paper order forms while looking at catalogs that just happened to be on computer screens. I comforted myself with the excuse that high-tech purchasers wouldn't come to a festival to order books.

I looked around and spotted Jack first. Once I'd found him it was easy to spot Bobby and Rebecca. They were standing at a table in front of Frank Manning who was sitting behind the table, hands behind his head, with his feet propped up on the table. He didn't seem to be overworked or the least bit stressed out.

Kent Fulmer was the Press employee who was working with Frank. He, at least, was standing and talking to potential customers. I'd met both Kent and Frank when the provost had asked me to help the Shelbyville police with their investigation into the Press director's murder. Bobby had told me that Frank had volunteered to work from noon on—just so long as he didn't have to work the early shift.

That reminded me. I'd learned that Kent and Frank regularly took a walk around 4:20 every day at the Press to smoke dope. The Festival closed at 5:00. I wondered what they were going to do.

I walked up and put my hand on Bobby's shoulder. She patted it without looking up. Frank was talking.

"Now you might want to try the fried gumbo. What the vendor does is batter and fry everything that they put into their gumbo—and season it with all the spice they use in making gumbo. You'll want to have beer with that."

I interrupted. "So, Frank, tell me how they batter and fry the liquid they put in gumbo."

Frank exhaled through his mouth, fluffing out his mustache. "Ah, Crawford. Glad to finally run into a responsible adult. Hazel will be so pleased."

Responsible adult? He must have decided to take his smoke break early.

"Dr. Murphy was most put out with me this morning. Last night, Mr. Fulmer and I inadvertently took the legal pads and pens that belong in the booth home with us." He stopped. "Well, to be perfectly honest, we took them as far as our cars and left them there."

I smiled. "So when Hazel got here this morning she didn't have anything to write on or write with. Did she curse you?"

"Really, Crawford, you misjudge Hazel. She is quite resourceful. However, my misstep yesterday caused her to wish for the aforesaid 'responsible adult.'"

"Okay. My guess is that Hazel Murphy would think there were four responsible adults standing in front of you. What now?"

"Ah, direct and to the point. So . . . adult." Frank lifted up his feet, swung around in his chair, and put his feet on the ground—sitting up in the process and revealing a plastic bag sitting on the table. "Voila!"

I picked the bag up and found two pads of paper, two stick pens, and a note—all clearly marked Property of The Festival. The note started out, "Dear Responsible Adult . . ."

I held the note out to Bobby so she could see it. "It actually is addressed to 'responsible adult'."

"Don't give it to me," laughed Bobby. "I'm determined to grow older but never to grow up."

Jack and Rebecca both lifted their hands, refusing to touch the note.

"What's the note say, O responsible adult?" Rebecca grinned impishly and I could see a family resemblance. Bobby had the same grin on her face.

Frank put his feet back on the table. "You can see the dilemma I was in. I hesitated to ask Hazel if she was sure I was responsible enough to pick out a responsible adult." He looked over at Bobby. "Shall we call him RA from now on?"

"Funny. Very, funny." I growled.

Jack piped up. "Have we determined that what Hazel is asking is reasonable?"

"The note asks that the supplies be returned to The Festival headquarters, specifically, to one Coba Boucher. We are to inform her that these are the very same ones she loaned the Press earlier today."

I smiled. "Okay, Frank. We'll return the pens and pads." It was the least I could do for Hazel. I'd once suspected her of killing her boss.

. . .

Once we were outside I remembered the EMT who had come straight across the grounds to Dot's tent. The one who'd gotten there first. The EMTs were set up next to headquarters so we should be able to cut across the grounds and get to the back of HQ faster than walking the pathway.

Normally, I would never have thought to take a shortcut and if there had been some of those please-stay-on-the-path signs there I probably wouldn't have.

"Follow me." We headed between the two booths, past where Kurt had briefed Ellen and Joyce on the accident, past the area marked off with crime scene tape, around a clump of bushes or two to the back of the only permanent building on the grounds. I was surprised at how close it was. The winding paths and the screening brush made it seem much farther away.

There were two folding chairs and an ashtray just outside the backdoor, which had a sign on it that said No Admittance.

I stopped to look around as the rest of my small group continued walking around to the front. I looked back at the fire scene. The remains of the fortune-telling tent were a black mess surrounded by the yellow crime scene tape. It looked like the fire had scorched some of the pine branches hanging over the site. It was a good thing the fire department knocked the flames down before the fire could get into the tops of the pines. There was a single, uniformed person walking around and taking pictures. I wondered if that was the fire marshal Kurt had mentioned. I shrugged my shoulders and followed my friends to the front door.

Someone had run a string fence along the pathway here—a token gesture to remind the public to stay on the path. There probably had been one at the other end but when the tent got moved it hadn't got put back. I stepped over the string onto the pathway, completing my act of rebellion. I glanced around. No one seemed to have noticed—or cared. I took the path, walked past the information booth, and entered The Festival headquarters.

The setup was the same as yesterday morning's—had it only been a day? People were waiting in line to talk to Coba. She was still seated at the table with the map of the grounds in front of her. She'd given up on the leather outfit and was back to the standard garb—Festival T-shirt, jeans, and sneakers. No, I corrected myself, not sneakers, more like sandals. Yesterday's boots must have been as hot as I'd thought.

The line was shorter than yesterday's and moving fairly quickly. Jack and Rebecca were standing near Bobby, but off to the side so no one would think they were in line too. I walked up just as Bobby got to the head of the line and spoke before Bobby could.

"Hi, Coba. I'm James Crawford—you remember I was with Chief Snoddy yesterday." She nodded but didn't speak.

"This is Bobby Slater from the University Press and her friends Jack and Rebecca. They came down all the way from Cranbury, Tennessee, to come to The Festival."

I'm not sure what I expected from Coba but her silent stare wasn't it. Maybe a thanks for coming? Welcome to The Festival? Any friend of the chief of police is no friend of mine? Whatever, she was all business today. Maybe it was just a delayed reaction to Dot's death.

"A coworker of mine, Hazel Murphy, borrowed some supplies from you this morning and she made us promise to return them directly to you." Bobby stepped in and broke the awkward silence. She handed the bag to Coba who dumped the contents out on the table, picked up another pad, flipped through some pages, and drew a line through an entry that had been written there.

"Murphy, right." Coba said. "Thanks." She stacked the pads on top of a stack of similar pads and returned the pens to a jar filled with their mates.

"Sorry about the tent that burned yesterday." I don't know what possessed me to try and extend the nonexistent conversation.

She looked at me as if she couldn't comprehend what I was saying.

"The fortune-telling tent? Dot's tent?" I prompted her.

"Oh. That. The tent wasn't Festival property. The Festival doesn't own any tents. Dot owned that tent. It has nothing to do with The Festival."

Bobby took my arm and we started leaving. "I'll tell Hazel that you got those pads and pens back." And on that note we all turned around and headed for the outdoors.

. . .

We were outside before anyone spoke.

"What was that all about?" Rebecca looked at Bobby and me. "I thought—that is—didn't you tell me that the tent the Press is using for a booth is The Festival's?"

"Well, that can't be." We all stopped and looked at him. Jack looked somewhat surprised to be the center of attention. "It can't belong to The Festival."

"That's what Frank said. He said he was sworn to secrecy and not to tell anybody but it was The Festival's tent." Bobby looked puzzled. "Where else would he have gotten it? And why would he lie about it?"

"I don't know about that but I do know that it's not labeled Property of The Festival and everything else sure is." Jack laughed. "Heck, I bet they'd have labeled the tent stakes if that tent belonged to The Festival. They label pads of paper and pens! How could they not label a tent?"

"Maybe The Festival doesn't want anybody to know they own the tents." Rebecca looked up at Jack. "Did you consider that? They may want to keep it a secret."

Bobby nodded. "That would explain why they made Frank promise not to tell where he got it."

"And it was the same deal for the AIDS tent." Now everyone looked at me. "Wanda—the woman at the tent—she told me the same thing. Sworn to secrecy."

"So there are two tents that belong to The Festival that aren't marked Property of The Festival? I'd just as soon believe somebody was lying about that," Jack smiled, "as to believe such a label-happy group could keep themselves from labeling a tent—no, two tents."

"Well, I think we can quit worrying about labels and think of other things." I looked around. "What about a beer? I'm thirsty."

Rebecca looked puzzled. "When did that happen? The last time we were here for The Festival you couldn't buy a drink at The Festival—I mean an adult beverage."

"Which can only be consumed by responsible adults, I remind you." From the looks I got everybody considered themselves adult enough for that. "Fair-weather adults. That's all I've got to say." We started walking toward the food court and Bobby began to explain.

"The Festival made the change two years ago. First off, you can't buy adult beverages on any day of The Festival except Saturday. And even then you can only buy beer and wine—no hard liquor."

"This is so American," said Rebecca. "We have the weirdest alcohol laws in the world. It's almost like we try to outdo each other."

"Could be." Bobby thought for a second. "Only I think this may be the weirdest. You can buy beer and wine but only beer and wine that was produced in Alabama—no national brands— just local. And here's the logic. The Festival is an arts festival and brewing beer and fermenting wine are considered arts! The vendors—I mean artists—are allowed to exhibit—sell—their works only on one day, Saturday, and only as an accompaniment to food. It is," Bobby took a few mincing steps and held her head high, "an artistic experience that only a few can truly appreciate."

Jack whispered to me. "How the hell did they get that by the licensing board?"

I whispered back. "The licensing board is the city council of Archibald. Do you have any idea how much money The Festival brings in? Besides, they prettied it up by limiting it to Alabama products and making people buy food with it."

Rebecca snorted in a ladylike fashion. "At one time there was a law in New Orleans that said you couldn't buy a drink on election day unless you bought food with it. Until the polls closed, of course."

"What? Like a sandwich or something?" Jack looked as surprised as the rest of us.

"That was probably the intent, but my mom said people would just order the cheapest thing on the menu so they'd serve pieces of chocolate pie with the double martinis."

"Gin and chocolate." I shook my head. "Sounds nasty."

"At The Festival we do things differently. When you get to the head of the line there are two cashiers. One to take your food order, the other your drink order. You just have to order your food first or have food in your hand."

"How civilized."

We got to the food court—the entrance of the clearing where the food vendors set up—and to one side there was a tall, lanky man drinking from a large cup of coffee. You could see his Adam's apple bobbing up and down as he swallowed.

I waved at him and he toasted me with his coffee.

"Rebecca, speaking of laws, there's somebody here I'd like you to meet. You too, Jack." I steered us toward the man as he started toward us.

"Oh," exclaimed Bobby, "it's Jim Ward. The policeman whose a friend of ours. I've told you about him, remember, Bex?"

Jim was dressed in khakis, plaid shirt, and a windbreaker—like a bunch of other men at The Festival. Only I was pretty sure he was wearing the jacket to conceal the fact that he was armed as much as to keep the wind off. It was either the underarm holster or the one for the small of his back. I think he preferred the behind the back one, but I'd seen both hanging over the backs of my kitchen chairs on poker night.

Andrew Boyd, the Shelbyville chief of police, required senior officers to carry a weapon at all times—for their own safety. As head of homicide, Jim was a senior officer and certainly had members of society—okay, the fringes of society—who undoubtedly did not wish him well. Sometimes Jim chafed at having to carry a weapon. Personally, I was glad he did. I don't have so many friends that I can afford to lose one.

Jim had started to put his hand out for me to shake when Bobby popped up between us and hugged him.

"Jim Ward, I want you to meet some of my friends!"

"It would be a pleasure." Jim winked at me over Bobby's head. "Any friend of yours—"

"This is Rebecca Perry and Jack Harlon." Bobby had to release Jim so Rebecca could hug him. "Rebecca's my sister-cousin and Jack's her husband."

"Nice to meet you, Mrs. Perry. And you, Mr. Harlon." He shook Jack's hand. "Is that Harlon with an *o* or an *a*?"

"It's Harlon with the *o* and I prefer Jack—with an *a*."

"And I go by Jim."

"How can you call me Mrs. after I hugged you! I'm Rebecca."

"I stand corrected, Rebecca. A hug in the South *is* a formal introduction." He turned back to Bobby.

"I believe I noticed a family resemblance in the hugging technique. You'll have to explain the sister/cousin relationship to me some time. I get confused beyond second cousin and have given up even trying to figure out the removes—once or twice."

I stuck my hand out and he gripped it. "A cousin close enough to be the sister you never had. Thanks for coming, Jim. Vivian not able to make it?"

"Vivian miss The Festival? She's shopping while I'm hanging around here waiting for you to show up. She's thrilled not to have me following her around saying we don't need any of the stuff she's going to buy anyway." He glanced around the circle we'd formed and shrugged his shoulders. "She claims I put a damper on the fun of shopping."

"You were waiting for us?" Bobby glanced over at me, a question in her eyes.

"For Ford here, anyway. He failed to mention that he was part of a party of four when he called last night."

"Have you been waiting long?" I pulled my phone out to check the time.

"Just long enough to get this excellent cup of coffee." He lifted the cup up again and took a sip. "It's not as good as the coffee you brew, and I had to pay for it, but I can recommend it."

"We were planning on trying the beer. At least," Jack tapped his chest, "I was."

Rebecca added, "I'm going to try the wine. I've never had an Alabama wine."

Ward shook his head. "Too close to breakfast for me, hence the coffee."

"We've been here long enough to work up a little hunger and thirst. Besides, we want to be hungry when suppertime rolls around." I looked around the group. "Look, I need to talk business with Jim—I'm in desperate need of his advice. Why don't y'all go on and look at what's for sale. I'm thinking Rebecca and Jack will need some time to decide what they want to eat—and drink. Heck, Bobby's going to have to study the wine list for a while."

"We can wait. I don't mind listening." Jack smiled. "If I did, I'd be single. Besides, Frank told us what to order."

"Did he mention which beer to order?" I asked. "There are supposed to be a couple of new breweries this year. I'm not sure what the choices are."

"Oh," Jack's face lit up. "If it's a scouting mission you're sending us on—food or drink, I'm your man!"

I grinned. "Absolutely. Get out there and see what's available!"

Bobby, Jack, and Rebecca went on into the clearing debating, as they went, whether it would be better to split up. We watched them walk off and then turned to face each other.

. . .

"Seem like nice people," said Jim. "Bobby's mighty fond of them apparently."

"Yeah. Just met them today. I was a little nervous—felt like they were coming down to see if I was good enough for Bobby."

"I've wondered that very same thing ever since I met her."

"Thanks, old buddy. You think I haven't wondered myself?"

"Don't worry about it. If she decides you are—that's all that matters. She's got a mind of her own, you know. Besides, you've got a pretty good track record. She could do worse." He took a final drink of coffee and dropped the cup in a nearby trash can.

"And that's the same thing I told Kurt Snoddy when he called asking about you."

"He called you? I didn't think he knew you."

"Oh, we've met a couple of times but he called my chief to ask about you and Chief Boyd told him to call me. Kurt must not have listened to me—otherwise he'd have shipped you back across the river."

"Thanks for the vote of confidence."

"Confidence? What the crap do you know about blackmail? Or how to investigate it? You know so much that you call a homicide detective for advice, that's how much you know."

"Hey, give me credit. At least I had enough sense to call you. I could have called Harry what's-his-name."

"Johns. And I wouldn't suggest you try to follow any advice he'd give you. It would be anatomically impossible is my guess."

"Oh." It's true that Sgt. Harry Johns and I hadn't exactly hit it off.

"He certainly wouldn't tell you that you were right. Follow the money as best you can. I'm sure The Festival would let you look at their books but you really need access to Dot's accounts."

"I know, and I'm at a dead end on figuring out how to do that. I don't think anybody's going to believe I've got her power of attorney."

"Even if they did, it wouldn't do you any good."

"How so?"

"Because powers of attorney terminate on death. How are you going to act for somebody when that somebody is dead. You're a private eye, you should know that—or did Perry Mason never mention it?"

"I don't remember. I'm sure blackmailers figured into some of the storylines, but I guess they were usually dead."

"So why don't you break into her house, find her financial records, and solve the case? That's the private detective approach, isn't it?"

"Little you know," I scoffed. "Both her house and her office are being watched by the police—well, law officers anyway."

"Sammy got his deputies looking after the house?"

I nodded absently. "After the tent burned, Kurt called him and suggested that he have the place watched. Besides, what are you doing advising me to break the law? I'd be bound to get caught."

Ward chuckled. "That's why I don't watch those shows on television. Somehow the villain always leaves incriminating evidence in a desk drawer and our just-bending-the-laws hero spots the connection as soon as he sees it. Why don't you get the police to go through her finances and tell you what they find? My guess is that some of those accountants trained in fraud detection would have a better chance of spotting it than you."

"What a great idea! I'll just walk up to Kurt and ask him to do that for me. I'm sure he'll take me right up on it just because I asked him."

"Maybe." He nodded. "Or maybe he'd tell you that you'd better call him Chief Snoddy from now on. I didn't mean you, jerk. I meant the board." Jim looked at my blank expression and added. "Of The Festival? You remember. The people who hired you to investigate?"

I shut my mouth as it had dropped open when I wasn't paying attention. "The Festival board?"

"If they want to find out if she was breaking the law by blackmailing people, they might also want to make sure she wasn't embezzling from The Festival. That will give Kurt a reason to get some subpoenas issued and financial information obtained."

"That's brilliant! What a great idea, Jim. Thanks."

"Ford, it's how law enforcement works. I do things like that most every day."

"Right." I was trying to think of a good comeback but nothing was working.

"Well, I'd best be finding Vivian." He punched me lightly on the shoulder. "She should be easy to spot by now—a bunch of packages with legs sticking out the bottom." He took a step forward.

"By the way. I told Kurt I hoped he got to see it."

I raised one eyebrow questioningly.

"When it all 'clicks' and you piece things together. Oddest thing I've ever seen."

I watched him walk off down the path and before long, he was lost in a sea of people—some costumed, some not.

. . .

Jack had decided what food he wanted to order, but he was still torn over the beer. He was going with the fried gumbo with a side of boiled crayfish Cajun-style. Bobby and Rebecca had decided to split a Greek salad and a chicken salad sandwich served in pita bread. They had perused the wine list and settled on two glasses of Zelda—a white wine from south Alabama made primarily from muscadine grapes. I went with the combo fajita hoagie (chicken and steak) covered with salsa, sour cream, and sliced jalapeño peppers.

To top it off I had the Redbone Hound Ale and Jack finally selected an Alabama Panther Stout Ale. They were from the Druid Oak brewery. For sides, the four of us split two orders of the fried spiral potatoes.

Jack and I had stood in line for the food and drink while Bobby and Rebecca found us space at one of the tables that were scattered around the grounds. Once the two of us got to the front of the line, Bobby joined us to help carry the food and drinks— plus a bunch of napkins—back to the table.

Once we were settled, conversation ended. Oh, there was the occasional comment, but mostly everybody concentrated on the food—and drink. Jack passed the crayfish around and we all agreed they were better when he'd added some hot sauce. We all got a bite of each other's food and everybody thought theirs was the best—always a good sign I think.

Jack and I were helping finish off the Greek salad—once I had seen the size of one, I knew why they'd decided to split it—while we were all finishing our drinks. The beer drinkers had gone with the twenty-four-ounce cup instead of the twelve. The women had exercised more restraint with the standard five ounces of wine. We were winding down now with little more than some empty, greasy, paper plates and mounds of used paper napkins in front of us.

We'd agreed to wait until later to have the fried dough for dessert. For one thing, it was much better right out of the hot fat than it was cold so waiting to get it made sense. The other being that we could create a little room for it after walking for a while.

Rebecca had come prepared with some of those hand-washing packets and she passed them around while I started to collect our trash. I'd just stood up when my phone chirped. I'd changed my ring tone so it took me a minute before I realized the noise was coming from me.

. . .

I pulled the phone out of my pocket and saw that the caller was Morgan Moore—Dr. Snake. "Hello!"

"Hey. How do you know Joyce?"

The voice was gruff but pleasant. "Well," I hesitated. I'd first met her when she'd been a suspect in a murder I was investigating. She hadn't been the killer, but I wasn't sure how to put it. "I really haven't known her that long."

"Never mind. Are you in Shelbyville? Or on the coast? I'm looking at those pictures you sent. Good pictures. Snake looks healthy, that's good."

"Actually, I'm in Archibald."

"Just across the river. I grew up there, on the west side of Shelbyville, did you know? Doesn't make any difference to a rattlesnake. Rattlers are on both sides of the river, but not the kind you have pictures of." He sounded like he was concentrating on the pictures and talking to me almost as an afterthought. When I had been at the university, I had seen a scientist dictating notes as he examined some specimens. I guessed I was listening to that same thing now. "The only big rattlesnake around Shelbyville and the northern part of the state is the canebrake. Some people call 'em timber rattlers. Same species. But an eastern diamondback is completely different and not found that far inland."

"You mean this kind of rattlesnake isn't indigenous to Jemison County? This isn't even a native species?"

"It absolutely is not from there. That's clear. Found in the Southeast primarily in coastal counties or a few miles inland. That one is most likely from Florida, Georgia, or South Carolina. That's where they're most common. Low country—Atlantic coast—far less common on the Gulf Coast. You sure you found it outside—I mean in the wild?"

"You're saying the rattlesnake is out of place, as it were?"

"You don't get eastern diamondbacks where you are." He added after a pause, "Unless someone brings them there."

"Then what the—" I needed to figure out just what the heck that meant. I hadn't heard of any "outside agitators" in Shelbyville in decades. "Thank you, Dr. Moore. I really appreciate your help. Thanks for calling me back."

I heard a snort on the other end of the line. "Thanks for what? Why are you interested in this snake anyway?"

"Well, it's been the center of attention here at The Festival since it killed somebody yesterday—"

"Killed somebody!" Dr. Moore's voice blasted across the phone. "A male, eighteen- to-twenty-five years old, who tried to handle the snake? Was alcohol involved?"

"Middle-aged woman. No alcohol involved as far as we know. There weren't any witnesses but we think she stumbled as she entered her tent and fell on the snake, which promptly bit her on the neck. Venom went straight into her bloodstream. She was pronounced dead at the scene. No chance of using antivenin."

Dr. Moore was silent. I was just about to ask if he was still there when he spoke. "On the neck, you say? She was in a tent? What was the snake doing there? Was it on display? Some kind of snake show?"

I shook my head though he couldn't see me. "There was a corn snake that was supposed to be in the tent. It looks like the victim knocked that cage onto the ground while she was in her death throes and it escaped. We figured that the rattlesnake was wild and got into the tent during the night."

There was another long pause on Dr. Snake's end. "Well, I guess somebody could have released their pet rattlesnake into the wild and it might have found its way into the tent."

"Occam's razor, right? The simplest answer. Somebody freed their pet rattlesnake after bringing it to Archibald."

I could tell he didn't like it as an explanation. Neither did I, but what were we left with? I thanked him again and he asked me if there was anything else he could do to help. I told him that other than finding out where the rattlesnake had come from I couldn't think of anything. He laughed and told me to call anytime. I promised I would.

The next thing was to let the police know the snake was a stranger to these parts. I muttered to myself, made a few phone calls, then stuck the phone back in my pocket.

. . .

Bobby and the rest had finished cleaning up from lunch and were waiting patiently for me to finish with my phone calls.

I walked up to Bobby and gave her a hug. "Look, I hope you don't mind, but I've got to go talk to Chief Snoddy and Ellen George. Kurt's at The Festival headquarters and they expect Ellen to be there shortly."

Bobby laughed. "Rebecca and I were just going to start some serious earring shopping and wondered if we should let you men go off on your own."

"Well," I turned to Jack, "I don't know what's going to be more interesting—earring shopping with two attractive women or investigating blackmail."

"I've shopped for earrings before but never investigated blackmail. I'll tag along with you if I won't be in the way."

"You're welcome to come."

At the entrance to the food court, we parted company: Bobby and Rebecca in pursuit of earrings; Jack and I off to ask favors and report findings.

CHAPTER 14
SATURDAY AFTERNOON

Jack and I cut through the crowd, walking with more purpose than those who were looking at the exhibits, artwork, artists, and each other.

It was Saturday afternoon in the fall and, in the South, college football would not be denied. I hear that there are pockets of similar behavior throughout the country and that may be true. But this isn't a pocket; it's a region covering multiple states, and in all of them college football reigns supreme.

Among the Halloween costumes were scattered college loyalists decked out in school colors to varying degrees. There were fans who were content wearing a shirt or blouse of the true colors, others with hats, jackets, and scarves branding their loyalty. There were also those who had to cover every inch of their bodies from shoelaces to face paint with the two colors representing their collegiate ties.

It was easy to spot Kurt Snoddy standing near the brick headquarters building. It wasn't because the tan Archibald police uniform was striking, it was the police chief who was. I pointed him out to Jack.

"Woof, he's a big-un."

As we got closer, I could see Kurt was stroking his chin with one massive hand and shaking his head. He looked like something was bothering him and I hoped it wasn't me. Since I hadn't gotten to talk to Ellen George yet, he couldn't be fretted by what I wanted her to ask him to do.

"Kurt, you got a minute?" I needed lots more than a minute but he didn't look like he'd agree if I asked for more.

He was staring off into space and spoke without looking at me. "You serious enough about what you're doing to bring your business cards this time?"

I pulled them out and handed him one. I wasn't sure why he wanted another but didn't think I'd ask. He glanced at it and stuck it in his shirt pocket. "Just checking. You may be teachable." He looked at Jack and then back at me. He pointed at Jack with his thumb. "Who he?"

I started to tell him when Jack stuck out his hand. "Jack Harlon—spelled with an *o*—Chief Snoddy. I'm from Cranbury, Tennessee, just north and west of Nashville, we just got in last night."

Jack's hand didn't disappear in the chief's grasp like mine had.

"You in the same line of work as Crawford here?"

Jack laughed. "Private investigator? No, sir. General contractor."

"Too bad. I think he could use some help." Kurt shook himself as if to break his train of thought. "Construction? Should have gone into that myself. Done something real. Saved myself the heartache of this job. You build something it stays built."

Jack snorted. "There's heartache in any job."

Kurt nodded, glanced around, walked a few paces away from the building, and signaled us to follow him by cupping his hand and flexing his fingers at us. It was such a classic law enforcement gesture that I wondered if they practiced it in police school. I didn't remember it from my days in the Shore Patrol but maybe I missed a day of training.

Jack and I followed him until we were standing farther from the foot traffic passing by.

"You got something for me?"

I decided that Kurt must be having a bad day. He'd been easier to deal with yesterday. And what I had to say wasn't going to make things better.

"I've got those pictures you wanted—the ones off of my phone." I handed him the disk and kept on talking. "And I sent some of them—pictures of the rattlesnake—to a snake expert."

"That fella Dr. Fines was talking about?" The disk followed my business card into his shirt pocket. If he'd been a smaller man, it never would have fit. "Dr. Snake from across the river?"

"Right! This morning I sent him the pictures of the rattlesnake, to see if there was anything he could tell us. He called me just a few minutes ago. The rattlesnake isn't from around here. Wrong species entirely. It's a diamondback rattlesnake from the coastal areas—more sun and sand."

Kurt rubbed his chin with the knuckle of his right index finger. "He say how he thinks it got here? Taking a vacation? Some kind of road trip?"

"No. He—." It wasn't that I was at a loss for words. That rarely happens. I was just trying to pick the right tone.

"Just goes along with everything else that's happened today. Come on." Kurt turned his back on the building and set out across the grounds straight toward the remains of Dot's tent. We dodged around some brush and then there we were.

. . .

"Fire marshal got here this morning and it didn't take him long to tell me that the fire had been set."

I nodded my head. "You knew that yesterday."

"Are you going to stand there and tell me what I knew or listen to what I've got to say? I don't know why I'm bothering to tell you anyway."

Yep, there was no doubt in my mind that Chief Snoddy was having a bad day.

"So it was set, huh?" Jack broke in. "What else?"

"There was an empty gas can that was found outside the tent. Ask him," Kurt nodded toward me. "He found the damn thing."

I stepped into the tent circle and squatted down. The floor had dried and you could see charred and twisted debris scattered around. I picked up a burned piece of wire to use as a poker and discovered it was attached to a lot of other pieces of wire all tangled together. I tried to match it up with what I'd seen in the tent before it burned, and failed. Maybe if I looked again at the pictures I'd taken. Whatever it was seemed to be roughly rectangular in shape, but how the thinner wires fit in with the larger ones I didn't know. Kurt kept talking.

"So today I learn for certain that the gas can was missing from the tool shed The Festival has back over at headquarters. Of course the shed was unlocked. As best the volunteers can figure it was over half full when anybody saw it last. So that was what the arsonist used as accelerant."

The chief frowned. "I told the fire marshal about finding the gas can and he said—right off—that whoever had done it, had splashed the outside of the tent with the gasoline, tossed the can away, and thrown a match on the tent. He said it was a classic case—typical in every respect. Happens that way all the time, he said."

"Well, that's clearly *not* what happened. The fire was set from the inside. What did he say when he figured that out?" I looked up at Kurt. "Or did he?"

Kurt and Jack looked at me and then glanced at each other.

"I just met him today." Jack said, shrugging his shoulders. "Don't look at me."

Kurt stared intently at me and growled. "And just how do you know the fire was set from inside?"

"Hey, I was with you when we saw it was on fire." I stepped back. "Can't be in two places at the same time."

"You could have used some time-delay trick so that the fire started after you set it. Give yourself enough time to be somewhere with witnesses when the fire starts. That's what the fire marshal figures the arsonist did."

I pointed at the floor of the tent—the plastic lip that kept ground water from getting into the tent. The lip that Dot had tripped over. "The lip is charred on the inside all the way around. Not so on the outside."

"Huh," said Kurt. "So was the canvas—what the fire marshal could find. Fire had clearly started inside the tent. That's what knocked him off his high horse and got him interested. Got him really working."

Kurt and Jack walked around looking at the remains of the tent. Nodding to themselves as they examined the charring.

"That's when he decided the gasoline hadn't been splashed on the walls from the inside either."

"Makes sense," said Jack. "You go tossing gasoline around inside a tent and you're going to get it on you. Not to mention the fumes. You'd reek of gasoline."

"Right," agreed Kurt. "And the fumes are the dangerous part. That's what goes boom."

"So what did he do? Pour it out of the can and make a pool of gasoline? I guess the flooring would have trapped the liquid, at that." I'd squatted down next to what should have been the entrance of the tent to get a closer look.

"That's the way the fire marshal figured it. It's a two-gallon can—over half full—say one gallon poured out on the floor. It wouldn't be that deep. He thinks it pooled up against that wall since the floor's not perfectly level. Then the arsonist lit a candle—one of those short, squatty kind—he called it something."

"Votive?" It was the only kind of candle I knew of that had a name—other than birthday cake candles.

"Yeah. Sounds like it." He nodded. "Anyway, they make them with a little metal disc on the bottom—holds the wick or something. He was looking for one of those."

"Would that work? I'd think the fumes would catch on fire." I'd always been a little nervous around gasoline.

"You never worked with gasoline much, did you, Crawford? What do you think, Jack?"

"I think it sounds like a great technique for burning up a tent. The candle flame would get lower as the candle burned, meanwhile the fumes from the gasoline would collect inside the tent." Jack walked around the remains. "I'd make sure the flaps were down to trap the fumes—and I'd probably use more than one candle. Just in case one went out."

Kurt nodded. "That's what the fire marshal figures, even though he didn't find any of those disks. We figure they might have floated away with all the water the fire fighters poured on the tent. You know what bothered him the most? The gas can being outside the tent. He couldn't figure out why the arsonist hadn't left it inside. Leave it there to burn up too. The Festival was still going on. Somebody might have remembered seeing a person with a gas can."

"Did the fire marshal have any idea how long the candles burned before the fire caught?" I started looking on the ground outside the tent for metal disks. I had a vague memory of what they looked like on the bottom of a candle. Jack saw what I was doing and started searching the other side of the tent.

"No. He told me that the candles are rated for burn time but they've got to be in the right candle holder for the times to be accurate. Still, he couldn't prove it wasn't some other kind of candle. He said a minimum of thirty minutes, but he was just guessing—and said so."

"He have any idea why somebody wanted to burn Dot's tent?" I was pretty sure I knew the answer to my question even before I asked it.

"Nope. He didn't even speculate—said that some people set fires just to watch things burn. There really doesn't have to be a reason."

He started counting on his fingers. "Myself, I figure we got a range of reasons. One, just to watch it burn. Two, to destroy blackmail evidence. Three, to get back at Dot. Four, to hope it spreads and catches most of The Festival on fire."

Kurt shook his head. "If the same people who broke in downtown are involved with burning the tent, I figure it probably has something to do with blackmail, but why would anybody think Dot would keep evidence in the tent? And who's to say they're the same people?"

His phone rang and he answered it. Whoever it was on the other end was doing all the talking. At first, Kurt just stood there nodding his head occasionally, then he pulled a small notebook out of his pocket and started taking notes. Jack and I went back to scouring the ground.

. . .

Don't know what good it would have done to find what was left of the candles but we were giving it the old college try. I wondered if we'd be more successful if we'd given it the old high school try and what the difference would be.

Kurt put up his phone and walked over to us. I put an interested expression on my face and waited for him to speak.

"When you get up in the morning you have no idea what the day will bring. Granddad used to say that all the time and then he would chuckle." Kurt himself chuckled. "I used to wonder what he meant but never asked him."

I glanced at Jack and then back at Kurt. "Sounds profound, Kurt. What has the day brought? If you don't mind my asking."

"Don't know what it all means yet, but I'm sure it means something. The woman on the phone?" He glanced at both of us. "Medical examiner—been doing autopsies for a couple of years now but had never seen a death by snakebite. Figured she'd never see another, so she wanted to learn from this one.

"You just got to love professionals like that, don't you? Let's sit." Kurt walked over to a picnic table and Jack and I followed him. He sat on one side; we took the other.

Kurt pulled back out the notepad. "First thing the examiner noted was that what Dot died of wasn't right for a rattlesnake bite. The cause of death wasn't right.

"According to her, rattlesnake poison—venom I mean—rattlesnake venom is primarily hemotoxic in nature." Kurt waved one hand in the air. "She went on to describe what that means but it doesn't really matter to us. Dot died from neurotoxic venom. The first attacks the blood system; the second, the nervous system." Kurt looked down at his notes. "The ME also said some rattlesnakes have been reported to have a measurable amount of neurotoxic venom but the jury is still out on whether it's enough to make much difference. Their primary venom is hemotoxic."

We were all silent. Jack and I stared at Kurt. Kurt stared at his notebook.

"And that means what," I asked. Sometimes you just have to spell it out for me.

"I have no idea what some of it means, but I know one thing, it means I arrested the wrong snake." Kurt sighed. "Near as I can figure it so far, the rattlesnake that wasn't even supposed to be here was—at best—a witness to the death of Dot Fields. Oh, yeah, there were multiple bites—wounds. Examiner said the snake that killed Dot must have bitten her twenty times or so."

"Twenty times!" Jack was shocked. "That's some mean snake. Or snakes?"

"Wait a minute!" I protested. "I was there. I saw you catch it. The snake was there—in the tent—and it was the only snake in the tent and it had a rattle on the end of its tail—still does, I assume. There's got to be some mistake about the venom—can that change?"

"Crawford—listen to yourself—the snake hasn't got any way to change what venom it's using. What do you figure? It wakes up in the morning and decides to load up with a different venom?"

Kurt looked at Jack. "Multiple snakes? Interesting idea. One problem. Where did they all go?"

"What kind of snake has the right kind of venom—the neuro-what-ever kind?" Jack, at least, was asking sensible questions.

"Could have been a coral snake." Kurt went back to his notes. "The ME really did her homework. Coral snakes are the only snakes in the United States that have neurotoxic venom and fangs. Except for those new studies she mentioned about rattlesnakes." Kurt looked up from the notebook. "But I don't think we need to worry about those."

Jack and I nodded as if we actually knew something about the subject, but we had sense enough not to say anything.

Kurt too nodded before looking down at his notes again. "Dot had puncture wounds—fang marks—from a pretty good-size snake. ME said she hadn't found out yet how far apart their fangs are—coral snakes, that is—but she made measurements of the bites—strikes—how far apart the fangs were on Dot."

"All twenty of them?" I was beginning to calm down. "Coral snakes aren't that big are they? Kind of slender, right?"

"Yeah," Kurt smiled, "our friend at the morgue says the snake must have been 'bad tempered' to have struck so many times."

I could tell I was thinking in circles. "But we don't have coral snakes this far north."

"You just finished telling me that Dr. Snake said the rattlesnake wasn't supposed to be around here either." Kurt didn't raise his voice, instead it got deeper. "You got one snake that isn't supposed to be here, what's a second? The more the merrier. Maybe Archibald is getting to be a popular vacation spot for snakes."

"There are artists from all over the country here this weekend. One of them must have brought both snakes with him and then they escaped. Traveling in one of those RVs they might as well bring their pets with them. Could have dropped the cages and busted them." Jack thought for a second. "Probably too ashamed to admit it—or too scared of somebody suing them."

"I could see that happening." Kurt looked at Jack and nodded approvingly. "I like the way you think. Yeah, embarrassed and ashamed. What do you think, Crawford?"

. . .

They turned to look at me.

"It was murder. Deliberate, premeditated, calculated murder." Immediately I felt better. I'd never felt right—comfortable—investigating blackmail—but murder?

I could do that.

Kurt and Jack looked at each other and then back at me. "What the hell are you talking about?" Kurt was shaking his head. "Blackmail not exciting enough for you? Now you want to introduce murder. Not just murder but murder by snake. Did they drop you on your head when you were little? How many times? Whoever heard of killing somebody with a snake?"

"I have." Now Kurt and I stared at Jack.

"Hadn't thought about it in years—but yeah," he nodded his head. "I certainly have—when I was in the army. I was a grunt, of course—just the one hitch—but the career guys all had stories. Some of them must have been true."

I thought about it. There had been stories in the navy, too. Usually they involved somebody "falling" over the side of the ship late at night and far from shore.

Jack continued. "We'd be out on patrol or in the bush, and come evening the bitching would start. And then somebody would mention that he'd heard of an incompetent second looie who had been such a danger to his men that he had to be taken

care of before he got everybody killed. It was simple—a hand
grenade in his bunker, a push out of a copter, a snake in his
sleeping bag . . ." Jack's voice trailed off.

We all sat there for a little while.

I broke the silence. "It's easier for me to believe that
somebody put the snake in Dot's tent than it is to believe that it
just found its way to her tent. Particularly when the snake's not
even supposed to be here."

"You've done this before." Kurt was rubbing his chin. "That
double murder a couple of months ago. You turned a suicide and
food poisoning into premeditated murder."

Jack's eyes widened. Maybe he hadn't been listening when
Rebecca—or Bobby—had told him about it. It was a cinch that
one of them had.

"I didn't turn anything into anything. It was just the truth."
Don't know why I get defensive when people act like it was
some big deal—but I do. "Can that medical examiner tell if it
was a coral snake, for sure? She's the one who's making a case
for murder."

Kurt took a deep breath. "I suspect she's already trying to
identify the species. She's a smart woman and this has got her
scratching her head trying to figure it out."

He stood up. "Damn. I've got a campground full of suspects
and almost all of them headed out tomorrow afternoon. Can't
keep them from leaving town. Don't know who's a suspect and
who isn't. I liked it better as an accident—damn if I didn't.
Crap." His shoulders slumped. "Now I've got to call Sammy and
tell him we think it's murder. And Andrew Boyd. This is going
to mean the countywide Multijurisdictional Homicide Unit for
sure." Kurt's smile was a little lopsided as he added, "Least
you'll get to see your friend Jim Ward now that it's a homicide."

I watched him walk away, pulling his phone out of his pocket as he did. He hadn't asked me if I knew who had done it and I was glad. I knew all right—or thought I did—but, as God is my witness, I had no idea how the hell I was going to prove it—or even if it could be proved.

Jack coughed and I realized I was staring off into space. I shook my head and stood up. "Okay, let's go over to headquarters. I still need to talk to Ellen George."

. . .

I almost went back and picked up one of the jumble of wires I'd found but realized that it was now a crime scene and the police would be tagging and storing items as evidence. It's just as well; they'd need it.

. . .

We went back across the grounds and into the HQ building. Same as the other times. Coba at the table, line of people in front of her, volunteers scattered around the room performing various tasks, everybody busy but chattering pleasantly. I wondered what headquarters had been like when Dot was running things then remembered that she would have been fortune-telling about now. So maybe things would have been this relaxed. Somehow I doubted it.

I'd hoped to find Ellen but wasn't having any luck. There weren't any other board members here that I knew, so we got in line. Coba might know where the board members were and one might walk in while we waited.

"Interesting, how quickly the chief agreed with you about it being—," Jack looked around the room and continued, "not what he thought it was."

I grinned. I was getting to really like Jack Harlon. "Oh, I think he hadn't been satisfied with the original explanation—as it were—from the beginning. I know I wasn't."

Jack shrugged his shoulders. "I was fine with it. I think most people were. I'll ask Rebecca. She's good about things like that. Besides she'll know half the people here before we leave."

I smiled. "Bobby's pretty gregarious herself."

"Sure." He nodded. "But not like Rebecca. Wait and you'll see what I'm talking about."

"I'll do that. How do you like your steaks?"

"That's right, Bobby said you were grilling steaks tonight. I like mine rare, but I'll take it whatever way it comes off the grill."

At that point we went off on grilling and grills, propane versus charcoal, marinades, dry rubs, and indirect heat.

"Yes?"

I hadn't realized that we'd gotten to the head of the line so I was surprised by Coba's question.

"Oh, hey, Coba. You wouldn't know where I could find Ellen George this afternoon would you?"

"Mrs. George does a lot of volunteering with the Friends of Music. Why don't you try their tent, there." She pointed to a spot on the map before us. I was glad to see that the map was upside down for her, which meant it was right side up for the Festival-goer.

"I understand that you were with Police Chief Snoddy at the fortune-telling tent site earlier."

The way she said it—without any rising inflection at the end—meant it was just a fact. And so it was. But most people make it sound like a question, not a statement.

"Sure enough. Just talking to him about what the fire marshal had to say. Why?"

"I was wondering if he'd given you any idea when we'd be able to clean up the site. That kind of mess isn't The Festival way. We keep our grounds neat and tidy."

"I'm afraid you're going to have to talk to Chief Snoddy about that. It's up to the police, but it shouldn't be much longer."

Coba gave a tiny snort. I wasn't sure if it was out of frustration or just what. "If you find Mrs. George, tell her I'm trying to get it cleaned up."

"Sure enough!"

Jack and I headed out of the building. He waited until we were out on the path. "A murder scene. And it 'shouldn't take much longer?' What's up with that?"

"You read a lot of murder mysteries, Jack?"

"Not up to now, I haven't. I'm thinking I've missed something."

I smiled. "Well, I've read a lot more of them than I've worked on, but I'll let Kurt Snoddy be the one that breaks the news it's murder—not me."

We took a few more paces. "Besides, she batted her eyes at me. I've met the woman three or four times and *now* she bats her eyes?"

Jack looked at me, shook his head, and laughed.

. . .

The Friends of Music had gotten a double space for their booth and it was even a little isolated—isolated for The Festival. Judging from the noises coming from the tent the isolation was deliberate. I remembered now. The Friends brought a bunch of different musical instruments to The Festival and encouraged "children of all ages" to make music. Judging from the bleats, squeaks, and squeals, talent was not a requirement. I was glad the Friends had only acoustic instruments. Kids were limited to their own lung and muscle power. It was loud enough.

I stuck my head into the tent and spotted Ellen right away. She was showing a young boy how to hold a violin under his chin and draw the bow across the strings. She spotted me and gave me a nod. The boy continued sawing away as Ellen gestured to another volunteer to come take her place. I backed out of the tent and Jack and I walked a few paces away from the entrance. It looked like the Friends of Music was doing great business attendance-wise. I wondered how often they encountered actual jewels-in-the-rough and if all the misses were worth the small number of hits.

The provost's wife came out of the tent and walked over to where we were standing—calm and collected as always. This time there was one strand of hair that had escaped her neatly arranged hair. I chalked it up to dealing with small children. I'd have pulled my hair out by this time.

"Mrs. George, I want you to meet—wait you probably already have met—." If the Georges were such good friends with Bobby and had known her for years, they were almost bound to have met Rebecca and Jack.

Ellen stuck out her hand. "Hello, Jack. So Bobby talked you and Rebecca into coming back for another Festival. Good to see you again."

Jack laughed. "It has been a while. Good to see you too. We missed the last couple of Festivals but this year Rebecca was bound and determined to get down here—for some reason."

"Are they off on their earring hunt? As I recall, they each buy a pair and then swap one with each other to make mismatched pairs. The trick is to find ones that go together."

"Got it in one." Jack smiled. "I know Rebecca and Bobby have several identical mismatched sets. Crawford here is just getting introduced to life with the dynamic duo."

"How's he doing so far?"

"Well, it's early days but he's holding up pretty well, I'd say."

"Has he gotten you interested in detective work? He's supposed to be investigating something for The Festival board even as we speak."

"He's letting me tag along with him while he's working."

Ellen turned to me. "I know you weren't stopping by the music tent just to introduce Jack to me. Does this mean you've got something to report? If so, why don't you wait until Joyce gets here." Ellen pointed down the path at the figure of Joyce Fines striding toward us. "That way you won't have to repeat yourself. She's early. Her shift doesn't start for another half hour."

"Dr. Fines volunteers at the music booth?" For some reason I found that surprising.

"She calls it the place musical instruments go to become instruments of torture."

"Ah. I see." I didn't really see.

"She doesn't play a musical instrument but always volunteers to help out. Says anybody can strike a drum."

"Over here, Joyce." Ellen waved. "James has something he wants to tell us."

Joyce looked at me questioningly. "Dr. Fines, this is Jack Harlon, a friend of mine from Cranbury, Tennessee."

She nodded at Jack and then to Ellen and me. "Are we having a meeting? It must be the blackmail investigation, yes?"

I shook my head. "Please don't repeat this until Chief Snoddy makes an official announcement, but I wanted to tell you that he has decided Dot was murdered. Somebody deliberately put a venomous snake in her tent—a snake that had been imported for the purpose, we think."

Ellen and Joyce stood stock-still. I watched as they processed the information. Joyce was the first to speak.

"The rattlesnake was imported? It wasn't indigenous?"

"Its species was completely wrong for here—apparently there are different kinds of rattlesnakes—but a rattlesnake wasn't what killed Dot anyway. There was another snake involved. The venom wasn't rattlesnake venom."

Joyce's eyebrows rose. "Even though it wasn't the snake that killed Dot it was still from somewhere else?"

"Right." Jack and I both nodded.

"How peculiar. Does this make sense to you?" Joyce looked at Ellen who shook her head.

I tried to explain. "It doesn't make much sense yet because we don't know enough to make sense out of it. But the only way it starts to make any sense at all is if Dot were killed— premeditated murder."

. . .

Ellen looked away and then back. "Someone got tired of being blackmailed and killed her?"

"We don't have a motive yet. That certainly could be a reason. Before we discovered it was murder, I had planned on asking the board to ask the police to investigate whether Dot had been embezzling funds from The Festival. But that's pointless now. Dot's finances will be part of the murder investigation."

The squawk of a mishandled violin hung in the air.

Ellen glanced at the tent and then back to me. "James, when you came into the tent, I thought you had stopped by to give me a status report on your investigation into the allegations of blackmail. Despite this new development, I believe we're still interested in knowing for certain if Dot had been using The Festival as a cover for her blackmailing."

I gestured helplessly. "I haven't gotten very far with that. I've got one person who says he was being blackmailed, but I can't prove that it was happening to anyone else. I talked with a police detective and we agreed that the best thing to do would be to 'follow the money.' I wanted to look at The Festival's books, but really needed access to Dot's records—bank statements, tax filings—any kind of paper trail that might show suspicious income. I'm guessing that part of Dot's blackmailing had something to do with the stipends your guest artists receive."

"Because this was the first year Chad Harris gained guest artist status?" Ellen was quick.

I nodded. "Something like that. It was a place to start. Is the stipend a fixed amount?"

"No. No. It varies based on the artist's needs, skills, and following." Ellen glanced at Joyce who gave her a confirming nod. "We revisit the amounts every year—on an artist-by-artist basis. Why do you ask?"

"Just wondering. How do you pick an artist to get a stipend?"

Ellen grimaced. "In theory any member of the board could nominate somebody but in practice the director makes suggestions. Both as to which artists and how large a stipend. The board votes yes or no but most of the time we go with the director's recommendations."

"Really?"

Joyce spoke up. "I see what you're getting at. It would be easy for Dot to tell an artist that she'd get him a stipend if he agreed to split it with her."

"Or just hand the whole amount over to her," I suggested. "The whole amount or more—depending on what she had on her victim. Were the stipends in the form of checks or cash?"

"We always wrote checks." Ellen looked thoughtful. "Each year there were certain artists whose stipends Dot suggested increasing. We make those decisions after The Festival closes— decisions about whom we are going to sponsor."

"Do you remember which ones?"

Joyce and Ellen looked at each other, then Ellen spoke. "We could come up with a list. Give us thirty minutes or so."

"Absolutely. You want me to keep working on the blackmail angle. Anything else? If not, Jack and I are going to see Chad Harris, and then we've got a meeting with Kurt— Chief Snoddy, that is. He told me I could call him Kurt." I grinned. "That is until he gets tired of me and tells me not to call him Kurt.

Jack stirred. "Don't forget Coba's message."

"Oh, right, thanks, Jack. I had forgotten.

"Ellen, Coba said to tell you that she's waiting for permission from Chief Snoddy to have the burnt tent area cleaned up. It doesn't look like the arsonist had far to go to get what he needed to torch the tent. He used The Festival's gas can that was in a storage shed."

"I told Coba not to worry about cleaning that up until after The Festival." Ellen didn't look pleased. I suspected that Coba was going to be reminded of what Ellen had said.

"Mr. Crawford. I hesitate to mention this because I don't want to make too much of it." Joyce paused.

"And what would 'it' be, Dr. Fines?"

"It probably isn't significant, but the artist you're going to see—Chad Harris—was once a student at the university. He graduated with a degree in biology, with honors, and started graduate school. He was considered an up-and-coming young scholar until he decided his skills working with glass were artistic not practical."

"And this could be relevant because?"

"Oh. I thought I said. One gets an undergraduate degree in biology. His graduate studies concentrated on herpetology."

"They did? Well, that is interesting. Thank you for mentioning it. I'll keep it in mind."

I looked at Jack and muttered, "Wonder if he keeps pets—or collects them?"

"James." I could tell that Ellen was thinking of something the way she said my name. I had the premonition of impending adult advice.

"Yes, Mrs. George." I felt all of thirteen—maybe fifteen.

"Chief Snoddy seems to think well of you. Has he complained to you about your involvement in his case—or your investigation of the blackmail?"

"Well, he was a tad testy a time or two, but he was having a bad day. I mean he hasn't told me to stop calling him Kurt like he said he would." Not yet, I added mentally.

"You know this isn't the kind of murder he's used to solving. He'll probably appreciate your assistance—particularly if you endeavor not to annoy him. Your tendency for flippancy might irritate him."

"Yes, ma'am. I'll do my best."

"All right. It's time I was back at my post—and time for Joyce to start. We'll work on the list of artists. Should we just leave it at headquarters for you to pick up?"

"Uh, any chance you could text it to me? Or email?" I pulled out one of my cards and Joyce took it from me.

"I'm glad to see you're treating your new career with a little more professionalism." She looked at the card and sniffed. "I wondered why you didn't have one when we met."

Dragon Ladies. The expression popped into my mind as I looked at Ellen and Joyce. Not women to underestimate—or to cross.

Ellen nodded at Jack. "Good to see you—give Rebecca my best."

Jack and I set off down the pathway toward Chad's booth while Ellen and Joyce headed in the direction of the discordant sounds coming from the Friends of Music booth.

As we were walking away, Jack said, "How you going to do that, Crawford?"

"What? Endeavor not to annoy Kurt?" I grinned.

Jack nodded and smiled.

"Beats the hell out of me."

. . .

Foot traffic was heavier than ever so it was slow-going along the paths. We'd slipped into single-file and were inching our way along when I got a text message from Kurt. The head of the security firm that patrolled the grounds at night was coming in to meet with him in thirty minutes. I acknowledged the text and wondered if I should text Bobby.

"Think we ought to check in with Bobby and Rebecca?" I'd read the message while walking but had to stop to respond to Kurt's text—unlike any self-respecting teenager.

"They know how to get in touch with us."

I nodded and started up again.

We passed Ted Lowe's booth. The picture of Dot was on display. It was still unfinished; he was trying to sell it as is. Cutting his losses I supposed. He was somebody who wasn't getting a stipend who was glad Dot was dead. I wondered if he'd ever painted snakes. Our murderer was somebody who knew snakes—knew enough about how to handle them to move them around and not get bitten.

I stopped so short that Jack almost ran into me. "Sorry. I still haven't learned how to type and walk." I pulled out my phone and typed myself a reminder: ask Kurt to have somebody check on doctors' offices, hospitals, emergency rooms, doc-in-a-boxes to see if anybody had come in for snakebite treatment lately, just in case.

There were several shoppers in Chad's booth and visibly fewer items on display. He was ringing up a sale when Jack and I got there so we wandered around looking at what he was selling while waiting to talk to him. Ringing up a sale? There was another phrase that had lost its meaning. How many cash registers ring nowadays?

In Chad's case, he didn't even have a cash register. A sales pad, lockbox, and credit card scanner attachment for his cell phone. I bet he had a point-of-sale app on his smartphone.

Probably emailing receipts to his clients—and capturing their email addresses too. Clever! All the while saving paper—good for the environment.

I wanted to show Jack the cat sculpture I'd seen in the booth but it wasn't where I remembered it. There was a small figure of a dog, that I hadn't seen before. It was on its stomach, forelegs straight out in front, tail wrapped around, head cocked to one side, looking up at the viewer. If I wasn't careful I'd fill the house up with knick-knacks.

I was trying to describe to Jack the way the black cat had looked encased in glass when a voice came over my shoulder. "That was my sculpture of Bast—the cat goddess—in the form of a cat. Glad you liked it."

I turned around and was face to face with Chad Harris. His hair was brown, lank, longish, touching his collar at points. He had a broad forehead that tapered down to a narrow chin, smooth skin without a hint of beard—almost baby-faced except for his eyes—they showed his age—early thirties, at a guess, and life hadn't been smooth for all of those years.

"Just sold it earlier today. Woman was thrilled to find it."

"You have another? Or will you make another?"

He smiled and shook his head. "No. That was one of a kind. Made it during my black period. He pointed at the sculpture of the snake I'd noticed before. "Like the mamba there. I was trying to stretch myself but I decided to go another way with it."

I noticed that there was a bandage on the base of his thumb. "Hurt yourself?"

He glanced at his hand. "Oh. Yeah, hazards of the trade—glass can cut you."

I stuck out my right hand and he shook it. "Chad, my name is James Crawford—most call me Crawford." I pointed at Jack. "My friend Jack Harlon."

Chad and Jack shook hands and I noted while Chad's hand was as long as Jack's, his fingers were delicate by comparison. I was getting a little tired of having my hand swallowed up.

I pulled out a business card, handed it to him, and gave him some time to read it. "Board of The Festival hired me the other night. The night you accused Dot Fields of attempted blackmail."

Chad's eyes flicked down at the card and then from Jack to me.

"I'm a general contractor out of Cranbury, Tennessee." Jack raised both hands and took one step back.

"I'd like to ask you about what happened that night. Jack's just along for The Festival."

"I could make myself scarce," Jack offered.

Chad snorted. "Don't know why I'm reacting that way. Hell, I refused to be blackmailed because I don't want to live my life that way. Hiding and denying stuff. No. If I did it, I'll own up to it." He walked over to where some director's chairs were set up—the tall ones that could serve as bar stools. "Do you mind? I've been on my feet most of the day."

. . .

It was one of those oddities of timing. He'd had customers when we walked in—had been selling stuff—and now his booth was empty except for Jack and me.

"Looks like you've been selling stuff right and left." Jack and I followed him to the chairs.

He eased himself up into his chair and stared at me. "Is that what you wanted to ask me about?"

"Nope." I pulled my phone out of my back pocket before sitting. "Sorry for the asinine comment. I'm new at this. I'll try not to do that again."

"New at this?" Chad cocked his head to one side. "Really? I would have said—oh, shit, now I'm doing it."

"It's a southern thing," said Jack. "We have to exchange a few pleasantries before we're comfortable getting down to business."

Chad and I looked at each other and then shrugged our shoulders almost simultaneously.

"Was she trying to blackmail you about the stipend?"

Chad snorted. "She was trying to blackmail me *for* the stipend. Said all I had to do was endorse the check and give it back to her. She'd not mention a word about you-know-what and I really wouldn't have lost anything because the only reason I got the stipend was she nominated me. And the only reason she nominated me was she knew all about how stupid I'd been."

"Look, Chad. Nobody gets blackmailed because of *being* stupid. They get blackmailed because of *doing* something stupid."

"Right. And there were two parts of stupid in my case. Doing something stupid and getting caught at doing something stupid." He shook his head and then leaned back in his chair. "How much do you know about exhibiting at The Festival? You know it's a juried event, right?"

"Yeah, but I'm not sure what that actually means."

"In nonjuried shows all you have to do is pay the entrance fee to display your works. Sort of a first-come, first-served approach. Church fundraisers, school fairs, flea markets—

community-based events are almost always nonjuried. For the public, this means there's no guarantee of the quality you'll find there. From the artist's point of view, it means you don't know what others are going to be selling and for how much. If you're starting out, you can do okay at craft shows like that or it can be really sucky. If you make mistakes and keep showing up at places where the customers aren't interested in what you're trying to sell, you can lose money."

He rubbed the palms of his hands with his thumbs, one after the other, as he talked. "Starving artist is such a trite cliché that it's embarrassing to be one. Trust me, I know. My parents weren't particularly pleased that I dropped out of graduate school to play around with glass. Can't fault them. College loans are hard to pay off if you don't make enough money to eat and it's hard to make art if you can't buy supplies."

Chad shifted his weight on the canvas chair then leaned back. "Getting accepted to a juried show is a way to break the cycle—the vicious circle. And once one show has accepted you, other shows are more likely to accept you—a cycle of success. The problem is getting that first break.

"The Festival was going to be my big break. I'd seen what got accepted—what prices people were willing to pay—and I decided I'd do anything to be able to show there—here. Anything."

"Uh-oh." I heard Jack whisper.

"I was working hard on getting a portfolio together—pieces to show—when a friend told me she thought the deadline for applying had passed. I freaked. I'd sent off for an application but hadn't done more than glance at it. I hadn't missed the deadline—it was the next day. All I had to do was fill out the

form, attach pictures of ten works of art, and get it to The
Festival offices before close of business."

Chad lifted his head and looked at us. "I had nine. Nine. I'd
even sold a piece the week before—if I'd known. So I sent ten
pictures of artwork in the next day." He took a deep breath.
"Nine pieces of art I'd created—and one I hadn't."

"You submitted somebody else's work as your own?"

"Yeah. Thought I'd gotten away with it too."

I leaned forward in my chair. "Who spotted it? Dot?"

He nodded his head, eyes staring off into space.

"Let me guess," I sat back. "She accepted your application.
You came to The Festival and were a hit—sold out. And then
she told you she knew you'd lied. Knew that you had
plagiarized—no that's not the word—what is the word—
presented somebody's work as your own."

"Yeah. Said the nine that were mine were good enough to
justify letting me in the show. That ten wasn't a hard and fast
rule. That actually the rules said 'up to ten.' So she'd pulled the
fake one out of my application and sent it on to the judges."

"Shit." Jack summed up my feelings perfectly.

"So, Thursday night she calls me over to her fortune-telling
table, shows me a photocopy of the original photograph, and
tells me she wants me to endorse The Festival check over to her.
I wouldn't have gotten in if it hadn't been for her. That I would
be blackballed from any future juried show once the word got
out that I had submitted somebody else's work as my own. Just
sign my name and go on about my business."

"Must have been hard to tell her no."

Chad shook his head. "It would have been—if she hadn't
made me so mad. She was smirking at me. Like she knew I
wouldn't do anything *that* stupid. That I'd do the sensible,

reasonable thing." He gave me a lopsided grin. "But being an artist wasn't the sensible, reasonable thing to do either."

. . .

I was wondering just what I was going to do with the glass dog as we headed back to HQ. I could put it on my desk, but I couldn't be sure The Black wouldn't knock it off. There was room on the mantle in the den. But TB had been known to get up on the mantle.

"Glad he had some customers before we left."

"He did look kind of despondent as we were leaving, didn't he?" I glanced over at Jack who'd escaped Chad's booth without buying anything.

"Not nearly as despondent as he was before you said that you saw no reason to repeat what he'd told you unless he turned out to be the guy who killed Dot."

"Yeah, shouldn't have mentioned anybody killing Dot. Kurt won't like it." I gave up trying to figure out a safe way to carry the dog that left my hands free. "There's Kurt over there. We must be early. I don't see anybody that looks like a security guard."

. . .

"Whatcha buy?" Kurt Snoddy pointed at the box in my hand with a toothpick. "Can't be food. I don't see any grease stains." The toothpick went back into his mouth.

"Late lunch?" I opened up the box and showed him the figurine.

"Hummph." He gave a thumbs-up.

I deduced that he liked the figurine and he had something stuck between his teeth probably because he'd just finished eating some Festival food—hence the reference to grease. I admit that not all the edibles for sale at The Festival were greasy or fried but I was feeling pretty good about my overall scenario—detecting-wise.

Kurt pulled the toothpick out of his mouth and flipped it onto the ground.

After all, I thought, it was biodegradable. Why not?

"Haven't heard from the examiner." Kurt glanced around the grounds. "Security guy's name is Guy Nelson. Used to be a law enforcement officer somewhere else—I forget. I've had no problems with him—he does okay. I asked him to come by early so we could talk. His firm supplies the nighttime security for The Festival. Has for years. He's not in grief over Dot's death but might still think it was an accident.

I thought for a second. "You going to ask him about the gate?"

He looked straight at me. "I'm going to ask him questions and he's going to answer me. If I don't ask a question you think ought to be asked, you can ask it. If I think it's a good question, I'll get him to answer it. If I don't, then it's up to him whether to answer you.

He smiled slyly, "He might have an attitude about answering your questions, but I'll let you be the judge of that."

Kurt turned to Jack. "How are you enjoying The Festival? Doesn't seem like you'd be having much fun following this fellow around."

Kurt and Jack were bantering back and forth, so I took a few steps back. Jack seemed to get along with everybody. I was trying to get all the pieces to fall into place—to get things to click. That's what Jim Ward called it—no, that's what he said I called it when I began to make sense out of what had happened in my first murder case.

. . .

"I'm glad to see you're not too proud to wear a uniform, Chief Snoddy!"

I looked up to see a man in uniform walking up to Kurt and Jack. He was wearing a dark blue Eisenhower jacket, gray slacks with a dark blue stripe down the outside of each leg. The stripe matched the jacket color. Light blue shirt with a button-down collar and what looked like a black bolo tie. I couldn't make out what the slide was supposed to be but at a guess it was a shield emblazoned with Nelson Security or whatever the company name was. His shoes were black sneakers and he had a ball cap with some kind of symbol on the crown.

I'd expected him to be fat and sloppy. I was wrong—way wrong. The uniform was crisp, clean, and tailored and he must know his way around the weight room. I was relieved to see he wasn't wearing jackboots and carrying a riding crop. He was the kind of guy who looked good in a uniform.

I deduced that my not wanting to be licensed as a uniformed security guard might have been misunderstood in some places.

The man stuck his hand out and Kurt shook it. "Guy, I want you to meet—"

"The asshole who was so repelled by the fact that the private investigator license also allowed him to wear a uniform that he refused that part? Is that who this dipshit with the shit-eating grin is—James Fucking Crawford?" He had squared off on Jack, hands on his hips.

"Nope." Jack's grin never faded. "I'm the asshole's friend. My name's Jack Harlon."

By that time I'd walked up to stand by Jack. I was grinning too. "I'm the asshole. Did you just call my friend a dipshit?"

Jack and I were standing there grinning while Nelson tried to recover. "Well, I'm just saying that if you're a friend of his then you've got problems too."

Jack turned to look at me. "I believe he feels that you are a bad influence and my associating with you is ill-advised."

"And we should believe him because—he's wearing a uniform? Or because he jumps to conclusions?"

By now, Guy Nelson's face was bright red. "Well ain't you the funny ones. You won't think it's so funny when I get through—."

"Shut up all of you." Kurt's growl was very effective. Guy stopped in midthreat.

I opened my mouth but the glare I got from Kurt kept me silent.

"I said shut up. That goes for you smart alecks and for you." Kurt stuck his head in Guy's face. "Were you about to threaten somebody in front of a law enforcement officer? Are you that stupid? At least behave yourself around me. Got it?"

Guy Nelson nodded his head and kept his mouth closed.

Kurt turned a menacing glance my way. "And you can cut out the jokes for awhile, got it? I don't want to hear them."

I nodded. There are times when my tongue runs wild and free but not this time—this time it seemed willing to cooperate.

"For the record," Kurt looked back and forth between us, "I think uniforms are a good idea. It makes it easy for the public to identify us as people who can help them. Gives them some confidence that a stranger could help. I used to argue with Dot until I gave up and just did it my way. She wanted my men to dress in civvies while on the grounds. Said the uniforms spoiled the atmosphere of The Festival, ruined the ambiance or some such. Made the crowd nervous." Kurt stopped short. "Huh, guess if you were taking advantage of The Festival to blackmail people, seeing officers in uniform might make you nervous." He looked around and chuckled.

"Can I just say something?"

Kurt looked at me. "You go right ahead, Crawford. I'm impressed that you asked."

"I'm retired—on pension. I didn't go into private investigation to put food on my table, a roof over my head, or the wolf away from my door. I didn't want to compete with those that do. That's what I was trying to say when I refused that part of the standard license."

Kurt rocked back and forth on his heels, glanced at Guy Nelson and then at Jack, then spoke. "You might have done better if you'd kept your mouth shut and turned down any of those jobs people were stupid enough to offer you. I'm thinking you'd make a lousy security guard. That's what I'm thinking."

Nobody spoke.

"Now," Kurt turned to Guy, "what you got for me? What was happening on the grounds Thursday night?"

. . .

It was obvious early on that Guy had known the blackmailing side of Dot Fields. He never admitted it, but it was clear he had been working for her under duress. Pride in doing a job right had been corrupted by years of frustration. I suspected that when Dot handed him the check for providing security at The Festival, he endorsed it and handed it right back to her. And the more he charged The Festival, the more money she got. It must have really rankled to pay income tax on income you never received.

The security he provided suffered as a result. Too few people on patrol, too long between patrols, and his people could sense his resentment. In short, nobody saw anyone tamper with The Festival gates. Dot's tent was off the main pathway so it got even less attention than the gates. The sound system for the music stage? That had gotten more attention but nobody who wasn't supposed to be at The Festival had been noticed around the equipment. As far as seeing snakes moving about either on their own power or with assistance, nothing.

. . .

"How about Friday morning, then?" Kurt had run out of questions and looked in my direction. I had mouthed the word "alibi."

"Where were you and can you prove it?"

"After working a night shift? Where I normally am—home asleep—alone." Guy looked at Kurt, opened his mouth, and shut it.

"What is it? I'm through asking questions. You got one?"

"Nooo," Nelson paused. "But you're asking for an alibi."

"Yeah," Kurt acknowledged it.

"Means that accidental snakebite story you gave out is a bunch of hooey. Somebody must have killed the bitch. What did they do—poison her and fake a snakebite?"

Kurt just shook his head and Guy kept talking. "Never mind. I don't really care about the details. Whoever did it did the world a favor as sure as I'm standing here. She *needed* killing."

We all stood there watching as Guy Nelson walked away.

"What did he do or not do to get blackmailed by Dot," I wondered aloud.

"Don't know and he's not going to tell us either." Kurt glanced at his wrist. "You got anything else for me?"

I checked my notes. "Yeah, how about checking around to see if anybody's been treated for snakebite lately."

He thought about it a second, then nodded his head. "Might be something there, might not. Be interesting to see. I'll let you know."

. . .

Jack and I ran into Bobby and Rebecca not far from headquarters. They both had packages, so it looked like The Festival was a success from their point of view. Rebecca had purchased a hand-made basket because she collects them but that hadn't kept them from availing themselves of its practical aspects. I added my boxed glass dog to the collection and then offered to carry the basket. An offer graciously accepted.

Everything was either wrapped up in newspaper or boxed, so there was no telling what they'd purchased but I could tell from the weight that it wasn't just earrings.

Both Jack and I had enough smarts to ask about the pursuit of earrings and had been informed that there were several pairs under consideration. The plan was to purchase them tomorrow.

We'd agreed that we were all ready to leave The Festival and headed for the gates. Everybody was ready to get back to some creature comforts—hot showers and clean clothes. I wouldn't have wanted it to rain on The Festival, but fall hadn't really started and the summer had been dry. We all, to varying degrees, were coated in dust.

At the gates, Bobby, Rebecca, and Jack headed toward the parking lots to find where they'd parked this morning while I headed for the shuttle bus stop. Jack took the basket with him and we agreed to look at each other's purchases over a cold drink at my house.

This time public transportation worked the way it should and the shuttle bus whisked me away while a line of cars were slowly creeping out of the parking lot—bucking the incoming cars of late-comers who wanted their parking spaces. It would be a while before Bobby and company got out of the lot, much less to my house.

When I got home, Tan greeted me enthusiastically and The Black feigned indifference—or maybe it wasn't feigned. I gave the house a quick once over and it looked presentable. Bobby had seen it look worse, so I had that covered. I'd spent enough time with Jack to realize he was going to take life in stride—deal with it as it came—and Rebecca, I suspected, was here to see if I was good enough for Bobby. Okay. So I was still a little nervous. The early returns looked promising but you never know. The Festival had been neutral ground. The house was not.

I hit the shower and, as the hot water worked its magic on tired muscles, my mind went back to Dot's murder. A snake as a murder weapon—I was still having trouble with that, Jack's story about second lieutenants notwithstanding. And sleeping bags are smaller and more tightly enclosed than tents. For that matter, it almost certainly hadn't happened in the United States. I knew snakes in other countries—on other continents—didn't behave like those in North America. Was it true that there were more venomous species of snake in Australia than nonvenomous? And what difference did it make?

As I was toweling dry, I realized that I was looking at this the wrong way—the snake weapon that is. What if somebody had been trying to kill Dot for some time? What if she'd had a series of accidents—or what seemed like accidents—and they were really failed attempts at murder?

I liked the concept but had no idea if it had any basis in reality. Had Dot mentioned anything about accidents? I tucked the idea into the back of my mind to let my subconscious work on it. I had guests coming over in an hour or so. Bobby said

she'd call before they came. I bet they were looking forward to
hot showers too.

The Black came into the bathroom and demanded I turn his
water fountain on for him. I was through with the sink so I
turned on the cold water faucet—just a small stream, he can't
drink very fast. It never would have occurred to me to spoil a pet
this way. But I had come back from a business trip to find TB
standing in the sink fussing at my stupidity. After I accused the
house-sitter of spoiling my cat, he admitted he'd turned the
water faucet on for The Black. His cat had trained him to do it,
and when The Black had asked, he assumed all cats did it.

It really wasn't that big a deal—except when I forgot to turn
the water off. Still, cats need fresh water—all pets do.
Something scuttled across my brain but was quickly gone. Had I
forgotten to give Tan fresh water? She shared a bowl with TB in
the house but had her own bowl outside. Might be time to refill
it.

. . .

Refreshed, I headed down the hall to the kitchen—turned
around, went back, turned off the water, and headed, once again,
to the kitchen.

The cat was walking with me, bumping up against my legs—
so much for the indifference. "So what do you think about my
idea, TB? The murderer knew that planting a venomous snake in
Dot's tent might not kill her. You can't be sure the snake will
bite. And even if it does bite, it might be a 'dry bite.' That's
when the snake doesn't inject any venom. Anyway the killer was
okay with it not working because it was set up to look like an
accident."

I was in the kitchen by then and TB jumped from floor, to counter, to top of the cabinets. Tan was working on an old rawhide bone—one with leather knots on either end. She had one end under her left paw and the other knot rested on top of her right paw so she could gnaw on it.

"If help had gotten to Dot before she died, that would have been okay too. Our killer could keep on trying, as long as the attempts were made to look like accidents. Eventually one of them would work."

I pulled the porterhouses out of the fridge and put them in the microwave so they could warm up to room temperature. The steaks were unusually thick—I'd had them cut that way—because that's what the recipe called for. The meat was safer in the microwave than on the counter. I'm not saying my pets are poorly behaved but I don't believe in putting too much trust in their ability to resist temptation.

I checked to make sure there was nothing in the oven—stopped to put the cookie sheet up where it belonged—turned on the oven to preheat for the potatoes and promptly turned it off again. I'd start preheating after Bobby called to say they were on their way. Meanwhile, I took the scalloped potatoes out of the fridge and put the casserole dish on a back burner.

That settled, I decided to get a glass of ice water. I was too thirsty to start with anything stronger. Thirsty? I got my drink and then walked over to the laundry room where the water bowl was. The bowl was full. "That's right, I filled it up before leaving." I stood and stared at the bowl like it was a clue or something.

"All animals can go without food for much longer than they can water." That was right, wasn't it? While I was standing there

Tan came in and started lapping at the water, splattering it all over the floor. Chewing rawhide dries out your mouth.

"Where was the water bowl for the snake—the corn snake, not the rattlesnake. Shouldn't it have still been in the cage or the tent? Stainless steel doesn't burn." Sometimes it's easy for me to figure out why something came bubbling up from my subconscious. Other times—like this one—I was clueless.

The phone rang and it was Bobby. They were clean, hungry, and thirsty. Was I ready for company?

Certainly! Yikes, I'd meant to feed my animals.

. . .

We had settled down on the screen porch with beers after introductions to Tan and The Black, plus a tour of the house. Rebecca and Jack had said all the right things—polite and enthusiastic, and Rebecca had brought dog and cat treats. She'd won Tan over right away but The Black was still being aloof. Fortunately, they both knew cats and weren't surprised.

Bobby had brought the ingredients for a spinach salad and Jack provided the wine for dinner—vintage zinfandel imported from a liquor store in Cranbury. He'd also brought me a bottle of single malt that the people at the liquor store had recommended. I hadn't had it or heard of it—not unusual—but it was a Speyside whiskey which was a good sign as far as I was concerned. Along with a bottle for the host, he'd brought a single-batch bourbon that I'd never heard of either. Jack was looking forward to our sitting on the screen porch performing our separate taste tests.

With all that to drink we'd started with beer. We'd learned to hydrate responsibly over the years and The Festival was thirsty-making.

. . .

"Well then, how did Tan get her name?" Bobby smiled at me. "Is there a tale behind that too?"

I'd just finished telling Rebecca and Jack the story of how The Black had come to live with me and had his name changed from Johnny to something more suitable.

"You've probably noticed that I don't have much of a high fashion sense." I was dressed in blue jeans, a knit shirt, and sneakers. The jeans were blue, the shirt white, the sneakers black, socks white, belt black. I could have varied it with a different colored knit shirt—as long as it was a primary color.

"Can't say I've noticed one way or the other." Jack grinned. "So that tells you something."

We all laughed.

"Well, you know how creative companies get with color descriptions? Cars aren't white, they're snowfall white, or cranberry red, forest green, ocean blue—stuff like that.

They all nodded their heads. "Same thing goes for pantyhose—or used to. They came in all sorts of colors—ecru, beige, caramel, taupe, nude—I forget how many—and they all meant tan but none of them were named tan."

Bobby and Rebecca giggled.

"That's just what Eleanor did when I complained about all the names for color they had on the pantyhose display."

"Let me guess," said Jack. "You volunteered—volunteered mind you—to pick something up before coming home, she asked you to pick up pantyhose, and then laughed at your choice."

"Not exactly. I decided to get one of every shade. I figured, what the hell, one of them would be right."

"Every shade?" Jack looked puzzled.

"Yeah, only they didn't have the right size in every shade, so I got one size larger and one size smaller for those shades. Then I discovered that some of them had sheer toes and some didn't. She hadn't said anything about toes. So I went back through the display making sure I had sheer toes and nonsheer toes for each shade-size combination. The trick there was that the packaging only mentioned toes if they were sheer. By that time I was figuring we could take some of them back."

"Wow," said Jack. "That must have gotten complicated."

"Yeah, it did. Then I realized that they came in patterned and un-patterned. That's when it really got complicated—keeping track of the selections—I mean."

"How many pairs did you come home with?" Bobby's voice was a little husky. Somehow Rebecca had developed the hiccups and Jack was wide-eyed and speechless.

"I didn't think then that was the point and I certainly don't now. You forget, I'm a geek and it was a geek's solution. If I'd had a cell phone I'd have called for instructions."

"And this explains why you named your dog Tan—how?" said Jack.

"It was the next weekend when we went to the shelter to adopt a puppy. Did you know that the people in the shelters will lie to you? Never mind, different story.

"You need to know that they've changed the process of pet adoption since then. The process I went through adopting The Black was much more complicated. Back then we settled on this little ball of fluff and were headed for the door while they were filling out paperwork. For whatever reason, they didn't have a record of this puppy that we were adopting, so a volunteer was filling out a form to record our adoption. She didn't want us to have any second thoughts or change our minds. So she was flying through the form asking questions as she went. When we got to hair color, she said brown—well brownish with a hint of red—should we call it auburn? Eleanor said, 'No, she's tan. It doesn't matter what shade it is, it's tan to him.' I figure the dog's lucky she didn't end up being called 'Taupe'."

Rebecca was scratching Tan's back near the base of her tail and she was ecstatic—eyes closed and the tip of her tongue sticking out. "Her fur is beautiful. I know people who would love to have hair that color, but I really wouldn't call it tan."

I opened and closed my mouth then looked at Jack who said, "I understand—completely."

. . .

I had put the potatoes in the stove when we'd gone out on the porch. When it came time to fix another round of drinks, I took that as time to start the propane grill. Normally the grill lives on the screen porch—up against the back of the chimney—but I'd moved it outside earlier. I was expecting a lot of smoke. I'd already put my seasoned cast iron griddle over the burners. It needed to be really hot before I put the steaks on.

Jack and I headed for the kitchen. Bobby and Rebecca had decided they'd wait until tomorrow for Gray Goose martinis, but they'd switch from beer to wine for a preprandial drink. I got out some wine glasses and a chilled bottle of white wine. As I was working the corkscrew, Jack and I discussed waiting until tomorrow to try the liquor he'd brought down and decided that we shouldn't wait. What if we didn't like them?

Jack took his whisky with a cube or two of ice while I take single malt whiskey straight up—with a side of water. We toasted each other and took a sip.

"Nice," I said. "Maybe a drop or two of water." I stuck my finger in the water glass, pulled it out, and shook it over the scotch. "Opens up the flavor in some malts."

"I'll tell the scotch guy at the liquor store. He's not a Scotsman but he knows his single malts—or so he claims." Jack tilted the bourbon bottle back to take a closer look at the label.

"How's yours?" I liked the impact the water had on mine.

Jack took another sip and smiled. He looked content—more than content. I picked up Bobby's wine glass and he got Rebecca's and we headed back to the porch.

"I was talking to TB this afternoon about an idea I had that made me more comfortable with the notion of a snake as a murder weapon."

"What's wrong with a snake as a murder weapon?" Jack sat down across the table from me.

Bobby shook her head. I like the way her curls bounce. "More to the point—what did The Black think of your idea?"

"I don't think TB's decided yet—still thinking about it." I looked at Jack. "A snake is not a surefire murder weapon."

Jack blinked. "I hadn't ever thought about it. Nothing's really foolproof is it? Not a big enough dose of poison. Bullets missing vital organs—same with knives and arrows. Hanging—well, no I guess—wait." He was really entering into being part of a murder investigation. "How about we say that no murderer can be sure of being successful if it is set up to be an accident. I mean, to look like an accident. If it doesn't matter if it looks like an accident or not, the murderer can just take another shot, right?"

"What if he's out of ammunition?" Rebecca looked interested.

Jack considered it for a moment. "If he's out of ammo, he can use the gun to beat the victim with."

"I'm with The Black," said Bobby, "I'd like to think about it a little more.

"And let me know when I should start the salad. I'll need ten minutes or so."

I'd stopped wearing a wristwatch—gotten out of the habit after I'd retired from the university. But I missed it when I was cooking for company.

"Excuse me."

I went into the kitchen, pulled my watch out of a drawer, and put it on my wrist, and glanced at the time. It was an hour off. Daylight savings time. It didn't matter. I could smell the potatoes by now. That meant they must be close to done. Time to get cooking before the evening got away from us.

. . .

When I stepped back on the porch, Jack, Rebecca, and Bobby had already moved on to the next part of the snake murder that was bothering me. So it wasn't just me.

"But whoever set it up so that the snake could bite Dot didn't use the rattlesnake—the obvious snake to use to kill somebody in the woods of north Alabama."

"West central, Jack." I corrected him automatically as I passed through. The grill was hot. The thermometers were all pegged. Since the probes were at the burner level, pegged didn't mean as much as it might. I lifted the lid, stuck my open palm over the griddle, and jerked it back—yep, it was hot—as if the red glow of the griddle hadn't been enough proof.

I headed back to the kitchen to gather up my primary ingredients—steaks, butter, and Dijon mustard—plus what I'd need for the sauce—brandy and minced parsley in a saucepan. I put the steaks and the rest of the ingredients on a big platter along with a very sharp boning knife and a long-handled metal spatula.

I carried the platter out to the screen porch.

"What sense does it make to have a rattlesnake on the premises when it's not the snake that killed Dot?" I was glad to hear that Bobby and I were puzzled by the same things.

"Good question! I'm about ready to cook these morsels."

"Morsels?" Jack got halfway out of his seat to get a better view. "I don't think you can call anything that size a morsel. Those are mighty fine-looking steaks, my friend."

Bobby stood up. "You're trying to tell me that it's time to make the salad? Then time out on talking about the murder! I don't want to miss anything."

Rebecca stood up and fixed a stern gaze on Jack. "I'm going to help Bobby with the salad. You can keep Crawford company but no talking about the case."

"Not a problem. You just make sure that you and Bobby don't cheat and discuss it."

"Jack?" A thought had just struck me.

"What's that?"

"Should we have opened the wine? Before now, that is?" I put the platter down on the table. "Sorry, I'm not coordinating this meal very well."

"You're doing fine. If I'd thought it needed it, I'd have suggested opening it when we got here." He nodded in the direction of the kitchen. "I'll just go open it and then be back out to watch you cook."

. . .

I heard Jack being greeted with laughter, picked back up the platter, pushed open the screen door to the outside with my butt, and stood there as Tan got up, stretched, and ambled out the door ahead of me. Once her tail was out of danger, I followed, letting the door slam shut.

Next to the grill there was a small table that I used as a staging area. I put the platter on it, uncovered the side burner, lit it, and put the saucepan with its cup of brandy on the burner. I waited a minute or so then opened the grill and looked at the griddle.

It was red hot in the center. Using the spatula, I placed the four steaks on the griddle tying to space them equally apart from left to right leaving an open space at one end—the smoke and steam made it hard to see—and closed the grill. I checked my watch and stirred the brandy. It was supposed to be reduced by one-third. The recipe called for three-fourths of a cup but I prefer to have too much sauce instead of too little. Besides, the recipe called for a nonstick sauté pan instead of a griddle. My way has some spillage issues.

When a minute had passed, I opened the grill back up and turned the steaks, again going from left to right. This time I moved the first steak to the open spot at the end and then moved the next steak into its place—a kind of rotation to even out the heat. The griddle had been hot enough—none of the steaks had stuck. I closed the grill and stepped back. The smoke and steam had gotten thicker.

Again, I gave the brandy a stir, adjusted the flame, and waited for the minute to pass. The recipe said to cook them a minute and a half a side, and I figured you needed to start the clock at the point the first steak touched the grill. Jack had come back outside and raised his glass in a toast to me. I nodded. The minute was up.

I took the steaks off the griddle, put them on the platter, closed the grill, picked up the knife, and slashed deep diagonal gashes about an inch apart in the steaks—trying to move quickly as the beef was continuing to cook. I put down the knife, picked up a spatula and spread butter across the steaks, forcing some into the gashes. On top of the butter I spread mustard—trying to do it evenly but speed was the issue. Once I'd finished, I put the steaks back on the grill—moving the one on the left end to the right end, as I had moved them across the griddle while cooking.

Did I mention the steam and smoke? It was even harder to see once the butter hit the griddle.

. . .

"Wow. Quite the performance." Jack nodded toward the platter. "I thought you'd cut a finger off for sure."

"Haven't yet." I laughed, stirred the brandy, and adjusted the flame—it was boiling down nicely. "I'm pretty good with knives." I nodded toward the kitchen. "Are they keeping their promise?"

"To not talk about the murder?"

I nodded my head.

"Pretty much, I'd say. Have your ears been burning?"

"Huh?"

"We missed the last Festival—one before that too—so I wasn't surprised when Rebecca said we had to come to this one. She'd said that before and then things would come up and maybe we'd come and maybe not—but not this year. She'd said something about Bobby having met somebody but it still took me a while to figure it out."

"So how am I doing?"

"You've got my vote for what it's worth. I'd give you a thumbs up, but my opinion gets solicited later. It's more of a confirmation or a warning—more significant if it supports Rebecca's opinion but still worth mentioning when it doesn't."

"They're talking about me?"

I checked my watch—two minutes—and went back into action. The recipe said to cook both sides of the steaks after smearing one side with butter and mustard but I didn't want to ruin the mustard crust that was forming. I didn't flip them, just turned them around, continuing to move them across the griddle.

"Rebecca was asking questions and Bobby was answering when I left." He pointed at the grill. "Has that got a name? What you're doing to the steaks."

"Yeah, it's called Sons of Rest beefsteak and I got it from a James Beard cookbook. He claims some saloon owner used to serve it free to a group of young men from good families as an enticement to get them to frequent his saloon—upped the tone of the place, I guess."

"Like those stipends the artists get at The Festival, huh?"

It was time to take the steaks off the grill for good, so I didn't answer Jack right away. I was determined not to overcook them. Once the steaks were on the platter, I cranked the griddle up off the burners until it was level with the sides of the grill. It made it much easier to deglaze the griddle. I wasn't going to leave the steak drippings behind if I could help it.

I poured some of the brandy on the griddle and it sizzled violently as I used my spatula to scrape the griddle, adding more brandy until all of it was on the griddle. I put the saucepan under one edge and carefully lowered that corner of the griddle so the sauce would run back into the pan—scraping bits of steak from the surface into the pan. The resulting sauce got poured over the steaks. Jack carried them in while I tidied up the cooking area and shut the grill down.

Tan had waited outside with me instead of following Jack and the smell of those steaks. "So what do you think, Tan? Who came up with the idea of using stipends to attract artists to The Festival? Or to keep them coming back?" She cocked her head. "Yeah. For some reason I'm guessing that if it didn't start with Dot, she expanded it—expanded it a lot."

. . .

Dinner was a great success. The steaks were rare, tender, and tasty. Bobby's salad was crisp and flavorful— balancing the tastes of the sour cream potatoes and red meat. Some French bread would have been nice but I'd forgotten to get any. Jack's zinfandel was a great hit too. We finished the wine sitting around the dining room table then got up and cleared the table.

Jack and Rebecca loaded the dishwasher while Bobby and I put up what leftovers there were—including a steak. Bobby and Rebecca had insisted on splitting one, saying they couldn't eat a steak that large. Jack and I hadn't had a problem with the size but didn't feel inclined to start on a second one after finishing the first. It was rare enough that I could heat it up a little and have another meal—with potatoes.

I fixed some after-dinner drinks—amaretto for the ladies, brandy for the gentlemen, if Jack and I qualified as such. We moved out onto the screen porch and went back to discussing Dot Fields's murder.

"The killer must have decided the rattlesnake wasn't the right kind of snake for the job." Jack was looking thoughtful as he peered through the brandy glass he'd held up to the light. "Good legs."

I don't serve brandy very often so I can afford to spend a little money when I buy it. I smiled, nodded, and took a sip. I felt the warmth spread down my throat.

Rebecca shivered. "I can't get over how whoever did it must have planned it all out in advance. It wasn't a crime of passion—it was cold-blooded."

"Cold-blooded?" I snorted at the pun. "Good one. What else could it be if you were going to use a snake or any reptile for that matter?"

"Wait!" Jack snapped his fingers. "What if the murderer decided to use two snakes? To make the odds of one of them killing the director better?"

At first, I liked it and I told him so. "Good thinking, Jack. Heck, who cares how many snakes were in the tent? The rattlesnake crawled into the bag and hid while the rest escaped."

Bobby looked dubious. "And the killer still wanted it to look like an accident? What did he do? Dump a cageful of snakes into the tent and run for it?"

"And where did the snakes go? Into other tents where nobody has noticed them?" Rebecca frowned. "That doesn't sound reasonable either."

"Does it make any more sense if it wasn't murder?" I glanced around the table. Gradually everybody shook their heads no. Dot's death didn't make sense unless it was murder. It wasn't that there weren't senseless deaths—they occur all the time. It was just that this wasn't one of them.

"So we agree it was murder and the murderer did what he did in order to kill Dot but not get caught. So the purpose of the snake was to kill Dot while misleading the police—and everybody else."

I thought about what Jack had said. "We know that at least two snakes were involved—the rattlesnake and the one that actually killed Dot. What we don't know is how the murderer got the snake to bite Dot, who put the snake in the tent, and where that snake is now." I sat back and picked up my glass only to find it was empty.

"Don't forget that you don't know what the rattlesnake was doing there either." Bobby smiled. "How about two murderers working independently who both decided to use a snake as a murder weapon?"

. . .

Bobby and her friends—who were now well on the way to being my friends too—had left. It had been a long day for all of us and tomorrow was likely to be even busier. All in all, it had been a pleasant evening—very pleasant. I smiled to myself as I washed the brandy snifters and liqueur glasses by hand. Dishwasher soap can scratch and I like using my hands while letting my mind wander.

I left the glasses in the drying rack, poured myself a small scotch, in a glass that could go into the dishwasher, and headed downstairs to my office. Tan was on one of her dog beds, softly snoring, and paid no attention. There was no sign of TB but he'd come out while we were on the screen porch and said hello, so he wasn't mad at me.

Sitting down, I tapped the spacebar on the keyboard and moved the mouse from side to side in order to wake up my computer. Out of the corner of my eye, I saw The Black come out of his cat carrier, stretch, and walk over to where I was sitting. I patted my leg. "Come on up, TB. You can help me look at all the pictures I've taken."

I'd moved his carrier out of the kitchen while I was getting ready for tonight's guests. In a day or so, I'd put it back in storage but I like to leave it around a couple of days before and after it's needed. That way when I bring it out it doesn't mean I'm taking him immediately to the vet—or anywhere else for that matter.

He jumped on the back of my chair and made his way over my shoulder and down to my lap. I had downloaded all the pictures on my phone already so I could give Chief Snoddy copies. I started comparing the pictures I'd taken after Dot's death to the ones I'd taken after the fire, trying to match up burned items with their before images. It wasn't too difficult, but it was surprising to me how much the fire had moved items around—sucking them into the middle of the tent.

"Don't guess I should be surprised about that, huh, TB?" He looked up at me almost questioningly. "That when the gasoline caught fire it moved some things and didn't move—others." I sat still for a minute, my mind racing.

"Well, duh." TB stirred in my lap. "The fire was set. The person who set the fire pulled things into the middle, poured gasoline over them, lit the candles, and got the hell out of the tent. It had nothing to do with blackmail and everything to do with murder."

The tangle of wires had been moved—wait—what about the firefighters? When they hosed down the fire wouldn't that have moved stuff around? Maybe I was going off half-cocked . . . but what if I wasn't?

. . .

The phone rang.

I hesitated to lean forward to check the callerID since it would disturb the cat, but then I thought it might be Bobby. It was Jim Ward—his personal phone.

"Jim?"

"Your guests gone?"

"Yeah, what's up?"

"Just had our multijurisdictional task force meeting on Dot Fields's murder. Kurt and I flipped a coin and I lost. Which is why I'm calling you."

"Whaa—?" I was dumbfounded. "Tonight?"

"Sammy doesn't waste time—particularly when a whole bunch of suspects are leaving town tomorrow afternoon and he's got no probable cause to keep anybody from leaving town—never to return."

I had to admit I was impressed, despite the sheriff's attitude toward me. "Wish I'd known about it." I didn't, really, I'd enjoyed the evening and would have hated to interrupt it.

"Kurt and I thought you should have had your plans ruined just like ours were, but Sammy isn't going to involve a private investigator in anything. In fact, he's not going to be happy if he finds out we told you."

"Told me what? I figured your first meeting would be organizational." At the university it had taken a number of meetings before a committee could get anything done—if it ever did.

"You figured? Crawford, the reason the task force exists is to be organized. We're already organized. The murder was in Archibald so Kurt should be in charge but Sammy has issues with things like that."

"I noticed," I said drily. "He seems to have issues with a number of things."

"Look, it's late and I'd like to quit for the evening. We've got one solid bit of evidence, only we don't know what the hell to do with it. The snake that killed Dot—well, the venom that killed Dot—was black mamba venom."

"That's African, right? Crap. I'd been thinking Australian." I had decided that no venomous snake from North America was a good candidate as the murderer—or rather the murder weapon. "How'd you find that out so fast?"

"Turns out black mamba venom includes some stuff that might turn out to be a better pain killer than morphine." Jim chuckled. "Small world. Guys in France have been working with the venom for a couple of years. Long enough to publish."

"The pain clinic—the one in Birmingham."

"Yep. Our gal here knew they knew something about some kind of venom. She copied them in on what she sent the CDC. Bingo."

"A black mamba." I'd already started searching the Internet. "Known to strike repeatedly—aggressive. Sub-Saharan Africa— known to attack lions and leopards. Sounds like a great murder weapon."

"Yeah, only how did it end up in backwoods Alabama? More specifically, in Dot Fields's tent." Jim sighed.

"And where is it now?"

"Excellent question. Sammy wants to make it that somebody got hold of the venom and used it to kill her. He's not partial to snakes—even as murderers."

"A black mamba explains the number of times Dot was bitten."

"Sure it does. It answers some questions while creating others." Jim yawned. "Look, I've got to go. We're supposed to 'sleep on it' and let Sammy know what we think tomorrow—bright and early."

"What time is 'bright and early' as far as Sammy is concerned?"

Jim laughed. "I'll wait to call him until I've heard from you. It's about time for things to go click, right? Goodnight, Ford."

"'Night, Jim."

. . .

About time for things to go click? Thanks loads for that, Jim.

A black mamba? I read some more Internet entries about the snake and decided you couldn't pick a better snake to use as a murder weapon. The venom contained a toxin that was a neuro- and cardiotoxin that would kill a victim within six hours. Injected right into the blood stream, it would probably work faster—and twenty injections would also hasten things along.

Absentmindedly, I began stroking The Black's head and he began to purr. He'd left my lap when I answered the phone and returned when I hung up. Somebody had let a rattlesnake loose in Dot's tent. And, if I was right, the same person had let an even more lethal snake loose in that tent—a black mamba. And there'd been another snake in the tent before that—the corn snake. That was a lot of snakes for one little fortune-telling tent. With the mouse, I selected the pictures I'd taken of the corn snake, rattlesnake, garter snake—no, Levi had said it was a rat snake—and one I'd found of a black mamba and arranged them in a slide show. I'd split the screen into thirds and fourths and had the images appear one-by-one on different sides, fading into other images in a random pattern. The picture of the black mamba didn't seem to fit, so I dropped it from the rotation.

It was almost hypnotic. Enough so that I forgot to keep petting TB. He gently bit me as a reminder of what was important in life. Him.

I looked at my wrist and was surprised to see I still had my watch on—too late to call people, but not too late to email them.

There was a pattern here. Maybe that was too strong a word—a potential pattern. I could feel images, memories, snatches of conversation, expressions start to coalesce then break apart, then swirl back even closer. All it needed was a little help to make it come together—and I knew the first question to ask—and whom to ask it of.

My nerves cut in about six and I couldn't go back to sleep. I gave up and got up. I hadn't been enjoying the dreams anyway.

I checked my email—nothing—not even spam. I reminded myself again that it was way too early for me to have gotten any responses from last night's requests unless I'd written to an insomniac.

Dressed in walking clothes, I clipped a lead on Tan's collar and set out for a short walk. Tan and I were going to The Festival today so I thought we'd review some commands—starting with the most basic—sit, heel, and down. Tan didn't find them challenging, which was comforting.

While we were working on our repertoire, I explained my plan for the day. This was the last day of The Festival and lots of the participants would be leaving at the end of the day. If we did our job right—Tan and I—Dot Fields's murderer would be headed for a jail cell. Provided that my theory—comprised as it was out of imagination laced with speculation sprinkled here and there with a few facts—held together. I needed to replace speculation with facts as the day progressed—and it would be nice if the facts fit in with my theory.

But Tan and I needed to be prepared in case I was right. It could come down to us.

. . .

After we got back from our refresher obedience course, Tan got a dog treat. I started the coffee, then checked my phone. No new emails.

The sausage, egg, and cheese sandwich had hit the spot—as it normally does. Usually Sunday was a day to loll around the kitchen or screen porch, drinking coffee and reading the newspaper. Today, I was showered, shaved, dressed, ready for the day, and on my third cup of coffee when my cell phone chirped—I had a text message.

The way I jumped you'd have thought I hadn't been expecting it. Actually, I wasn't. I was waiting for a phone call. The text was from Dr. Moore—aka Snake—asking if it was too early for him to call. I shook my head. "He's doing *me* favors and asking if it's convenient for him to call?" I texted him back and wondered if I'd been as polite as he was being when I'd asked for help last night.

There was a pad of paper on the counter and a pencil holder filled with pens and pencils—most of which worked. The phone rang. I grabbed a pen with one hand and the receiver with the other.

. . .

I was staring at my notes when The Black stood up and stretched. He must have jumped up on the counter while I was on the phone—funny I hadn't noticed.

"That was Dr. Moore, the snake expert." TB yawned. "He was very helpful—just like the last time. Did Tan tell you what we talked about on our walk?"

Tan was on her dog bed. Her tail thumped against the floor either in confirmation or because she'd heard the word "walk." TB sat back down, wrapped his tail around his feet, and looked inscrutable.

"That part I got right. He's got a hunch of his own that he's checking on. Meanwhile." I paused and looked at The Black. "Jim's wrong. It's really not a click. It's more of a snap. One thing snaps in place and everything else gets clearer." The phone rang and I picked it up without looking at the callerID.

. . .

It was Sunday—Sunday morning at that—and I had a few things to attend to and errands to run before Tan and I could head out to The Festival. Fortunately I was able to get in touch with the people whose help I needed before church services or maybe they'd gone to early morning service. The Catholics, I understood, could have gone to church the day before. I didn't ask, they didn't volunteer, and nobody asked me. That's life down here in the Bible Belt.

I was humming to myself when I got back to the house. Things had gone better than I deserved. With a little bit of luck—with a little bit of good luck, I corrected myself—this could work. I could feel the now somewhat familiar excitement building. It was going to be tricky.

I opened the door into the backyard and Tan bounced into the room. It wasn't that my excitement was contagious. Tan could tell that we were about to take a ride and she loved to go anywhere in the car. For the first time, I wondered if I didn't need to rethink my refusal to carry a weapon. It was one thing when I was putting myself into a potentially tight situation—another when it was my dog.

The Black appeared from somewhere. I gave him a thumbs up. "Looking good so far. I know where it isn't and that's almost as important as knowing where it is." He walked up and rubbed himself against my leg which is as much of a seal of approval as I've ever gotten. Tan lowered her head, they touched noses, then The Black jumped up on the counter. It looked like he was going to sit there until we got back, but I knew better. He'd be asleep in a patch of sunlight before we even got to The Festival grounds.

. . .

It was late morning but traffic still wasn't bad. When I got to the parking lots, they weren't crowded either. I knew The Festival always started slow on Sunday. I wondered if it was because people were in church or was it because they didn't want to be seen anywhere else other than church on Sunday morning. This private eye business was beginning to make me cynical. I laughed to myself—beginning?

I found a parking spot that was within a couple of hundred yards of The Festival gate, parked, got out, and went to open the hatch for Tan. The 4Runner was ideal for loading and unloading dogs—dogs big enough to jump in and out that is. As soon as the hatch came open, Tan jumped out onto the ground. Maybe my excitement *was* contagious. I made her jump back into the car so I could put the leash on her.

We started out with Tan at heel but after she calmed down I released her and we ambled up to the gate. There was a cream colored 4Runner parked in the director's reserved parking spot. It was an older model than the one I drove, so I wasn't surprised that Coba could afford it on an assistant director's salary. She might not drive her car often, but at a distance it looked to be in good shape. Better, I admitted, than mine did. Coba was ready for her trip to Atlanta, leaving from The Festival after the closing ceremonies.

I showed my pass to the young ladies who were more interested in meeting Tan than they were in making sure I'd paid my entrance fee. This was the reason that so many college boys had dogs. They may not be able to attract the coeds but their dogs can.

After a few pats, some ruffled fur, and conversation about her probable ancestry, Tan and I headed on into The Festival. There were a few other dogs already there and some of those were dressed in costume. The ones in costume either looked embarrassed or—in the case of the smaller ones—like they had a chip on their shoulder. I never have understood why anybody wants to put a costume on a pet—dog, cat, bird, whatever. My lack of understanding certainly didn't keep people from doing it.

We moved on down the pathway heading toward the Press's tent. Bobby was working for a couple of hours this morning while Rebecca and Jack slept in. They were going to join her for lunch—at least those had been the plans last night.

While we were walking, I did see a dog that actually looked good in his costume and it acted like it thought so too. It was a golden retriever—mostly—whose owner had been inspired to paint black stripes along her legs, flanks, and back with some kind of washable paint. She looked more like a tiger than you'd have thought possible.

. . .

Tan and I stopped at the AIDS booth since it was on our way. Wanda was manning the booth all by herself so the volunteers could all go to church before coming to The Festival. I had hoped to run into her here at The Festival once I found out that the phone number I had for her no longer worked.

Wanda admired Tan and she graciously accepted the kind words and pats then went back to sniffing the ground. Here at the end of The Festival the ground must be filled with wonderful smells—people, food, drink, other animals. She might even be picking up some of the odors from the fire.

"I've been thinking about that immigration lawyer you mentioned. How did you hear of him? From Coba?" I had to be careful not to—what did they call it—lead the witness. I wanted her true memories not ones I suggested.

Wanda looked up from patting Tan. "No. I actually told Coba about him—gave her his contact info—and told her to be sure to mention her connection with the university." She looked puzzled. "Who *was* it that told me about him? Let me think." Wanda frowned. "You know what's funny? I saw him on television last night. Can you believe it?"

"The lawyer? Advertisement?"

"No, he was on the sidelines at the game in Knoxville last night. Maybe you noticed him? He stuck out standing next to the players in his business suit looking all lawyerish."

"He was at the game?" Bobby wasn't really a football fan—neither were Jack and Rebecca—so I hadn't had the game on last night. I'd recorded it, of course, and planned on skimming through it later on.

"Didn't I tell you he was a football fanatic? He goes to all the university's games no matter where they play. Bowl games, season tickets, and all that." She snapped her fingers. "It was Chad Harris!"

"Chad Harris? The guy Dot tried to blackmail?"

"Right. That's the one. It was at a fundraiser and he had contributed a figurine to be auctioned off. Somebody had told him the problems we were having with Immigration and he told me about this lawyer."

"Chad Harris, huh? It's a small world isn't it?"

Tan and I looked at each other. Wanda gave me the lawyer's name, Ben Gibbons, and his phone number and email address.

. . .

I stopped just outside the tent to make another phone call—another piece of information that might be evidence and might not. I glanced at my wrist to check the time and realized that today I wasn't wearing the watch so I pulled back out the phone that I'd just stuck in my back pocket and looked at it. Habits. It's funny how you can think they're broken then revert to them so quickly.

I heard laughter coming from the Press's tent. It sounded like Frank Manning was telling stories. I was glad to hear his voice. He was Bobby's relief and it was getting close to noon—the first performance of gospel music of the day—and I wanted to be down at the performance stage when the choir walked in.

Tan's ears perked up and she tugged against the leash so I dropped it, interested in whose voice she recognized. Or laugh, I corrected myself, she'd not met Frank before.

"Whoa! Who's that?"

I walked past the edge of the booth so I could see inside and spotted Tan sitting on her haunches at Bobby's feet, tail sweeping the floor while her ears were being scratched.

Bobby, Rebecca, and Jack were seated in something of a row facing the opening of the tent. Frank had pulled a folding chair from the side and was sitting with his arms folded on the back of the chair with his back to the entrance. Not surprisingly, Frank did not look like he'd come to The Festival after attending church services. Still the blue jeans were clean if wrinkled.

"Whose dog is that?" Frank stuck his hand out and Tan backed away from it. "Bobby, don't tell me you've adopted one! I warned you about the Metro Shelter's booth!"

I made a clicking noise, caught Tan's attention, and snapped my finger at my side. Tan backed up between Bobby and Rebecca so she could go around Jack and come to my side, giving Frank the widest berth she could—all the while dragging her lead.

Frank turned around, exhaled through his mustache fluffing it out, and said, "Crawford! I knew you had a cat but what a great dog! Did you train him yourself?"

"I gave her the book." I shrugged. "We both read it. I think she got more out of it than I did. Come on, let me introduce you. Stick your hand out and hold it still."

Frank looked puzzled but did what I said. I'd never had a dog that was as afraid of strangers as Tan was, but we'd worked out a system. I stepped up and Tan followed.

"Good girl, Tan. It's okay."

Tan leaned forward and stuck her muzzle out as far as she could without getting any closer to Frank. She sniffed and as she did her lips curled back, showing her teeth.

Frank blinked at the dental display.

"Okay. It's okay, Tan."

The dog looked back up at me and then at Frank. Her tail started to wag, slowly at first and then with her customary vigor.

"You didn't have to do that with us. At least, if you did, I don't remember it." Jack looked puzzled.

Frank tentatively scratched Tan under her chin and Tan closed her eyes and looked blissful.

"She's different at the house. Don't know what it is." It really wasn't a lie—well, not much of one. I was as nervous as I've ever been, all the while hoping nobody noticed, trying to make sure I'd covered all the bases, trying to make sure I did indeed know who the killer was, and Tan sensed it better than anybody except The Black.

"I've told you what the difference is." Bobby tossed her head and her curls bounced.

"Bobby has her own interpretation of how Tan thinks."

"Well, we're both female. When I met Tan," Bobby looked around, "Ford greeted me at the door, The Black checked me out, and then Tan came in from the backyard. I'd been vetted. There was no reason for Tan to worry. Not the same here."

Rebecca nodded her head. "Makes perfect sense to me. Last night, we came in with Bobby who's gotten a seal of approval and Crawford was glad to see us. Frank just didn't have the credentials."

While we were talking Tan had worked her way into such a position as to maximize petting opportunities. Frank, Bobby, and Rebecca were each scratching, stroking, or patting Tan who looked like she might die of happiness. It was rare to see her stick just the tip of her tongue in and out—happy dog.

I glanced at my wrist then pulled my phone out. "Look, I'd like to be at the stage when . . ."

"The choir marches in." Bobby finished my sentence as she stood up. "This is not a part of The Festival that I'm familiar with but I'm looking forward to it."

"Ms. Slater made it quite clear to me that I'd better be here in plenty of time so she didn't have to miss this," said Frank. He

stood up as Bobby, Rebecca, Jack, Tan, and I made our way out
to the music stage.

. . .

We were seated on the first row of the metal bleachers as the
gospel choir started forming. On stage were the empty three-
tiered risers where the singers would stand. Most choirs trooped
in as they were supposed to fit into the stands—sopranos, altos,
tenors, and basses—first row, second row, third, fourth—but not
this choir. Okay, so it was just for show, but what a show! I
loved it.

The audience was gathering—the bleachers filling up—when
the choir director walked in front of the stage. She was short and
stout and dressed in her Sunday best—no choir robe. None of
the choir members wore robes. Every so often someone would
step out of the crowd walk up to the director, lean their head
down to hear something, then go onto the stage and take a place
on the risers. Eventually there was a steady stream of individuals
approaching the director, bowing their heads, and taking their
place among the others. As the numbers on stage grew, you
could began to hear the sound—the notes the director had
assigned—coming from the choir.

There may have been some overall pattern to how the choir
director assigned members to come on stage but I hadn't been
able to detect it before and had long since given up trying. As
more and more members marched in, the sound grew and grew
until the choir was assembled and singing the chord the director
had picked.

The hair on the back of my neck was standing up—just like
always. I like to think that when Delia, Mary, and Levi add their

voices I can tell a difference. The director continued to stand with her back to the stage until the crowd settled down. Then she raised both hands, fingers extended, over her head, paused, then clenched them. The choir immediately fell silent. The director turned to face the singers—hands still over her head—everybody silent until she dropped her hands and the choir exploded. "Hallelujah!" And the performance was on. Same deal every year and every year I get goosebumps.

After the concert, we made our way toward the food court for our final meal at this year's Festival. The gospel singing had thrown us later than usual for lunch and Jack was fired up to try the liquid gumbo or shrimp étouffée. Normally I would have ordered one and let him order the other, but my breakfast had stuck with me this morning. I really wasn't hungry. He compromised with a cup of gumbo and a bowl of the étouffée.

Rebecca and Bobby had decided to split the chicken salad salad. I had thought it was a typo, but it wasn't. Bobby called it truth in advertising—adding chicken to a salad didn't make it chicken salad, but adding chicken salad to a salad made it more than what people expected when you said chicken salad. At least, I think that's how her reasoning went. I had a little trouble following it. I finally settled on a fish taco without the hot peppers. The ladies ordered water, Jack got sweet tea, and I opted for lemonade.

Tan watched intently as we settled down at a picnic table to eat. Last night, I had explained to Jack and Rebecca that anybody who fed one of my pets at the table would end up taking that pet home with him or her, so Tan soon lost interest and lay down at my feet. I'd brought some dog biscuits and would let her have one—once we found one of the watering holes set out for the pets. Like most things The Festival did, it did Pet Day well. When it did allow you to bring pets, it made sure to be pet friendly.

My phone rang. It was Dr. Moore. I excused myself, answered the phone, and stepped away from the table. I didn't have much to say but that was all right, he had plenty. I hung up after thanking him profusely and promising to "come see him" if I was ever in Alton, South Carolina.

"Anybody ever been to Alton, South Carolina? Sorry, I didn't mean to interrupt."

"No problem." Jack waved his hand dismissively. "We were just trying to figure out what else we wanted to see. Did you say Austin?"

"That's in Texas. I said Alton—Alton, South Carolina."

Bobby spoke up. "There's an Austin in Colorado—Arkansas too."

"That's horse country—Alton, South Carolina. Pretty little town, I hear. They play polo there." Rebecca took a sip of water.

Bobby looked admiringly at her friend. "Bex, you never cease to amaze me. You know the oddest things."

"Let me guess," said Jack drily. "You ran into a polo player one time who was from Alton?"

Rebecca shook her head. "I think he was moving there for the polo. You remember, we met him at the bar while we were waiting for a table at the brewpub five or six years ago."

"Right." Jack nodded his head. "Of course I do." He looked at me over her head and mouthed. "No, I don't."

"Why did you ask about Alton?" Bobby brought us back to the beginning of the conversation.

"Oh, I just promised Dr. Morgan Moore, aka Snake, that I'd come see him if I was ever in Alton. I was just wondering how likely that might be."

"You've got to come to Cranbury before you dart off to Alton."

"I'll come to Cranbury and then we can all go to Alton."

There was a pet watering hole just outside the food court with not much of a line of thirsty pets so we waited for Tan to get a drink. Bobby and Rebecca each gave her a biscuit, so when the dog in front of Tan, a basset hound, finished dunking its ears and splashing water everywhere, Tan was happy to wash down the crumbs.

Two- and four-footed, we set out for a final sweep of the booths, rested, fed, and watered.

. . .

"So, are you waiting for the end of The Festival before going back to private-eyeing?" Jack was helping me load one of my purchases into my car. It was a metal flower—well, three blooms of a flower—three to four feet tall set in a concrete base. It really wasn't that heavy for stainless steel, but it was clumsy to handle. I was glad for his help.

Once the sculpture was in place there was no problem loading everybody else's purchases in the back of the 4Runner and still have room for Tan. My car was the one closest to The Festival entrance so we'd agreed to load it up and let the others retrieve their purchases when I came to Bobby's cocktail party this evening.

"Do we really want to see the closing ceremony?" Rebecca glanced around and saw, as I did, people who were tired and dusty. "If it's like the choir's opening, then it's worth staying, otherwise . . ." She let her voice trail off.

Tan hopped into the back of my car and lay down with her paws hanging over the edge of the hatch as if she was ready to leave too.

"You thinking that if we leave early we can help Bobby get ready for the party?" Jack looked at Rebecca and smiled. "And maybe get off your feet for a little while?"

"Why don't you go ahead," I suggested. "I've got to—I want to catch the closing ceremony like I did the opening one. Tan will keep me company. You three go on."

I snapped my fingers and pointed to the ground next to me. Tan stood up, jumped to the ground, walked over, and sat by my side. I stepped forward and closed the hatch.

"Closing is at five. Guests are invited for sixish, right, Bobby?" I pulled my phone out of my back pocket and checked the time. "It's twenty 'til five. If you leave now you'll avoid some traffic. Staying for the ceremony might run you late—you never know." As I was talking, I gradually became aware of Bobby's silence—and a steely glare.

"If you think I'm going to miss whatever it is you think is going to happen, you've got another think coming." She glanced at Jack and Rebecca. "There are some picnic tables just outside the gates. Why don't we go sit there and wait for the—ceremony? Just in case—something comes up? It might be interesting."

Rebecca looked at Bobby. "Is that why he's so jittery? I thought he seemed distracted."

Bobby shrugged her shoulders. "You saw how much he ate for lunch and that was before the phone call."

Jack and Rebecca exchanged a glance, communicating in the way that couples who know each other well can do.

"Great idea. We'll stay," said Rebecca.

"Sounds good to me," added Jack.

I took a deep breath, let it out, and met Bobby's gaze. "Wish me luck then." No use struggling against the inevitable.

. . .

Bobby, Rebecca, and Jack were comfortably settled at a picnic table just outside the gate. They'd picked up some soft drinks and water and were trying not to look interested in whatever it was I was doing. I didn't think they'd win an Oscar, but it shouldn't matter.

With Tan on her lead, I walked over to the 4Runner parked in the director's reserved spot. It was still in the shade, the windows down about half an inch. The tinted rear windows made it impossible to see what was in the back—same as with my model. Tan was interested in the smells and I followed her around the car, stopping at the right rear tire—the one that couldn't be seen from The Festival grounds. I knelt down and Tan licked my face. I handed my end of her lead to her so my hands were free.

. . .

Tan and I walked through the gate, she still had the end of the lead in her mouth—she was proud of it. I'd folded it so it didn't quite drag on the ground. We were within the letter of the law: pets must be on a leash or otherwise confined. The fact that Tan was on both ends of the lead was stretching things a bit.

I was going against the foot traffic, Tan following behind. The crowd was thinning out, most people were ready to call it a day. They were looking to catch a seat on the shuttle bus, get their car, and get on the road. It was time to take the purchases home, show them off, and get back to the Sunday afternoon routine. A few people were hanging on, waiting for the closing ceremony. I saw Rufus George and Joyce Fines in the crowd, along with Lenora, some other volunteers, vendors, and the like.

The people who had spent the last three days working hard to make the yearly event a success were coming together—tired and content, proud of another job well done, glad to share the common experience they'd all had.

Here and there, I noticed people who hadn't been at Dot's party. Some of them looked familiar. I headed over to a small group of men. They were trying not to be conspicuous, but I can pick out a bunch of cops pretending to be Festival-goers. It helped that I'd met most of them. Heck, one was a good friend.

Jim Ward stepped out from the group, clapped his hands, and went down on one knee. Tan spotted him and shot forward, tail wagging ninety to nothing. I followed at my own pace. By the time I got up to the group, Chief Snoddy was leaning forward holding his fist out so that Tan could sniff it. Jim had gotten to his feet. Sheriff Sammy Thompson was eyeing Tan skeptically. I didn't know if it was because she was my dog or if that was his attitude toward dogs in general.

Harry Johns, Ward's assistant, was part of the group as was Sammy's driver. Harry and I didn't speak and were both happier that way. I didn't know the driver well enough to do more than nod at him. Throw in another Archibald law enforcement officer and, unless I missed my guess, I was looking at Jemison County's Multijurisdictional Homicide Unit.

"What kind of dog is that?" Sammy pointed at Tan. I don't know to whom he addressed his question since he wasn't talking to me.

Tan, who up to that point had shown no interest in the sheriff, decided she didn't care to be pointed at by a stranger. She left Chief Snoddy, circled around Jim, and hid behind me, peering out around my legs to see if he was still pointing at her.

"She's a brown," I heard myself say. "On both sides. I've got her papers." I was talking about her adoption papers, of course.

"A brown?" Sammy looked puzzled.

Jim Ward coughed into his fist. "Technically Tan is an Austrian brown. It's fairly rare in the United States, but those familiar with the breed just call them browns."

"Yep." Chief Snoddy nodded in agreement. "A kid down the street had one when I was growing up—great dog. All us kids in the neighborhood loved it. You can't beat a brown for putting up with children and the silly stuff they do." He looked at me. "You know, childish pranks. The kind of thing they're supposed to outgrow."

Jim nodded at Kurt's remark. "I'd heard that about them too—patient. Real good with children. Tan's a particularly pretty brown, don't you think?"

Sammy shrugged his shoulders turning his attention away from Tan. "I never had a dog growing up. Only dogs I'm familiar with are police dogs."

"Really? I was raised by a beagle. She did a good job, but I do occasionally want to bay at the moon." No one commented on my remark so I added, "I don't think browns would do well as police dogs—wrong temperament."

That met with general agreement, nodding heads all around.

I turned back to Jim. "Any luck?" He shook his head no. I was pretty sure I'd have heard if any of the other possibilities had come through, but it was better to ask.

"How about a search warrant?"

"On a Sunday, the day after an away game—a night game at that?" Jim snorted. "How about some probable cause? Plain view is still your best chance."

"Besides," Kurt patted my shoulder. "Looks to me like you've got it figured out—provided you're right."

"Provided we're not here on a damn fool wild-goose chase."

"Nice way of summing it up, Sheriff." I looked up the pathway to the headquarters building. "Real supportive. I appreciate it. We should see just how much of a damn fool I am pretty shortly."

"Tan." I clucked at her and she sat at my left hand. I raised my right hand and gave the group a little wave. "Gentlemen, Sheriff Thompson, if you'll excuse me. Tan, heel."

. . .

I walked back through the gate and worked my way behind the crowd of people that had formed in front of the gates. It was up to Tan and me now.

Someone had brought out the block of wood on which to prop the ends of the gate. Without it, the ends wouldn't meet in the middle. I wondered why the blacksmith hadn't tried to add an additional leg on which to prop the gate, making it even heavier. Who knows? Maybe he had put it on, discovered it made it worse, and removed it.

Coba was walking down the path from headquarters, flanked by Ralph Stark and Ellen George. From where I stood, it looked like Coba was giving them detailed instructions on doing things that they already knew how to do. Coba was to perform the closing ceremony and then hit the road to Atlanta in order to make a meeting with Immigration tomorrow morning. At least that's what we'd been told.

The three stopped some ten feet from the gates. Coba continued to talk for a few minutes while both Ellen and Ralph nodded their heads. I glanced at my phone for the time. They needed to hurry it up if The Festival was going to end when it was supposed to.

Somebody carrying a wireless microphone walked out of the group of volunteers and approached the threesome. She stopped next to the group, fumbled with the microphone until we could hear her handling it over the public address system, and then spoke into it. "Test. Test."

Somebody had been thinking ahead. Dot's voice hadn't needed amplification. The same could not be said of Coba's voice.

"Test. Test. Test." The volunteer turned around and held the microphone out to Coba.

"Coba." The microphone picked up Ellen George's voice. "We know what we're supposed to do and even if we didn't you'll be back—." Coba grabbed the microphone, turned it off, and whatever else Ellen had to say was lost.

The volunteer, her duty done, turned and walked away. Ellen and Ralph separated, walking to opposite ends of the gates, and suddenly Coba was alone in front of the open gates—the center of attention. She hesitated for a long moment and I wondered if stage fright was going to overwhelm her, but she lifted the microphone to her lips, having remembered to turn it back on.

"It is with mixed emotions . . ."

So she was going to say something nice about Dot, something about how she was proud to perform the closing ceremony while sad at the same time. The horrible accident, life cut short, humbled to follow such a person. I tuned her out. I hate speeches like that unless they are very well done, and I've rarely heard one that wasn't poorly done. It was one reason I hated office parties at the university and didn't go to them— including my own retirement party.

Glancing around, I saw a few people who appeared to be enjoying the ceremony. But most looked bored or were chatting with their neighbors. Par for the course.

Ellen and Ralph started carrying the ends of the gates toward the middle where Coba was standing. Their movement jerked me back to the present and I tuned in to what Coba was saying just as the gates were closed. She'd finished with her personal remarks and had moved on to the closing ritual.

"So be it! The gates are closed and The Festival is over! Keep the feeling, the hope, the promise alive within you until next year when the gates will open again! Let the spirit of The Festival live within us all until then!"

If The Festival was dated in any way, it was the opening and closing ceremonies. I could imagine smaller crowds, younger people, denim and tie-dyed clothes, long hair, bare feet, beards, mustaches, incense, peace symbols, and heads nodding at the ritual words.

I found myself joining in when the crowd shouted, "The Festival." I kept myself from adding "Power to the People."

And then it was done. The Festival was over and people began wandering off—buyers and spectators going to their homes; vendors, to their packing; volunteers, to their cleanup duties. The ceremony marked the end of the common experience—the shared experience—and a return to individual lives.

. . .

Coba looked a bit forlorn standing there alone on the other side of the gates. She turned away from the gate and the woman who had brought her the microphone reappeared to take it away. With that final task completed, Coba turned and headed for her car. She reached into the small purse hanging from one shoulder and pulled out a set of keys.

That was my cue. I started toward her, angling through the rapidly departing crowd to reach her before she got much closer to her car. She caught sight of me and stopped—suddenly alert, a wild animal that has caught sight or scent of a human—poised and ready to flee.

"Ms. Boucher," I waved and smiled broadly. "I didn't want to tell you until you'd finished the closing ceremony, but I just noticed that you've got a flat tire—flat as a pancake—must be some kind of leak. You're going to have to use your spare." Since I had said tire's valve stem core in my pocket, I was pretty confident about the leak, the flatness of tire, and the need to use the spare.

She wasn't buying the folksy act. Her eyes cut from my face to the 4Runner's tires—the three she could see.

"Oh, it's the back right—passenger side—tire." I turned slightly so I was a little bit closer to her and pointed to the back of her vehicle. "You can't see it from here. The only reason I noticed it was Tan here. I've got the same model car and she must have thought it was our car. She was sniffing around and I spotted the tire."

Coba still hadn't spoken. She glanced at Tan when I mentioned her and Tan promptly got behind me so I was between her and Coba. I had hoped that Coba liked dogs so Tan would inspire trust—that didn't seem to be working. Not much was working—so far.

"Like I said, I've got the same model, so I thought I'd offer to help with the tire." I held out my hand. "Just toss me the keys. Changing tires on cars like ours can be tricky if you've never done it before. I just need to set the brake and stuff."

"The Festival has a pump. I'll just get it filled with air."

"It's really flat—pancake flat. You don't want to drive on it at all—until it's fixed that is. You could damage the tire, the rim, or both." Damn. All she had to do was give me the keys. "I'll change the tire and you'll be on your way to Atlanta in no time."

Coba shook her head no. "I can handle it. I can take care of it myself. Go away!" She made a shooing motion with her hand. It was the hand the keys were in. This was not going well at all.

Kurt Snoddy could move. Back in the day, his times in the 40 were no doubt lousy. But offensive linemen need an initial burst of speed; they don't need to keep it up. He still had it. I'd never have guessed how quickly—and silently he could move.

In the flicker of an eye, his hand engulfed her hand—the one that held the keys. "A pretty girl like you changing her own flat tire with all these men standing around?" His voice boomed. "You're not from around here are you?" Kurt released her hand and lobbed the keys at me.

It was just like we'd planned it, if I'd been smart enough to plan it. I hadn't realized just how unlikely it was that Coba would give up those keys. My stupidity never ceases to amaze me.

Kurt kept on talking, drowning out her voice if she was trying to say anything. "Too many southern gentlemen around here for you to get your purty little hands dirty!"

I grabbed the keys, relieved to see the remote control fob, back-stepped, and pointed to Coba's car while pushing the hatch release button. I was staring at the back of the 4Runner and Tan yelped as I stumbled into her.

"No! Leave my car alone! Don't touch it!"

. . .

That, as my law enforcement friends advised me, was the point where the rules of admissible evidence began to get interesting. Interesting, you understand, to defense attorneys, prosecuting attorneys, judges, courts of appeal, and the like.

Most law enforcement officers don't care for evidence that's acquired by interesting methods.

Coba's exclamation, I assumed, could not be construed—would not be construed—as approval to search her vehicle.

I stared at the back of the 4Runner. Did you know that law enforcement officers can act on evidence they see inside vehicles? Provided, of course, that the evidence is in plain view from the outside. They can't enter the car to see if there might be anything interesting in there. I was pinning my hope on the plain view doctrine—if I could just get things into plain view.

How long, I wondered, how long does it take for those stupid pneumatic supports—lifters—to open the hatch after it's been unlocked? Jim had pointed out that those things wear out—get too weak to work.

There. It had started to move, hadn't it? I remembered one of the features I particularly enjoyed about my 4Runner. All you had to do was to get the hatch close to closing and it would automatically take over and close itself. Under my breath I cursed Toyota and safety-conscious engineers. As far as I was concerned, once I'd pushed that button the hatch door should have flown open knocking anything or anybody out of its way.

The hatch continued to move, picking up speed as it did so. I grabbed Tan by the collar and unhooked the lead. I kept hold of her collar as I crouched down so I could peer straight into the back of the 4Runner.

By now, Coba realized that the back of her vehicle was opening and her commands to leave her and her car alone were becoming shrill.

With a sudden acceleration the hatch opened fully and the cargo area between the back seats and the door was revealed.

My first thought was that Coba traveled light. Sitting in the middle of the cargo area, secured with bungee cords at all four corners, was a rectangular plastic box. That box was staying where she'd put it and so was what was in it.

I'd been worried that she might hide the cage from view with her luggage. Tan and I would have had to deal with that if it had occurred. But it hadn't.

The cage was just like the one she'd carried the corn snake in—clear plastic on the sides; heavy mesh wire on top; bottom of the cage covered in what I had learned was orchid bark bedding, safe for all reptiles. And sitting on that bark was a grayish-green snake—not much to look at.

"Doofus. What did they teach you in Boy Scouts? Be prepared!" I was talking to myself as I clawed at my back pocket trying to get my phone out. I could see Tan looking at the hatch and then back at me. I got the phone loose and started taking pictures.

"Stop!" Coba was twisting in Chief Snoddy's grasp. She'd have to do something more than that to break his grip. "Stay out of my car!"

I snapped my fingers and pointed—Tan leapt into the back of the 4Runner as I switched to video.

. . .

Once in the car, Tan approached the cage slowly, sniffing the air and the smell of the snake as she got closer and closer to it. Tan's not a big dog and the cage wasn't particularly large, but there wasn't that much room in the back of the 4Runner.

The snake struck. Its neck spread like a cobra's hood and there was a splash of black as it hit the side of the cage.

Tan jerked back and started barking. The snake pulled its head back. Its mouth was open and I could clearly see the blue-black color on the inside of the snake's mouth.

"Tan, come." I killed the video and emailed it. Took a few more pictures and sent them off too. Tan was sitting at my feet waiting to be praised when somebody knocked me to the ground and began to pound on my head and shoulders. Tan started barking again and then Coba was lifted off of me.

Harry Johns and Jim Ward were each holding an arm. Coba was cursing in some foreign language and trying to get loose. I wasn't sure what she was saying, but cussing sounds like cussing no matter what the language. There was fresh bright blood on Kurt's hand and it was dripping. I was pretty sure how Coba had gotten out of his grip. I guess there isn't that much biting in football games.

I glanced around and saw that a small knot of people had collected near the parking lot. The sheriff was standing to one side looking askance. I pointed to the interior of Coba's car. "It's a black mamba. We've found the murder weapon."

My phone rang. It was Dr. Morgan Moore. He'd been waiting by his phone in case I got pictures I could send him. I answered the phone.

"Dr. Moore—" I had to stop talking to keep from interrupting. I waited until he paused. "Thanks for the confirmation. Do you mind repeating that to the sheriff of Jemison County?"

I held the phone out to Sheriff Thompson. "But don't take my word for it."

Sammy looked at my phone like it might be a snake but finally took it out of my hand.

. . .

Coba began to speak in English. "That's not my snake! I've never seen that snake before! Somebody must have—."

I had to laugh. "Must have what? Brought one of the most dangerous reptiles in the world and stuck it in your 4Runner? Packed it suitable for travel? Strapped it in so that there was no chance of that snake escaping between here and Augusta?"

"I'm going to Atlanta!" Coba began to squirm again in Harry's and Jim's grasp. Both were careful to keep all parts of their bodies out of reach of her teeth. "I've got an appointment— everybody knows about it."

"True enough. You've told everybody about your appointment. But what you've told them is only partially true. You have to go through Atlanta to get to Augusta. Augusta is your destination. And you do have an appointment, only it's not with Immigration. It's with the man who sold you the black mamba—as well as the eastern diamondback rattler, the yellow rat snake, and, your favorite, the corn snake. You were a good customer and he remembers you."

Coba's voice was so soft I had to strain to hear what she was saying.

"She was an evil person. She said she was going to fire me. Not give me a reference. Make sure I never worked in Alabama again. I'd have to move and start the naturalization process all over again . . ."

"You set up a couple of snake traps to catch the mamba after it had done its job. You stored the traps in Dot's tent the day before. You slipped in the back entrance, replaced the corn snake with the black mamba, and took the corn snake away with you, didn't you?"

I hadn't liked the way Coba stared at me when I first met her—what was it—four days ago? That look had been a little off-putting. This one was filled with pure hatred. I was meeting Coba's glare when suddenly her eyes lost their focus.

"I have nothing to say. I want a lawyer."

"You knew Dot would enter the tent, stick her hand in the cage without looking, pull the snake out, and try to drape it around her neck. She did it all the time with the corn snake.

"I saw her do it myself. She didn't care about the snake. It was just a decoration for her—a prop. It bothered you the way she treated the corn snake, didn't it? Just once you wanted the corn snake to react, to attack her. That's what gave you the idea, wasn't it? You thought about putting a snake in there that would strike back."

"I want a lawyer." Her voice was flat. "I do not have to speak to you."

"True." I paused for a second. "By the way, your immigration attorney—Ben Gibbons, isn't it? He tells me that he doesn't have an appointment with you on Monday. He says he never schedules appointments on a Monday after a university football game. He also said to tell you that you don't need an immigration attorney to go to jail. As he doesn't do criminal law, he's going to go ahead and invoice you for the balance you owe him—and he's retroactively canceling your discount.

"And the man in Augusta won't be able to take the mamba back. It's evidence in a murder case."

Chief Snoddy had a handkerchief pressed against the base of his thumb where Coba had bitten. The blood was still seeping through the cloth. "Jim, you mind getting cuffs on Ms. Boucher?"

Jim Ward took out his handcuffs and locked Coba's hands behind her.

The chief looked over at me. "Hope she didn't rough you up too much. She surprised me with that bite."

She hadn't bitten me, but I was beginning to feel the sting of scratches on my face. "I'll be fine. But if I were you, I'd make sure she's had her rabies shot."

Sammy stepped up and handed me back my phone. I wondered how he'd treated Dr. Moore. He wasn't a potential voter but he wasn't a private investigator either. I'd have to remember to ask Snake.

Sammy turned around to look at the members of the task force. "Okay, I'm convinced. A damn fool way to try and murder somebody, but she confessed to it." He glanced over at the Festival-goers and volunteers still clustered together in a small group near the parking lot. "We've got witnesses to the confession. Chief Snoddy, it's your jurisdiction. Take her into custody. We'll see to things here. I'll call the district attorney's office."

Snoddy shrugged his massive shoulders and began to read Coba her Miranda rights as he and one of his men led her toward an Archibald patrol car.

Sammy turned back to where Jim and Harry were standing. "Make sure you get the evidence secured. Get the names of some of the witnesses who are civilians—no cops and no official connection to The Festival. See if one of the veterinarians in town will take care of the snakes."

He paused. "Forget the veterinarians. Get in touch with Jeff Forte of the university police and get the names of some snake scientists out there. See if they'll confirm that the snake is a black mamba and hold all the snakes for us. The university ought to be good for something." He nodded to himself as if checking items off a mental list. "That should do it." He dusted off his hands and nodded at his driver who headed for the squad car at a trot. "Good work, Captain Ward, you and Sergeant Johns. I'll be sure to mention it to Chief Boyd."

. . .

I was standing behind Sammy and could see that Jim's face hadn't changed expression. He stared at Sammy, raised his hand, and with one long finger pointed past him. Following the gesture, Sheriff Thompson turned and found himself face to face with me. Tan hid behind my leg. "Oh yeah, Crawford." He paused for a second. I could see him struggling with what to say.

"Your dog did a good job."

With that he spun on his heel, walked over to his police car, got in the passenger side, and rode off—siren howling and lights flashing.

Jim Ward just shook his head from side to side as he watched him leave. "Sorry about that, Crawford. I thought you did at least as good a job as Tan did. Maybe better. You didn't bark as much."

I felt somebody standing next to me and was surprised to see Jack Harlon at my elbow. For a big man he moved quietly. Bobby and Rebecca were walking up behind him.

Jack nodded in the direction of the rapidly disappearing sheriff. "Talk about somebody who needs killing."

I laughed. "Seeing as how the good sheriff didn't assign me any official duties, let's go to Bobby's and have a drink. But first I have to take this afternoon's heroine home and feed her."

Jack turned back to speak to Bobby and Rebecca. He pointed to the rapidly disappearing patrol car. "Crawford solves the case and all the sheriff can say to him is 'your dog did a good job.' What a jerk. Least he could have said was you and your dog—."

I had squatted down next to Tan and was patting her when Bobby reached out, patted the top my head, and cooed, "You did good work too. Good boy, Crawford. Good boy." And with that, everybody laughed. I laughed so much that I lost my balance and sat down—hard.

Tan began to enthusiastically lick my face, so I hugged her around the neck and barked at Bobby. She had that million-kilowatt smile of hers going so it took a second or two before I saw Ellen and Rufus George walking up behind her. From my viewpoint I couldn't tell if they were amused or not.

As I started to get up, Jack stuck out his hand. I grabbed it and found myself being lifted to my feet almost effortlessly. General contracting—at least the way Jack Harlon practiced it—certainly keeps you fit.

I dusted my hands off on the back of my jeans, and waved at Rufus and Ellen.

"I see that the assistant director of The Festival has been taken into custody," said Rufus.

"She killed Dot?" Ellen's question was more to the point.

I nodded my head and started to speak.

"Congratulations, James." Rufus put out his hand and I took it. "We Georges seem to keep supplying you with murders to investigate, but, James, Shelbyville is really a small town. We can't keep having people die for your entertainment—or employment." He gave me a languid wink.

"What made you—" Ellen began.

"Ellen." Bobby raised her hand. "We're headed back to my house for cocktails and appetizers—and an explanation from Crawford on how he figured out whodunit. Want to join us?"

"Since that's exactly what I came over here to ask Crawford, it sounds lovely—much more comfortable than standing around in a parking lot." Ellen glanced in her husband's direction. "Cocktails at Bobby's. Entertainment by James. Appealing?"

Rufus smiled his agreement. I had my doubts about how interested he was, seeing as how he hadn't particularly cared how I had solved the murders he'd gotten me involved in.

"I'll take Tan home, feed her, and get back over to your house as soon as possible." Bobby was shaking her head no before I had barely started.

"Do you think I'm going to let you go home and tell that cat how you solved the mystery before I hear about it? The Black can wait to hear and Tan can wait to eat. Besides," grinned Bobby, "I've got some food at home that Tan can eat."

"Okay!" I grinned back at her. I saw no reason to mention that I'd already discussed Coba with The Black.

I pulled in behind Bobby's car. She couldn't get out of her driveway, but she shouldn't need to. Judging by the cars, I might be the last to arrive. I'd taken Tan for a short walk on the pet path before loading her in the car and it had given everybody else a head start.

Tan hopped out of the back as soon as I opened it and immediately went to sniffing. She'd never been at Bobby's townhouse before, so all the smells were new and different—I guess. Since I don't have a sense of smell anywhere close to Tan's I never really know what she's smelling. I can testify that she finds it fascinating.

I walked up the short brick sidewalk and stepped up onto the threshold. "Tan. Come." She tore herself away from a particularly yummy-smelling patch of grass and immediately transferred her attention to the doormat. Bobby had left the front door open with only the glass storm door closed, so I could see people standing around in the living room. I opened the door and urged Tan in.

I closed the door behind us and Tan followed me into the room.

"Crawford!" Stan Dowdy raised his glass to me. "I understand you solved another one."

"Don't say anything about it, James." Rufus put up a cautioning hand. "Bobby says you're the evening's entertainment and we're not to let you spoil it."

"Where's Ellen?" I hadn't spotted her or Bobby.

"She's here. In the kitchen helping Bobby and Rebecca with the food."

"That's great." I shook Stan's hand then Rufus's. "Looks like you two have found the bar already."

Rufus pointed across the living room to where Jack was standing next to a liquor cart. "There's the bartender, but if you want a beer, the cooler is on the patio." He nodded at the sliders that led to Bobby's patio and backyard.

Stan scratched Tan on the head after making sure she remembered him by holding out his hand for her to smell. "I hear that Tan was the hero—according to Sheriff Thompson, that is."

I laughed. "She played her part, that's for sure. She made it very easy to identify the murder weapon."

""Whoa!" Frank Manning walked up, beer bottle in hand. "Don't ruin the surprise! I was working the booth and missed everything."

I decided he was drinking from the bottle because it made it easier to get the beer past his mustache. If he'd used a glass the foam would have caught in his facial hair.

"By the way, am I right in crediting you with Bobby's improved taste in beer?"

"That's good detective work, Frank. Yep, I left some Red Stripe here and ever since then it keeps replenishing itself." I glanced at Rufus and Stan. "She treats me better than I treat myself. I usually make do with Yuengling."

"Crawford." Bobby's voice came from the kitchen.

"Excuse me, gentlemen. My hostess calls."

. . .

Bobby's townhouse was spacious—for a townhouse—but you can't put three people in a kitchen and it not seem small. When you add a fourth plus his dog, it gets downright crowded.

I got a quick hug and an energetic kiss that was far too short. It had great potential.

"Why don't you and Tan go out onto the patio. And take the rest of the guests with you. I've got Mr. Whiskers locked up in my bedroom and need to let him out before he decides to destroy something."

"I didn't think he'd come out what with all these people here." There really weren't that many people here, but I wasn't a cat and this wasn't my home.

"Oh he wouldn't if he wasn't locked up. But he is, so he wants out, so he can find all these people in his house and go off and sulk."

"Makes sense in a cat sort of way. Come on, Tan, let's shift this party outside."

. . .

We'd moved outside in good order, closing the sliders behind us. People had cheerfully rearranged Bobby's patio furniture into a configuration that made sense to them even if it hadn't to Bobby.

Frank—along with his date, the St.-Pauli-Girl-look-a-like-only-more-so from Thursday night's party—had moved out into the small yard where the breeze would sweep away his cigarette smoke. Interestingly enough his date's name was Pauline. I never found out who had given her the costume she'd been barely wearing.

The cooler was filled with Yuengling, Red Stripe, water, seltzer, and an assortment of soft drinks. I grabbed a bottled water to start with. There was still plenty of adrenaline in my bloodstream that I didn't feel like mixing with alcohol. Tan found a spot to curl up in—after she'd sniffed all over the backyard. Bobby had provided a rawhide bone and Tan was happy to entertain herself with it.

Bobby, Ellen, and Rebecca brought the finger foods out on trays, carried them around, then set the platters down, placing them on small tables scattered about on the patio.

Jack appeared with their drinks—Bobby's Gray Goose. I'd given the recipe to Jack. Rebecca, Ellen, and Bobby sat down and took sips. The martinis seemed to meet with their approval.

"All right," Bobby set her glass down. "Everybody got something to drink and eat?" She surveyed the patio and was greeted with a series of nods or raised glasses. She looked at me.

"Okay, hotshot. How did you do it? What did you see that all the rest of us missed? How did you know that Coba was the murderer?"

I'd been leaning against one of the columns that support the shade-providing pergola trying to figure out just how I had come to that conclusion—or, more accurately, how to explain it.

"First of all, not everybody saw everything that I saw."

Jack, who had been swirling the small batch bourbon in his glass and holding it up to the light, took a sip, swallowed, and said, "I want to know why you decided it was murder in the first place."

"It wasn't one thing. It was a bunch of things."

"Like what Jim Ward says—it just all goes 'click,' right?" Bobby nodded then cocked her head at me. "Where is Jim, by the way?"

"Meeting one of the university's herpetologists at his lab on campus. It took a while to find somebody out at the university who had the facilities and the inclination to house a black mamba, along with the other snakes."

"Why didn't he have that assistant of his do that?"

"Harry?" I laughed. "Turns out Harry Johns is scared spitless of snakes. He promised Jim he'd do anything if he didn't have to deal with the snakes."

Bobby looked questioningly at me.

"Coffee. Every workday for a month. Starbucks, extra large or whatever they call it. Jim likes his coffee."

"We're still waiting," said Stan. Jack must have fixed his rum and coke for him. Stan would never have used a wedge of lime and a stirrer.

I bobbed my head. "Sorry. You see there was all this stuff that went wrong at The Festival that made me wonder."

"Something goes wrong every year," Ellen objected.

"I'm sure it does," I agreed. "Up to and including the director getting killed. But think about it. On the first day, the gate was broken and the sound system was messed up. Both things that had worked perfectly the day before. Then Dot finds a snake in her tent, gets bitten, and dies. That night her tent is burned down. Oh, and the night before she'd been accused of blackmail."

"Speaking of which," I looked at Ellen George, "can you tell us what the board found out about Dot's sideline?"

Ellen didn't answer immediately. She looked down at her hands, which were resting in her lap. "I don't see why not."

She brought her gaze back up. "Dot had left her last will and testament in The Festival office along with a duplicate set of keys and some other items to make it easier for whoever was responsible for cleaning up her affairs." Ellen was momentarily pensive. "Remarkably thoughtful of her when you think about it.

"In any case, Lenora Maisano and I decided that as members of The Festival's executive committee we should check out the contents of the old gun safe in Dot's house. To be sure nothing belonging to The Festival was in the safe."

Ellen looked directly at me, as if she thought I might challenge her assertion. I gave her a half smile. "Makes sense to me."

"Lo and behold, the safe was filled with envelopes and boxes, each marked with a person's name."

Ellen paused for so long I was about to ask if she had finished, when she spoke again. "The executive committee has decided to treat the packages like lost and found items. If we can locate the owner, the unopened package will be returned to him. Or her. If not, the package will be destroyed."

She looked around the room to see if there were any questions but there weren't. I wasn't surprised at what they'd found in the safe. Lenora had said that Dot told her she 'stored her protection in that safe.' I'd been pretty sure she hadn't been referring to guns.

All eyes turned back to me.

. . .

"What was with the sound system?" Frank smoothed his mustache with a curved forefinger. "It was fine when I got there but somebody told me it was squawking up a storm that morning."

"Feedback. Mose told me somebody had messed with the volume controls on the amps—just the volume. The other knobs hadn't been moved. Somebody came along after the technicians had finished and turned the volume all the way up."

I looked around. "They were still working on the sound when I left the grounds Thursday afternoon. Mose tells me it took them until quitting time to get the sound right. He also says they charge by the hour, but I'm not going there."

Everybody chuckled.

"And the gate?" Ellen was keeping me on track.

I shrugged my shoulders. "It opened up fine on Thursday, but Friday morning was a different story. Jack, you talked to Ralph Stark about that, didn't you?"

I thought the way he'd been staring at his glass Jack might not be paying attention, but I was wrong. "After the gate was closed on Thursday evening somebody unscrewed the top bolt of the hinge on both sides of the gate—and tossed the bolts away. They had to have done it while the gates were closed and sitting on that block of wood they put in the middle. Too much weight on the bolts otherwise—never get them to turn."

"So, why couldn't it have been some prankster or practical joker who did those things? Why a killer?" Rebecca looked puzzled.

"Right. That's what I thought at first—because none of that had anything to do with Dot blackmailing people."

"Whoa!" Stan held up his hand. "Stop right there. If those things had something to do with Dot getting killed then why wouldn't her blackmailing people be related?"

I took a pull of water out of the bottle and wiped my lips with the back of my hand. "Actually, the blackmailing issue muddied the waters, made it harder to figure out what really happened. Coba could have used the blackmailing to distract us—if she'd known about it. Because Dot's blackmailing isn't what got her killed."

"You really think Coba knew nothing about the blackmailing? The kickbacks from the stipends or anything?" Ellen looked thoughtful. "Lenora and I wondered if she was involved when we started putting things together."

I shrugged. "It might have been easier for Dot to have an accomplice, but Dot detested Coba."

Jack looked thoughtful. "So how did blackmailing make it harder to solve the crime?"

"Because I assumed that the murder and the blackmail were related. I really went down the rabbit hole on that one."

"How so," asked Bobby.

"Dot had been successfully blackmailing people for years. My guess is that a good blackmailer has a sense of which people to blackmail. People who are more likely to kill you rather than submit to blackmail aren't the kind of clientele a blackmailer wants. For instance, blackmailing murderers would be dangerous—embezzlers not so much. My mistake was assuming that a blackmailer was more likely to get killed than an ordinary person. Faulty logic."

Rebecca was frowning. "Why faulty?"

"Because blackmailers are just as likely as anybody else to drop dead of a heart attack or die peacefully in their sleep at age one hundred and ten. First rule of successful blackmailing: make sure your victim knows that killing you won't solve anything— their secret will be revealed if you die."

. . .

I threw my hands up in disgust. "I'm sorry, I'm doing a lousy job of explaining how things fit together. Let's see if I can tell a straightforward tale.

"I'll try one strand at a time. Thursday I met Coba for the first time. She was carrying a snake to Dot's fortune-telling tent for the photo shoot that Stan had set up at Dot's behest. It was in a cage—the snake that is, not the photo shoot—and the cage was covered with a cloth. Coba was dressed like most of the volunteer workers—Festival T-shirt, blue jeans, open-toed sandals."

"Right," said Stan, "I was there."

"You remember, then, how Dot jerked the cloth off the cage, reached in and grabbed the snake, then draped it over her neck. All without really paying attention to the snake."

Stan nodded.

"I could see that Coba didn't like what Dot did. She opened her mouth to object but didn't say anything. Dot had heard it before."

"I didn't notice Coba wanting to speak, but I can believe it. I thought Dot was a little rough on the snake, myself." Stan poked at the lime wedge with his straw.

Rufus stirred in his seat but didn't speak. I was pretty sure he got it.

"Right. The next day I saw Coba leaving the opening ceremony carrying a snake cage—just like the day before."

"Dot sent her on with the snake while she dealt with the broken gate," Ellen remembered. "She wanted Coba to put the snake in the fortune-telling tent."

"The cage she was carrying didn't have a cloth over it and she showed the snake to people on her way to Dot's tent. She made a point of showing it to me—I could testify that it was the same harmless snake I'd seen the day before. That day Coba was wearing a leather skirt, leather vest, knee-high boots."

"Is that supposed to mean something?" Frank had a carrot stick and was waving it in the air. "Sounds like it was opening day and she dressed up."

"Frank, the only day she wears boots is the day a snake gets into Dot's tent and kills her."

"Oh!" said Bobby. "She was wearing boots for protection! From the snakes!"

I nodded. "Something that occurred to me after the fact, but, yes, that's what I think."

I shrugged my shoulders. "She was smart enough to dress so the boots went with her outfit, but the outfit wasn't right for the day.

"She was dressed too warmly so the boots wouldn't look out of place. And she had ridden her bicycle to work. It was parked in the assistant director's parking spot."

Bobby frowned. "Did she? I don't remember its being there."

"It was only there the one day. Every other day Coba walked to The Festival—including Thursday. She left her bicycle at home—locked up."

"Locked up? Was it locked up at The Festival?" Rebecca had fished one of the olives out of her martini and was nibbling at it.

"No. She left a lock and chain on the bike rack in Archibald—at the offices—so she didn't have to carry one back and forth from home to work."

"But no lock at The Festival." The way Jack said it, it wasn't a question. "Because she never rode to The Festival."

"Right."

"But she did on Friday." Jack nodded. "Anything special about this bike?"

"Just a regular bike with a rack over the rear wheels—designed for those saddle-bag like things bikers use. You know—" For the life of me I couldn't remember what they were called.

"Panniers." Everybody turned to look at Pauline who promptly blushed. "The saddlebags are called panniers."

"Right!"

Jack sighed and leaned back in his chair. "I don't suppose you saw the panniers on the bike?"

"No. She took them with her into headquarters. They were next to her under the table, I think." I looked over at Pauline. "Do panniers look like small soft-sided coolers?"

She nodded her head. "The ones you use for groceries do."

"Oh! When we sent Coba away to take a break she took them with her—I think. Or was that some other day? The days of The Festival all run together. I wish Joyce were here. She'd remember."

"We can ask her." I smiled reassuringly at Ellen. "But since Friday was the only day the bicycle was there, I'll bet that's the day you remember."

"So that's what made you suspect Coba? That's all of it?" Jack was smiling.

"No. Actually I started wondering what was going on when I found out that both booths—the booths that started out on either side of the fortune-telling tent—had been provided by The Festival."

"What?" Ellen looked around. "But The Festival doesn't provide tents—never has and never will! That decision was made years ago when—"

"But that's what—" Frank interrupted. "Coba told me . . ." His voice died away.

"If you'd really looked at the tents, you'd have known they weren't Festival property." I turned to Ellen.

"The AIDS director told me the same thing. The Festival wanted them to be able to attend but didn't want anybody to know they'd provided the tents—or waived the entry fee."

Ellen shook her head. "We don't do that."

"How was I supposed to know the tent wasn't provided by The Festival?" Frank sounded aggrieved.

"Frank! It wasn't labeled."

He looked puzzled.

"Property of The Festival."

"In big black lettering," added Jack.

"Duh!" Frank slapped his forehead.

"Everything that belongs to The Festival is labeled—pens and pencils, pads of paper, gas cans, trash cans, folding chairs, everything—though, I admit the wooden stakes aren't labeled."

Ellen laughed. "Technically, the stakes don't belong to The Festival. Long story."

"Good to know." I said. "I wondered about them.

"Since the tents weren't labeled, I realized The Festival hadn't arranged for the Press and the AIDS Outreach program to have booths at The Festival. Nor had The Festival placed those booths on either side of Dot's fortune-telling tent. A prime location if it hadn't been next to Dot."

Ellen put a hand up to her mouth and cleared her throat. "We've always had difficulty placing vendors next to Dot."

"Dot's tent could be reached quickly from headquarters just by cutting across the grounds. Makes sense for the director to be able to get to HQ quickly."

Ellen nodded her head.

. . .

"But Dot wasn't the only person who wanted to be able to get to the tent and back again quickly—and unnoticed. Actually Dot didn't care about being noticed. But the murderer did care—about being noticed by people in the two side booths. The AIDS director complained to me about how her tent blocked the view to either side and behind. It was the same for the Press's tent. The two tents were the same style, with side flaps and a solid back. They were strategically placed to either side of the fortune-telling tent.

"The booth operators," I made a mock bow to Bobby and then Frank, "if you will, in both tents had been given a plausible reason not to tell anyone about how they got the tents. The style of the tents and the way they were positioned made sure that anyone approaching from the rear wouldn't be noticed. Add to that the broken gate and the malfunctioning sound system. Only one person could have made all those things happen: Coba Boucher."

Jack was leaning back, hands on his stomach. "We were at Dot's tent—or what was left of it—talking with the chief of police." He was twiddling his thumbs; a small smile tugged at his lips.

"We were talking about how the fire had been set and the chief got the call about the black mamba venom. I've never seen lightning strike a man before. So I waited to ask. You knew who did it then, didn't you?"

I made a mental note to never, ever play poker with Jack Harlon.

I shrugged my shoulders. "I'd already decided it was murder. But that's when I started trying to prove who had done it. Not quite the same thing. When I realized the arsonist had destroyed Dot's tent—the murder scene—but hadn't damaged Festival property, the only name that made sense for the arson was Coba Boucher. Which meant she was also the murderer."

"Damn," said Bobby. "That's what Jim Ward calls 'the click,' isn't it? One of these days I'm going to get to see that." She looked at me. "What else did you realize?"

I looked at the bottle of water that was in my hand. "Let me get a beer and I'll finish the tale."

Jack stood up. "Would anybody like a fresh drink? I'm fixing."

. . .

In the midst of everybody milling around freshening drinks and taking bites of the excellent snacks, Jim Ward walked through the gate and into the backyard.

"So this is why you're not answering the door? Because you're all outside? I thought maybe you were avoiding me."

"Why didn't you just open the door and come in?" Bobby protested. "You knew we were here—and where's Vivian?"

"Vivian got a ride home when it looked like I was going to be tied up with police business and there's an angry-looking cat at your front door." Jim stopped. "To answer your questions in reverse order."

"Well, get a drink. Crawford was getting ready to explain everything to us." Bobby waved at the liquor cart. Jack lifted up the martini shaker he'd been pouring from. "Martini?"

Jim shook his head, "No. But I'd take a taste of that small batch bourbon Crawford mentioned—with just one rock."

. . .

"Okay." We'd all gotten our drinks and Bobby had brought Jim up to date on what I'd said so far. "We've got Crawford at the point where he's convinced that Coba is the murderer based on the fact the arsonist hadn't destroyed the gas can."

Jim took a sip of bourbon and smiled. "I hope the rest of his story is as good as this bourbon."

I had everyone's attention again.

"Dot was going to fire Coba, make sure she never worked in Alabama again, so Coba said. That would have meant starting the whole naturalization process all over, no small thing. It might even have meant being sent back to South Africa. So Coba decided to kill Dot. And Dot showed her how. Dot would essentially kill herself—by making the snake bite her.

"Once you've got a snake as the murder weapon"—Jim shifted uneasily in his chair, still resistant to the idea—"by replacing a pet snake with a venomous one, all the pieces start to fall into place.

"The Festival was the logical place to murder Dot. Outdoors. Lots of people coming and going, but not entirely randomly. Coba could control some of the variables at The Festival. And she could come and go without anyone noticing."

I turned both hands palms up. "Dot needed killing. Coba decided to make it happen.

"Thursday evening, Coba stayed on at The Festival grounds. If anybody saw her they wouldn't be surprised, she was just working late. She tampered with the gate and the sound equipment, then she went home, changed, and went on to the party.

"Friday morning she loaded up her—" I looked over at Pauline. "Panniers!" She nodded and gave me a slight smile. "Coba put the rattlesnake in one, her carpetbag with the mamba inside it in the other, and biked to The Festival grounds. She put the bike in her reserved parking space, carried the panniers and bag into headquarters, and started doing whatever she needed to do to get ready for the opening ceremony.

"The corn snake was at the headquarters building. When Dot came in that morning she brought her fortune-telling equipment with her. She'd used it the night before. It was in that large carpetbag that she called her magic bag."

I took another swallow of beer. "Dot had planned on taking her magic equipment and the corn snake to her tent before the opening ceremony, but the gates were broken. She couldn't get the snake, take it and the magic stuff to her tent, and fix the gate in time for the opening. So she told Coba to get the snake and take it to her tent—just as Coba intended for her to do."

"Suppose Dot hadn't told her to get the snake?"

"I don't know, Stan."

"We'll probably never know for sure," said Jim Ward, "but I'll bet she had a Plan B."

"Maybe," I said. "But she didn't need it. Dot ordered her to get the snake and carry it to her tent. I was standing there when Coba started up the pathway. She spoke to me, reminded me that I'd seen the corn snake the day before, and attracted a group of people who saw her take a nonvenomous snake in a cage to Dot's tent."

Stan raised his hand. I was going to ignore him but he started waving it.

"What?"

"Did the fact that she'd used the cloth cover the day before but didn't that day make you suspicious?"

"Yes. When I started going over things, but not at the time. I was more interested in why she was wearing boots. I figured she'd be sweating to death by lunchtime."

Jim Ward was spinning a toothpick between his thumb and forefinger—it must have been in one of the appetizers. Frank had lit up another cigarette and Jim was an ex-smoker. I don't think he even knew he was twirling the toothpick. "What about the—what did you call it—magic bag?"

"She had that over her shoulder too—well, she had her bag over her shoulder—the one with the mamba in it."

Jim cocked his head. Meanwhile out of the corner of my eye I could see Rufus slowly nodding.

As I opened my mouth to go on with the story, Jack held up his hand. "What's this about two carpetbags?"

"I can answer that," said Ellen George.

Jack dropped his hand.

"One of the exhibitors gave those bags to Dot and Coba. They were reversible, sturdy, waterproof, capacious—and identical. That's one of the reasons the vendor had them to give away. She'd made a bunch from the same fabric and they didn't sell. People don't come to craft shows to buy something that looks mass-produced.

"Dot was always picking up the wrong bag and blaming it on Coba." She smiled. "Coba tried to keep the opposite side out— the one Dot wasn't showing. But Dot would dump the contents out of her bag, turn it inside out, and then blame Coba when they looked alike."

"Okay," said Jack. "Sorry. I'll stop interrupting."

"So Coba was carrying her own bag—with the snake in it— instead of Dot's. I know that because we," I gestured toward

Bobby, "saw Dot getting coffee after the opening ceremony. She took her coffee mug out of the bag."

Bobby nodded her head. "She got it refilled."

"Back to Coba. She heads on up the path when Dot starts the opening ceremony. Once she's in the tent, Coba sets the cage down on the floor, gets the corn snake out, puts it in a snake bag, and ties the bag shut. Exit the corn snake.

"Then she retrieves the snake traps from under the table where she had stored them with supplies—incense, lighters, batteries, light bulbs, tissues, stuff like that. None of which belonged to The Festival. Coba made sure of that. She didn't want Festival property in the tent when she torched it.

"The snake trap was a wire cage with a one-way entrance. She set a couple of them on the floor at the edge of the tent."

"Did she tell you all this," asked Stan wonderingly.

"No." I took another swig from my beer bottle. "She wasn't exactly forthcoming with details of how she pulled off the murder. Most of it we deduced."

"You mean, you did," said Jim Ward.

"You and Kurt would have reached the same conclusion I did. It was just a logical deduction based on what we know happened."

. . .

"How in the world did she get the black mamba into the cage?" Rebecca looked around at the group. "Can you imagine dealing with something that deadly? She must really have hated Dot."

"I think that's safe to say," replied Jack with a slight smile. "I guess most murderers hate their victims." He looked thoughtful. "Except maybe the ones who kill strictly for monetary gain."

"And contract killers," added Bobby.

"And maybe—"

Rebecca interrupted Jack. "Anyway she took an incredible risk getting the mamba from the sack to the cage. Didn't she?"

"It was a risk, certainly. But according to Dr. Moore, it was more in the nature of a calculated risk. She'd left a snake stick and tongs at the entrance to the tent and she knew how to use them. Dr. Moore says she would have untied the neck of the sack, used the stick to pull the sack open, picked up the snake with the tongs, dropped it into the cage, and closed the lid."

Rebecca shook her head. "More of a risk than I'd want to take."

Jack gave his wife a quizzical look. "So if you ever kill anyone it won't be by using a deadly snake as the murder weapon?"

"Of course not," said Rebecca with a grin. "You've told me that I could talk somebody to death. Why use a weapon?"

"What happened next?" Pauline had been so still and quiet I'd forgotten she was there.

"Coba puts the cage back on the table, sticks the snake stick and tongs by the back door, puts the snake sack in her own carpetbag, takes a look around, and leaves by the front door, or flap if you will. The stage is set for murder."

"Sounds like the title of a murder mystery," volunteered Ellen.

I smiled at her. "It does indeed."

Ellen smiled back. "I apologize for interrupting. Do go on, James."

"It's easy enough to imagine what happened when Dot got to the tent. She dumped her magic bag on the table, turned on some of the electric candles, stuck a few gaudy rings on her fingers, wrapped some scarves around her head, opened the snake cage, grabbed the snake as she always did, and draped it over her shoulders."

My audience was silent, thinking about what would happen if you flung an ill-tempered, highly venomous snake around your neck.

"Any single bite could have killed her—and nine or ten other people."

Bobby spoke very softly. "I wonder if she even had time to realize her mistake?"

"I don't know. We do know she was struck on the neck and was conscious long enough to tear her flesh trying to get the snake off. She thrashed around, knocking over table and chairs, fell to the ground, and died."

Jack spoke up. "Chief Snoddy thought she'd fallen over the entrance lip and was on her hands and knees when the snake bit her, which would explain how it could reach her neck."

"Kurt had never seen Dot yank a snake out of a cage and toss it around her neck."

"Crawford's right." Stan looked a little pale. "I bet Coba had fantasized about that corn snake turning on Dot."

"How did Coba figure on covering up the crime?" Jim Ward had a handful of peanuts and was popping them into his mouth one peanut at a time.

"I'm guessing about the next bit, but it had to go something like this. Coba knew Dot's fortune-telling schedule. Before any customers arrived, Coba cut across the grounds to the back entrance. She had her carpetbag with her—this time with an eastern diamondback rattlesnake in it. The plan was to frame the rattlesnake for Dot's death. It might have worked if she'd known enough to get a rattlesnake that was indigenous.

"She shone her flashlight into the tent and saw the mamba in one of the snake traps. I think if the snake hadn't been in the trap, she would have just turned around and gone back to headquarters. I would have."

Jim snorted. "You wouldn't have used a venomous snake to kill somebody. Get on with it."

"Right," I nodded my head. "Coba needed to put the rattlesnake in the mamba's place, and she needed to do it in a hurry. Furthermore, being Coba, she needed to do it without harming any of the animals."

"The human mind is remarkable." It was the first time Rufus had spoken since I'd begun my explanation.

"True. But what prompted that comment?"

"Ms. Boucher's deep and sincere concern for the reptiles she was using in a plot to murder a human being." Rufus gazed off into the distance. "An apparent paradox."

"You wouldn't get her to agree, Rufus. Coba firmly believed Dot needed killing, whereas the snakes had done her no harm at all. She would have gone to great lengths to avoid hurting them."

"You are no doubt correct, James."

"So where was I?"

Bobby spoke up. "Coba has the rattlesnake and the mamba both in the tent. She needs to make the substitution. Fast. Before people start arriving to have their fortunes read."

"Right. Coba's got two snakes and two carpetbags. She uses the snake stick and tongs to reverse the procedure she used to get the black mamba into the cage. Then she transfers the rattlesnake from sack to carpetbag, figuring the snake can easily make its way out."

"But it doesn't." Jim was looking thoughtful.

"Get out of the bag? No. It was still there, with blood on it, when Kurt and I were looking around the tent."

I brought the bottle to my lips and took another swallow. The beer was no longer cold. "Now Coba collapses the snake traps, slides them back under the table, grabs her carpetbag with the mamba inside, puts the snake stick and tongs back in place, steps out of the tent and around to the front, flips the sign to The Gypsy Is Within—Please Knock, walks back across the grounds to headquarters, and waits for somebody to bring her the news about Dot's terrible accident."

I looked at the empty bottle in my hand.

Jack stood up and handed me another beer. "You'll need this, because we've got questions." He turned to Jim Ward. "You're head of the homicide detectives or something like that, right?"

Jim smiled. "Something like that."

"So how does this plan of Coba's stack up—premeditated murder-wise? Good, bad, indifferent—inspired? I mean for getting away with it of course."

Ward chuckled. "It used to bug Crawford that the murders I work on aren't like the ones he reads about. I'd say this one has all the elements for a satisfactory mystery plot. But as for getting away with murder, Coba was plagued by the same problem most perps encounter: in order for her plan to work she needed a sizable dose of luck." Jim tilted his glass upside down to get the last few drops of bourbon and then set it on the table beside him. "She didn't get it."

"Do you think she really expected to get away with it?" Jack wasn't letting Jim off the hook so easily.

I absentmindedly screwed the top off the bottle of Yuengling and took a sip. It was a good thing I hadn't tried that on a bottle of Red Stripe—I'd have torn my hand up.

"Maybe. It's been my experience that murderers, by and large, are pretty much optimists." Jim scratched his chin. "I don't really know about murder by snake. Not a lot of precedence for snakes as murder weapons—even in literature."

"That's what my friend Dr. Snake says. Says even Sherlock Holmes and Rex Stout got it wrong—their stories about snakes that is."

Jim looked at me. "I was talking about police procedurals—not garden-variety murder mysteries."

"Really? Well, according to the man who identified Coba's corn snake, rattlesnake, and yellow rat snake as not being from around here—as we say—and even managed to identify the man who sold those snakes to Coba, and sold a black mamba to her as well—according to that guy, both authors screwed up describing snake behavior—Arthur Conan Doyle in *The Adventure of the Speckled Band* and Rex Stout in *Fer-de-Lance*. Snakes can't hear and fangs by themselves can't poison people."

"Wait a minute." Jack Harlon held up his hand.

"Don't," said Jim Ward, shaking his head at Jack, "just let him explain it his own way. In the end it's faster. Trust me."

. . .

"So where did Coba get all the snakes?" Bobby was looking a little dazed. "She was responsible for acquiring them, right? The rattlesnake, the corn snake, and the mamba?"

"She was, as well as the snake I saw next door to The Festival's downtown office. Early on, I sent Dr. Moore pictures I'd taken of all the snakes. Except the mamba of course." I glanced over at Bobby. "Remind me to tell Levi he was right about that snake at the Bird House not being a garter snake—or from around here."

I turned back to my audience. "The snake next door was a yellow rat snake, and isn't native to Jemison County any more than the corn snake or rattlesnake. They were all from coastal areas, East Coast coastal that is, or from Florida.

"When Dot elected to keep a snake as a pet—well—when she decided being a snake handler might make the fortune-telling more lucrative—she commandeered the corn snake. Coba still needed something to take care of the rodents. So she ordered another snake—another pretty one—that she let go outdoors at the Bird House."

I shook my head. "By taking the corn snake, Dot actually made it easier to find out who killed her. By that time Coba had become a regular customer of the reptile dealer in Augusta.

"When I told Dr. Moore that Dot had been killed not by a rattlesnake but by a black mamba—at least by black mamba venom—he was fascinated. Said if you were foolish enough to try using a snake as a murder weapon, a black mamba was a good choice. He volunteered to do a little investigating for me."

"You should be sure to tell Joyce that Dr. Moore was instrumental in solving the mystery. She will be pleased to know that."

"Thanks, Ellen. I'll let her know." Tan, who had been happily gnawing away at her rawhide bone, walked over to the water bowl Bobby had set out for her. She lapped noisily before wandering over to where I was sitting and leaning up against my leg. I scratched between her ears then gave her a pat. She made her way back to her bone.

"Where was I?"

Jack spoke up. "Dr. Snake has just volunteered to investigate for you."

"Right. He called me back within fifteen minutes. A snake dealer in Augusta, Georgia, had provided a coastal corn snake, a yellow rat snake, an eastern diamondback rattlesnake, and a black mamba to the same customer within the last six months—the black mamba some three weeks ago.

"And get this. If a customer isn't satisfied, for any reason, the dealer's policy is to refund the purchase cost, minus a 25 percent restocking fee, within thirty days of purchase. Coba called him a few days ago. Said she was planning to return the mamba on Monday."

. . .

My beer bottle was empty. "Can I have some of that single malt now?"

Jack got up and headed to the liquor cart. As he picked up a glass he spoke. "Not if you think you're through answering questions."

"I've told you everything I know!"

"Not quite." Jim Ward was shaking his head. "You told the chief you knew it was murder when he caught that rattlesnake."

I held my hand out to take the glass from Jack and he pulled it back.

"Oh that. That was after Kurt found blood on the snake—remember I mentioned that?"

"Right," Jack pulled the scotch further away from me. "And as far as I'm concerned that was just more evidence that the rattlesnake had gotten blood on itself when it bit her."

"Yeah," agreed Rebecca. "It made the idea of an accident believable. Dot stumbled, lost her balance, and fell on the snake."

I closed my eyes and spoke more to myself than my listeners. "Let me think. The tarot cards were clean. In fact, they looked brand new. That's right." I opened my eyes. "It was when I was giving Dot CPR. I couldn't stand to look at her, so I looked at what was on the floor. There was no blood on the tarot cards or on the outside of the carpetbag."

I reached for the glass of single malt that Jack held out to me. "I didn't realize what I'd seen until I watched Kurt wipe blood off his hands after handling the rattlesnake. The reason the cards were clean was that they had been inside the carpetbag when the snake struck, which meant someone had dumped them on the floor after Dot was killed. Who else would it have been but the murderer?" I looked around the semicircle of people on the patio.

At first, no one spoke as they mulled over the facts and suppositions. Then Jim Ward looked up.

"The break in. Who and why?"

"I don't think The Festival's going to push for the crime to be solved." I glanced over at Ellen. "At least I hope they aren't." She shook her head no.

"Okay. It was Chad Harris. The one who so publicly refused to be blackmailed. He'd lied on his initial application to The Festival. He wanted to destroy it." I smiled. "I'd say he's been watching too much TV, where the hero breaks in and finds the evidence—right before the commercial break. My guess is that he tossed the plaster around to cover up any tracks he might have left."

I took a healthy sip of the single malt. "Any other questions?"

Jack shook his head like he was waking up. "I've got one. If I'm ever accused of murder, can you practice in Tennessee?"

KEEP READING FOR A PREVIEW OF
THE DEACON NEEDED KILLING
BOOK 4 IN THE NEEDED KILLING SERIES

It had been a while since I'd had lunch with Stan. His workdays can be a little crazy and it's hard for him to commit to a particular place and time. It wasn't so bad when we both worked at the Department of Technology—either one of us could bail on lunch at the last moment and the other could adjust his plans. It was for sure that we were both going to eat.

Nowadays, since I'm retired, the logistics are more complicated and last-minute cancelations more inconvenient. I tease him about having classic male commitment issues.

Today, we'd made arrangements to meet for lunch and, if possible, Jim Ward would join us—it would depend. For some reason Jim can get away with his lack of commitment to lunch dates. I think it's because he's head of Shelbyville's homicide department. Stan, on the other hand, does video for the university. "Does video" isn't an adequate description of all that he does—but it's the shorthand description he uses. Who am I to challenge it?

He hadn't called to say the meal was off so here I was at the Happy Buddha, a Chinese restaurant in an upscale strip mall near the university, sitting by myself at a table for four near the wall, menus on the table, silverware wrapped up in napkins, and no Stan—or Jim.

I particularly like going to the Happy Buddha in the fall and spring. The owners have taken something of a minimalist attitude toward heat and air conditioning—physical comfort-wise anyway—and we are talking about Shelbyville, Alabama. Most restaurants are like meat lockers during the summer—but not the Happy Buddha.

So the temperature was comfortable but the longer I sat there by myself occupying a table for four as the restaurant filled up with the lunch crowd, the more uncomfortable I felt. I'd ordered iced tea, but had held off on ordering anything else. It wasn't that I didn't know what I wanted—I'd learned the menu pretty well while I was working and it hadn't changed. The issue was that if I ordered, my food would be here before my friends. The Happy Buddha didn't waste time.

"Sorry I'm late." Stan pulled a chair out, sat, and grabbed a menu. "I had some faculty member show up with 'a simple question, really,' of course it was neither simple nor a single question." He sighed and shook his head.

"Faculty," I observed, "what can you do? Don't have a job without 'em, can't kill them."

"Were you talking murder, Stan?" Ward's deep voice came from behind me. He must have gone to the restroom first to come to the table from that direction. He edged around me and I pulled forward to give him some extra room. "If so, I suggest discussing it with an attorney, not a private investigator. At least the attorney could claim client privilege." Jim sat and pushed the table out a little to give himself some more room. I don't know if Jim had been reading Westerns or if it was one of those continuing education courses every professional has to take, but lately he'd taken to sitting with his back to the wall—just like a sheriff in the Wild West—as if somebody was out to get him.

I guess it says something about me that I'd noticed the change and it says even more that—until now—I'd never considered the idea that maybe somebody *was* out to get him. Homicide detectives aren't universally loved.

. . .

"Is it safe to be sitting with you?"

Jim didn't respond. He flipped the menu over to the lunch specials side and started running his finger down the page.

"Huh?" Stan sat up straight and turned in his seat to look around at the other customers. "Why wouldn't it be safe to sit with a policeman?" He turned back around to look at Jim and me.

"Pay no attention to the comedian." Ward flipped the menu back over to see what was available for supper, I guess. I hadn't had as many lunches with Jim as I've had with Stan even though I've known Jim longer, but it seemed to me that Jim never remembered what was on the menus of the places we'd frequent for lunch. Or maybe food wasn't as important to Jim as it was to people like me—and Stan.

"Ready to order?" I didn't recognize the waiter, which was hardly surprising. The waitstaff turnover was pretty steady, mostly students working their way through college.

He glanced at me first. I suppose because I'd already ordered a drink. "General chicken, hot and sour soup, and fried rice. No, make it steamed rice." Food was important to me, but so was fitting into my clothes.

Stan shrugged his shoulders and ordered. "Chicken and mushrooms, steamed rice, hot and sour soup, and water, no lemon."

The waiter looked at Jim who paused and then rattled his order off. "Egg drop soup and the combination fried rice. Oh, and hold the egg roll will you?"

"Hold the egg roll." The guy nodded. "What to drink?"

"Eh?" Jim glanced at the table and saw what I was drinking. "Iced tea with a glass of water too—no lemon."

The waiter walked away.

"So why don't you take off your jacket, Jim? I'm sure you'd be more comfortable." For some reason I wasn't willing to let the back-to-the-wall issue drop. Stan and I were in shirtsleeves but Jim was wearing a suit, just as you'd expect of the head of homicide.

Ward glared at me but it was Stan who spoke. "What's going on? What am I missing?"

I pointed at the empty chair with it's back facing the lunch crowd. "It used to be that Captain Ward would have walked right up to the table and sat in that chair. Today he comes in the only entrance to the restaurant, checks to see who's here, even goes so far as to check the restrooms in the back, works his way around to our table, and then takes a seat with his back to the wall, even if I was somewhat in the way." I was talking to Stan but looking at Jim.

"He's wearing his underarm holster instead of the one he usually wears—you remember, the one that fits at the small of his back. The underarm holster makes a bulge in his coat and, for some reason best known to him, means he keeps his jacket on." I paused. "But it means he can get his gun out faster."

The waiter took this opportunity to deliver the drinks. Not that he was waiting for a pause in the conversation. The timing was just right. He put the iced tea down in front of Jim and gave him the water without lemon, Stan got the other water, and he took my glass off to refill.

"It's no big deal." Jim took a sip of water. "The guy is stupid and belligerent. He'll be back in jail before too long. Meanwhile—." He shrugged his shoulders.

"Mama Ward didn't raise no stupid children." I smiled, relieved. "Glad to hear you know who it is."

"Yeah, he's too stupid even to make it anonymous. Had to shout his threats out in front of witnesses. Chief Boyd heard about it and now I'm under orders to take 'all reasonable precautions.'"

"Does that include not eating alone?" Stan grinned. "Having others at the table probably means he'd hesitate to shoot, right?"

"Not this guy." Jim peeled the paper strip off the rolled up napkin and silverware. "I told you he was stupid."

. . .

The waiter reappeared with my tea and two egg rolls. He put one plate in front of Stan and the other in front of me.

Stan and I looked at each other and shrugged our shoulders. I'd never been able to get any member of the waitstaff at the Happy Buddha to "hold the egg roll," despite years of trying.

"Maybe it's the suit," said Stan.

I looked up at the waiter. "Spicy mustard?" He reached into his apron and pulled out a squeeze bottle, put it on the table, and disappeared.

Stan spooned some of the red sweet sauce onto his saucer. It was always on the table at the Happy Buddha along with the salt, pepper, soy sauce, and a bowl of crunchy noodle things. I squeezed some hot mustard onto my plate, dipped a corner of the egg roll into the pool, and considered why the mustard wasn't left out too.

My eyes filled with tears and I wondered, not for the first time, why I did that to myself. I was never sure how spicy it was going to be and never prepared for how spicy it could be. Maybe the Happy Buddha didn't leave it out because of liability issues.

I could hear their attorney. "He requested the mustard. Not our problem."

Jim was sitting back in his chair eyeing the room. "I think they use some of what's in that stuff in tear gas."

I blinked and looked at Jim through the film of tears. "That reminds me," I gasped. "Wanted to talk to you about defensive weapons."

Jim and Stan exchanged glances. They both looked puzzled. I took a swallow of tea and started to feel more like myself. "The tear gas comment reminded me. You know how some people carry pepper spray or stun guns for defense."

They both nodded as the waiter returned with our bowls of soup and a bowl of the crunchy noodle things. Good deal, since I'd eaten most of what had been on the table while I was waiting.

Stan nodded. "Sure. The kinda thing you carry in case you're hassled. Don't want to hurt anybody but—"

Jim snorted. "You two guys are something else. What did you call them? Defensive weapons? A weapon's just a weapon."

"Oh, come on, Ward. Some weapons are more defensive than others—like pepper spray and stun guns. You know what I'm trying to say." I picked up my spoon.

"Tranquilizer dart guns and rubber bullets." Stan chimed in. "Stuff like that."

Jim just shook his head, took a spoonful of egg drop soup, and swallowed. "A weapon's a weapon and that's all there is to it. Oh, you may use it defensively, but it doesn't mean you couldn't use it offensively. Don't kid yourselves. If it can protect, it can attack."

Stan and I realized we were on shaky ground arguing with a man who had a pistol tucked under his arm. I was glad my soup was good. I had the feeling I was about to have to eat my words as well. "Okay, okay. I had just been doing a little Internet research and wondered what you thought about them."

"Defensive," Jim hit the word hard, "weapons? Why were you doing that? You figure Bobby needs extra protection now that she's hanging around with you?"

As that *was* the reason I'd started poking around investigating different weapons on the Internet, I didn't have much to say. It had come to me that private investigation might be hazardous for friends of the investigator as well as the investigator himself.

"Pass the crunchy things would you?" Stan pushed the bowl toward me and I picked it up and shook some of them into my soup.

We all sat quietly eating for a minute or so. The waiter returned with our main courses and, after sorting out who'd ordered what, we continued eating in silence.

I decided to man up. "Well, the thought had occurred to me."

"Well, thank God for that, anyway." Stan ducked his head and concentrated on his chicken and mushrooms after his outburst.

"I agree," Jim sprinkled some soy sauce over his fried rice. I'd wondered if the Happy Buddha had cut back on salt in order to serve healthier food or to save money. Judging by the amount of soy sauce Jim was using they weren't saving money. "Glad to hear you might be developing some common sense to go along with that Sherlock stuff you do. You still against carrying heat?" He shook his head. I didn't have to speak. "I know, I know. Guess I'll have to be pleased that you're thinking about learning how to walk instead of wishing you'd learn to run."

"I carried a pistol in the Shore Patrol—a .45 caliber something—and didn't like it—or the feeling it gave me."

"You ever use it?" Stan looked curious. He had paused with his fork in the air.

"That was the Colt M1911. It was a bitch to hit anything with."

"Right. I was told by a bunch of instructors I'd have a better chance of hitting the target with a baseball."

Jim snorted. "Drill instructors aren't very original with their insults. The U.S. used that pistol from WWI to Vietnam. It hit plenty of targets."

"Is that right?" I turned back to Stan. "Never had reason to fire it. 'Carrying heat,' as Jim puts it, effects people in different ways. Some of the other guys in the Shore Patrol were a little more—" I groped for the word. "Enthusiastic, if you will, about having—no, getting—to wear a weapon than I was. For them it was a fringe benefit of the job—along with the nightstick."

"So what about carrying a nightstick?" Jim was peering at what was left of the mound of fried rice that had been on his plate, poking at it with his fork. "Clubs are pretty good weapons too."

"Actually, I was thinking about canes. The other day I came across a site—"

"Something wrong with the rice, Jim?" Stan had noticed the same thing I had.

"Just trying to see how many shrimp you get in the combination. There's plenty of chicken, some beef, but I think I've run out of shrimp."

Stan and I looked at each other. I spoke.

"And you were expecting?"

He looked up from the plate. "Equal amounts of each, why?"

Stan and I laughed. We'd figured that out years ago. "You got equal amounts. You've just got to measure by cost—not quantity!"

ACKNOWLEDGMENTS

I have a bunch of people who—by now—know that I rely on them while I'm writing—and, as in the past, they've come through for me. You all know who you are and I thank you once again for your help.

Special thanks to Whitfield for all-things-snake in this book. Without his help I'd have had to come up with a different murder weapon. Any reptilian-related errors that might have crawled into the text are mine, not his.

Thanks to Ann for pointing out Ford's poor potato storage habits, Van for spotting the voice-activated phone error, and both of them for suggesting Crawford be less hard on himself; to Audrey for noticing the scene I'd forgotten to include and for other helpful suggestions; to Jill for her legal expertise and knowledge of police procedures; to Christine for the number zero; to Donna in Clarksville for her continued enthusiasm; and to my extended support group—Anita, Wayne, Donna, Leigh, Paul, Katie, Alston, Marie, JoLee, and all the Ann(e)s in my life. Careful, or you just might end up in one of my novels

Writers do not create their works in a vacuum. Or so I believe. They are influenced, sometimes consciously, often unconsciously, by the world around them—by the people they know, the movies and TV shows they watch, the plays and concerts they attend, and, of course, by the books they read.

From the Hardy Boys and Nancy Drew to Perry Mason and Nero Wolfe, I was raised on a steady diet of detective stories. Later, I added to my reading list such authors as Dorothy Sayers, Dick Francis, and Robert B. Parker. They and other writers helped shape my understanding of how to construct a mystery and fueled my love of a good whodunit. Authors outside the genre, notably Robert A. Heinlein, kindled my imagination as a young reader and engendered in me a love of reading that continues to this day. I thank them all for the many wonderful hours I have spent in cloud-cuckoo-land, from the English countryside to the streets of Boston to the far reaches of outer space.

I also owe an odd kind of thank you to the tornado that swept across parts of the South, including Tuscaloosa, Ala., on April 27, 2011. My wife and I came through the tornado physically unharmed, but our lives were changed forever. Like others who have survived an event of such enormity, we began to assess our needs and wants, our hopes and dreams from the perspective of survivors—with the visceral understanding that life is short and the future uncertain.

As a result, I retired from the University of Alabama in September 2011 and took up writing mysteries. I am having a wonderful time, and I hope you enjoy reading my books as much as I enjoy writing them. It's too late for me to keep the day job.

VISIT BILL'S WEBSITE AT BILLFITTSAUTHOR.COM FOR RECIPES, TESTIMONIALS, AND INFORMATION ABOUT HOW TO ORDER PAPERBACKS AND EBOOKS IN THE NEEDED KILLING SERIES.